Mary Brock Jones lives in New Zealand but loves nothing more than to escape into the other worlds in her head, to write science fiction and historical romances. Sedate office worker by day; frantic scribbler by night.

Her parents introduced her to libraries and gave her a farm to play on, where trees became rocket ships and rocky outcrops were ancient fortresses. She grew up writing, filling pages of notebooks and filling her head with stories but took a number of detours on the pathway to her dream job. Four grown sons, more than one house renovated and various jobs later, her wish came true.

To keep up to date with her latest news and releases, sign up to her newsletter here:

www.marybrockjones.com/

Or find Mary here:

http://www.marybrockjones.com/

https://www.facebook.com/MaryBrockJonesAuthor

https://twitter.com/MaryBrockJones

By Mary Brock Jones:

A Heart Divided
Swift Runs the Heart

Hathe Series

Resistance: Hathe Book One
Pay the Piper: Hathe Book Two
Toil and Strife: Hathe Book One and Two
Aftermath: Hathe Book Three

Arcadia Series

Torn

TORN

Arcadia Book One

Mary Brock Jones

Mary Brock Jones

Auckland, New Zealand

Author: Mary Brock Jones
Published by Mary Brock Jones
Remuera,
Auckland, New Zealand 1050
www.marybrockjones.com

Publisher's Note: This is a work of fiction. Names, characters, places, and incidents are a product of the author's imagination. Locales and public names are sometimes used for atmospheric purposes. Any resemblance to actual people, living or dead, or to businesses, companies, events, institutions, or locales is completely coincidental.

Book Layout © 2017 BookDesignTemplates.com

Cover design by Amygdala Design. www.amygdaladesign.net

Torn/ Mary Brock Jones. – 2nd ed. (2019)
ISBN: 978-0-473-50863-0

CONTENTS

CHARACTER LIST AND GUIDE TO PRONUNCIATION

Mountain region names describe a person's closest family connections. The emphasis is usually on the first syllable, but this can vary.

Sounds:

- 'ch at the end of a word - like the Scottish ch.

- 'h in the pronunciation guide indicates a degree of aspiration in the sound.

- a further, slight aspiration is shown by an apostrophe just before the letter in the pronunciation version (italicized - stress syllable shown in bold)

CHARACTER LIST

MAIN CHARACTERS

Fioruisghe ingh Bram an Scathach den Coille (also known as Fee den Coille by non-mountain Survey): - eco-engineer and leader of a mountain Survey team.

*Fee-or-'hrish-gay ine Bram arn '**Ska**-tha'ch den Coyle*

Fioruisghe, daughter of Bram (father) and Scathach (mother), of the family Coille.

Fioruisghe ingh Coille beann Caleb den Winter (Fee's married name)

*Fee-or-'hrish-gay ine Coyle bee-**arn** **Kay**-leb den **Win**ter*

Fioruisghe, daughter of the family Coille, wife of Caleb, of the family Winter.

Caleb Winter: - eco-engineer and leader of a Plains Survey team.

Caleb mar Sol duine Fiorughte den Winter (Caleb's mountain married name)

***Kay**-leb mar Sole d'win **Fee**-or-'hrish-gay den **Win**ter*

Caleb son of Sol, husband of Fioruisghe, of the family Winter

FEE'S FAMILY.

Scathach ingh Coibhneas bean Bram den Coille, (Mam).
Doctor and mother to Fee.

*'**Ska**-thar'k ine **Coy**'-nee-ars bee-**arn** Bram den Coyle.*

Scathach, daughter of Coibhneas, wife of Bram, of the family Coille

Bram mar Gliocas duine Scathach den Coille (Da). Father to Fee and head of den Coille

*Bram mar **Glee**-o-cas d'win '**Skar**-thar'kh den Coyle*

Bram, son of Gliocas, husband to Scathach, of the family Coyle.

Cumchdach mar Bram an Scathach den Coille. Fee's eldest brother.

*Coo-'var'kh mar Bram an '**Ska**-thar'kh den Coyle*

Seolta mar Bram an Scathach den Coille. Fee's second brother.

*See-**ole**-tar mar Bram an '**Ska**-thar'ch den Coyle*

Samhchair ingh Bram an Scathach den Coille. Fee's sister

*Sarm-'**hair** ine Bram an '**Ska**-thar'ch den Coyle*

Ceart mar Bram an Scathach den Coille. Fee's third brother.

*Kee-'airt mar Bram arn '**Ska**-thar'ch den Coyle*

Aigherach mar Bram an Scathach den Coille. Fee's youngest brother.

*Aye-ger-ar'kh mar Bram an '**Ska**-thar'kh den Coyle*

Den Coille: – name of the festia pollen company owned by the den Coille family.

CALEB'S FAMILY;

Sol Winter: - Caleb's father and head of Winter Solaris

Helena Bascombe Winter : - Caleb's mother.

Ethan Winter: - middle brother
Silas Winter (Si): - youngest brother
Winter Solaris: - the solar energy company owned by the Winter family, usually shortened to Solaris.

PLAINS SURVEY STAFF

Kal Mendip: - an eco-engineer, specialising in the interaction of plant & soil.

Gerard: – an eco-engineer, specialising in economic calibration

Marabeth: – cook

Jim: – head wrangler

Adam: – hydrogeologist

Bob: – communications officer

Chaba *(Char-bar):* – engineer

Jareth (**Jare**-eth): – engineer and Marabeth's son

Ben Crane: – zoologist

Viv: – veterinarian.

Suze: – medic

Frank: - Botanist

MOUNTAIN SURVEY STAFF

Seamach *(Shay-mark)*: – security and communications.

Ronan (*Row-nan*): – flyer pilot.

Joseph: – botanist and arborist.

Caerthida *(Kare-thee-dar)*: – geologist, cousin to Fridha

Fridha (*Fri-thar*): – zoologist and cousin of Caerthida

Kebhyn (*Ke-'vin*): - Horticulturist.

Sorcha - (*Sor-shar*): — engineer.

Rannach (*Ran-nak*): — meteorologist.

Carnach (*Car-na'k*): – geotechnical engineer

Aillis (*Aye-liss*): – microbiologist

OTHERS

Fox – Survey regional commander. Fee and Caleb's boss.

Representative Joe Gibbs: – Planetary Upper House representative for the plains region.

Councillor Seilach ingh Craobh bean Stobach den Bunachan: – Lower House government representative for the Mountain region.

*Sye-lach ine Crou'sch bee-**arn** Stow-bar'k den **Boo**-nar-'harn.*

Douall mar Ceart duine Caerthida den Coibhneas:

***Doo**-ell mar **Kee**-art 'dwin Kair-**thee**-dar den **Coy**-nee-ars*

Head of security for Councillor den Bunachan, second cousin of Fioruisghe, husband of Caerthida, of the Survey mountain team.

Marco an Fallon: - Supreme Field Commander of the Federal Police of Arcadia.

Sharach (*Shar-a'k*): - Survey eco-engineer, old friend of Fee

Dard: – Survey eco-engineer, old friend of Fee.

Finola Aknutk: – Survey communications field coordinator.

Anya van Lissen: - lead presenter and interviewer on Today, a leading vid-cast news programme.

Representative Coinneas mar Coille duine Falamh den Cleireach: -

***Coy**-nee-as mar Coyle dwin **Fell**-ass den **Clare**-ee-ark*

Upper House Representative, Mountain region.

OTHER TERMS

Festia: – tree cultivated for its pollen.

Baullnia (***Bow**-ll-nee-a*): - very large tree forming the base for cities built in the forest canopy

Beith (*Beeth*): - trees with a light, dappled foliage. More heat tolerant than mountain trees

Chaullnea (***chorl**-nee-a*): – perfumed flowering shrub

Cetaeven (*Ke-**tai**-ven*): – a stimulant and painkiller.

Feldwesten – third continent of Arcadia.

Manascraoch (***Man**-ass-crou'sch*): – den Coille home city.

Beod project (***Bee**-odd*): – a basin occupying much of the central desert of Feldwesten.

Rakki: – a small pet animal that makes a 'chittering' sound.

Nieten (***Nye**-ten*): - domesticated native herd animal. Used for food/hides/ fibre.

Alliance: – Alliance of Human Worlds. Interplanetary organisation, with ultimate power to ensure that the settled planets abide by agreed treaty rules.

MEASUREMENTS

Arcadia uses decimal based, Standard Galactic units for distance, time, mass etc. They have been expressed here in current day terms i.e. second, hour, day etc. However, that is only a current day translation. The Standard Galactic units used throughout the Alliance, irrespective of planetary or deep space location, are based on Natural Units of measurement i.e. on universal physical constants independent of planet or spatial location. On Arcadia, they are roughly equivalent to the following current Earth measurements.

DISTANCE

1 Standard galactic metre is roughly equivalent to 1.5 metres or 5 feet.

Standard galactic kilometre (generally referred to as Kays) = 1000 SG metres.

TIME

Standard second is equivalent to 5 metric seconds.

Standard minute = 10 standard seconds.

Standard hour = 100standard minutes, and is equivalent in usage to an hour, but in time is almost 1.5 hours

CHAPTER ONE

A place of endless light and untouchable horizons. That was Fee's first impression of the plains regions east of her mountain home. Vast, empty lands opening out to sky and wind that looked nothing like her native forests. Her second impression came when the flyer landed and she stepped out into air so hot it threatened to sear the skin from her body. She would have stepped right back inside, but the pilot passed her bag over and made it clear he was waiting for her to get off.

"Someone will be along to meet you."

She had no choice but to walk down the ramp. Then he hit the hatch button and took off, leaving her stranded on a lonely dirt road in a place bare of anything resembling life as she knew it. No trees, no dancing leaves to offer escape from the fierce heat, only the wooden railings of an old fence line standing derelict on the side of the track. She hitched herself up on the first rail, fingers clinging to the familiar roughness. How she wished she could jump into a flyer and scurry back across the mountains but she had work to do and a planet to save. The once beautiful world that was Arcadia deserved better. She tucked herself up another rail and stared out at this strange land.

A man walked down the road towards her. He had to be the one sent by the Survey. An ecological engineer like her, so she'd been told, and yet nothing about this man looked familiar. There was a stillness about him, his feet scuffing up the dust on the road the only sign of his passing. She scrunched back against the fence, stepped up another railing, and waited.

She had been dropped off in this remote place to keep her arrival quiet, and the man looked like he'd walked all the way from town for the same reason. Not that it appeared to bother him. He was as one with the road; hat, hair, shirt and boots fading into the dun-coloured background. A man who belonged here.

She did not. Too dark, too restless, her hair a cloud of tangled curls and her hand playing a staccato of fidgets on the wooden planks. Everything about her was made for mist-drizzled forests, not hot, scorched plains.

He came to a stop in front of her. Tall and self-contained with his hands stuffed into his pockets and eyes the colour of light on a high mountain tarn in the cold of winter. They studied her now, looking her straight in the face with little sign of welcome.

"Caleb," said the man.

That was all. Fee would have liked a whole lot more. At home, she would have given her full name. Fioruisghe ingh Bram an Scathach den Coille, daughter of Bram and Scathach of the family Coille, and bowed in honour. But this was not home. She settled for a brisk nod.

"Fee." His home; he could make the first move.

"You the one sent by Central?"

She nodded and eased herself as upright as possible. The man, this *just Caleb*, kept his hands in his pockets. No hand shake, no attempt at one, just those eyes watching her. Unfortunately she couldn't stay perched up on this rail all day. She slid down to the earth. "You know why I'm here?"

He nodded and stepped back. "You coming?"

She supposed she was.

"To your home?"

He shook his head. "Down to the office."

She waited.

"Home's a bit farther on," was all he added, the set of his shoulders showing clearly that was all she was going to get.

She almost gave up, but Central had sent her here, and that meant she had to stay. One deep breath and she hoisted her pack onto her back to scramble after the man. He didn't stop but did slow down to let her catch up. So whatever she was here for mattered to him too. Would it be enough? Her orders had been brief, far too brief, but had made it clear they'd have to work together.

A flurry of dust sent her into a fit of coughing. He kept walking but did turn slightly to see she was all right, passing her a bottle of water and pulling her bag off her back, to lift it effortlessly onto his own. She muttered thanks, gulped down the water, and grit her teeth as he shoved a hat on her uncovered head. An hour later, and she was grateful for that too. Was there no cloud cover in this land?

Yet another hour of hard slog passed before the first buildings appeared. She guzzled more water, and refused to register the grimace on the man's face. Water was precious here, rainfall scarce. Her studies of the area before she came told her that, but reading about something and facing the reality of it were quite different.

She'd always imagined the plains were dead flat, yet that wasn't true either. Like a hastily thrown quilt, the land rose up in knobs and hummocks; an upward slope here, a hollow there. The town coming into view was built against one of the rising hummocks.

"Protects us from wind and helps temperature regulation," said the man beside her.

It didn't look much of a town. All the buildings were single-storied, many tucked back into the dirt of the hillside and each one capped with a distinctive roof: low-slung, and covered with a silvery woven cloth that merged with the silver straw of the local grasses. It was too distinctive, too unique to be for decoration only. Solar power generation was her guess, and the man beside her had to be the source. No one else here had his training. "Your design?"

"Partially." There was a closed look on his face and his hand waved her on. "The office is over there."

It certainly wasn't inviting on the outside. Small even by the scale of this town, the office was no more than two windows, a door at front, the low-slung roof and, over the door, a weathered sign proclaiming 'Ecological Survey Office'. By now, Fee didn't care as long as the inside was dark, cool and had drinking water. She had a sinking feeling that only the last was likely.

She followed Caleb inside and found she was right. Baking hot sunlight poured in the uncovered window and the temperature control system was singularly ineffective, but there was a water chiller over to one side. She poured out a mug and let her fingers dabble in the cool drops forming on the side as she sank gratefully onto the closest chair. The man Caleb had already taken the chair on the other side of the large desk and was sending a call through to their boss at Survey Central. Audio only, which told her even more about the security of this operation. Minimising data transfer cut down the risk of outside snoopers.

That suited her fine. It meant she could stay sitting right where she was.

"What's the story?" said Caleb after the preliminaries.

"Fee there too?" said the man on line they both knew as Fox. He had a long, important sounding title but all it meant was that he ran field operations on this continent.

"Here, boss."

"You've both received your portfolios and the logins to the operational file?"

Caleb grunted a yes. Fee nodded. "Yeah."

"I'm activating the file now. Read it tonight. I need your final plan as soon as you can scope out what's needed."

"Isn't that your job?" said Fee.

"Not this time." She didn't need visuals to see Fox's reaction. His voice was curt enough. What did he expect? That she'd be happy about being pulled out to this back end country. Right now, she was hot, tired and too on edge to care.

Caleb leaned forward. "This important?" he asked the boss.

"Of course."

"Why the two of us?"

"The profile analysis recommended your pairing as the most effective team. Your skill sets show the required compatibility."

Fee really hated it when Fox spoke in disembodied jargon. It usually meant he was hiding something—and that it would come back and bite her one day. "How long have we got?" she asked.

"Soon as you can—real soon." With which the man switched them off.

Fee scowled at the red light, and noticed Caleb was doing the same.

"There's a secured com point over there." He waved towards the wall, and she saw there was a smaller desk on the side. At least the docking console looked like it was made this century. She wished she could use her wrist pad, but orders ruled it out. Maximum security on this project.

What the hell was the Survey up to?

She took the seat, plugged in her remote point and brought up her screen. Luckily it used the standard Survey setup, for her so-called colleague showed no signs of helping her if she did have a problem. She logged in and pulled up the flagged file. A cursory glance at the summary, and on to the bit she most needed right now. The background file on her partner, or whatever this man Mr just Caleb was.

Full name: Caleb Winter. It fit, somehow.

Family: he actually had one. Quite a large one. Mother, father, two brothers and numerous cousins, uncles, aunts and assorted hangers on. She knew how that felt.

Grading: Ecological Engineer, First Class. Same as her, right down to rank. One of the top in a profession tasked with maintaining the environmental engineering of Arcadia to suit the planet's human settlers.

Specialisation: passive wind and solar utilisation. So the low-slung houses and special roofs had been a bit more than *partly* his design. Not that she had any intention of calling him on it.

"You're water and transpiration effects?" the man said now. He'd also checked her file first. "Not much call for that around here. Any water we get, we treat like gold."

She shrugged, forced to agree. Yet there was a reason she was here. The Survey rarely made mistakes. It couldn't afford to, not with what was at stake.

She stared a moment more at the tabs on his file, then switched back to the start. Time to find out what they were supposed to achieve here.

"No." The man's chair crashed to the floor. "Those bastards."

Now he was glaring at her. "This your idea? You mountain folk—you always wanted this place."

"What?"

"This scheme." He paced the length of the room and glared at her again. "You really don't know?"

She shook her head and turned back to the screen, feeling him watching her all the time.

She had to read it through twice, the first stage and the reasons for it. No wonder he was furious. "It appears simple enough," she ventured.

"Yeah. Simple. A great, big lake, dumped right in the middle of this sector—and that's just the start. It'll destroy this place."

She was still reading, still trying to get to grips with the data and figure out what was really going on here. It wasn't as if one lake would make much difference, not on its own. This had to be more about the big picture, the war the Survey was fighting to save their world from its own people. One lake would provide water for irrigation, would let the people here grow grass rather than hide from the sun, show them they could live in a kinder world. She looked at the projection figures.

"So what was here two hundred years ago," she said.

"Shrubs, open forest, tall grasses."

"And now?"

For a minute, she almost feared for her safety. He actually growled at her. "Shorter grasses, sparse scrub, herbs. So?"

"And the transition zone between your grasslands and the mountain forests?"

"Almost a single line. A clean cut." He was back to pacing. "The change; it's too abrupt. I know that. It's going to get drier here, dead, if nothing is done."

"This isn't just about the plains."

He looked at her as if she'd said he was an idiot. "Yeah, I get that. The Survey's playing a bigger game, but why do they have to start here?"

"Because you know these people," she guessed.

"Hearts and mind. But you know something? These plains, our world: we like them just as they are.

He kept pacing, one eye on the screen, reading even as he walked, till he finally ground to a halt. She gave him the dignity of silence, as he glared at the screen, then at her.

"Seems your services are needed."

It was a poor kind of concession but all she was going to get. She did her best to ignore him as he sat down again and went back to intently studying his screen.

For half an hour, only the occasional grunt or angry murmur broke the silence as they each pored over the rest of the plan. Words and images began running in circles in Fee's head.

Finally she shoved back her chair and stood up, looking round the room.

"Have you got a holo-field here? I need to get a proper handle on this."

He stood as well, looking no happier than her, and punched a code into his unit.

"Full security on?" she asked as the holo-field shimmered into life.

"For this? Hell yeah, at maximum."

The field settled, revealing a three-dimensional aerial view of their continent. Arcadia was a simple world. Two main continents, one circling half of the southern hemisphere, the other, her own, straddling the opposite quadrant of the northern, plus a scattering of islands and a small third continent in the seas between. Right now, it was her own land she was interested in, watching closely as he zoomed in. Other Survey teams could sort out the mess elsewhere.

From the short, coastal margin in the west, across the towering forest clad slopes of the main dividing range that was her home country, to the dry baked foothills and plains on this side. He set it to slow scan, hovering at easy speed over the brown grasslands of his home territory, out to the dry centre of desiccated sand and rocks with the occasional scrubby patch, to the lifeless centre, and on to the east, the washed out coastal hills before the land plunged into the eastern sea.

"And North?"

He changed direction, bringing it back to the dead centre, before swinging up to the great metropolises hovering on the edge of the sub-arctic region. Water was no problem there, fed by the great northern ice sheets and the generous rainfall as the hot central air currents hit the cold stream from the north. That's why the major cities were there.

He paused over the largest; a great expanse of tower blocks and traffic ways. The capital city, Urbis. They'd both been to college there—it had the only remaining school of eco-engineering—and was home to Survey head office.

"You visit often?" she asked, unable to quell her curiosity.

"Not unless I have to."

She wasn't surprised. Urbis had nothing in common with this fierce plainsman.

"Couldn't breathe there," he suddenly muttered.

A second comment. A breakthrough? Don't fool yourself, Fee. The man looked as surprised at admitting it as she was at hearing it.

But now was not the time to push it further. So her gut said anyway, in a sudden jittery swirling. "Can you extrapolate forward ten years, based on current ecological trends?"

His fingers stabbed at the com unit. The holo-field settled into a new pattern, one that shoved his mouth into a dead straight line. He added rainfall averages and prevailing winds, and it was Fee's turn to gasp, her eyes locked on her mountains in shock.

"You've read the figures," he said. "What did you think they meant?"

She stared at the dark band of gale force storms bearing down on her beloved trees. "We'll be destroyed. No planting will stop that." She stepped forward, jabbing at her unit to take control of the field, and zoomed in on her home town. A mighty sheet of water poured down the hillside, scouring away trees, tearing up rocks, overflowing old, familiar water courses. Her home tree, a mighty baullnia, the largest tree type of this world, stood square in the path of the torrent. Then it stood no more.

Her family's home was built within those branches. She stared in horror, the controls slipping unheeded from her hands.

"Sit," he shoved a chair in behind her, "before you fall."

So now she knew how he felt, and the twist of the corner of his mouth said he saw it. She had to fight hard to get herself under control, before surrendering charge of the field to him. She'd seen enough of her home's fate.

"Bring the scan back to this region, with no change."

The quirky twist disappeared and she was venal enough to feel pleased. He zoomed south again, and she recognised his town and the building they sat in, surrounded on all sides now by dying grasslands. Brown stalks, tough woody scrubs and stony ground. She remembered the view as she came in, hovering over long rippling waves of grasses. Dry, yes, but not leached of life as it looked in this projection.

A cluster of buildings stood out, some distance from town to the east. Towering over them was a field of waving pillars, silvery groves of tall metal flashings with endless flexi thin panels of sooty grey floating between them.

"What's that?"

"The nearest solar plant. It's not as big in this time, and there are open bush lands and animals around it still."

"And the buildings?"

"Houses." His face closed up. He shrugged, and relented. "My family compound. The main house is a bit farther away."

Aah. Hence the wealthy education and the air of command. Suddenly, she realised who he must be. She should have made the connection sooner—or Fox should have warned her.

Winter Solaris, the name behind the solar energy company that dominated the plains' economy. Usually known just as Solaris, but their logo included a large and florid W.

"They must have been thrilled at your choice of career."

The ghost of a smile but no explanation. She let him be. He'd read her file; must know she was a den Coille though he'd said nothing. "Add in the lakes; the first one we're building to start with, then the rest, along with the other changes they make possible."

He switched views again, putting in the new water sources, the new plantings and cross sculpturing of the landforms. She gasped. The change was impressive. Still mostly grasses and shrubs, but so much richer. Touches of green, along with animals and more houses. The solar array was smaller, but still substantial.

He moved the scan again, across to the centre. Grass, scrub, solar arrays again, but filled with so much more life, and back to the mountains, to see trees marching up the lower parts of the eastern slopes where only scrub stood today.

"Now add in the full scheme."

Both gasped.

She stepped forward, fascinated. "I've seen that before."

"Yeah. At college." His voice sounded as stunned as she felt. "It's straight out of the historical surveys from the first landings. Some of the plant types are imported and there's organised farms with sustainable cropping, but overall, that's what this world looked like before we came."

Fee stared. She knew the theories, her reports were part of the puzzle that gave it proof, but to see it brought to life like this…Their planet was unique, one of the few with carbon based life forms fully developed into a flora and fauna capable of supporting human habitation. The original eco-engineers had only to tweak what was here already. Except the money took control and the settlers did more than tweak.

The weather patterns in her home continent were well enough understood. Water laden winds streamed in from the western oceans, barrelling in soggy triumph over the narrow coastal flats and filled to greedy saturation, until they hit the dividing ranges. The clouds ruptured, dumping vast floods of their watery burden on the western slopes, and what was left had to supply the whole of the eastern plains. At the time of settlement, that rain had been enough to support extensive grasslands in the east. All that had changed.

Thanks to her family and others, today that western coastal strip was no longer a healthy mix of meadow and forest, but almost entirely covered by densely packed plantations of festia trees, source of a nutrient-rich pollen that was the basis of her family's wealth. The Den Coille company dominated the festia market as much as the Winter's did Solar energy production, power bought at a high cost to the dangerously unbalanced mountain slopes.

Solar power had dealt to the inland prairies. The energy barons, with Winter Solaris leading the pack, had stripped away any plants in the way of their vast arrays of sun-soaking panels. Not the only way to harness the sun's energy, as her new partner had shown with his roof designs, but by far the most profitable. The resulting desertification was a bonus as far as the solar barons were concerned.

Now, the mountain range was no longer the main problem. It wasn't high enough to explain the widening disparity in rainfall between west and east. No, that came from the catastrophic clash between the increased density of the forest on the western slopes and the hot rising thermals of the increasingly denuded plains. The rain clouds gathered their harvest of water from the oceans and across the thick forests then raced up the divide to smash headlong into the red-hot currents swirling up to the peaks. As if hitting an impenetrable wall, the clouds now dropped their load almost entirely on the west. The only water making it to the east had to travel underground, water that must wend its way through tunnels, cracks and aquifers before dissipating into the thirsty interior.

It was a pattern of damage repeated all over the planet, extremes in local ecosystems clashing with those of equally driven neighbours. Only the Survey stood between the powerful money lobby behind it all and the catastrophic environmental disaster that must come.

Yet something in her still hoped to be wrong. "Add in the populations able to be supported." She was holding her breath, she discovered.

Together they studied the new figures superimposed over the field. "About the same as now," said Fee. Caleb Winter nodded. "And without the plan?"

The figures settled, clear black against the underlying images. "On screen, number comparisons only," demanded Fee, even as his fingers worked.

The columns sprang to sharp life on his screen, the figures undeniable. This was what waited them if nothing changed.

"They are so low," Fee breathed.

"About a third of today's population, and that's only from the mountains."

"Your town is down to twenty percent."

"It's settled then." He looked no happier than her, glaring at the screen as if willing the figures to change.

She could sit still no more. "Strategy?"

It was as if he just remembered her presence. He swung round, his gaze raking over her from her small, softly-shod feet, up her dark leggings and leaf-green tunic to her face and hair. She looked different from him, did not fit here. She knew that.

"Not tonight. Not yet." He stood. "I'll show you where you're staying."

She stood too. Was forced to hurry after him to catch his long strides.

"And after?"

"We talk strategy. Just—not tonight."

Within minutes she was deposited in a small room in the attached annex. It had all the essentials, but she wasn't foolish enough to feel welcome.

"Don't leave the building. The fewer know you're in town, the better. And remember, if anyone asks, you're here on a routine calibration visit."

He stepped back, nodded a cursory farewell, and strode swiftly away. As if he couldn't rid himself of her presence quick enough.

CHAPTER TWO

Fee opened the bunkroom door and stopped out into a morning already warmer than any day she was used to. The harsh sun cut into the shadows and chased away the night's chill.

She had slept last night after a fashion. Not a restful sleep, rather one fraught with hazy images of danger. Her home tree, crashing down in a gale; dancing spikes of brown grasses jeering at her fears; and dust storms rising from the ground, racing to engulf her. In the middle of all the mayhem, the tall figure of Caleb Winter strode relentlessly forward.

Her hand jerked, and she took a hasty swallow of the bitter dask in the mug she held. Honest dask was how the man had described it last night as he gave her a brief rundown of the kitchen.

The annex layout was simple enough, much like all the other Survey quarters she'd stayed in. Bunk room, basic kitchen, laundry and combined dining/living area. Built to hold all the members of a research party, the space felt far too big and echoing for one person. Making it worse, her so-called colleague had barely checked she was settled before rushing out the door.

Escaping. That's how it had looked to her.

"Morning." A man walked down the street. Tall, dressed in a faded shirt and tough trousers like Caleb, he waved a laconic hand and went on his way. Not a curious people, these plains folk, it seemed. She lifted her mug to take another sip. It did bring you to life, she had to admit, and by the third sip came close to thinking it not such a bad drop after all.

Another person ambled down the street. A woman, dressed in similar, stout work clothes to the man. The shirt had once been red, she would guess, but was now a washed-out blush of colour. "Morning," she called to the woman, and got another laconic wave back.

A few more passed by as she stood on the doorstop. None showed much interest, but all gave her a friendly enough salute. She stood, watching the morning come to life, the sun quickly rising in the sky and the sheltering shadows of the early dawn burn off under the hot rays. She squinted into the distance. The office's front door opened onto the main street, but the annex looked out onto a side road at the edge of town. Across the road the surrounding plains faded into the distance. Vast and empty, threatening to dwarf any who failed to stand against the power of that unending panorama.

She watched the next person wander down the road. Again that slow lift of a hand in hello, the deliberate amble, seemingly slow but covering the ground easily and with a deliberate sense of purpose.

And all so much taller than her. Alien did not begin to describe how she felt. She stepped back inside and shut the door on the burning sun.

She'd only just finished breakfast when the door banged open and a familiar figure strode through.

"What the hell were you thinking? The whole town knows you're here," said Caleb Winter.

"Good morning to you, too."

He scowled back in answer as she tucked a falling strand of hair back behind her ear, wishing she had the courage to look down. Her buttons were all done up?

"Dask," she tried.

"You were meant to stay out of sight."

She remembered his farewell words of last night. "Why?"

He gave that about as much consideration as the dask mug she passed him, gulping at the burning liquid as if at water. It didn't appear to help much.

"I went into the store this morning and what's the first thing I'm asked. Who's the *pretty* stranger up at the quarters?"

"I just waved hello to a few passers-by."

His fist clenched the mug handle. "We don't do *passing by* out here. The only accidental *passer-by* was the first one. After that, you had Jenny May Scree, biggest gossip in town, the Mayor, the Chief Warden, and the owner of the general store— my third cousin—who just happens to also own half the rest of the shops in town."

It wasn't sounding too good. She thought of shrugging, but a strong sense of self-preservation stepped in. She tried looking meekly apologetic instead.

"Don't. I've seen your file. There's not a meek bone in your body." He gulped down another mouthful, a long deep swallow as if attempting to find sanity in its restorative powers.

She backed up, putting space between them to diminish the effect of his height. "Okay, sorry or whatever you want me to say, but I really don't see the problem. You must have had Survey staff visiting before."

"Not one planning to leave a whole damn lake behind when they left. Especially not where Central claims this one should go."

"It's in the wrong place?"

"No." It was dragged out of him. "Not for what the Survey wants it to do." He banged his mug on the table, thrust a hand through his hair and paced across the room. The man seemed to do that a lot. "You need to see it. From the ground."

Finally something that made sense.

"Finish your breakfast. We leave in half an hour." He tossed his unfinished dask into the waste chute, pushed the mug into the washer, grabbed open the door and slammed out.

Fee didn't move, sipping at the remains of her dask. It was cold. She screwed up her nose in disgust. Nothing for it but to get a move on. She hurriedly ate and showered, washing off the stale feel of the troubled night, stepped out and pulled her bag open. On top was the plains gear pack the Survey pilot had shoved into her hand as she'd entered the flyer, telling her to leave her own behind.

"No use where you're going," he'd said with little sympathy.

She'd kept hers anyway, tucking it like a talisman below the new one.

Caleb came back in exactly half an hour. He said nothing, just raked her from head to toe, studying her new gear. Tramping boots, still with that just-bought shine, khaki trousers unmarred by the persistent dust of the region. Ditto her long-sleeved shirt and cap. She had followed to the letter the guide in the pack, but all she got for her trouble was a brief nod before he picked up her bag and strode out, clearly expecting her to follow. *So he hadn't been able to criticise her gear. One very small point to her.* She hurried to catch him up, though wondered why she'd bothered as she still had to walk double to keep up with his strides.

He glanced at her. "We have to call in on the family compound on the way. They know you're here, now the whole town has seen you, so you'll have to meet them. Too many questions otherwise." A frown touched his face. "I run the Winter livestock operations. We'll say you're coming with me to check out the grazing near the ranges. The family is used to me taking Survey staff out there. It's an easy way for them to see the land, and keeps the Survey away from the areas that matter to Solaris."

She nodded, not sure what else to say. He knew his people. "My family must not find out what is planned," he added.

"You know best." So they had something in common, apart from their Survey link. Both of them must lie to those they loved. A dubious link.

Despite the basic look of the town, she was relieved to find they were to ride out in a modern skimmer. But too soon, the vehicle carried her into a world far from anything familiar. Out here, the vegetation felt even more forbidding. Tough scrub, spiky succulents, and bleached to near translucent grasses; and hot, so hot and dry. Nothing like her forest home on the far side of the mountains where she could dance in the rain, race down a tumbling stream, lift her cheeks to a fine mist on a summer's morning. She tugged her hat farther down her head and glanced across at the man Winter, wondering how he survived this heat.

Then recognised the look on his face as he stared out at the scrub and rocks. He loved this land as much as she loved her own, and that was something she must not forget.

They passed the third array of solar panels. So far, all had been the same. State of the art, simple, but extraordinarily ugly. She pointed at the last one.

"Why not use your roofline material instead?"

"Does the same job, yeah, but on a smaller scale and it's too expensive, so I'm told." There was a wry twist to his mouth; the nearest to any hint of empathy he'd shown.

Just then, they crested a slight rise and a house came into view. She gasped. Not just any house, not this place.

The Winter Homestead.

"My mother rules here," said the man beside her, in what she was coming to recognise as typical understatement.

She looked, and felt something inside her break. Trees. There were real trees, towering around the large, airy house. It should have looked incongruous, the design of it quite unlike the ground-hugging design of the houses in town. This house was double-storied, surrounded by wide porches on both levels, and light and cheerful. Surrounding it, a garden of rare beauty, mixing trees and brightly coloured flowers.

Here was a house that said "This land is mine" rather than "I belong to this land". Yet for all its alienness, it looked right. She could only stare in wonderment.

She tried calling on her training to make sense of the incongruity. Was it the clever transition from native to exotic in the garden margins, trees and shrubs merging into trees and foreign bushes and flowers, so that by the time the eye made it to the velvet green patch of lawn in front, there was no shock of transition? All, and yet none of that quite caught it.

"Your mother's not from here?"

He shook his head. "My great-grandmother. She was an off-worlder, from Earth. No one since has dared change it. My mother's a plainswoman but she loves it here. The native edging is hers. My father didn't want to change anything, but she made him."

If Fee hadn't been nervous already, that finished it. How formidable was this woman? She'd heard all her childhood of the reputation of Sol Winter, and had guessed more from the little Caleb said and the vast litany he left unspoken, but she had hoped for an ally in his mother.

What to hope for from a woman who could stand up to the head of Winter Solaris?

Caleb pulled up to the imposing front portico. A strange choice for a family member. The small driveway heading off to the side of the house had the well-used look that said that was how most came to this house, but she said nothing. The man looked near to uncomfortable as it was.

An awkward grimace, as he opened her door. "It's tradition, when someone hasn't been here before."

He marched up the wide steps leading to the front door and shoved a blunt thumb against the pad. The door slowly opened. An older man bowed slightly, a warm welcome on his face. Fee's nerves settled fractionally.

"Your mother is waiting in the green room, young Ser."

Caleb's smile was equally as warm and he touched the man on the shoulder before marching in through the doors, leaving Fee to follow in his wake.

"A colleague, James," was all the explanation he offered, but the man bowed low and gave her a formal smile of welcome.

"This way, Sera," he said as his arm waved her in. She hurried to catch up. Caleb was opening a door, and she followed after him into a truly beautiful room. Walls sprang to life with a pale swirl of green and white, leaves and flowers mingling together in harmonic serenity, and the furniture was a mix of the decorative and the stunningly comfortable.

She halted as she noticed the tall woman rising gracefully from a chair. The likeness to her son was undeniable, especially when the woman raised her eyebrows as she looked pointedly at Fee, standing just behind her son.

"A colleague, here on a calibration visit," said Caleb.

The woman's eyebrows rose a notch higher, and her son shrugged in a kind of surrender.

"Mother, may I present Sera Fioruisghe ingh Bram an Scathach den Coille. Fee, my mother, Helena Bascombe Winter."

Fee wasn't sure which stunned her most: that he'd taken note of her full name in her file, or that the man was capable of formal courtesies.

She bowed her head to his mother and spoke the proper words of greeting from her homeland. Her new Survey clothes obviously fooled no one, for the woman looked unsurprised and returned with the accepted mountain reply.

"May you and yours flourish. You are welcome under our canopy." She gestured to a chair beside her. "Please, be seated."

"We can't stay, Mother. We're heading out to the west range to check the stock. The Survey can only spare Fee a few days."

Huh. Fee had assumed this assignment would take weeks, rather than days. This man had some explaining to do. When they were alone, that is. For now, she took the seat indicated and blandly met his mother's gaze.

"Den Coille? Of the festia plantations?" Her face cool, the woman's mouth twisted in distaste.

Fee nodded. "My family's home is directly across the ranges."

The mother dipped her head in assent but left it at that. Her son rose abruptly. "We have to get going."

"Your father will want to see you."

"Is he here?"

"Out in the sheds with Ethan."

Another of those indecipherable looks on Caleb Winter's face. "Tell him I called in." Then Fee was forced to gallop after him again. Just once, she wished he would remember she needed two steps to each one of his as he strode out the door and through the complex of buildings lurking behind the homestead.

He stopped at a plain, square-built shed, quite unlike the environmentally attuned buildings of the town. Inside, a man input data to a screen and another lounged against the back wall, watching. Caleb nodded to them.

"Cay." The young man leaning against the wall nodded back. When he saw her, he straightened up, a very interested smile on his face and a twinkle in his eye.

"Hel-lo."

Caleb frowned at him. "Down, Si."

"So," said the young man, taking a step forward.

Caleb frowned again, gave one of those disgruntled shrugs of his and gestured at the grinning man. "Fee, my baby brother Silas. The one making himself useful at the table is our tech wizard, Jake." The man at the screen briefly glanced up to acknowledge her then turned back to his screen. "Fee's here on a calibration trip. She's busy, working."

"Unlike some of us," said Si with so much laughter in his voice Fee got the feeling that teasing his big brother was one of his chief delights. "Don't listen to my surly brother, pretty lady. I'm sure you can spare me one evening to let me show you the pleasures of our humble town?"

She couldn't stop the smile touching her lips and reluctantly shook her head, aware of the dictates of security. "Sorry, but Caleb is unfortunately right. Ask me again if I come back," she couldn't resist adding.

The graceless rogue took her hand and bowed low. "With the greatest of pleasure, sweetheart."

She could almost feel the fire of Caleb's eyes burning a hole in her back and reluctantly dropped the hand. Suddenly, a gruff shout ratcheted through the air from outside and the laughter was wiped from the young man's face.

"Damn," said Caleb. "Back door?"

"Too late," said Si. "He'll know you're here."

Another moment, and a large frame blocked the doorway.

It didn't take the age of the man to tell Fee his name; the likeness to Caleb was too strong. Older, broader built, but with the same lean features and rangy height.

"Pa," said Caleb, the formality of his voice belying the familiarity of the word. "Ethan."

Only then did Fee notice the second man standing behind Sol Winter. A man with the face of their mother, but the same height and stance as his brothers and father.

"I heard you were here," said Sol Winter.

"I'm on my way to the west range."

"And the girl?"

If Fee had any illusion the man hadn't seen her, which she didn't, it would be gone now. The older man scanned her from head to toe, lingering on the badge on her shoulder that matched the one on his son's.

"Survey," he spat, "and mountain stock, from that face."

"She's here on calibration, as legally required."

"Just make sure she stays on the western range."

Legally, she could go anywhere needed for her work, but now did not seem to be a good time to remind the head of Winter Solaris of that fact. As it was, the man at the table had shut down all data screens as soon as they heard Winter Senior shout. Shut them down so Sol Winter wouldn't think she'd seen what was on them, she realised now.

"Fee; my father Sol Winter and my brother Ethan." There was a hint of a wearied sigh in Caleb's voice as he answered. Did his father hear it too? His other brother stepped forward, giving her a brief nod, his face as cool as his mother's.

"Ethan manages the solar side of the business."

"Since my eldest son sees fit to spend his life elsewhere, someone had to."

Caleb's eyes darkened and he glanced over at Ethan. "We're going now," he said.

"In that Survey skimmer of yours, I suppose. At least take a family vehicle with a tracker to let us know if you get into trouble."

"The Survey one in the skimmer works fine. They can find me as well as any of your trackers."

There seemed nothing more to say after that. Sol Winter shoved into the room, forcing her and Caleb to step back and down the steps. Young Silas winked at her as she left, and the older brother, Ethan, glared at Caleb with such a look of pain in his eyes.

Family. Yes, she and Caleb definitely had that problem in common, and felt a huge rush of relief as their skimmer set out from the Winter compound to head west.

"Can they track us?"

Caleb didn't bother asking who she meant. "No. The Survey's tracker unit will shield us."

She got the feeling she wasn't the only one who suddenly felt free as they left the Winter homestead. Next stop, this new lake. A lake site Caleb Winter hadn't told her the full truth of yet.

CHAPTER THREE

Hours later, they pulled up beside a small hut. That was all Fee could call the building in front of her. Four walls, a roof, and not much more. She was already feeling crabby. Being stuck for hours beside a silent man who clearly didn't want you there did that to you. Then she stepped out of the skimmer into the full blast of the heat. The sun was right overhead and blazing down at full strength. All she wanted was shade and food, not some stupid stop over at a shack in the middle of nowhere.

Caleb Winter pulled his bag from the back, then picked up the other Survey kit.

"Bring your gear."

She stared. He was really taking out his pack. *This* was their destination? She looked all around, searching for something other than flat, scrubby dirt.

"We're supposed to be going to the lake site."

"Lunch time," was all he said, and walked into the hut.

Food did sound good, and the hut was at least out of the sun. She climbed out stiffly, hoisted her bag onto her back and followed him inside.

It looked no more promising than the outside. Caleb was doing something over a solar cooker on the other wall, and in the middle was a simple table and bench seating. Very hard, planked seating.

"Sit yourself down," said Caleb.

That better not be an amused smile on his face.

She began to cheer up when he pulled out a condensation splashed bottle of water from a chiller set under the bench. He lifted an eyebrow in query and she nodded vigorously as he sloshed some into two mugs.

Soon after, he produced two plates of food that smelled absolutely heavenly, and her hopes began to rise. Fortunately he said nothing, just began to eat, lifting his mug in silent toast. To what, she wasn't sure, but felt impelled to join him. Then shrugged at her moment of weakness, and lifted her fork to begin.

It was amazing what food and drink did to a body. She might even start to like this plainsman. But it was a momentary weakening only, abruptly banished as he finished and stood up, sweeping everything back into his pack and the concealed units of the rough looking room. "Better get a move on. We've still a way to go."

Outside, he disappeared behind the hut—only to emerge leading two horses, and pulling out saddles from a locker on one side of the shack, or she guessed that was what the objects over his arm were. She'd only ever seen horses or their equipment on readers.

She stared in consternation at the large beasts. Very large beasts.

"You don't mean…?"

But he did. She watched him saddle up the larger horse. Halfway through, he looked over at her as if to say *get on with it*.

"Err—you do realise I've never ridden before?"

For an instant there was a hint of real emotion on his face. Surprise. To quickly vanish again, leaving that contained face of his making her feel even smaller.

"She's quiet enough. I'll saddle her up in a minute."

"Couldn't we take the skimmer?"

He shook his head. "Too unusual if we're seen. Technically, this may be public reserve out here, but it's been under Winter control as long as anyone remembers. We only run stock on it, and horses are best for stock work."

"And we don't want any questions. Not this early in the project," she added sourly.

All too soon, she was standing beside a horse that towered over her and listening to a curtly delivered set of instructions.

"Lift your left leg back." Next minute, she was flung into the saddle, landing with a thud. The horse jigged forward a step then halted as the man tugged on the rein. "You're lighter than I expected."

Was that supposed to be an apology?

He passed up both reins. "Hold these, don't move and wait till I mount up."

He walked over to his own horse, leaving her in sole command of the beast. She tensed all over, even more so when the horse began to walk forward. The man swung up onto his own horse and effortlessly turned it as he grabbed at her reins, bringing her mount to a halt.

"Relax," he ordered in a disgusted voice. "Tightening your legs like that makes Janie think you want to move off."

Relax. Easy enough for him. Her hands clutched the spur at the front of the saddle. He looked her over and pulled one of the reins out of her grasp, leaving her the other. "I'll lead till you get your seat. After that, you'll have to learn to ride." He tugged gently on the lead, and she clung tighter as she felt the horse move under her again. "Don't worry, we're only walking today."

Maybe he meant to sound reassuring, but after a very few hours, Fee was a mass of aches and tired muscles. They had kept to a walk as he promised, but within a short time of starting, he'd tossed the leading rein back to her, along with a string of instructions. She made herself listen and learn, just to stop the lecture. The sun was still high overhead, beating down relentlessly, and she was near begging for release from the continual plod and ache of pulverised seat muscles. They had seen some stock on the way, Caleb marking them on his data pad, and taking screen shots of what he called the condition score points.

Finally, he pulled on the horse's reins and directed them into the shadow of a cluster of blue-gray bushes. She urged her horse forward, drinking in the illusion of darkness as she escaped the sun.

Caleb climbed down, loosening his gear, and she followed suit with her own horse. It was beginning to be too much of a pattern, her following in his wake.

"Bring your gear. This is the project site."

At last. She untied the Survey bag Caleb had roped to the back of her saddle, and reached up to grab the spare water bottle.

He noticed, and gave a nod. "But save it for emergencies. That canteen has to last the day."

He pulled out two dishes from the back of his saddle, put one in front of each horse and poured water into them before looping their reins over a scraggly bush. Then set off up the slope on the other side of the bushes, leaving her to scrabble after.

As yet another stone slid from under her feet, she stopped and let loose a string of curses. She was sore enough as it was, without risking a twisted ankle. She'd be lucky if she could still walk after this trip was over.

Caleb had disappeared over the top of the rise in front. An imperceptible rattle of rocks above and he was back. Another point against him, she grouched to herself. He moved over this hellish soil of rocks and gritty sand as silently as if he were threading through the branches of home after game.

"Do you want the whole territory to know we're here?" he said.

It was too close to her own thoughts for comfort. "This isn't my usual place," she muttered back.

Her skin was burning, her head hurt and her legs felt like jelly from that dratted horse. She grabbed her canteen out for another long swallow, only to have it snatched off her and the cap screwed back down. The man sloshed it, judging the level inside.

"Save it. That's got to last—and put your hat back on." His hand grabbed at her belt, pulling out the cap she'd shoved through it.

"Hate hats," she grumbled.

"Sunstroke's worse."

Mr Bloody Perfect. But he did give her time to breathe, to squat down on the side of the hill and gingerly feel her ankle.

It would do, she decided. He said nothing as she stood slowly and carefully tested the ankle. She took a step, then a few more. He raised an eyebrow and she nodded. They set off again, but this time he stayed beside her and took it much slower. Near the top where the slope evened out, he waved a hand downwards. She copied him as he crouched close to the ground.

"Follow me exactly," he said.

At last, an order that made sense. Her muscles still ached, but this kind of work she understood. They crawled the last metres, heads carefully below the tops of the tough grasses. She began to appreciate the long sleeves and trousers of her plains gear, but gave no thought to complaining as the rocks tore at her hands and knees. She was almost as silent as he, and for the first time he gave her a nod of approval.

At last, they were at the top of the hill. She huddled down, wishing for cover more like she was used to: a tree, a shrub, even a spiky bush. There was nothing on this hillside but long grass to protect them from unfriendly observers as she inched forward to peer over the brow of the hill. Down below, a dusty creek bed meandered through a natural hollow, butting up steeply by this hillock before spreading out to meld into the plain. She had seen the plan, and now looked for the proposed shoreline.

"It looks a fair site for a lake."

The man beside her stiffened. What had she said now?

"See that rock down there?" He pointed to the centre of the hollow

"The big black one by the bend in the creek bed?" It was more a boulder, standing taller than two men and with a wide, flat space on top.

He nodded. "The Council Rock, we call it. When I returned from college, I stood on that rock to pledge myself to my family and people. I promised them I would keep the grasslands safe."

Legally, it wasn't a lie, but that was no help. He hadn't promised there would be no change, but that's what his people would have heard. She got that. She also knew he had no choice. She'd done the same to her people.

"They believed me," he said.

"We need a lake there."

"And you'll get one. And trees, and shrubs, and winds that don't kill every plant in their path above leg height. But see this?"

He lifted a rock, one of the many littering the soil and digging into her body as she lay there. Beneath it was a crusty piece of—crud, was all she could think. Not much bigger than her thumb and looking like a piece of dried-up dung covered in crusty lichen. His finger gently traced the length of it.

"Just a few drops of water is all it takes. *Billyups* we call them. Always ready for a drink, like the bloke who keeps asking 'Billy up yet?' It's hibernating now, but when the rains come, that outer shell absorbs every drop of water it can get. Within a few hours, you've got a kind of slug with legs that eats grass, pollen, insects, anything."

He gently lowered the rock back over the thing, his mouth crooked. "You bring the lake in and old billyup will be done for. He only survives here because there are few creatures that can make it through the dry spell. He gets that first bit of water, feeds himself up as quick as he can, and lays a whole bunch of babies that dig deep before any other creature comes round. And then old billyup dries his skin layers up again with all that water stored safe inside him until the next rains. That's how he survives. You make the place wet, those other creatures will outdo him every time and old billyup will disappear."

"Your people will survive. They can build new kinds of houses, grow crops, earn money by something other than solar farms."

"But will they still be my people?"

It was a question she must answer too. Not yet, but soon, if the Survey's plan was to succeed, and the answer was irrelevant. There was no choice, and no point telling him that. He understood it as well as her.

The planet had spoken. *Change, or I will. Flood, storm, drought. Don't bother taking your pick because you're going to get the lot.* The Survey had run the models so many times, and always the same outcome.

Only no one believed them. Ecological engineers like Caleb and her had once made this world; now they were universally scorned, their skills valued only when it suited.

More trees on the back slope, said her father. More festia blossoms in spring, more sap in autumn. The lifeblood of her family, the blossom pollen was rich in nutrients, the sap a widely used fuel source. Problem was, festia trees loved dense plantings, feet bathed in a swampy sponge and moist air. No room for useless, empty meadows on her father's mountain slopes.

She had plenty of anger inside her already. Caleb Winter had no right taking his out on her.

"So you lose this Council rock? People can just find another place closer to town. This is hours away."

"That's what you think. It's that easy?" He stared hard at the rock, his body rigid. Finally, he shimmied back from the edge and rolled over to face her. "You think it'll be the same? That rock, it's like a sanctuary. Once up there, anyone is safe to speak."

She was starting to feel guilty, and didn't like it. "This is what you use for…"

"…Name blessings, proclamations, the important stuff? Yeah. It's where a young couple brings their wedding flowers; and where our youth spend the last night of their childhood."

Her anger rushed out of her. "We have a tree boll like that. Beneath it, I pledged to serve after my graduation. But we did not promise *how* we would serve."

"No." His fist grabbed at a clump of grass, yanking it out by the root. "The Survey, it's our only hope. I know that." He stared down at the clump of burnt grass in his hand. "Do you know the current wattage price of solar power?"

She shook her head. "I know my father moans about it a lot."

"I do, to multiple decimal points. My whole family does. The Old Man would like nothing more than to clear every last plant and spread solar arrays all over our land. He only paid for me to go to college so that I could sign off the environmental consents."

"You don't know that."

"Yes, I do. He told me before I left."

"So what happened?' Fee kept her voice dead even, fearful of stopping him.

"There are certain facts you can't deny, not with our training." He rolled back onto his stomach and stared down at the rock.

"Lots do," she said, and thought of her own family.

"Yeah." He was silent. Until, as if dragged out of him, he added. "One day, with luck, I'll have children. I'd like for there still to be a world here that they can live in."

She shuffled carefully forward, reassessing the site, seeing the natural contours of the land and where the beaches could go. Too high, and the water would endlessly seep into the land, undermining the roots of the shrubs they must plant; too low, and the surface area of water for transpiration would be insufficient to seed the surrounding region and thrust back the encroaching desert. Thinking hard, she ran an eye over Caleb's rock.

She did it again, from three different angles.

"There's no way to save it," she finally said. "It will be at least two metres under water at the minimum possible depth."

He looked surprised. "And at the optimal?"

"Three metres down. Barely visible."

It was the nearest she could come to an apology, and he seemed to realise it.

"Thanks for trying." There was a slight easing in his shoulder and when he spoke again, his voice was once more set on business. "So show me exactly where the shore line is to be."

She took his lead and let her training take over. For the next half hour, she pointed out the shore line, where the beaches must go, where she needed deeper-rooted shrubs to hold the bank. He in turn looked at the wind patterns, pointing out where the plantings must go to allow the maximum transpiration without letting all the precious water vapour dissipate uselessly.

She had to concede that the man knew his home country. He was intimately familiar with the wind patterns and how the surrounding land affected them, from where the water laden breezes came and where the scouring dry storms that leached the life from all plants.

Surprisingly, they worked well together. The holo-map of the proposed lake lay before them as they sprawled in the dirt. He made changes to the plants she proposed, and she modified the shoreline levels as he pointed out the lie of the land and where it affected the outcome. She got so wrapped up in the work, that it was not till she moved to smudge in a new headland that she realised how long they had been lying there.

"Urgh." A nasty tweak from a neck too long bent. He looked up as she reached to rub the abused area.

"Time to take a break," he said, beginning to shuffle backwards.

Gratefully, she followed his lead, still keeping below the sight line of the vegetation till they were once more within the shelter of the blue bushes. The horses waited patiently, their trough now empty, and they licked greedily at the square nutritab Caleb offered them both.

They were mounted and on their way before he said anything more about the project. "You seen enough? Best you don't stay here longer than necessary. I'll keep my links open and we can finalise the rest of it tomorrow."

She nodded agreement. "How long before we can set the charges to start filling?"

"Depends on the weather."

She had wondered where they were going to get enough water for the lake. The dusty creek bed seemed a poor embryo for the lake she envisioned. "So you need rain?"

"Yeah. Everything has to be set to go by the first month of the wet season."

"Wet?" She looked around in disbelief.

"It's all a matter of degree," he said with a chuckle. "You've seen the geoprofiles. Most of our rain falls close to the ranges—what water makes it over from the trees on your side—then gets lost in the aquifers under the plain. That dry creek bed can be a raging torrent for all of a day then it disappears. But hidden underground, there's a sea of water. That's where most of what we use comes from, after purification and ion removal."

She had read of some of this, but listening to his slow drawl and watching his hands bring the words to life made it real. As real as the storms and thunder of her own country she loved so much. She had quite forgotten the aches of the morning, and it wasn't until the afternoon sun caught her in the eye that she took note of their direction.

"This isn't the way back to the hut?"

He chuckled again. Twice in one day! "Remind me never to let you set the direction."

Fee wriggled in her seat, beginning to feel the effects of muscles never exercised in quite this way before. "How much farther are we going?"

"Don't worry," was all he said, and kicked on his horse. They stopped late afternoon at a hidden spring to water them, Caleb pulling it up into the troughs and adding a tablet.

"It precipitates out the salts," he explained. "The horses know to drink only from the surface." They refilled their own bottles as well, and he suggested she taste it before he treated them.

One sip was enough. She spat it out.

"Not good?" he asked meekly.

"Definitely not good." She was still trying to get the bitter taste from her mouth. Salty and decidedly nasty. "There was a point to that?"

"Easiest way to make sure you never depend on untreated water. Doing that can kill you round here."

It wasn't the only thing likely to kill him, she thought darkly, wishing that for five minutes she could set the man down in her forest home. See how he liked being the outsider.

Not long after that, she heard the jets of a flyer landing. Her ride home, she guessed, and she discovered a sudden bite of regret with the realisation that she'd found a degree of peace in this strange ride she'd not have thought possible a day ago.

They were in a flat bowl, hidden from the east by a low lying series of hillocks. A perfect place for a surreptitious changeover.

"Your family?"

"They're used to Survey staff coming and going. But best they don't get to see a Survey flyer up close."

That she understood too. Letting her father ever see the level of technology at the Survey's command would raise far too many questions. Not when he thought it a small, useless department that did nothing much.

"I'll send the rest of your gear over with the next outwards Survey packet."

She nodded acceptance, hoisted her bag into the flyer and thrust out a hand in farewell. She could be all business too. "I'll scan you my notes once I write them up"

He took her offered hand, a short clasp, no more. "I'll input them into the overall scheme and send you the plan updates."

There was little to be said after that. They had a lot to do in the next months, but nothing more needing to be decided now.

Then he bent down, touched his lips to her cheek and stepped back, saying nothing. She lifted her hand, feeling the place his lips had been.

"Keep safe," he murmured, and watched her climb into the flyer.

CHAPTER FOUR

She was back on the plains. The wet was coming, said meteorology; time to get that lake filled, ordered Fox. Fee stepped down from the flyer and into a furnace. This was supposed to be the wet? She'd thought it was hot last time she was here, months ago at the start of the dry. Now, it was as if someone had taken a blow torch to the land. Burnt grasses and the smell of baked earth filled the air. Caleb Winter better have atmospheric controls in his skimmer. Then she heard the neigh of a horse, and a rider appeared over the horizon.

Leading a second horse. *He must be joking.*

The flyer lifted off, abandoning her again, as Caleb rode up and lifted a hand in greeting. "Sera Fee."

"Caleb." They'd had been in regular contact since she left, first name contact. The man needn't think she was going to start using formal titles. His mouth quirked in answer, and he climbed down from his horse. His very high horse. Both animals looked quiet enough but she still looked hopefully about for a skimmer—or any proper kind of vehicle.

No such luck. Caleb lifted her backpack and tied it to the saddle of the second horse. "Two riders are harder to track than a vehicle," he said. "One visit by a den Coille is suspicious enough for Solaris. Two looks like an invasion."

He pulled the hat and water bottle from the back pocket of her pack and shoved the hat down on her head.

She glared back, but it had no effect on the plainsman.

"Heat stroke's dangerous."

He lifted her into the saddle and she had to clutch tightly to the pommel as her horse lurched after his. He quickly grabbed the reins from her. She made to grab them back. "You taught me what to do last time."

"When you remember it properly, I'll give the reins back."

She opened her mouth to argue, just as the horse gave a slight stumble and she clutched at its mane. Worse, when she looked up, he wore the trace of a hastily buried grin.

"Fine."

They rode on all morning, following a seemingly random line across the plains. He gave the reins back after an hour, taking her through a series of riding lessons. She needed to be able to do more than sit on a horse like a sack of victuals, was his explanation. They might have been fun, if she hadn't been plain terrified. Some of it wasn't too different from her treks through the forest canopy, her body falling into a natural rhythm as if on a wind driven branch. Trotting was weird, but she got the motion of it; the slow canter was easier; but her brief attempt at a gallop left her white faced and the plainsman clearly stifling laughter. After that, he agreed she knew enough to get by; or maybe he didn't want to kill her quite yet. She wasn't totally sure which.

For the rest of the morning, they seemed to wander aimlessly about the plains. They passed a few herds of nieten, a native animal now domesticated, so she had to assume he was making it look like they were checking the stock as he'd claimed the last time they came out here. Finally, she recognised a rise of land, and not before time. For the last hour, she'd fought to keep awake, battling the lure of escape from the heat and the plodding horse under her.

They tied up in the same place as last time, under a group of scrubby bushes. Fee slid off and bolted for the scarce patch of shade. Caleb said nothing, attending to the horses and pulling out what looked blissfully like a cooler pack holding lunch, but never taking his eyes off her. Once finished giving the horses their water, he stalked over.

"Sit, before you fall." He opened the cooler, and passed her a bottle of something liquid.

Cold and wet, that was all that mattered right now, but it turned out to be sweet, juicy and absolutely delicious as well. She grinned. "I needed that. Thank you."

His face closed suddenly over, as if she'd surprised him.

I'm not fragile, just alien to this place.

No, they had a job to do. Worrying about how he saw her would get them nowhere.

At least he put an excellent lunch together.

Afterwards, they walked round the spur of the hill to come onto the lake site just below the ridgeline. She had studied the holo-vids of it so often, but seeing it again crystallised all the figures and diagrams in her head. Over there, they would dig channels to improve the flow; to the left would one day be groves of Beith trees. One day, when they had changed the local microclimate enough.

Seeing it, making it real, for the first time she began to believe they could do this. "You and your team have done a good job here." She gazed around, setting in the wider picture. "When do I get to meet them?"

"Soon enough."

Damn him. Just when she'd begun to think he might be half human. "Make it soon. I can only spare a few days."

He hadn't even sent her his team list yet—for security reasons, he'd claimed. Like her mountain team, the rest of his team worked undercover, hiding the extent of their Survey duties under an innocuous everyday job. Only Fee and Caleb openly worked for the Survey in this area, and their role had always been kept deliberately low key. The Survey only worried about results, and had learned long ago that corporates and the public would block most open restrictions on their activities. There were environmental laws, and all the regions paid lip service to following them. But not enough, nowhere near enough to stop what was happening to Arcadia. So the Survey worked behind the scenes.

Yet Caleb could have told her the names of his team—if he trusted her. No, he kept their names secret for the same reason she hadn't told him of her own group. Not till she had proof, till she believed deep in her gut he would not betray her people.

The man beside her glanced up at the sun. "Time to go."

The afternoon matched the morning. Endless roaming through parched lands. She was fast losing patience; hot, dirty and feeling ever more useless. There better be a reason for all this trekking about. She gulped at her water bottle, realised it was empty, and thrust it back into her pack. Caleb Winter silently passed her another, his own canteen.

"No, you need it."

"I have another, but that's all there is."

One more point against her.

Just then, another horse appeared on the ridge line ahead with a young man on its back. Fee was getting very good at reading body language, and the man beside her showed too little surprise at seeing the newcomer. "You know him?"

Caleb Winter nodded. "One of our stockmen."

She sat unmoving on her horse as the two men greeted each other.

The stranger was looking pointedly at her, and his horse nudged Caleb Winter's. Grudgingly, Caleb waved a hand in her direction.

"Ben, Fee. Fee, Ben."

Well, that told her a lot. But the younger man grinned and put out a hand to shake. Good manners made her return the clasp, and she gave a polite smile back.

He immediately brought his horse around to the other side of hers, filling the silence with endless chatter as they rode. When pumping her about her background failed, he moved on to constituting himself her unofficial tour guide.

After a time, she had no choice but to give in to his cheerful goodwill. He looked younger than her, but not by much she guessed, and beneath his banter lay a wealth of knowledge of this land and the animals that lived here.

She had thought the plains empty till Ben pointed out the hunting bird so high in the sky she could barely make it out.

"What's the point of being so far up?"

"No good for us," he agreed, "but perfect if you have the eyesight of a top rate telescanner. Prey can't see him but that fellow up there sees anything that moves down here. Just watch him now."

The bird had drifted lower, seemingly uninterested in the ground below.

"Now watch the near ridge," said Ben quietly, his hand softly lifting. "See that spot beside the orange rock."

They were still riding on but the other two had slowed. Beside her, Caleb Winter's hand smoothly checked her horse though he said nothing.

A black slash through the sky, a plummet of a bullet shape and a puff of dust. Then the bird was pulling up again with slow beats of its powerful wings and a small bundle dangling from its claws.

"It's a ganda, a small, ground-dwelling native. They hide down their tunnels when they think old Jack Robber's around, but that one was on sentry duty and never saw it coming.

"How sad," she said.

"Just nature," said Caleb Winter. "Just is."

She knew that, but the speed and violence had been so swift, the end so complete. "They both have to live," she said, as much to herself as to the others. "Jack Robber—is that a local name or the bird's real one? I haven't heard of it before."

"Local," said Caleb Winter abruptly.

"Real, like ganda," said young Ben. "We're not hot on names given by outsiders round here. Our own tell you so much more."

What could she say to that? Nothing, it appeared, as they came up over the ridge of dry grass and all thought of worrying what they thought fled. The men carried on, but what Fee saw in the flats below had her tugging sharply on her horse's reins. Caleb Winter's horse was over the slope and starting on the clearly marked path down the other side before he noticed she'd stopped. He pulled his horse in and looked back.

"And this is?" She was feeling decidedly nasty.

"Base camp."

"Camp? More like a mini town. Bet you even got showers and real cooking down there."

"Yep. Everything you need," said Ben helpfully, also stopping. It took him a minute longer than Caleb Winter to realise his mistake, but at least he let it show on his face.

Fee stared down at the collection of buildings below, buildings complete with antennae and solar roof coatings telling of up to date amenities, all built in the style she recognised from the main town, a style owing much of its design to the man sitting on the horse in front of her.

"I thought you didn't want me to be seen in towns?"

"It's not a town. It's the base camp for the Winter cattle range. Only stock workers live here."

"And it's safe?"

"You have my word."

She stared hard at him, challenging that. His steady gaze gave her back her answer, and finally she gave the smallest of nudges to her horse's flank, loosening the reins to let it follow the other horses down to what she guessed was their home stable.

"We talk tonight. I don't like working blind."

"And I don't like outsiders here."

Ben leaned over. "Don't worry. If the boss gets too much, you can bunk up with me."

Winter glowered but it made no impression on the young man. "You might enjoy us more than you expect," Ben added.

Thoroughly nettled, Fee wished for the umpteenth time for a sight of one, large honest-to-goodness tree and the welcome feel of rain on her face. Anything that spoke of home.

The next few hours were a bustle of arrival and meetings. Most of the buildings were for work, she discovered: a stable for the horses, grain and supply stores, a communications suite that stunned her with the level of equipment, and administration offices. The remainder were the living quarters of the staff, around twenty men and women who drifted in as Caleb Winter showed her around.

More tired than she cared to admit, the stock crew remained a blur of faces and voices until well into the evening meal. Most of the talk passed over her head and she gratefully subsided into a pile of cushions on a bench after the tables were cleared as one after another brought out musical instruments or talked of their day. There was a harpist and a singer of rare beauty, and a hush fell over the room as they launched into song. It was nothing like the music of her mountain home, yet somehow it fit this place. Too soon, they were finished and the volume of talk rose again as she blinked hard on heavy eyelids.

"Go to bed," said the voice of Caleb Winter beside her. "No one will be offended."

She suddenly realised what the firm but comfortable cushion under her head was. Caleb Winter's shoulder. She jumped back, abruptly and disconcertingly awake.

"I'm fine," she muttered, edging away from him and thoroughly embarrassed. He said nothing, and after a while she began to relax again, listening to the talk around her. Really listening for the first time to talk, it dawned on her, she understood all too well.

She waited a bit longer, just to make sure.

"You're all Survey!"

Heads turned, and young Ben grinned, for which he would pay later. As for Caleb Winter…

He turned that cool gaze of his on her. "Of course. How else could we keep the Survey plans for out here secret? Or maybe you think my family won't notice a large lake and plantings in their back yard?"

She no longer knew what to think.

"Introductions needed, Boss," suggested young Ben, still with that amused grin on his face.

Caleb Winter stood and pointed out the various staff members, who each waved cheerily at her as their name and specialisation was called out. It turned out Ben was a zoologist. Among the rest were a botanist, hydrogeologist, hydrologist, meteorologist, horticulturalist, agricultural scientists, engineers, a veterinarian—to monitor the effects of the changes on the stock, said Caleb—pure ecologists and two other ecological engineers. Over them all and bringing everything together were Caleb and herself. Or that's what she remembered her orders saying. Whether the man beside her had ever read that part of the plan, she seriously doubted.

"You couldn't have told me this earlier?"

"No." It was uncompromising. "They all come from this region and most have families who have no idea they work for the Survey."

She hunched her shoulders. "You think I don't understand the risk of being found out? That my family know what I really do for the Survey?"

"Who knows what mountain folk think."

She stood, hating that blank stare in his eyes. "I wish you all good night," she said to the assembled company, feeling their awkwardness and seeing too many shuffles. But they all wore the sun-lined faces of plains people, faces that sided with the man beside her. She turned back to him.

"Yes, Ser Winter, I am from the mountains. But I am Survey, first and last."

With which she marched off to her lonely bed.

Caleb watched her go.

"Well done, Boss," said Ben. He wasn't the only one thinking that, by the looks on the faces around him.

"And you think there's none of the Old Man in you," said a woman sardonically.

He'd known Suze since they were both babies. "She's a risk. One we can't yet discount."

"Maybe," said Gerard, one of the other ecological engineers, "but you've read her reports."

He gave a single nod of his chin in confirmation.

"Then you know she's got as clear a brain as comes, and a backbone of solid steel in that tiny frame."

Yes, he knew that, and more. "I'll talk to her tomorrow."

It was all Caleb could promise. Yes, he had read her reports. Yes, he had worked well with her these last months, and yes, they made a good pair.

When he wasn't trying to avoid noticing the utterly feminine shape contained in that exquisite body of hers.

"In the morning," he repeated firmly, and called for the daily reports, firmly banishing any more mention of their disconcerting mountain colleague.

"About tomorrow. Jareth, you and Chaba ready?"

"We'll lay the final charges first thing," said a man at the back of the room.

"Bob, what about surveillance?"

"We'll be driving the herd south all day. As long as you join us at the start and before the end, we can keep your father's drones fooled with the dust kicked up by the animals. Too hard to pick out any man clearly while the herd's moving, plus we'll be feeding a pre-recorded stream to his spy cams by the lake site."

That seemed to be it. "Thank you, everyone," he said to the wider room. "We've worked a long time for this. It will change our land, in ways I know many of you find challenging. But these changes are necessary."

There were some moments in life that ought to be marked. He nodded to Jim, his head wrangler, right hand man and the one, true stockman among them. On cue, the older man pulled a bottle from under the desk, kept especially for this night, then passed it round with a generous slosh into all manner of receptacles.

"To our new lake," said Caleb, lifting the bottle high.

"To the lake," came charging back.

The staff began to drift off soon after that. Caleb stood to join them, but old Jim hadn't finished with him yet. He planted himself in front of Caleb, barring escape.

"What about the girl?"

Caleb wasn't stupid enough to ask 'What girl?' Not to the man who'd taught him to ride his first pony. "She's mountain folk."

"And it was her help that got us to this day."

"Maybe."

"So she deserves to be there when the charges blow. What if the filling doesn't go to plan?"

"It will," said Caleb.

"And you know that, how? You seen enough floods go bad, but you ever seen a man-made one?"

He shrugged, ignoring the question, but the old man refused to move aside, not yet. He'd never given way before, so why should Caleb expect now to be different?

"She's mountain," Caleb repeated.

Jim stared straight back. "You heard her," the old man said. "She's Survey first."

CHAPTER FIVE

It had been a long night for Fee. Unable to bear the suffocating dark, she finally gave up on sleep and pulled out the plans for the lake. Something niggled at her peace, something from the day before that she couldn't quite put her finger on.

It had to be near dawn when she finally fell asleep. She woke much later, sore from the day before in both body and heart, and it was with a serious case of nerves that she ventured out of her guest suite and made her way to the common room for breakfast.

The quarters were silent. The others must still be sleeping off the effects of last night's party. She'd heard the cheers, burrowing under her cover to hide from the knowledge that she was the only person on base not welcome to join in.

But when she walked into the dining hall, only Marabeth was there. The friendly woman had been introduced to her last night as cook, guardian and chief-in-charge of everything that mattered to a body, as an older man had put it. Right now, the woman was stacking dishes into a side cupboard.

Putting them away. That was wrong.

"What's to eat," she said, in the most cheerful voice she could muster.

"Don't worry, young Sera. I've saved some for you. Those lumpkins didn't eat quite everything before they left."

"Left?"

Marabeth nodded. "First thing. Best to drive stock before the heat sets in. The boss makes sure of that."

The boss? Surely her annoying new partner hadn't deserted her too? "I needed to talk to Caleb."

The woman shook her head in apology. "He won't be back till late. They're taking the herd south to fresh range land."

"All of them?"

"Well, yes. There's a few thousand head to be mustered up and got going."

All day on horseback. Fee rubbed the abused muscles of her backside. Maybe being an outsider had its advantages after all. Another day of riding was more than she cared to contemplate right now. "That's all right then," she said, feeling almost cheerful.

Marabeth pulled cereal from another cupboard and moved over to the dask machine, picking up a mug from the stack there. "Was it something important?"

"Not if they're only driving stock. I need to get him to shift some of the charges."

A crash, and the mug shattered on the floor. "The charges?"

Fee's inner alarm screamed into life. "You are Survey?"

"No, not me. Worked for the Winters all my life. But my son Jareth is a Survey engineer. They're setting the charges for the lake right now. The boss, him and Chaba."

If Fee had a mug, she would have dropped it too. "They can't. They have to shift the placement of the western ones."

"My Jareth? He's in danger?"

She didn't try to lie. "Yes."

The woman flung her apron onto the nearest bench. "You have to get out there, now. That's my son. Please, Sera, you have to save him."

Of course, was the answer. No other choice was possible. But how?

By getting on a horse and riding at breakneck speed across this forsaken land in a direction she barely remembered, it turned out. All the fast, cross country skimmers in camp were code locked for security. Normal practice, said Marabeth, when all the stockmen trained to use them out here left camp. Only the slower transporters were free to use, and they needed properly formed tracks, not the rough, unforgiving terrain lying directly between here and the lake site.

Marabeth had saddled up a horse, thrust a directional beacon in Fee's hand and tossed her onto the animal's back before she knew what was happening.

"The horse knows this land. Just keep her on the right path and she'll get you there."

The woman slapped the horse's flank, and Fee held on for grim death as it took off. She only hoped there was a more direct route to the lake site than the one Caleb Winter had led her by yesterday. It would be so like that devious man.

She was beginning to know him. Or hoped so. She was staking his life on it.

Once clear of the buildings, the horse broke into a trot. To be quickly followed by another change, one that had her clinging tight with hands, legs, everything she could, as the horse broke into a fast run. She'd seen Caleb do this yesterday, shifting his horse easily from a nice quiet walk to this fast, flying run and had briefly tried it. Very briefly, and had never wanted to do it again. A gallop, she suddenly remembered he called it.

Caleb had never looked in danger of being flung dangerously to the ground.

"It's fast. That's what matters."

Her knuckles clenched down so tight her fingers hurt like the devil, and the only reason her legs weren't collapsing as she clamped them to the horse was fear of what would happen if she relaxed.

"It's like a tree in the wind. Go with it." She bent forward, flattening herself as best she could against the horse. It seemed to help. Sort of.

The beacon pinged. Right, it ordered. She briefly lifted her head, saw a rising slope that way and a sandy mire on the left. Change direction. She tugged on the right rein, hauling hard against the horse and prayed fervently till she felt its head come round.

No, too far, you stupid beast.

Her hair whipped in her eyes. Pull it round properly. That was it. Now, they were over the rise and off straight again.

The horse knows what to do. Marabeth said so.

Maybe, but it didn't feel like it.

The next half hour was a nightmare. No other word for it. But her fear of not making it in time always loomed over her terror of the moment. The horse showed signs of slowing. There was nothing she would like more than to stop and collapse onto the safety of the ground.

She thrust her heels into its flanks. "Faster, faster, you horrible beast."

She could only briefly glance at the beacon, haul roughly on the reins whenever the pings told her to change direction.

Not far now.

A boom echoed through her horse and up into her body. Little sound, but that unmistakeable vibration of an explosion. The start of the planned sequence of charges that would bring water gushing up from below the rising ground and into the waiting basin.

Her horse jerked, a second shudder, hooves thudding to a halt, and she was sent flying through the air.

There were sandy areas, soft and forgiving, all over this land. She'd had to avoid so many on her way here. That wasn't where she landed. Over and over she rolled, clawing desperately for an anchor, only to end up in a pile of shale and dirt.

Her head hurt, every bit of her bare skin stung and one arm hung uselessly.

Up.

She lurched to a stand, the pain of her arm almost too much to bear. She hadn't dreamed that unmistakable crunch of bone.

"No time to worry now."

Hauling her belt off to use as a sling and wrapping her arm tight against her side, she set off again. Over the top, jogging painfully slowly, shouting as loud as she could. A stumble, a downward thrust of her right arm to stop her landing on her left. Then off again.

The edge of the rise. They must be just over the other side, sitting on top of the bluff. Solid rock, they all thought, safe to hide behind from the power of the charges below. But last night, unable to sleep and tossing fitfully over the scenes of the day, a picture in Fee's head had suddenly clicked into focus. The vegetation on the beachhead below; it didn't fit the geotech surveys. That wasn't solid rock they sheltered on, not with that evidence of seepage in the resurgent plants below.

She was too winded now to shout, too winded to feel more than despair as yet another charge went off. Too weak to stand against the shockwave and too hurt in body to stop her fall as the looming ridge gave way under her feet, sending her down the bank in a flurry of rock and dirt. Only the tall, hard body of a man flinging himself forward stopped her before she shot over the edge of the bluff.

"What the… What are you doing here?"

Her arm had been banged again. Pain threatened her with oblivion, but she had no time, not for that or the anger in his voice. "The charges. West bank. Don't blow." Then the darkness took her.

A slosh of water, and the looming face was back. He shoved the wet strands of hair away, and she saw on his face what she must look like. She dragged back another useless strand of hair.

"What happened to you?"

"Not important," she gasped out. "Don't blow."

"The charges, yes, I got that." He turned and looked up at a woman. "Chaba, tell Jareth to hold off."

The darkness came back, but this time a man's strong arms held her safe and she had no more reason to fight.

She came awake to the feel of cool water trickling down her chin.

"Drink, damn you."

She struggled, but stilled as the break in her arm ratcheted tight in a pang of sheer agony.

"Not thirsty."

The trickle stopped, and she opened her eyes slowly, catching something fleeting in Caleb's face. Only to disappear as the stark lines of necessity hid all emotion. "How badly hurt?"

She took a deep breath, holding her body still and mentally forced herself to separate out the roiled up clouds of pain. "Broken arm, banged head, rest are scratches only," she got out finally. "Left one," she said as he started prodding her right. He switched and she could only gasp, pleading, "Don't touch."

His hold gentled, skilled fingers finding the break and holding the arm to ease her pain as he spoke into his wrist com. "Jareth, get that medpac here, now." He lowered her slowly down to lie flat on the ground, keeping her arm absolutely still

"Thank you," she mumbled as the hard ground anchored her again.

A grimly straight mouth. "Not needed."

"Is…" she tried, struggling to make him listen.

"Not," he said, glaring, as she caught that fleeting something again. "Oh hell. Enough." He struggled, took a deep breath, then another, and his face closed over again, all except those too bright eyes. "Enough. You can tell me the rest after we get you cleaned up. What happened?"

"Horse. Stupid beast didn't like explosions."

"You rode here?"

"It seemed a good idea at the time."

He shook his head, and she saw the first sign of respect enter his eyes. "You're a damn novice."

"Only way to get here in time."

"Remind me not to underestimate you again."

He lifted a finger in front of her face, and she shoved it back. "I'm not concussed."

"Let me decide that." But he took the finger away and began to check her cuts instead, leaving the arm wrapped tight in its makeshift sling.

The woman beside him sat back on her heels. "So we hold off, or what? We already ran the geotech scans and Kal cleared it. Those charges are fine."

Fee struggled up, levering herself with her good arm.

"Lie still," snapped Caleb, arms grabbing her. Fee ignored him, she had to, and spoke to the woman he'd called Chaba.

"Three weeks ago. There's been rain upcountry since. Do another scan."

The woman had no intention of doing any such thing by the look on her face

Another man came up the hill. Jareth, she would guess.

"What's going on? There are two charges still to go."

Chaba pointed at Fee. "She wants us to run the scans again."

Caleb had listened to them, but his eyes had never moved from her face. She gave him back stare for stare.

"You sure about this? Kal's our soils eco-engineer. He didn't see any problems here."

"Maybe, but water does funny things to dirt, and knowing the theory is different from seeing it in action."

He wasn't convinced, but he did turn and look down at the creek again, at the shrubs and the charges. Then back to her face, holding her gaze in that silent communication that may have told him plenty but gave nothing away. Closed up, watching her, seeing the pain she couldn't hide from him.

"Run the scan," he said.

The two engineers looked disgusted, but could do nothing while Caleb laid Fee carefully back down before pulling the portable ground monitor from his bag. He pointedly turned to her, asking her where to set the probes, then passed them over to the engineers with orders to do exactly as Fee said. They stumped off down the bank.

"Thank you," she said.

"And if you're wrong?"

"It's still 'Thank you'."

A few minutes later, the others came back, flinging themselves on the ground and watching while Caleb set the scan to start. Marabeth's precious son whistled a particularly flat tune that added to the pummelling in Fee's head but there was no point asking him to stop.

The scan was taking a long time. Too long. She levered herself up to peer over Caleb's shoulder.

"Sit back and rest," he ordered. "I'm just running a reverse check."

She felt tears threatening and hated her weakness.

Soon Caleb was finished and set the display running. Jareth and Chaba lolled over to watch. Then both sat up abruptly.

"There's water there."

"A whole honeycomb of soft rock."

"If we'd set that last charge…"

"We could all have been killed by a collapse of this bluff," finished Caleb. "Thanks are due, Fee, it seems, and apologies." He glared at his two subordinates, but both were too busy taking in the rolling data, horror scribed on their faces.

Jareth jabbed madly. "That was solid rock in the last scan."

"It can happen with these particular rock types in areas of erratic rainfall," said Fee wearily. "The rock cavities silt up with soluble matter, and the composition of packed dirt and rock can be near enough to the same that density differences are hard to pick up without specialist scans."

"So where do we set the charges?" said a chastened Jareth. He brought up a holo-map of the basin and she leaned over, pointing.

"Here, for the western one. And take out the last one. It will only cause a bad flare up."

After a discussion over the com unit with the tech team, one she was too sore and too exhausted to bother deciphering, the two engineers set off. They seemed to know what they were doing, and she lay back again and shut her eyes. The dark called her again.

When she opened her eyes, she was alone and in a different location. Higher on the bluff, over a proper rock base by the looks of it. A scrabble of stones and the harsh face of Caleb Winter filled her gaze. It had that closed-in look she was becoming far too familiar with, but there was a welcome lack of fuss in his voice.

"You've been out to it. I gave you a shot to block the pain and straightened your arm. Can you manage till I can drive you out of here?"

She made to flex her hand. Her arm did feel easier. "I'm fine." But her throat was too dry. "I'm tougher than I look." He said nothing, merely rechecked the arm and handed her the bottle of water before opening his com unit. "Jareth, Chaba, set the charges and get out of here. I want you safe with the rest of the crew if anyone comes snooping around, and take her horse with you."

He bent to the control box on the ground beside him. There was a row of red lights, blinking one by one to green.

A buzz on his wrist com, and he bent to listen. She so wished she could listen in. To her right, she heard the whoosh of a flyer pulling away.

"Jareth and Chaba. They've cleared the charge site."

He sat, watching the last light. It changed, but still he did nothing. Just stared down into the hollow below.

What was wrong? Her body was beginning to ache all over as the pain meds wore off. She huddled against the hard dirt, waiting. "You finished yet?" she finally muttered.

He said nothing, his fingers poised above that last button. She lifted her head, staring at the row of red lights.

"Just push it."

His finger hovered then pulled back. His hands clenched and he kept staring down into the hollow.

"That simple, is it? Push the button, all done, and you can get out of here? Back to your trees and mountains, and your greedy rushing rivers?"

She refused to feel guilty. Refused to let him blame her for this. "Yes."

He surged up, fists grabbing at the dirt of this land of his. "Look down there."

As if she had any choice with those hard eyes on her. She lifted her head, looking down into the basin. The smell of bruised, dried grasses cloaked the air and baked into the stones.

The hollow looked the same as on that first visit, so many months ago. A flattened basin of grassland, broken only by the gouged out, crazy crackling path of the dry stream bed. It completely lacked the vibrant life of her home country.

"That lake will bring life to these plains," she reminded him softly, and then wished she'd kept silent as he turned and she saw the fractured shadows in his eyes.

His arm lifted, pointing to the flat slab of dark stone, set above a hook shaped bend in the creek. The rock he'd told her about before, where he'd stood and perjured himself to his council.

"If you lie on that rock in the afternoon sun and shut your eyes, all the sounds and smells of the plain surround you."

"You know this is necessary."

"Yes, I know."

He wasn't going to do it. "We need that lake," she reminded him.

"I know the science as well as you."

"Without a lake, there is no water for crops."

"We manage fine now. Our biggest income is from solar energy."

"And in the long term?"

A growl, frustrated and from deep within his body. "I know we have to do this. Why do you think I'm here?" He stood, looked one last time down at the hollow, then bent swiftly and punched his finger against the button. From far below ground, a wave of energy rocked through her. It was done.

CHAPTER SIX

They waited until the first dark stains proclaimed success. Water seeping up into the dry stream bed. Fee suddenly realised she was holding her breath, and very carefully released it as she watched the spreading stain and studied the banks. So far, so good. No sign of eminent collapse.

"It'll take a week at least to fill," she said.

He knew that already, but said nothing. Just took one last look at that tell-tale discolouration before he reached over to check her arm as he helped her up.

"I can walk." She did not want him picking her up, did not want to feel the comfort of those arms. He looked relieved and nodded agreement. Yet he still watched her closely and eased his long stride back to match hers. Then she stumbled and he swore, lifting her up anyway.

She opened her mouth to argue.

"Don't. I want home today. This is quicker."

She subsided. He might hate her for what he had just done, but his arms were strong and safe, and she was too sore to argue.

"Thank you," she muttered.

"Don't thank me yet. We'll have to take the long way back to base. If Solaris find out you're here or what happened to you, they can't find out it was here you fell off."

"You're right, we can't risk any questions about this site. I'll manage."

A grunt in answer, but she caught a glimpse of something new in his face. Respect. Not that she'd push it further. She half expected him to throw her up onto the seat, but he placed her gently, settling her belts in place. She closed her eyes in bliss as a blast of cooled air hit her face.

Caleb hadn't exaggerated about taking the long way back. It was well into the afternoon before they neared the main camp site. She was half conscious only, dreaming of cold showers and hot dask—in either order.

The brakes slammed and the man beside her cursed. She shook her head blearily and struggled to sit up.

"Stay down," he ordered.

She ignored him, pulling herself up just far enough to peer over the control panel and down into the flat. The base looked much as before, except for the arrival of a grey, all terrain vehicle, much like the one they sat in. Caleb leaned forward with a scowl.

"My father's."

"Oh."

Down at the camp, an older, broader version of Caleb climbed out of the truck and stared up at them, waiting.

He'd seen them.

"Damn it. No way to hide now." Caleb set the skimmer into motion down the track. "Don't talk unless you have to. You're badly hurt, remember, and you do not want to go to the Winter compound."

"All … right."

"My father's only interest is the solar arrays. He will fight anyone that puts them at risk, den Coilles being top of the list."

Well yes, she had picked that up.

His fists clenched on the controls, as if hating having to explain his family to her, to an outsider. "You've seen the figures. Cloud cover up by ten percent with the first lake; and by twenty-five percent once the full chain of lakes is finished. That's a lot of money lost."

He braked to avoid an outcrop of rock, and she gritted her teeth as her arm was jolted.

"Sorry." His eyes were still on the track and the words were automatic.

Caleb pulled up beside the other vehicle, but made a show of climbing out slowly. She went to open her door, but he gave one, barely seen negative shake and she subsided.

His father stalked across. "You're not with the herd?"

"We had an incident," Caleb said. "A visitor decided to go for a ride on her own and got thrown."

The door beside her was wrenched open and the older man glared in at her. She clutched her left arm and huddled back against the seat, trying to look as pathetically hurt as possible.

"Her, here again! Why?"

"Survey business," she said, trying to sound both pathetically injured and staunchly defiant. Not a good idea, from the man's face.

"What were you looking for?"

"I just wanted a try at riding without anyone around to see my mistakes. Stupid of me, I know." She made her voice breathless and threw in a hint of tears. Truth to say, the way she felt right now, it wasn't a hard act.

Caleb moved forward and leaned down to pick her up, forcing his father to move backwards. "I'm about to arrange transport back to her home for treatment. She's broken that arm and been concussed."

"You got a first aider in this crew?"

"Me," said his son. "Arm's splinted, I've checked her over and given her some meds to keep her over the trip."

He set off inside, marching into the bedroom that had been assigned to her and laying her on the bed. His father followed, glaring suspiciously.

"That girl's den Coille. You know how much of the food basics in this area use that blasted festia pollen, and her father controls the market."

Caleb shrugged. He made a show of checking her arm and feeling her pulse.

It did nothing to deter his father. "There'll be real hunger around here if the den Coille's slap us with a trade embargo. You have to go back with her. Make sure that wily Bram den Coille doesn't do anything stupid. "

"No."

"Your blasted Survey caused this, boy. They sent her here. So you take her home."

"I'm busy," said Caleb.

"Doing what? Rounding up a few scrub nieten? You've got men enough to do that. You can leave for a few days."

Fee saw the frustration on Caleb's face. There was no way he could tell his father why he couldn't leave now. Nor was the man going to back down. If only he'd leave, but the chances of that were about nil, she reckoned.

Caleb looked down at her, and she nodded back. "Call in your mountain evac team," he said, looking thoroughly disgusted.

She took the com unit from him, punched in the emergency numbers and spoke to the Survey field operator on the other end, using the codes for full Survey security. Then lay back, feeling as exhausted as she hopefully looked, and waited for the arrival of the ambulance.

Caleb watched the evac team land. The Survey was skilled at camouflage by necessity and they had done their job here. The flyer was forest dun in colour and the accent of the man who disembarked and snapped out an unfriendly demand for *our patient* came straight from the western slopes of the mountains. Only the discreet Survey salute reassured Caleb who the man really worked for. His father stood beside him still, watching aggressively, and saw nothing in the quick flick of fingers against brow.

"Inside," said Caleb, giving a one-thumbed indication, the other hand stuck in his pocket. "We'll ship her gear on later."

"I'll take it now. All of it," said the man. "She won't be back."

"Not a good idea," agreed his father in a surly tone.

The man gave an arrogant lift of brows, then signalled the woman emerging beside him to bring up the floater. A doctor, from the insignia on her tunic front.

"This way," said Caleb.

He led the newcomers into Fee's room. The woman checked Fee's pulse and eye reflex, examined her injured arm and felt her ribs. But he recognised the Survey instruments embedded in her wrist com and the slight head tilt that told of a connection to a personal vid display.

She turned to the pilot with the floating stretcher. "Strap her rigid. I can't say exactly how much damage she's taken to her torso and abdominal tissues."

Caleb had scanned her himself, knew there was nothing broken except her arm. But bruising from a horse fall could hurt like hell. The girl would be a mass of black and blue, but he wasn't about to suggest the doctor lift her shirt to check. Even bruised, Caleb would dearly love a view of the body under that shirt, but no way would he let another man see it. Most definitely not his father.

"Time to go," said the pilot. He and the doctor carefully placed the floater struts around Fee, easing her off the bed. A slight grunt, the only sign she gave of her pain.

Marabeth had collected up Fee's gear and handed the bag to the mountain folk as they loaded her into the flyer. Caleb had deliberately kept back from the open hatch, but it made no difference. His father shoved his way forward.

"My son will be joining the girl."

The pilot went to shut the door in front of him. "Not possible."

"Not only possible, but you don't leave here without him."

Caleb knew that tone of voice, and didn't make the mistake of taking it lightly. "And if I refuse?"

"That flyer's not leaving."

The pilot went to get on board anyway, though Caleb knew it was pointless. There was a reason Caleb's crew were so careful to hide their Survey activities. Unless his team used risky blocks on them, his father's spy bots monitored and controlled everything that happened in the region. Including blocking the movement of a Survey flyer, no matter how sophisticated.

Worse, if the flyer did manage to take off, his father would know immediately how advanced was the Survey's technology. Which was something no one outside the service must find out, not if they were to save the world.

"Wait up, Captain. I'm coming with you."

It only took him ten minutes to throw a bag together; ten minutes too long. For once, he was relieved to see the soil of his homeland receding beneath him. He looked over to where the mountain girl was strapped in and being worked on by the doctor. No, she had a name. Fee. But that was too familiar, and he did not want to let this girl in. Did not want to think of her as anything but an inconvenient colleague forced onto him by head office. The doctor sat back.

"How is she?"

"Not as bad as I feared. The arm is a clean break and the rest is mere bruising. A few days of taking it easy will sort that out, and the arm will mend in a couple of weeks."

The girl tried to sit up but fortunately the floater restraints held her down. "How long before I'm operational?"

"Depends what you define as operational. Central wants you ready now, but they'll have to wait."

"She's done her bit."

"I'm ready to go now."

"Her work's done," he pointed out to the doctor, refusing to look at the girl.

The damn woman was still trying to sit up.

"You're hurt. Lie back. The last time I took a tumble like that from a horse, I couldn't move for a couple of days."

"And how old were you?"

"Eight," he admitted.

Her lips tightened, but she stopped fighting the restraints.

The doctor stepped in. "You are on compulsory medical leave for two days, Fioruisghe."

That made it official. Not even Fox could overrule it, which meant Caleb was stuck with going all the way to the mountains with her before he could get back. A whole day wasted. He slumped into his seat and glared out the window.

"Son of a ... Turn around. What do you think you're doing?"

The pilot didn't even bother looking round. "Flying you back to the lake site. Orders from central."

Caleb swore, thrusting a finger out the window. "See that patch of low scrub to your right? And that rock beside it? Those are spybots, courtesy of Winter Solaris. My father's patrol craft will be boring down on us in five minutes, exactly, unless you turn now."

"Okay, but I'm calling Central."

"Do, and patch them through to me."

The pilot looked at him like he was some half-cocked idiot. But there was more than a bit of Sol Winter in Caleb's genes, and the pilot shrugged and made the link, before passing the flyer's controlled com over to Caleb with a 'your funeral' shrug.

It was the duty coordinator. "Put me through to Fox." He could hear the irritation in the voice but had no time for a charm offensive. "Emergency code X34b," and might have laughed at the obscenity he caught if it hadn't been so serious. Not that it mattered. The code got him patched through.

"Winter, what's the fuss?"

"That lake. No one is to go near it for a day minimum. Not even shielded."

"No can do. Too much risk of flooding if the seepage gets out of control."

"And my father is a suspicious SOB who will have his watchers putting this area on the highest priority for the next couple of days. He knows your mountain woman is a plant, but thinks she's working for the den Coille family."

The string of epithets that came back was impressive, and reassuring. Fox was a pragmatist at heart.

"Agreed," said their boss. "Get to the mountains, deliver the girl and get back. And don't give your name to the den Coilles. We don't need both sides more suspicious than they are now."

The girl beside him coughed. "Um, not a good idea, Sir." She was struggling to sit up, again.

"Sit back before you tear something."

She paid him as much attention as ever. "My family will know who he is within minutes of arrival."

"How, by scanning a guest in their house?"

It's what he would expect from his father. Then again, the head of den Coille was probably no different.

She shook her head. "My mother," she gasped through the meds. "A full DNA scan is her way of greeting a stranger."

"Not without my cooperation."

The girl didn't bother to answer that one. She both made a point and gave him a warning. *The den Coille matriarch is that good, so keep your wits about you.*

He subsided back into his seat, still holding the girl's eyes. After a time, she gave him a curt nod, satisfied with whatever she saw in his face. She was that good, too.

"This crew?" he said now to the doctor.

"All mountain born and bred," she said, barely looking up from her patient. He had a feeling she had picked up on every bit of his strange conversation with the girl.

He indicated the girl. "Family?"

"No. Fioruisghe is the only den Coille brave enough to stand against her family. But we are Mountain Survey—Fioruisghe is ours."

This was a day for warnings. "A full formal greeting with all honours then. Agreed?" he said to their boss.

"Agreed," Fox said, his voice as glum as Caleb felt. "Just be sensible. Two days, and you're back at the lake, Winter. Den Coille is to follow as soon as she gets medical clearance."

Caleb glanced at Fee; saw the pain shadows in her eyes. "Yes, sir," he said with as much semblance of honesty as he could dredge up, and was relieved to hear the com signing off.

The pilot had completed his sweep and they were heading now towards the mountains. Soon he would be lifting up, into the clouds, over the other side into the legendary mists of the west. What waited him there was another matter.

CHAPTER SEVEN

Through the fog of drugs, Fee felt the lurch in her stomach that meant they were starting down the far side of the mountains. The doctor leaned over, infuser in hand. "No," she managed to get out.

Which brought Caleb Winter right in her face. "You need the meds. If they wear off, it's going to hurt, bad."

As if she didn't know that. "I *need* a clear head."

"You need bed rest, and that's what you're getting," said the doctor, readying the infuser again.

"Not with…My father … Can still talk lying down."

The plainsman's face turned away a minute. "Her father, Doc? What's he like?"

"Biggest name in this neck of the woods, and knows it. Sorry, Fioruisghe," the woman added half-heartedly.

"You've met mine." His eyes scrutinised her. "Yours is…?"

"A good match for yours."

Did the man always talk in half sentences? They read each other so easily, too easily.

"Leave off the meds, Doc. Use something that keeps her mind clear. She needs that more."

A problem solved, and maybe it wasn't so bad to let Caleb Winter fight a battle for her. So far, he did it well. She drifted off again, half dozy with the pain and drugs. At the same time, she noticed a change in the smells in the cabin. A touch of loam and water, and the precious smell of home. Then her abused muscles and bones told her what they thought of her refusing her meds. The mildest of bumps had her biting her lips.

"Lie still, woman." Caleb's face loomed into view again.

"How far out?"

"We land in thirty minutes," said the doctor's voice from behind him, before she began yet again checking her signs. Fee shook her head in frustration.

"No time. Winter, Caleb, whatever … how much do you know of mountain protocol?

He was back in view again, with the tail end of a shrug. "Some. Why?"

That could mean anything. "Say my father's full name."

That threw him, part of her was pleased to learn. "You can't, can you?"

"Bram den Coille. He'll have to do without the middle bit. We don't do that on the plains."

The doctor looked shocked. "On this side of the mountains, Ser Winter, we take manners seriously." She frowned as if at a recalcitrant boy. "Get some sleep, Fioruisghe, while I endeavour to prevent this barbarian giving the entire city apoplexy."

She was forced to accede, her head pounding. Rest: she could do that, but sleep was not an option, not without those meds. She shut her eyes anyway.

Caleb watched the girl, Fee. Did she know of the crease that cut into her brow when she was worried?

A sharp rap of knuckles on his arm. The doctor was talking to him.

"She's as fine as can be expected, and none of your concern."

Good point. He dragged his eyes away from his—colleague, that was a safe word—and listened to the doctor again. He had a good memory and soon had the full names of her parents and siblings, his pronunciation fair enough to pass muster. *How did these people ever talk to one another? They must spend all day exchanging names.*

"It will have to do," said the doctor's frustrated voice.

So maybe didn't quite pass muster. "Too much polish would sound suspicious," he pointed out.

"Maybe, but a little would help."

"He's right, Doctor," said the pilot. "Sounding too much like us will put the den Coilles on high alert. Why would a son of Winter Solaris bother learning mountain protocol unless he was up to something?"

"Thanks," muttered Caleb.

"You're welcome," grinned the pilot. "No time to do better, anyway. We're landing in a few minutes. Go back and strap down."

He took his seat near Fee. No, on this side of the mountain, she was Fioruisghe ingh Bram an Scathach den Coille. He preferred Fee. Short, blunt and to the point, just like her. She was awake and bracing herself from the clench of her jaw. For the landing, or what came after? The doctor had her in hand so he had nothing to do but strap down for the descent. Out of the window, a solid carpet of unfamiliar green rushed up. The mountain cities were fabled as marvels of engineering and Manascraoch the largest of all of them, an entire city built within the massive trees that were native to this region. Homes, offices, shops and public spaces wound within the mighty branches. He could see little of it here; a spire protruding here, a glimpse of winding walkway there, but that was all. Nor did he look for more. The only thing that interested him today was where in all that solid wall of leaves they were to land. His question was answered when a platform rose to meet them from the branches and he sat back to wait for the greater trial; meeting and fooling the den Coille parents.

She'd been an idiot to refuse the pain meds. Fee dug her fingers into the side of the pallet. The strapping stopped most movement, but each small jolt jabbed a knife through battered muscles as the flyer settled on the pad.

Why did injuries always hurt more after the event than at the time? It wasn't even as if she could blame a lack of adrenaline to mask it. Too much of it was surging through her veins right now.

The pallet settled and voices echoed around her. Next came the smell and voices she knew best; her father and mother hovering nearby. *Stop being a coward.* She opened her eyes.

"It's just a few bruises," she assured them.

"So why are you still in so much pain?" Fee could never hide any hurt from them. The down side of having a mother who was a doctor. "What is she on and when was the last dose?"

"She has been fully checked in flight and is being transferred to Manascraoch Central," said the evac doctor.

The woman should have known to save her breath. In no time, her mother had arranged for her transfer to the private, medical wing of the den Coille cluster. Her father hove into view, glowering angrily, with, looming beside him, one tall, sparely built and plains-burnt problem.

"Perhaps you can explain how you came to need hospitalisation in the first place?" said her father.

"Bram den Coille, she is in no state to answer questions."

"So who should I ask them of?"

He was like an unstoppable force of nature, but Fee tried regardless.

"Father, meet Caleb Winter of the Plains Survey office. Caleb, my father, Bram mar Gliocas duine Scathach den Coille."

The hasty lessons hadn't been a total failure. Caleb Winter gave a semi bow and uttered the required salutation. A pity there was no warmth in it, but nor was there any in her father's reply.

"Eldest son of Sol Winter, owner and head of Winter Solaris?"

"The same," said Caleb in an equally cool voice.

"What's your business here, plainsman?"

"Sera den Coille was injured on Winter territory. It was only courteous to ensure her safe transferral home."

Was the man looking for trouble? Her father said nothing, dead silence. Not a good sign. Caleb Winter was silent too, and that, she was coming to learn, was a worse sign.

The two men stood staring at each other, one either side of her pallet.

It finished as quickly as it had begun, and she heard her mother's very slight huff of relief.

"I'll have a room made up for our guest," she said.

"My thanks, Sera den Coille."

The words were polite, but there was little of ease in the plainsman and the last she saw of Caleb Winter was his stiff handshake with the cousin detailed to escort him. She hoped a Winter could recognise a security man.

After that, it was a day before she knew anything but drugs and the tedium of pain.

There was a knock and her nurse entered her room. "You have a visitor. Ten minutes only."

Caleb Winter followed her in, and must have heard the sour note of mistrust.

"Can we be private? It's work related," he said.

The woman sniffed but couldn't argue with Fee's nod of acceptance. "I'll be right outside," she said, as she stalked from the room.

Caleb came to a stand beside her bed, ignoring the chair, and his eyes carefully scanned the room.

"You look better."

"Compared to how I looked yesterday, that's no compliment." She forced a smile, but still his eyes searched. She lifted her chin as she shuffled up towards the headboard, and saw the instant he lit on the sensor above the call pad.

"If that's all you're worried about?" he said.

"All I know to worry about," she said, and caught the nod of acknowledgement. There was probably another audio pick up, but she had yet to find where. "It is good of you to stay on."

"You were under our protection. My father expects courtesy towards guests."

"And your work?"

"Will have to be managed by another."

Such a strange conversation, pocked with riddles below warnings. She had so many questions. Why was he still here? It wasn't part of their original plan, so what had changed his mind? He couldn't leave the lake to fill unsupervised; nor could she. For a day now, water had seeped into that hollow unwatched by the two eco-engineers best qualified to catch the first signs of something going wrong. Had the Survey contacted Caleb? Could they even contact him on this side of the mountains without raising suspicions?

"You can do nothing for now," he said softly. "Rest, get better."

She put out a hand, touching her finger to his. He took it, folded her hand into his, and his nod this time was one of a promise.

"Get better," he said again, and her slight smile and bow was an equal promise. They had work to do.

"And you?" she now asked.

"Have reports to write," he said, and looked directly at the camera.

Did the man have no sense of self-preservation?

Caleb left the room, feeling more frustrated than when he'd entered but also with a strange kind of peace, of having resolved a problem. Her mother had told him it'd be another day before Fee could get out of bed, which meant another day before Caleb was free to return to the lake—if she was safe.

In her own home, surrounded by family? Even he had to admit it sounded crazy. It changed nothing. From the instant he'd seen her ringed about with den Coilles, all asking questions, and seen the buried signs of panic on her face, he was lost. She needed his help, his protection, and she would get it.

So how to fill in his time without straying too far from the hospital ward?

There was more than enough to explore here. He'd seen phase two of the plan and knew what the Survey intended for this region. He would have a part in bringing it about, his knowledge of the effects of wind flows on an ecological system essential to its success. He shrugged on the ubiquitous poncho worn by everyone around here to keep off the rain and shoved open the door.

"Can I help, Ser?"

There was always a man at his door, ready to *assist* him. Well muscled, and he would bet that was a weapon hidden on the man's hip. He halted on the wooden stoop, refusing to look down. "How do I get to ground level?"

"Is there something you need? I can fetch it for you."

"Soil, dirt, ground beneath my feet," he growled, figuring honesty would do him no harm. The den Coilles and their ilk would probably be thrilled to hear this tree top city of theirs was getting to him.

The den Coille's city of Manascraoch might be considered a crowning glory among the engineering miracles that were the mountain cities. Didn't mean everyone had to like it, and he certainly did not. Houses, offices, parks and gardens wove through the treetops, spilling haphazardly down the hillside and winding in and out of the giant baullnia trees that grew wherever the spreading plantation of festias allowed.

He put a hand against the mighty trunk beside him. Baullnia were the true natives of the mountain, with roots digging deep down into the poor soils, holding the hillside tight in protective custody. But baullnia did not yield the rich pollens of the festia.

The guard said something into his earpiece, turning away to stop Caleb hearing it. He was sorely tempted to thrust past the man and vault down the first set of stairs he came to. Only the suspicion that he would be thoroughly lost in minutes stopped him. So he waited.

"This way," snapped the man. Caleb refrained from giving in to his malicious grin, as he followed the man down a coiling maze of stairs, corridors and platforms.

At last his boots squelched in forest litter and the smell of dirt and dead leaves rose up to greet him. Pungent, foreign, but the ecologist in him recognised the life in it and felt more at home than any time since coming here. He dug his heel into the upper loam, scraped back the top layer and found what he sought—dirt, real dirt. Gritty, wet as all hell, but genuine dirt. Dry it out for a few hundred years, change the mix of elements, and it could be the dry, sandy grit of home.

He'd glimpsed a rocky outcrop from his window that morning, and asked the guard to show him the way to it.

"Why?" said the man sullenly? "It's a fair climb."

Caleb shrugged again, with just enough in it to goad the man but not enough to cause Fox a serious heart attack. "Got nothing better to do," he finished with. "You?"

Anything you care to mention, he would guess. But the guard confined himself to a disgusted grimace and set off up the hill.

As the man had said, it was a fair climb. Finally, the tree canopy began to clear and Caleb felt his foot strike hard rock. He scrabbled up, renewed, and climbed over the outcropping.

It felt like limestone with a heavy inlay of quartz and granite, the edges smoothed by years of rain and wind. There was a break in the clouds now, a rare surcease from the constant rain.

Caleb lifted his head and felt the familiar heat of the sun on his face.

A few steps more, up onto the highest boulder, stepping carefully over the still slippery surface, and he could stand, free in the open air at last. He stretched out his arms, taking in the breeze and massive, dark green carpet spreading out all around. The only clue to the margins of the city were the changes in colour of the vegetation as the smaller-leaved baullnia gave way to the denser green of the festia plantations that dominated the rest of the slopes.

This was a created landscape. Man had made this.

"Get down from there. Do you want to kill yourself?"

Caleb shook his head. "Not with plains boots on," he said, looking down at the man's flexible shoes and showing his own well-ribbed heels. Caleb grinned, and took the time to study the slopes, amusing himself with deciding where he would make the changes the Survey needed. Thin that ridge out over there and restore the baullnia trees, fell the gullies below and replant with shrubs, release the dykes and let the mountain streams gush down the hillside again, with the festia remaining only in the dank hollows for which it was designed.

Caleb took a last, leisurely sweep, drew in a deep breath of the open air and descended once more to the gloom of the forest.

"You're mad," growled the guard, stalking back under the shelter of the branches.

Caleb smiled to himself. Only a matter of viewpoint. A drop landed on his nose and he shook it off in disgust.

Two more days. That was all. After that, he was off—back to a *proper* country.

CHAPTER EIGHT

There was a very old song her mother had sung to her as a child whenever she was sick, and she whined about when she'd be better. "One more day," her mother would say, "wait one more day." There was a lot of truth in that, Fee had to admit this morning. She still ached in every muscle, but her head was clearer and she could get out of bed without collapsing.

About time. She had things to do. She called the nurse and demanded her clothes.

Half an hour of arguing later, the woman finally brought her a simple tunic, leggings and slippers; probably more from fear that if she didn't, Fee would injure herself hunting them out and get the nurse tossed back to a job with real patients and real work.

The woman nearly won though as Fee painfully forced her injured arm into the tunic sleeve. Only the I-told-you-so look on the nurse's face kept her going.

She had to be up and about. Too much depended on her. Not least the safety of her disturbing colleague.

"The plainsman who came in with me? Where is he?"

The nurse's mouth pinched tight. "He's out on the slopes, down at *ground* level."

Of course he would be. The last place any true mountain dweller would go. "He's Plains." She shrugged. "Is he back?"

The woman put through a call in her earpiece, confirming what Fee had suspected from the start. Her less than friendly nurse was part of her father's guard corps.

"On his way up, now," she said.

"Can you ask if he would come in here?"

"You're not dressed!"

Fee glanced down. The man had seen her torn and bruised, and had been her field medic. "I'll put a wrap on," she finally said. It was the most she could manage.

Her guard nurse looked no happier. "Sit down in that chair before you fall down. I'll fetch the wrap."

The woman might be right, but Fee had no intention of looking like an invalid in front of Caleb Winter. It would take him a fair time to get from ground level to her family's complex, high up in the apex of the Baullnia groves. Enough time for a short nap and maybe she could fool him.

The noise of his coming jerked her awake, giving her just time to hastily smooth her hair down and take up a nonchalant stance, leaning against the table, before he slammed through the door.

With both of her parents flanking him and an armed guard behind.

"Get this ape off me," he growled.

"Tell us what you're doing here," barked back her father.

"Sit down, Fioruisghe—now." That from her mother, in full maternal mode.

None got any satisfaction.

Caleb eyed her up and down, before glaring at her father. "Making sure your daughter is fit after her accident on *our* plains. It's called taking care of your guests—an old plains tradition."

"So what were you checking, up on that bluff?"

"Just getting some fresh air in this blasted tree prison of yours."

Probably true, thought Fee. "Have you seen the plains?" she said to her father.

"Of course."

"So you can understand why our forest is hard for a plainsman. I know the plains were bad enough for me to deal with."

She sensed the outraged stiffening of the plainsman, but dared not look at him. Not when her father was at last listening to her. "He could barely spare the time to come here. That he did so is a sign of good faith, not anything else you might imagine."

"Like building more solar arrays pushing up into mountain country?"

"No."

"I have little to do with the solar arrays," said Caleb, moving to stand beside her. "I look after the stock side of our operations."

Her father snorted.

"Animals, is what he means, Da. He looks after their grazing animals. You need grasses for that, not solar arrays.

"This true?"

Caleb nodded curtly.

"You're not here as proxy for your father?"

"No."

Fee somehow doubted Sol Winter would agree with that, but she believed him.

"I came to ensure the well-being of a colleague who was injured on my watch," Caleb added.

Fee was starting to feel the effects of getting up too quickly. She leaned discreetly back against the table and returned her mother's searching stare with one of bland enquiry.

"Fioruisghe is home and safe. There is no need for your concern," her mother said.

Her father thrust forward again. "That's right, young man. My daughter is fit enough now. Time you took yourself back to your own side of the mountains."

"I will—when I'm ready," said Caleb.

Fee could have stamped her feet at all of them. Caleb wasn't going anywhere, that was clear, and her father was worse than Caleb's Jack Robber bird when an idea took root. Time for a backup plan. If only she had one ready. But, as one of her lecturers had once told her, 'flexibility is the key.'

"He can't go, not yet." The scowl on her father's face deepened. "I need his input on a Survey matter," she added, on a blind piece of inspiration.

"Yes?" said Caleb.

She stood as straight as she could, trying her hardest to appear fit and well.

"Just before I came back, one of my team sent in a report about some leaf signs on the festia in the north gulley. I'd like a second opinion from Caleb. He has experience in wind effects I don't have."

Hopefully Caleb caught the reference. She'd sent him all the initial draft plans for this region.

But: "I can look in the morning. You're staying here," is what he said.

"You don't know my forestry team. I'm coming."

"No, you're not," said two voices in unison, and her father looked at Caleb in surprise.

She flung up her hands in frustration. "So there is something you can agree on, but does it have to be this?"

Her father ignored that. "You get back to bed and rest, young lady."

Caleb said nothing, but glared agreement. She flexed her fingers, stretched out her arm tentatively. The glue and grafts were taking well and her mother had said she was already up to fifty percent tensile strength. "I'm fit for light duties, as long as I take care."

"Light duties is not careering over bloody trees and stomping through swamps," said Caleb.

She focussed on her father. "Can I have one of the skimmers for transport? I'm going regardless, but it would be easier with proper equipment—and your help, Ser Winter."

Neither man looked like budging a micron, and her mother's face wasn't much better. Plan B needed to be a bit bigger.

"I need to go, Da. Seamach mentioned brown vein margins on the leaves."

Her father's face paled, and she felt a twinge of guilt. "You're sure?" he said.

"No, which is why I need to get out there. Checking on potential environmental problems is my job; one I'm legally obliged to do, and you have no one else here better."

She had him beat. His face tight, he turned to glare at Caleb. "You better keep her safe."

"On my honour," said Caleb, looking no happier at having his hand forced.

"Much good that's done so far."

"I'll keep her as safe as she will allow," Caleb said instead, and was rewarded with a hastily smothered grunt of laughter.

"You're learning, boy." Her father scowled at her. "Pleased with yourself, aren't you?" She grinned back, knowing she'd won. "Not till tomorrow morning, only under the conditions your mother sets and you take den Coille security."

Her mother was the only one smiling after that.

Caleb took one look at the crowd ready to board the flyer next morning, and nearly turned right back round again. "I should have gone home."

"And miss the tour? Stop grumping."

Her parents joined the waiting mob.

"Morning," said Fee.

The damn girl was looking very pleased with herself today. Caleb grunted and gave a nod to her parents. It was more than Bram den Coille deserved, but her mother was another matter. Scathach den Coille was a doctor.

"You sure she's up to this?"

From the look on her face, the mother in Sera den Coille said no. But it was the doctor who replied. "Her arm is recovering well, and the head scans are all clear." Which meant *Yes* in medicalese, he guessed. "Fee is sensible and knows her limits."

Were they talking about the same woman? The one standing beside him wearing that dubiously demure smile?

"We fly out, check the trees, and fly back. No scrambling over branches, no digging, and I use a stick if on the ground. I have the list."

"Then follow it," her father said.

Caleb wished the man sounded more hopeful. "She will," he growled.

If nothing else, it punctured that false smile of hers—and did it matter that he felt like dirt for doing it? It was a relief to shut the flyer door against her parents.

Nothing more was said until they were well clear of the ground. Then the pilot's voice came over the speakers. "All clear, boys and girls. The cone of silence has been lifted."

"Ignore Ronan," said Fee.

"Yeah, he's a cartoon blimp," said the man sitting across from him. He leaned forward and Caleb straightened warily.

"Seamach. Put it there." A big hand stretched out, and Caleb was shaking it, even as he saw the size of the grin on Fee's face.

"Meet the team," she said.

He lifted an eyebrow.

"My Survey team." She waved a hand, one by one pointing at the others in the flyer. "The big hunk in front with the permanent stain under his fingers is Joseph, our botanist and arborist. Caerthida beside him is our geologist. Her cousin, Fridha, next to her is the team zoologist, and behind her is our horticulturist extraordinaire, Kebhyn. Our resident genius who has chlorophyll in his blood and dreams of cropping plots. Across from him there's Sorcha," the woman in the far seat with weird spiky hair waved at him, "a proper engineer, as she keeps telling me, and Rannach beside her is the team meteorologist. You'll meet the others at the site."

She had that pleased look on her face again. He frowned. "Clearance category?"

"All highest level. You're safe to talk."

"And the flyer?"

"Was swept for sensors before and after take off."

"Don't worry, plainsman. You're with Survey here," said the big security man. "We don't bite colleagues, even when they do come to cut down our trees."

He was still trying to get his head around it. "This is….?"

"My mountain team. The ones who've been working on the exploratory work for phase two ever since Fox dropped it on us."

The geologist leaned forward, fingertips pressed together and speaking as if laying down each word in a complex pathway, deliberate and precise. "Fioruisghe showed us the overall plan as soon as it was cleared by Central. The first phase is ready for implementation, pending final plan approval."

"For which we need your input," added Fee beside him, and he bet that cost her every bit as much as it had him when an outsider was planted squarely in his home project.

"You're ready to start development?"

"A trial area only. Central wants the lakes established before we start in proper."

He was impressed. He'd stood where this tiny woman stood, knew what she'd had to set in progress while still dealing with the shock of what was planned here. The enormity of change to a land you loved. There were parts of his own project he still kept from her, but maybe that was a mistake. He'd decide later, after he'd spent time working with her mountain team.

"So today? Is that where we're going?"

She nodded. "You've had all the preliminary data. I'll send you through the trial outline now and the valley schematics."

He studied her face for any underlying message or resentment. There was not—or none apparent. Maybe she was as good at acting as he.

Then he caught it; that faint lift of the corner of her mouth. She was thoroughly pleased with herself.

He allowed himself a small grin back, and was rewarded by a hint of a blush on those pretty cheeks. Take that, little Sera.

Their plan was good. Even without an intimate knowledge of this land, that was obvious. He could see parts where he might make modifications, yes, but not till he saw the ground and felt the winds.

Suddenly they were directly over the site. A deep cleft in the ever crumpled mountains. The plans he'd been sent included a virtual view, but the reality was something again. The colours brighter, the cascade of water spilling over the rocks, the ferns bathing in the spray, and the contour of the slope creating a mathematical symmetry that an artist would savour for years. The sameness of the trees marching down the hillside was the only flaw.

Fee turned her head toward him and for an instant her smile shared his wonder. "Ronan, put the canopy back and take us for a slow circle," she ordered.

That was when the true beauty of the place hit him. A rich scent filled the cabin: warm sunshine, pristine water and a unique floral fragrance. He'd smelled it once before in a high level parfumerie in Urbis when he'd been trying to impress a Senator's daughter. Yet that far-off memory was only a pale whisper of this. Richer, headier, more intense.

"There is a grove of chaullnia bushes by the bottom waterfall," said Fee. "They're in full flower at the moment. The harvesters come next week."

"Those bushes are worth …" He couldn't think of a sum big enough. "And you're going to disrupt this place. You can't keep what you're doing hidden for a minute!"

"Don't worry. Got it covered."

She had? He glared at her, forgetting for a moment that she was beautiful and irritatingly alluring. Right now, she was just plain irritating. "There's nothing in the plans."

"I know." A slight twist of her lips. "We have a scheme in place, but to make it work you must know nothing of what comes next. Trust me, it's for the best."

Trust her?

Protect her, help her, make love to her if she would let him.

But trust her? Not by a long shot.

They landed in a small clearing at the top of the gully, where a bluff overlooked the folded land below. Waiting for them were the others in her team: a zoologist, microbiologist, forestry scientist and marching up the slopes, scanner in hand and eyes casing the changing terrain, a giant of a man was introduced as the team's geotechnical engineer. An essential person in this inherently unstable country.

Propped up in her seat in the skimmer, she was all business again, his little Sera, introducing her new members and gesturing the rest forward to describe their part in the master plan. It was done well; the layered ordering of it building to an exhilarating and outrageous whole. At the end, he walked forward to the edge of the bluff, needing silence and space to set it all in his head. Fitting the pieces of what was here now, and what was to come, into their place in the pattern.

This was what he loved about his work. The interlocking magic of all parts of a living system and the careful shifting of pieces to make what was needed.

Change is minimal. Only do what is necessary. The mantra of his favourite lecturer. Her profile said Fioruisghe den Coille had studied under the same master, and today he saw it confirmed. What was planned here was a tapestry of subtle shifts, a starter for what must come to the whole western side of the ranges.

It would work. A few changes needed, now he'd seen the actual site, but nothing major.

His eyes traced the hillside again, from ridge line down to the bottom of the hollow where the precious Chaullnia bushes squatted in non-descript splendour, their tiny flowers hidden beneath blue-grey leaves.

He turned back to the skimmer. "The new plantings will start at the top?"

She nodded. "From a distance they'll look like festia plantations for the first few years. The clearings will be on the lower slope; there, and over there." Her fingers pointed to the areas where the ground flattened out, natural breaks to be sheltered by planned groves of new tree types.

He studied the festia. "Those trees don't look that old. Won't your family query replacing them so soon?"

"No. We recycle the plantations frequently. The best pollen comes from just maturing trees."

It was too pat, but he didn't know enough about the den Coille operations to argue. Unfortunately.

So he better find out was setting off his inner alarm system. He leaned into the skimmer to pull out the pack holding his scanner units.

Fee made a move to climb out and join him.

"You're staying with the skimmer," he said with little hope of agreement. But to his surprise, the rest of her team joined in with a chorus of denials, backing him up.

"Sorry, pipsqueak. Orders from your mother, and she can be one scary lady when she's crossed.' said Seamach.

Even more surprising, after a long stare at all the faces set against her, Fee sat down again, leaned back against the head rest and pulled up the plans on her screens.

Her mother had said she was sensible. Or maybe she'd known how battered her daughter's body still was, and had counted on it doing her work for her. Whatever the reason, he was grateful. Now to hope Fee would stay put till he'd finished his work.

After taking his readings, he walked the slopes to get a feel for the terrain. It was something he always did and had learned never to skimp. Feeling the wind, walking the ground, seeing the land and sun at play; these were the touchstones. The proof of what the figures might say. Sometimes there was a disconnect, reality and figures playing different games, and there was always a reason.

So far here, both matched. However he tried to deny it, Fee den Coille knew what she was doing and was good at it. The lakes project needed that kind of expertise.

Once she was fully recovered—and when he had learned to see just an eco-engineer and not a maddeningly enticing, fascinating, utterly gorgeous woman.

He made it back to the skimmer just in time. The stubborn woman was clambering out the back, pack in hand.

"Not another step."

She swung the pack up to hoist it onto those slim shoulders. He solved the problem by lifting it off her and tossing it to Seamach, who grinned in reply and swiftly stowed the thing back where it belonged: in the luggage hold.

"I'm finished," he said to her, "your team are finished. We leave now."

The rest of her team agreed so quickly and packed the skimmer up in such swift time, he might have felt sorry for her if he hadn't seen the blue marks of exhaustion haunting the hollows beneath those extraordinary eyes.

"Time you were back resting, like you should have been all day."

From the set of her mouth, that was exactly the wrong thing to say. Too bad. Someone needed to make sure she looked after herself.

On the way back, he took advantage of the skimmer's Survey security to contact his own team. They were making good progress, they reported, but it didn't stop the frustration eating at him. Holo-pics and tables of figures could only tell so much.

Fee leaned across to see and he switched the view screen from personal to her channel. She pulled up the lake filling stats and visual display. "Looks to be going well."

He nodded, having heard the same note in her voice as ate at him. Looked to be, but was it?

A muddy hole in the ground. That's all that could be seen so far, but already the rising water lapped half-way up the base of the Council Rock. Did she know the small depression now filling was where you put your first foothold when clambering up? He changed views.

She said nothing and switched her channel to the flow rates and the subterranean surveys of the ground seepage. "Seems stable," she said, peering with a frown at the display, "and the rate of filling will exceed transpiration. Anything else is your department."

He nodded. "Yeah, looks fair enough." He didn't add what else he needed, that same gut feeling as on the slopes here to tell him if it was really working. Nor could he know the mood of his team. He knew what the sight of that water lapping at the base of the Council Rock did to him. What of his team?

All were desert born, most raised in his home region. All had worked as hard these last months and had as little time to get over the shock of what they must do before plunging into the Survey's work.

He needed to be home. He looked across at the woman sitting opposite.

She caught his scrutiny too quickly and ducked her head. But she could not hide the shadows on her cheeks, the fading bruise on her shoulder reaching up her neck, the awkwardly held, still healing arm.

She had been so badly hurt.

"Cone of silence back down," the pilot's voice said. "Entering den Coille surveillance zone. Please secure all valuables and interesting device usages."

There was a general chuckle and a shuffle of com units. Fee switched off her channel. "Sorry, Caleb. You better shut down, just in case."

"Your family can crack Survey security?" Solaris had been trying for years to do exactly that.

She shook her head, "But they can detect the Survey trace, and we don't need them being suspicious of us. Not today."

There was something in the way she said it that he thoroughly mistrusted. He glanced out of the windows and saw they were coming in to land. No time to find out what was going on, but it didn't stop the cold brush of warning at the back of his neck.

A full scale reception party stood waiting. Her father, a crowd of siblings and cousins—and her mother, standing to one side with a seriously ticked off look on her face.

They enveloped Fee before she even set foot on the landing pad.

"Just answer them truthfully in that standoff plainsman style of yours," said the pilot softly as he passed him, heading with the rest of the team towards the control room before Caleb could ask any of the questions buzzing in his head. He had a very bad feeling.

"Winter, is this correct?" The tide parted and Bram den Coille stood glowering at the far end of an aisle of mountain folk, a suspiciously forlorn looking Fee standing beside him.

The man might choose to bark at him across the entire length of a landing pad, but Caleb wasn't about to reciprocate. He deliberately walked across to within normal talking range. The rest melted back, leaving them in an island of space. What was that about? He looked at their faces, felt the tension in their rigid bodies, arms tucked tight to their sides and suddenly registered what he was seeing — fear.

"Is what true?"

"You found no signs of environmentally caused decay?"

"Not a sign."

"No wind burn, no broken leaves, no physical damage from wind or weather?

He thought of that magnificent hill side, the bloomingly healthy festia and chaullnia, the magical aroma filling the air.

"Normal wear only," was all he said, keeping his gaze firmly fixed on the man and away from his benighted daughter. The same one Bram den Coille now turned to.

"So the reports are true?"

And the woman nodded, without a trace he could see of shame.

It was as if all the puffery in the man collapsed in one burst. "That's it then. It's parasynth. Put out the quarantine order and send in the destruction corps immediately."

"In progress," said Fee with that fraudulent sweetness back in her voice. "Kebhyn put out the call as we came through, pending your final order. Kebhyn—set to go?"

It was the serious man from her team, the horticulturist, looking as completely absorbed in his work as on the way out. Bram and the others looked at him, all with a respectful air.

The horticulturist played on his com unit, looked slowly up and said in that steady, absolutely believable tone. "The quarantine is now in place and sensors on the boundary prevent entry to the north gulley. The team is assembling and will be leaving within the hour. I must go to join them."

"Yes."

Bram den Coille looked visibly shaken. Caleb was forgotten, much to his relief. He used the chance to discreetly input the words 'parasynth' into his com unit.

The answer came back in his ear, on his personal top security channel. "Parasynth—Parasynaesthesia. A highly virulent disease of festia trees, caused by ..." There was all the usual technical data, even in the shortened form, but the bit that stood out came at the end. "Highly contagious. No treatment available. Only option is destruction of all potentially infected trees, followed by re-cropping with non-related species.

No wonder the man in front of him looked shaken. His delightful daughter had just threatened him with the loss of his entire business. And he thought he was tough.

"You'll give us a copy of your findings?"

Belatedly, Caleb realised the man was talking to him.

"No. Survey property," and didn't care if he sounded too abrupt. Let Bram den Coille anywhere near his report—the one that made no mention at all of disease? Not likely, not ever. Yet he shouldn't take out his anger on the man.

His daughter, now.

Strangely, den Coille didn't argue, only looked at him with more loathing than when he'd first arrived.

"I'll be in my room, finishing my reports," Caleb snarled at Fee—no, at Fioruisghe ingh Bram an Scathach den bloody Coille, the architect of all this, and marched away while he still had some chance of controlling his temper.

It didn't last. Not when the girl banged on his door and thrust her way into his room before he was even halfway to getting a lid on his anger. "What in hell?"

And swore when she stuck up a hand for silence and plugged a code into her com unit, before shutting the door precisely and turning to face him, chin shoved out in challenge.

"What in hell," he repeated just as precisely, "was that all about? Parasynaesthesia? You got a grudge against your family?"

"It was necessary. Quarantining the area is the only way to keep out prying eyes and let us get on with the clearing and re-planting."

He crossed his arms and thrust his face at her. "And you couldn't have warned me?"

She held his gaze, making no attempt to look apologetic. As if she was in the right here.

He lifted a hand in disgust. "You mountain folk sure have a different definition of family."

"And yours is so marvellous?"

"No, my family is completely and utterly jacked over. But I've never done anything remotely like that; not in public, even to my father."

"Huh," she said, crossing her arms as well and hugging them tight to her body.

Then uncrossed them, wincing as she repositioned the injured arm. It did not soften his mood, or not much. He waited.

A scowl now. "We couldn't tell you beforehand. We needed a completely honest response from you."

He lifted an eyebrow.

"You were being scanned. Any false emotions would have been seized on. That Plains outrage and straight talking of yours are exactly the response they'd expect to an undeclared parasynth outbreak."

"Undeclared?" That prickling in his neck was back.

"Yes. Undeclared to the Survey, and that's exactly how it would have stayed if you weren't here. Do you see any obvious Survey presence here, except me?

Okay, now she had him listening. "Not even your father is above the Survey. It's government." They didn't use them often—the public backlash usually made it not worth the trouble—but the penalties for blocking the Survey's actions were financially vicious. They had to be, given the corporates they were up against.

"He can limit their presence. Why do you think the rest of my team work undercover?"

Like his team, but he wasn't about to give her any points at the moment. "You have a public office?"

She nodded. "And do all the usual Survey jobs; the ones everyone knows about. Da accepts that he has to let his staff help me. The team, that is. They all work as contractors to the Survey, or that's the arrangement he knows about. It gives him a real thrill to think he's getting one over the government by getting them to pay his staff to do den Coille work."

"Staff whose first loyalty is actually to the Survey?"

It was a question he absolutely needed the answer to.

She glared at him, that ridiculously pretty chin of hers shoved even higher. "They are Survey first, their loyalty tested time and time again. I trust every one with my life."

"I'll take your word for it. So where do I fit into this charade?"

"We need that quarantine, and we couldn't get it without an independent witness to give Da no choice," she lowered that chin a fraction, "and as independent witnesses go, they don't come much better than you."

It wasn't a compliment, said those eyes of hers.

"You're Survey. Central knows you're here, and you are the eldest son of Winter Solaris. Da can't touch you."

He certainly hoped not. His own father was no soft touch, but Bram den Coille was turning out to be downright lethal.

"All right, you win," he said. It seemed to make her no happier than it did him. "Give me the plan—the whole plan."

Nothing on her face changed yet something in her shifted, as if a too tightly wound spring had relaxed enough to keep working a bit longer. She nodded agreement, and the jolt of air lodged in his chest escaped in a whoosh of relief. She reached out her hand, touching her com-unit to his for a direct data transfer.

"Safer," she said.

He skimmed over the files and looked up sharply.

"This plan—it's not what happened up there."

She tucked her arms against her chest in defence, and that felt all kinds of wrong.

"We modified it. Look at the updates."

He checked the dates on the file changes. "This version…?"

"…came together last night."

Not possible. "You were near unconscious."

"I have a good team."

"So the disease strategy, that wasn't yours?"

"No, that was mine." No trace of apology or shame in her voice. Rather, she defiantly shoved her chin out as far as it would go. "Parasynth is the only thing scary enough to keep den Coille out of the north gulley. We're a hard crew to stop."

"Your land, your strategy." But never his, not like this, and refused to admit to hypocrisy, given what he was doing to his own family.

Those pursed lips of hers said different. "Yeah well, I'll leave you to your work." She swung round to go, but suddenly swivelled back, leaned forward, and poked him hard in the chest.

"You think I like this? My Da, he's a good man. But these mountains, our mountains? There'll be nothing left of them if the Survey loses. I do this because I have to."

She crashed the door open and was gone before he could stop her.

Then the room was empty.

CHAPTER NINE

"Tomorrow, if Fee is well."

If one more person asked when he was leaving—just one—he wouldn't be responsible for the outcome. This time, it was the security guard outside Fee's quarters. Her mother came out of the room and heard him.

"She will be, as long as she rests. Come back later."

"She's safe?"

"Safe? This is her home."

He had no answer to that, not to her mother. But he still wasn't leaving this city, not yet. So where to go while he waited? He couldn't leave the den Coille complex. The tension in the city was ratcheted to a breaking point as news of the quarantine spread, and a Survey enforcer from the Plains was just the spark that would set the place alight.

"I'll be in my room if she needs me. I have to contact my people about the work I had to leave."

Hours later and Fee felt no better. She ought to be used to lying to her family by now. So why did this time feel so much worse? Why did she feel as if she had used Caleb Winter in a way he would not forgive, and why did that matter so much? She wandered aimlessly round her room, touching and discarding one object after another.

Next moment he was back, looking no happier than when she'd stormed out on him.

"Sit down," he growled at her, "before you fall down."

So much for showing him she was fit enough for him to leave. "You've been in touch with your base camp?"

He glared up at the corner of the room, at the exact spot she'd told him there was a sensor button, and nodded. "The herds are fine, spreading out into the new range area."

The lake was filling to plan. Is that what he meant?

"You need to get back there?"

He nodded, and slung himself into the chair opposite.

"You're not the only one who needs to get back to work." She glared at her stupid arm. It would be another day at least before she lost the supports for it. He thrust his body forward and suddenly his chair seemed far too close.

"No you don't. Not in this state."

"Yes, I do."

He sat back again, to her relief. "You can't. Not without your mother's clearance, and she is one tough lady. The work can manage without you."

"No, it can't." She could be as stubborn as him.

He glared at her, then up at the corner again. "I need air."

She knew how he felt. Anything was better than this nightmare of half-guessed truths. "I have a place I like to go."

"Can you see the sky from there?"

"Yes, though I can't promise it'll be a cloud free one."

But he looked at her arm, and shook his head. "Someone else can show me the way."

"No."

She stared straight back, refusing to be beaten by his black scowl. Finally, he lifted a hand, rubbed the back of his neck and sighed in defeat. "Only if you use a chair. You've done enough walking and hiking around today. "

She allowed herself a small grin. "The nurse will get me one." Whether she likes it or not.

The woman fussed around as Fee settled into the flitter chair. She hated the need for it but had to admit she wasn't up to walking far yet. Her nurse's face couldn't have looked more grim. "You have a comtab on you?" Fee lifted her wrist to show the band. It was Survey issue, but she doubted the woman would realise that. The grim look stayed, but it did stop her protests. Fee was free to go with Caleb.

Or was until Caleb's guard stepped in behind to follow them. She chopped a hand at the man.

"Stand down, Jaresh."

Unfortunately, Jaresh had known her since childhood and the demand had no effect. "Orders."

"Countermand them."

"Go against your father? Not likely."

Beside her, she sensed the plainsman fighting for control. "She's safe with me."

It was true, in ways that still surprised her, but if Caleb Winter thought to reassure Jaresh, he was wrong. She lifted her wrist. "I have a com-tab and we are not leaving the estate."

She remembered beating up Jaresh at school for precisely the grin he gave her now. Problem was, she was bigger than him in those days.

He leaned forward. "Your father agreed to this little jaunt?" His grin spread wide at her lack of answer.

The plainsman beside her whirled, heading back. "Forget this."

"Stop." Her hand caught at his arm. He looked ready to explode and she half expected him to throw it off, but he came to a halt. She threw a dark look at Jaresh. "Pass me your comtab and patch me through to Father."

A lift of his shoulders and he passed it over. Caleb watched, still tensed to leave. She held his eye as she switched the channel over.

"Father. It's Fioruisghe. Call off Jaresh, or I'll have the Survey lift both of us out of here in one hour."

She switched the com unit to silent till the sensor said her father had run out of bluster.

"The Survey, one hour," and passed the unit back to Jaresh—who held it at arm's length while he listened to her father's orders, scowling at her all the time.

"I should have remembered you play dirty." He gave her the most perfunctory of salutes, with a slight flick at Caleb. "Plainsman."

Even before he disappeared from sight, Caleb was striding off and Fee had to switch the flitter to fast to keep up with him. He barely glanced at her, and his hands were clenched tight. "By the sands, get me out of here."

She swirled around him. "Next on the left and up a flight." The walkway vibrated under his boots and she thought he had for once forgotten how high they were above the ground. Up another flight, around a corner and she stopped in front of a nondescript door, coded to her palm print only. She had set it many years ago. This was the entrance to her own special place.

It opened and he went to stride on through.

She screeched a warning and managed to grab hold of his shirt, halting him right on the threshold just before he plummeted over the steep drop on the other side. He stared in horror. "Are you trying to kill me too?"

"It's quite safe if you're careful. There's a flotation belt hanging by the door. "

His hand clung tight to the door frame and he stared out at the canopy as if at a nightmare. "Maybe I can do without sky."

"I rode a horse; you can climb a tree."

He looked at her carefully strapped arm. "Look where that got you."

"We need to talk, and up here is the most secure. Ride on the back of the flitter. You'll be safe there."

He looked no more convinced, but after yet another tug of her arm, he relented and took a step back, and up onto the chair.

"Fasten that belt," she ordered.

"What about you?"

She could have argued, but slipped on the spare belt. She was pushing him hard enough already.

He clung to the seat back and she kept the pace slow. Out along the thick branches, lifting easily under and over the cross-branches. She wouldn't have bothered on her own, steering straight for her objective, but he seemed more comfortable with something solid below him.

"Oof. Watch out." His head caught an overhead, nearly toppling him overboard.

"Sorry." She slowed right down. "Nearly there."

She brought the flitter to a hover just in front of a fork in the main branch and began to clamber out.

"What do you think you're doing?"

She leapt onto the branch, using her good hand to hold onto the thinner of the two forks. The tree swayed with her weight and she went with it, glorying in the life below her feet.

"Come on, it's safe enough. The gravity belt will hold you if you slip."

He looked as her as if she was insane, but did remove his boots, so unsuited to the living branches of her mountain city, before pulling on a pair of the flexible mountain slippers. So he'd learned something of her home.

With his natural strength and loose limbed ease, he could have done without the help of the flotation belt, but Fee kept her smile to herself when he kept it at full strength. This wasn't his home and he wasn't ready yet to feel what she did; the give and sway of the living tree beneath her feet. It was her own billyup, the heart of the mountain she loved.

He climbed out of the flitter, one hand clutched tight to the seat railing and the other reaching desperately for the branch on the other side of the fork.

"Through here." She pushed through the gap in the branches, watching carefully as he followed. Each of his footfalls cautiously placed; a thin frown on his face and the colour of it bleached waxen, but he was moving forward.

She gave him her hand, and he slipped only the once, his fingers clutching tight to hers in sudden panic till his belt brought him safely upright.

"This better be good."

A thick bank of leaves blocked their way as the cluster of branches came to an end. She pushed through, ignoring the twinges of abused muscles and wished she had both arms. This time, it was his hand steadying hers as he followed her through the living curtain.

Then halted. "This is—"

On the very edge of the city, it hung between tree and sky: a balcony woven from living branches. The last rays of the sun arrowed down and, far out to the west, a crimson glimmer marked the border of sea and air. She took her favourite spot on one of the benches set on either side, leaned her head back against the supporting branch and let her chest fill. Breathed in, out, absorbing the play of wind in the leaves and the scent of fresh rain on tree and moss.

He walked without a word right to the edge, hand just touching the railing, and threw his head back to let the last warmth of the sun fall full on his face.

"Thank you. Sometimes—the trees. A man can't breathe."

He dropped his gaze to the rails and let his fingers run lightly across the interlacing pattern of leaf and branch, eyes tracing the woven basketwork of living tree that made up the small hideaway, all supported by three thick boughs underneath. The room moved with the play of the wind, but never so much that it felt unsafe.

"It's beautiful," he murmured. "So fragile."

"Don't worry. It's strong enough to hold us."

She stood up and came across to take the small space left beside him, drawn to discover how he viewed her home.

His gaze rested on the waves of trees enfolding the hill side. "Impressive."

"The view from the Bluff is reckoned the best one in the city. I heard you went there."

A slight lift of his shoulder. "This is better."

She smiled. "I think so. I used to come up here as a child, just to see the treetops."

My trees, was her private thought. The forest had shared her dreams as she grew up and she couldn't remember a day when she hadn't been in love with the wonderful complexity of the interlocking parts of her world.

He shifted slightly, and turned to look down at her, the dying light catching on the suddenly hard edged lines of his face, betraying the barely held backwash of temper still riding him. "How private are we here?"

"I swept it for sensors before I left, and there's no sign anyone's been here since. We're safe to talk."

He pulled out his Survey issue scanner and ran his own check, regardless. "All clear," he confirmed moments later. "Now, sit back down before you fall down."

He fit his words to action, wrapping his hand around her and gently nudged her back towards her bench.

She shoved back, but deep inside felt the tremor of barely recovered muscles pushed too far, too soon.

"You do not want me to carry you."

He was right about that. "Fine." She reached behind her for the seat and sat down again, pulling her feet up and cradling her head against the soft wall of leaves behind her. "Better?"

The faintest hint of a smile touched the corner of his lips and he gave a slow nod.

"So what was the news from the lake?" she said crossly.

"The water intake is on target. Still seepage only, but on schedule. Kal had no concerns."

"But—"

His face had tightened at the question. He breathed in hard, releasing it with a short gust of temper-fuelled air. "Do you ever give up?"

She pulled her legs farther up, tugging on her knees. "No."

He was much bigger than her, but she held his stare. She'd grown up with four brothers, and this was too important. "You have to get back?"

He nodded, a curt dip of his head this time. "There's only so long my crew can cover for me—or fool my father."

"And me? Fox was quite clear—we get the lake under way first. The mountain project comes later.

"You're not going anywhere. Not till that arm is healed."

She tucked her legs in tighter as he leaned over her. She still had to argue back. "You need my input. None of your crew knows as much about water systems as me."

"You can work from here by com unit."

"It's not the same—and stand back. Give me some room."

"Why. So you can put up all those defences and fool yourself into thinking you're up to leaving here. Let you imagine you're in control of me? Can feel *comfortable?*"

She shook her head, desperate for space between them, but damned if she would give way on this. "No. So I can do my job."

"Your job!" His finger jabbed at her. "That lake is on my land, in my country."

"And it doesn't matter to me what happens there? That lake is important to all of us, and you need my input to make it work."

He shot up at that, strode back to the balcony edge and clung to the rail. She felt every footfall in the shiver of the wood beneath her.

Then he turned, and she forgot the living wood.

"Survey be damned. That fall, from that horse. You nearly died back there."

Her mouth dropped open. She must look like an idiot, and scrambled to close it as she half rose.

"Don't."

One word, but something in it had her sitting back down.

He shifted, lips drawn tight.

Desperate to change the subject, she shoved her hands into her stomach to still their tell-tale restlessness. "So when do you go back?"

"A flyer is on call whenever I need it."

A deep breath. "Thank you for staying so long."

"Don't. Not that polite rubbish, not to me."

Don't. That word again. What did he expect? Suddenly she found her courage.

"Why stay so long? You're needed back there. We both are."

He glared at her now, the anger plain. "You were hurt."

He flung himself onto the second bench opposite her, setting the whole room swaying. "You needed me."

She hugged her knees into her chest, unable to deny it. The crowds when they landed, her family, the suffocating concern in their faces and the knowledge she must betray them soon. "Why does that matter to you? You've made it clear enough you don't want to work with me. That you'd prefer I had nothing to do with your lake, or your land."

He glared back, looking more rattled than she'd have thought possible. "I don't know, but it does. Deal with it."

CHAPTER TEN

"Deal with it." What kind of answer was that?

The only one you're going to get, said the fixed set of his jaw.

He swore and shot up again, pulled the Survey tab from his pocket and handed it over. "Here's Kal's update."

While she read the latest data, he stared at a point somewhere over her head.

Deal with it. Sure, plainsman, about as well as you.

She took the tab, set it to scroll through the figures and schemata and shoved her new problem to one side. Not too successfully, at first, but then she looked more closely at the data.

He was right. He should have been long gone. They couldn't hide this much longer, but that wasn't all. They both needed to get back. She pulled up the latest images, the deep scans of the aquifer channels, teeth chewing on her bottom lip.

"No problems reported, you said?"

"No," he said, but there was that note in his voice again, that forced surety. "They're all in the predicted range."

Just. She pushed the schematics over to him. "Look, here and here." His eyes went to where she pointed, a slow nod following as he too tracked the colours of the water soaking the substrata and creeping towards the new lake.

Her finger jabbed down, setting a second screen shimmering in the air between them, figures marching across in an undeniable reality.

"Marginal?" he said, his tone a question but his face said he knew.

"For now. It's holding, can be managed, if you know what you're doing."

His mouth set tight. "You can do it from here."

She shook her head. "Not as well. That filling rate needs close monitoring; the kind that only you and I have the experience and training for."

He said nothing, stubbornly refusing to listen. But she'd seen Kal's profile and Caleb knew the man even better than her. He was good, very capable, knew what those soils could take. But he didn't know what water could do, how quickly it could change from friend to vicious enemy, not in his gut.

She zoomed in on the area most vulnerable. "You want a collapse of that aquifer?"

A brisk flick of his hand, the idea not worth answering. Of course not, said his face. "I'll head back there soon, once you're fit enough to leave."

She felt like stamping her foot, no matter how childish. The man knew as well as she that he had no choice. That he had to head back to the lake site before something broke. He just needed convincing of it.

"I'll head back soon," he said again. She glared at him, only to have him glare back as ruthlessly. She finally threw up her hands.

"Your funeral."

Except it wasn't his funeral; it was Arcadia's if they got back too late.

He would protect her at the expense of the planet?

Thoroughly rattled, she dropped her gaze and went back to checking the records. That was when she noticed it. The second tab, with a label that made her heart grow cold. Phase two.

"This wasn't drawn up today."

She turned it around, showed him the new file. A very familiar terrain holo-map, her mountain region, now scored in damning detail; red for change, green to stay the same. There was a lot of red.

Why she felt so betrayed, she refused to consider. All she knew was that a cold knot of something foreign coiled tight inside her. "So why exactly do you find the view up here so much better than from the bluff?"

His mouth tightened. He wasn't going to answer her. Then a shrug.

"It's higher up, so the patterns of growth are more readily seen."

"How much of my home—how much of my family's fortune do you plan to destroy?"

She leaped off the seat. His hand reached out to steady her but she twitched away. She'd had never thought herself capable of violence, but right now she could do this man some serious damage. His eyes narrowed in recognition and he turned back to the view below, stonewalling her with the flat voice of a disembodied professional as each stab of his hand laid out the reality of his words.

"Bring in some open meadows down on those flats, restore the creeks your people dammed to provide controlled drainage and plant baullnia in place of the festia. Its rate of transpiration is half that of the festia and its roots go deeper. Those festia plantations turn everything into a swamp." He glanced up at the clouds. "The wind patterns here will help dry out the land, but won't scour away the top soil. Not with the new plantings."

She looked at the schematics, at his annotations. There was too much truth in them. Her own team's reports said much the same, though not as clearly or as brutally complete.

"What about the festia? They feed a lot of this planet, don't forget."

"Will survive—in lower numbers. Their pollen isn't the only food source possible on these lands."

He moved back as far as he could in the confined space. "Your people do have choices. You said as much today with those food shrubs you're planting in the north valley."

The rational side of her knew that, but this land belonged to her. She stared out at the kaleidoscope of green, the hills under a blanket of trees, and tried to imagine the changed version. She looked at the holo-map, at the rich green slopes of her home.

"It's what used to be here. That's what you told me about the changes to my homeland."

He was right in that too. It had all been so much simpler with the north gulley project. She could cope with that. But this plan? This was her home. "It didn't help you."

"No, but I did understand why it had to be done."

"Just not by an outsider?"

He nodded. "Still don't, not even one as skilled as you in water management."

She lifted her head in shock.

"That system of channels keeping the festia plantations here thoroughly soaked all the time; it's very clever—and quite unique."

She squirmed. "Not really."

"Yes, really. I checked your Survey records. You designed it."

She couldn't look at him. "Not all of it."

He snorted. "The bits that work best; they're yours."

She shrugged. She couldn't deny it. That system had brought her another year at grad school.

"Now you work for the Survey."

If he could have moved even farther back, she was sure he would have. She did it for him, retreating back to her seat, and pulling up her feet onto the bench, as if creating a wall to hide behind.

"The Survey is important to me," she said.

"I know what my lands will lose by that lake, and what we risk without it. The desert grows year by year: and not even billyup can live in the dead heart of it now. What do you have to lose?"

She tucked her feet in tight. Would this man understand? Did she even want to try to make him? She took a deep breath. "If we keep on as we are, these hills will disappear. Washouts, mudslides, just plain rot and decay."

A twig dropped in her lap. She glanced up, and had to brush away the grit that followed. The wind was getting up.

"We need to get back. Weather's coming."

He scowled and leaned back against the thin balcony wall. "You were going to say?"

There was a creak, and a message running through her feet. He leaned back on the railing, so angry, so tightly contained.

Another crack, loud and ominous.

A piece of shirt, that was all she could grab, but it was enough. A yank on cloth that sent him toppling right on top of her as the balcony railings crashed into oblivion.

They landed hard on the thick branches underlying the leafy floor and her free hand clung tight as the full weight of him smashed down on her.

Stars, and blackness, and the screaming redness of pain.

"What the … Fee, come back."

A slap on her face and a weight lifting off her.

She tried to talk, took a breath, tried again.

He knelt beside her, fingers probing flesh already screaming in agony. Then mercifully stopped and leaned back.

"Nothing broken. The arm's still intact, but your bruises and ribs have taken another drubbing. "

He helped her to sit up, before pulling off his shirt. Those muscles—what did he think he was doing?

"Umm."

"Don't be stupid." His big hand set to, rending the material into strips, and in no time he had her arm and ribs strapped tightly in place with a very serviceable field bandage. The pain eased and she sighed in relief, only to grit her teeth again as he lifted her up.

"Sorry. I'll make this as easy as possible."

She nodded and leaned into his chest. The man was seriously ripped; must be all that horse riding.

"That, and other stuff," said an amused voice. The burn in her cheeks was hotter than the fire of the pain.

"That wasn't meant to come out aloud."

He chuckled and she relaxed. It was such a strange sound in the circumstances. His hands holding her told a different message. He was not relaxed at all.

"Can you call the chair closer?"

She nodded and held up her wrist so her fingers could reach the control strip.

"And call in your parents."

"Not a good idea," she mumbled, catching a flash in his eyes. Guilt? "You do know you could have died back there?"

He started to shrug, stopping only when the movement brought a gasp from her. "You saved me, and hurt yourself again."

So he still owed her, did he mean? Or they were now even? Talking to this man was like crossing a swamp at night, bog holes beckoning with each footfall.

He lifted her and swung them both into the chair, cradling her on his lap as he took the controls. Her head pounded, her body ached, but the warm smell of his body surrounded her and she leaned back tiredly into the security of his chest. One strong arm anchored her in place and he took the chair slowly back to the first doorway.

It swung wide, to reveal a whole troop of people waiting for them on the landing. Her father was dead centre. She had a very bad feeling. Her feet were already moving to stand, only to feel Caleb's hand pressing down on her shoulder.

"Put her down and step away, plainsman." Her father's face was as black as she'd seen it, focussed on Caleb's bare chest and arm holding her. The weapons his men smacked into place decided it. Caleb set her carefully down on the skimmer seat and stepped off, hands held wide and high. The muzzles pointed and he turned round, hands yanked behind his back and secured with cuffs. Two large men shoved him into place and the rest of the weapons stayed armed and focussed on him.

"Father?"

"Stay out of this, Fioruisghe. Plainsman, you're under arrest for plotting, industrial espionage and the deliberate introduction of a prohibited disease organism."

"And—" Caleb's face was totally self-contained but something deadly sat behind it.

"You will be detained until we're sure you're no longer a threat, or Winter Solaris gives us a suitable undertaking."

Caleb didn't bother with claims of innocence. "You do know I have nothing to do with the Solaris business?"

"Then I hope you like trees."

"Father," she cried again, struggling to get up.

"Sit back," snapped Caleb. "She fell and hurt herself again," he said to her father. "Get her help."

It was a damn cell. Caleb paced the bare room. Four steps one way, five the other, the only extras a built in hygiene unit and a narrow bunk. They had stuck him in a jail cell.

He marched back the other way and slapped the far wall. Solid as hell. In this whole city of lightweight flexible structures, did this have to be the one room they built properly? He didn't even know if he was high in the branches or down at ground level. After cuffing and bundling him off, they had stuck a bag on his head and forced him up and down so many flights he had no idea where he was now.

He paced back again, slamming into the solid wooden door on the other side. Above it was the only opening in the whole blasted room. A grille set so high that if he'd been the same height as most of these mountain people, he'd have had no chance of seeing through it. As it was, he had to stretch up hard, only to see a passageway as bare of anything useful as the cell he was stuck in.

Caleb Winter, eldest son of Winter Solaris, and they had stuck him in a cell. His father was going to raise all hell when he found out. No one did this to a Winter.

At least Fee was safe.

How long would they wait to message his father? Why did they risk holding him?

How badly hurt was she?

Questions, damn questions. All he had, and he didn't look like getting answers to any of them in a hurry.

Without light, there was no marking the time. A couple of meals came, slid through a server hatch, and the changes from quiet to local sounds to quiet again said it was late in his second night here. A light permanently shone through the hole in the door, but there was none in his cell. Only a faint glow from the far top corner telling of a sensor. Because of that sensor, all his rage must stay locked inside. Pride of a Winter; his father's favourite saying.

A scrape of the door and a scratch of a lock released. He poised, the cell door swung open and he sprang.

"You!"

Small and dark, she slipped his grasp and was across the room—not her wisest course. It left her trapped in the far corner. He stood near the cell door, one eye on the sensor, and watched to see what Fee would do.

She put up a finger, gesturing for silence. So now she thought him an idiot as well.

He kept his arms out from his sides and did nothing that could be taken as a threat. That sensor must be recording their actions and some guard would come barrelling in here any minute. With her in that corner, looking like she was under threat, the guard might shoot first and ask questions later.

Hopefully the man would check the room before acting, and Caleb had no intention of making the situation look any worse. Or not more than her father already thought it.

He lifted his arms in query, pointed to the sensor and waved a hand in front of her face. She shook her head but kept a finger over her mouth.

It could hear sound but no visual feed.

Silently, as flexible as a small desert rat, she slipped noiselessly across the room and out the door, waving a hand at him to follow.

A trap? Maybe, but it was better than doing nothing.

She slipped into a small side passage, dark and mercifully looking like it was clear of sensors. After that, he reckoned there had to be a 3-D maze in her head, she led him down so many twists and back ways.

They emerged high in the canopy of the baullnia. No nearer freedom than at the start of this mad trip, and his one glance down sent a sickening lurch through his guts.

Ahead of him, she walked out onto a branch, surefooted even with only one arm. She expected him to follow her onto that scrawny limb?

She stopped, turning effortlessly on the narrow bridge. "It's the only way," she mouthed. "I come this way all the time. It's perfectly safe."

He glanced down again; way, way down.

"Don't do that—don't look. If I can ride—"

"A horse, I can walk across your skinny twig of a branch?"

"Keep your eyes on my back. Concentrate on that, nothing else."

She set out again, slower this time, and he followed, rigidly upright.

Keep your eyes on my back, she'd said. He found a better version; the butt swaying delightfully in front of him. Only that proved one very bad option. It might take his mind off the fall below but was too distracting in so many other ways.

"Nearly there," her voice said.

Another step and she disappeared between two branches. One more, and he pushed through the leafy curtain after her. Only to see a thicket of cross-hatched branches and logs. He didn't believe it. They were in another tree.

"There are more crossings like that?"

"Not too many. This is the best way to get far enough from the city centre for the Survey to make a pick up without setting off alarms."

"The sensor in that cell will have done that already."

An earnest shake of her head. "I fiddled with the system. We're safe till the next guard change in a couple of hours."

That meant only one thing. "You're coming with me?"

"It's the only option. At least till Father cools down."

"What did you expect when you pulled that disease con? It didn't occur to you that he'd blame the obvious suspect, the plainsman outsider?"

She blushed. "Well, yes, it was a possibility. But throwing you in a cell? He's lucky it wasn't one of your brothers. We really don't need any border issues."

"You think I'm not tempted to start one?"

A twist of a grin on that deceptive face. "Tempted, yes. Start one, no. Not with the lake site bang in the middle."

Some vote of confidence.

The next half hour was one of the more hellish of his existence and the Survey flyer at the end the most welcome sight in a long time. Along with everything else, he could see her steps beginning to flag, her hand having to shoot out more than once to grab a supporting branch. When they got to the flyer, she stopped and lifted her arms, waiting for him to help her in. Something deep inside him clenched tight, something that changed him forever.

He picked her up and lifted her into her seat.

"Last chance," he said. "Your father may bluster, but you're safe enough."

"Maybe, but he will ask questions. Ones I can't answer."

"You do know we'll have to hide you when we get there?" He adjusted her webbing, buckling her down. "My father will find out I was thrown in a den Coille jail." She opened her mouth to argue. "No. Trust me, he will find out."

She looked up at him, so solemn, so brave. His anger evaporated and he leaned down, touching her cheeks with his lips. So soft, her scent a unique mixture of woman, leaf and flower. "Don't worry so. I will keep you safe."

He took the seat opposite, and they lifted off. He glanced across as they cleared the tree tops and caught her staring out the window. Her eyes were fixed on the trees, and she leaned forward as if desperate to capture that last possible image. The loss on her face—

He quickly looked away, unable to intrude longer. He recognised that look too well. She was Survey all right, through and through.

"Hold tight for landing," said the pilot. Fee clutched at the webbing. They were coming in cloaked and that was always bumpy.

A blast of hot air hit her as soon as she stepped out. She heard the pleased grunt of the man beside her and watched him tilt his head back to let the sun's heat bathe his face. They had landed in the middle of a cluster of long grasses and shrubby bushes, thick enough for camouflage, and two of his men hurried forward to greet him. Her, they ignored. So they knew she was coming. The lack of response said they expected her, but welcomed her? No, definitely not that.

Caleb stretched in the welcome sunshine, with a pleased grunt as he recognised the two men. Adam, their hydrogeologist, and Jim, his head stockman. They might disagree with his actions, but they would obey orders. Yeah, and tell him what they thought of it later.

A brief flick upwards of the eyes of both men as they took in the silent, injured girl standing behind him, but that was all. So far. He tilted his head for Adam to get on with collecting their bags. "How's the lake?" he said to Jim.

"Filling."

He raised an eyebrow.

"No sign of your Da, yet." The old man had never been one to waste words.

"I'll check on progress and head back to the homestead tomorrow."

Jim nodded, then led the way back to the skimmer.

The girl only had one light pack, same as himself. She looked tired, worn down. Hell, she was supposed to be still in bed. He helped her into the cab and climbed up after her, nodding to Jim to head off. "Straight to camp."

She squirmed round. "What about the lake?"

"Not for you today."

She didn't argue, a worrying sign. "How long before we see your family coming after you?" he said to distract her.

"I left a note. It may give us a week, if my mother has the say."

Hmm, he had to admit her mother's word could do it. "Why would she give you that?"

"I threatened to apply to the Survey for a transfer if they followed me. She knows I mean it. As for Da, even if it wasn't personal, he needs my skills. Where would he find another eco-engineer for the same pay rate?"

He could see the effort of will keeping her upright. "Lean back. My shoulder is wide enough." He pulled her gently in, cradling her in his free arm and shooting a sharp warning glare to the others about any wisecracks. She let her head fall, and something in him relaxed. She was safe, for now.

"It wasn't business to your father back there. That prison cell felt personal."

She frowned. "Mmm, very." That was all.

At camp, she still gave no argument when he consigned her to her room before setting out for the lake. She settled back on the bed, her face pale and the circles under her eyes a dark reproach.

"You have meds with you?"

She nodded and waved him off. It didn't free him of worry, and he put a call through to their medic before he left. "Check her over thoroughly. My guess—she's still meant to be hospitalised."

One the way out, he linked through to Survey Central. His father could wait; the Survey would not. There was an ominous backlog on his com unit, all demanding replies.

"Nice of you to drop in," said Fox when he hailed him. Their boss was not known for subtlety, and the edge on his voice today made Caleb thankful the man was halfway around the planet.

"I'm heading out to the lake now. My crew haven't reported any problems though."

"Being all highly experienced eco-engineers. Wait. No, that would be you and Officer den Coille, one injured riding an animal she knew nothing about, the other too busy playing nursemaid to do his job."

The opposite side of the world; opposite sleep times.

"We're back now."

The boss must be mad. It took him a full second to pick up on that one. "We?"

"Fee and me."

"She's not—." Silence, for a blessedly long time, then a sigh. "We facing a major interzone issue here?"

"Nah. She's resting at camp. I'll send a full report through later. You could let her mother know she's safe and our medic will send her scans through. But probably best to let them think she's in some other place."

This time there was a real groan. Luckily they were nearly at the lake, and he had an excuse to sign off, breaking off the connection just as they pulled over. He walked up through a low depression in the slope surrounding the filling basin, keeping as low a profile as possible.

Then he saw it. A flat plate of dirty brown, glistening in alien triumph against the dry banks. A giant puddle stuck right in the middle of his baking home land. Brown, turbid, with foaming patches where the breeze had stirred up the sediment, but most definitely it was water. Not beautiful, not yet, not like the artfully sketched plans they had all pored over, but it would be. One day, if they could hold off his family.

The footsteps of change. Small but unbeatable, or that was what they hoped.

Kal had been working down by the edge. He came over, taking a break from sampling, and stood beside him looking down at the filling basin.

"She's something," he said.

Caleb kept staring. "Yeah."

They both stood, watching their dreams come true and their fears materialise.

"Planting starts next week. She's on target, perfectly so. Once you give the go ahead, we'll be onto it."

No, it was Fee who had to do that. Fee who was the expert in water usage patterns. Fee who had crystallised his gut feeling about the filling. "Yeah, 'bout that," said Caleb.

CHAPTER ELEVEN

The light breaking in the window woke her as a woman bustled in the door, with that unmistakable efficiency of a trained medic and nurse. Fee tried to sit up, but yelped as the twinge of abused muscles caught her. "I told mother …" Then she saw the style of the woman's clothes and memory pounced back. "Morning," she mumbled.

The Plains woman rolled in a tray. "Ready for breakfast?"

Fee was about to shake her head, just as the heavenly smell from the plate woke her senses. "Yes, I think I am," she said, surprising herself.

Time for a quick internal inventory as her new nurse bustled around. Bruised still, yes, but not too far off operational. Hopefully. "Give me a few days and I'll be back on board," she said.

"That's good to hear."

"Yes." Then recognised the look on the woman's face. "I'm needed now, aren't I?"

"Now, don't you go worrying yourself."

"Let me see Caleb."

Relief brightened the medic's face. "He set out this morning for the main house. You can talk to him when he gets back tonight."

Fee struggled further up. "No, too late. Get me one of the other eco-engineers."

The woman hurried forward to restrain her, and Fee cursed her inability to hide all pain. So maybe not quite operational yet. When Caleb fell on top of her, she'd suffered more damage than she cared to admit. "Get me some painkillers, then get Kal in here."

She hoped she had the name right. The one who'd seemed least sympathetic to her.

"Hey now, not yet. No one expects you up today. Not if you're to get better quickly."

"I know exactly how badly I'm hurt and none of it is life-threatening."

The medic finally gave way, and even left Fee alone when asked. Her stupid pride; she should have asked for help. It took a long and painful hour to dress, shower and ready herself for the eco-engineer, and her relief when the meds kicked in was disgustingly sobering.

She glared at herself in the mirror, seeing a pale face and dark circles. The woman came back in and clucked sympathetically.

"Make up," snarled Fee. "He's a man; he won't notice."

Kal arrived just as she was finishing up. She had to bat the tube into a nearby drawer and hide her fingers behind her back, but she'd also been right. He didn't notice a thing.

"You ready to start work yet?"

"Soon as you can get me out there. I'm still mostly one-handed."

The curt nod of his head said 'Follow me'.

The nurse thrust a bottle of water in her hand, yelled to their retreating backs, "She's still under medical orders," and watched as Fee hurried after the man. Not that Fee remembered him being so brusque the first time they had met; but he'd been talking to a plainsman that day.

It was a slow and bumpy trip out to the lake and the man made no effort to help her scrabble her way out of the skimmer or climb the bank. Her first sight of the lake made it all worth it.

No beauty; she'd not expected it.

"It's water, real water." She made no attempt to hide the smile on her face and the man beside her almost joined in her pleasure.

"Filling on schedule." Legs braced, he looked down on the dirty pond. "Another week, and we can increase the rate of flow."

She shook her head, remembering those latest reports. "Too risky. That aquifer network is marginal, only just holding."

His head bent curtly towards the sky. "It's fine—and there are other risks."

"Oh." Caleb's hurried trip to the Winter homestead. "The Survey will keep Sol Winter at bay. Their lawyers are almost as good at their jobs as we are."

The man just stuck his hands in his pockets. "Old Man Winter finds out, he'll do everything he can to stop this lake."

She grimaced. "It seems to be going around among fathers."

Enough. Whatever this man thought, she had work to do. Fee set off down the slope, striding quickly and taking no care against sliding downwards. She turned back and yelled at Kal. "We going to get this lake finished or what?"

He was staring after her like she was some kind of crazy woman. He might have a point, but he picked up his backpack and set off after her. When she stumbled at the bottom, landing on the shoulder of her injured arm, he was there to pick her up. "You sure you're up to field work?"

If she hadn't needed his help to get up, she would have shaken him off. But she did, and could only mutter a less than gracious "Thanks," grab her own pack again and stalk over to the water's edge.

"No problem," he growled back. So much for repairing bridges or whatever was the man's problem. As long as he worked with her.

The relays she had set up beforehand were still working. She flicked through the scans, monitoring the incoming channels, the flow rate and the porosity of the lake margins.

"What's your speciality?" she asked the other man after awhile. She ought to know. The local specialities were in her briefing notes but she had concentrated more on the physical part of the lake files.

"Interaction between plant and soil type; soil stability," he said.

Of course. It was Kal who had decided on the placement of those first blast charges, the ones she had so cavalierly forced Caleb to shift. It explained some of his behaviour, but she had a feeling he would have resented her regardless, and mentally shrugged. His problem. She had enough of her own. "And the fourth eco-eng?"

"Economic calibration. The lawyers love him."

"Unlike the rest of us." It was an old eco-eng joke, one that actually brought a quirk to the man's mouth and a short nod.

"Yeah," he said. "Pity Gerard wasn't more appreciative of them. He's one of the good guys."

They all were. It was hard to remember sometimes, when family whined or Central rode roughshod over the locals. Without the Survey, her home world was in big trouble.

She bent down to her scanners again.

"That week I said it would take before we could increase the flow rate? I was right."

"We'll see." *What would a mountain girl know?* said the curl of his lip. "I've got samples to take. You?"

"Just about done. You go ahead. I can wait on the bank while you finish."

Hopefully the man couldn't hear the tremor in her voice, as her body told her enough was enough. It would nicely finish off his assessment of her.

He tromped off around the lake, probing the soil at intervals and only occasionally glancing back at her. She managed to stay standing and looking busy till a friendly patch of scrub finally hid him from view and she could collapse onto the ground, shutting her eyes in relief. She would probably burn to a cinder in this hateful sun but right now she didn't care.

A clatter of rocks signalling Kal's return brought her back to awareness, forcing her to open her eyes again. She pulled the water bottle from her pack, took a swig and immediately upgraded her previously irritating nurse into the camp of the angels. It was laced with electrolytes and in a thermal bottle that kept the contents blessedly cool. She gulped it down, adding a couple more tablets from the stash in her belt, and sighed in relief as the beating at her temples and the throbbing in her arm came back to bearable levels. She pushed up, awkwardly manipulating her vials one handed to fill them with water from the growing puddle.

It really did look like a puddle—a very muddy, very big puddle. She tugged at the hat on her head and couldn't resist a small giggle. So much effort, so much at risk, all for a big brown *puddle.*

Kal stomped back into view and she forced herself to thrust away the smile. She strongly doubted Kal would see the funny side of all this.

Would Caleb?

At that moment, Kal waved her up. "You finished?"

So much for working together. There was no talk on the way back and the med tablets had long worn off by the time their vehicle pulled into its bay. Another skimmer sat in the next bay.

Caleb was back.

She stumbled out of the cab and made instinctively for the tall, familiar figure coming towards them. She was so glad to see him. No, that wasn't right. There was no reason in it, no reason for wanting to grab onto him and hold on tight or that suddenly all the aches of her body seemed easier. He was a work colleague, that's all. He didn't even *like* her.

Then stopped still as she took in the rigid set of his shoulders, the tension in his face and neck.

"What in hell do you think you're doing? Get back to bed."

That was all she got before he turned to the other man. "Kal, urgent meeting in the hall. Now."

Fee was not invited—that was clear. She chose to ignore it, waiting till the man had walked off before inserting herself into the back of the hall. With the amount of tension going free, she doubted anyone would notice her, certainly not Ser Caleb Winter himself.

Caleb stepped up to the stand at the front of the room and the fidgeting stopped dead. Fee had to angle her way to the side to have any hope of seeing him.

His message was short and simple. "We're on Plan B. You all know what to do." The silence thickened to a turgid, fear-filled soup and Fee shrank back further into the shadows as Caleb's orders sank in.

"Kal, you and Adam start scoping out the site. We start digging tonight. Jareth and Chaba will organise the charges. The rest of you are on transport and cover."

Fee was stunned. Bodies separated, moved purposefully out. She snagged the nearest. "What's happening?"

He shrugged her off, as if a discarded fruit peel. "Boss will tell you what's needed."

It was the only answer going. No one else would stop to talk. Finally she tracked down Marabeth. The cook was stuffing saddle bags with field rations.

Fee tried for nonchalance. "Are we heading somewhere?"

Marabeth's hands kept moving. "Not you, Sera."

"Someone is, and tonight by the looks of it."

Marabeth nodded.

"Why?"

No answer. Fee copied the woman's actions, strapping down full bags and adding to the growing pile. Marabeth nodded in approval and made no comment about her awkward movements, waving a hand to the back wall. "There's a stack of water canteens there—start filling them."

Fee waited till they settled into a pattern of working together, before trying again. "What happened, and what is Plan B?"

A familiar voice in the doorway answered her. "My father's on his way here," said Caleb Winter, "and he's found out about the lake. Plan B will hopefully save what we can of the project— and you are supposed to be resting."

"In the middle of all this?"

"Especially in the middle of all this. We haven't much time. I need you to follow orders."

Marabeth strapped down the last of the bags. "She's helping and she is not in the way."

"She has to be fit to travel tomorrow. The Old Man cannot find her here."

Fee coloured. "I'm fit enough."

"No, you're not. I don't know what will happen tomorrow. Get to bed."

Fee had never felt smaller or more useless. Marabeth put a kindly hand on her shoulder. "Best do as he says."

She could only nod and walk out, head high. A lump clogged her throat. She must be more tired than she realised; she never let things get to her.

It was a long night, not helped by the constant noise of movement in the camp. Something was underway, something she should know about, and she was locked out in every way that counted.

That last order, for her to be fit tomorrow, effectively stymied her, and she strongly suspected Caleb Winter had known that. Rant and rail against it, yes, but she would do nothing to endanger the work of the Survey.

She twisted round in her bed. The Survey—that strange, amorphous leviathan of a government agency that had first caught her attention in college. Ripe with enthusiasm, shocked at what her lecturers had revealed and terrified for the future of her world, she was prime for the plucking. Gullible even. Would she have joined up, she had often wondered, if she had properly examined each and every aspect of the Survey.

Anti-democratic, anathema to much of the idealism at her heart, overly secretive and manipulative; the Survey was all these.

But the purpose, the aims; those were true.

No matter how many lists of counter arguments she came up with, the evidence could not be denied. So many years after the original eco-engineering of their planet, mankind was playing a dangerous game on Arcadia. So many harmless interventions, an accumulation of small changes designed to aid the economic well-being of a region or business. All too easy to justify. But put them together, combine their effects; that was a different story.

The expansion of the desert to increase the non-polluting solar arrays for the Solaris Corporation. The ordering and fostering of the festia plantations on her side of the mountains to provide much needed food. The festia's pollen had made her family rich and powerful, just like the solar arrays did for the Winters of Solaris. Corporates too big, too powerful to allow any deviation from their ways, both refusing to see how the changes they had made were destroying this region. And both viewing the other as a rival, a threat to their constant drive for expansion.

A rattle of stones outside; another heavily laden transporter pulling away. What were they up to out there?

She tossed again, trying hard to find a comfortable position.

Soft voices and a smatter of orders. The gruff bass of Caleb Winter's voice, briefly heard. She rolled over again. How had she landed herself in such an invidious position?

The Survey. It all came back to that. Her father thought it some minor government department. So did most other Arcadians, only aware of it because of the annoying number of legal powers given it by various governments to interfere in the business of hard working Arcadians. For what reason, most could no longer remember. Still, official rules could be managed by an astute company. That's what her father said, and Solaris no doubt thought the same...

If either of them thought to look harder, they would have found that the Survey's machinations sent tendrils into every corner of the world, all with the covert approval of the authorities of that region.

The big business corporations might not know it—*must* not know until it was far too late—but this time the government meant to win.

Fee tugged the cover over her head, fruitlessly attempting to shut out the noise outside her window. Was she the only one trying to sleep tonight? The only one prey to so many doubts?

It had all been so easy once. She remembered a session in her college library. Desperate to refute her lecturers, she had delved into the papers locked away in those academic treasure houses, intent on finding where the truth lay. Was it in her father's brash opinions, his gleeful increase in wealth and power with each new planting, or was it in the sudden downpours that scoured away whole beds of new saplings, the howling dust storms that raced across the plains, the sudden devastating squalls that had sunk an entire fishing fleet the year she first left home?

All her life, she had seen the patterns of the living world and been fascinated by the intricate interlocking of plants, animals and planet; the air, the soil, the sun and water that gave them all life.

She had fought, denied her eyes and the knowledge in her heart, but in the end it was useless.

Last night she had openly betrayed her family and showed them the Survey came first. There was no coming back from that.

She had put the Survey first for so long, even before family, but did she truly trust it? She barely knew the names of the senior managers. They changed too often to track; the internal politics of head office too convoluted to follow. Like most field staff, she left Central to its own games and got on with the real work. But now, the Survey had changed her life and she had a feeling she should no longer ignore Central. The Survey was too powerful, its hold too ubiquitous. She suddenly realised that she didn't even know where its money came from, yet the resources at its disposal were impressive. Could it really all come from government budgets?

She tossed again, hearing voices outside. Calling, urgent. Survey voices.

Trust.

These people, men and women like her own team at home, Fox and her immediate superiors, the scientists and lawyers labouring away in the big cities of the north, the lonely explorers collecting data from the most remote corners of the world.

Yes, these she trusted absolutely. They were like her, their commitment total. The commitment of people who had taken the trouble to look beyond their own interests and past their back fence. That same back yard she had vowed to protect; to keep safe from the ravages of extremism threatening them all.

Enough!

A chink of moonlight broke through her window screen. She thrust back the covers and threw her clothes on. Pulled out her backpack and filled it with the basic essentials—hat and water canteen on top—then marched out.

Organised chaos greeted her, everyone hurrying purposefully, clearly familiar with what they must do. They had to have rehearsed this. She kept in the shadows, unable to help without hindering.

A convoy of vehicles roared out of the far side of camp, while others worked on the buildings, covering the labs with screening mesh that made them look like storage barns. She wandered closer, always keeping out of the way. Peering into a lab, she saw workbenches and technical equipment disappear into a basement in the floor, and the startling transformation as shelves unlocked from the walls and a facade of barrels of grain and bins of spare parts slotted into place. Even the dust smelt different; of horse dung or machinery oil.

Overhead, a Survey flyer hovered, lifting massive containers of gear before swinging silently away in the night air to disappear towards the foothills.

"What are you doing up?"

She hadn't heard him, his tread deceptively quiet in the bustle. Caleb. She swung round to find him watching her from the dim light cast by the camp night glows, his face hidden in shadow.

"I couldn't sleep."

"Your injuries hurting?"

She shook her head and gestured at the hustle around her.

He glanced briefly over his shoulder as if dismissing it and turned back to her. "We leave camp in four hours." A second quick study, taking in her pack. "Get some more water and trail rations from Marabeth. Count on being away for up to a week." That was all, enough to satisfy him he'd done his duty, it felt like, and he strode off, disappearing around the side of yet another freight wagon about to leave. This one looked like it held some serious digging gear. Just what was going on?

She was ready long before the time was up, tried to get some more sleep but failed, and ended up sprawling in the chair as she waited in her room for want of anywhere better. There was no place for her in the well-run evacuation outside. Finally, young Ben stuck his head around the door, took in the made-up bed and the pack at her side, and gave a brisk nod.

"You've with me. We're on horseback again, sorry."

She had half expected it, but said nothing.

"You able to ride?"

"Yes," she said, hoping it was true. She had strapped her healing muscles and arm to keep them safe, but she still had some movement. She *should* be fine. A clap of hooves and a cluster of horses gathered by the corner of the building, most already mounted. She saw the one from her last memorable ride, and was relieved to see that it had come to no harm.

"Don't worry," said Ben. "We can mount you by the porch."

He held the horse steady, keeping it close to the decking so it was an easy step up from porch to saddle.

Or would have been, if the roar of trucks careering into the compound and the squeal of brakes hadn't spooked her mount. Trucks marked with the logo of Winter Solaris.

"Blast." Ben shoved her head down out of sight as one of the others grabbed her horse's reins and forced the animal back against the porch.

"Get her up on there, fast."

Next minute, she was swung into the saddle, landing with an "Oof," and scrabbling for the reins. She just had time to clutch onto the front of it and grab the reins before a hand slapped down on her horse's rump, Ben leapt into his own saddle and they were off at a furious gallop around the corner and away from camp.

She caught a glimpse of the man climbing out of the lead truck, and dug her heels sharply into the horse's side.

Old Man Winter, early on the scene and upsetting all their arrangements.

Caleb caught the flurry of horses leaving, saw Fee's small figure clinging to the reliable mare in the middle of the group and hoped to hell his father hadn't seen her. *Keep her safe, Ben.*

He walked down his office steps and towards his father's cab, his face set tight to hide any sign of what he felt.

"Damn it all. What have you done now, boy?" said the Old Man.

Caleb had long ago lost any qualms about lying to his father. "I have no idea what you mean."

A glare, and his father turned to look at the dust train left by the galloping hooves. "They're in a hurry?"

Caleb shrugged. "There was a report of a large foxllar hunting out on the south flats."

His father returned his stare, glint eyed and hard, then gestured to the man in the second truck. "Mac, follow them."

Caleb cursed silently as the man gunned his vehicle and drove off after the horses. Young Ben could lay as tricky a trail as any man of his father's but Fee was no rider and barely recovered from that latest fall.

Just a couple more hours. Couldn't the Old Man have given him that?

"Breakfast's still up if you want something," he said.

"No time for that, boy. I'm here to find out the truth of a report I've received."

"Oh, and what might that be?"

"Get in the cab and you'll find out." He gestured brusquely to the open doorway. But suddenly swung back, red faced and narrow eyed with rage. "The Council Rock? You care so little for who you are?

Caleb ignored him, walking across to his skimmer. Two of his father's larger offsiders planted themselves on both sides of him, blocking any movement.

"I said get in, boy."

Caleb stopped, turning slowly back to face his father. "You sure about this?"

The Old Man was every bit as skilled a card player as Caleb, better in these kind of hands. He would call a bluff every time. Now, he gestured at the two men to grab hold of Caleb. But included in the myriad of facts his father did *not* know was how his son had spent the wilder of his nights at college, nor what he'd learned in basic field training. A few judicious moves and the two men were buckled over in pain while Caleb still stood there, watching his father and braced to meet the rest of the men piling out of the other Solaris trucks.

The men cut off his escape but none tried to touch him again, and still the Old Man waited. Caleb had only been making a point, and his father knew it. Now, Caleb stepped forward. His father made him climb in the cab first, and another stooge climbed in the other side, weapon prominently displayed on his hip.

The convoy cut straight through the desert, trampling over carefully planted shrubs and precious gravels carefully graded to hold water flows. A year's work gone. He would need all his patience when they got to the site. His team had all left but he still scanned the area to make sure there was no sign of them when they pulled up near the lake hollow.

Bare dirt and the grinding of stones under foot as the trucks screeched to a halt. A jerked order from the weapon in his guard's hands and Caleb followed his father out of the cab.

Silently, they climbed the slope and stood at the top, staring at the brown puddle below. The foamy wash lapped at the base of the Council Rock. His father's face went white with shock.

"Is nothing off limits to you?

"We need storage water for the stock, and this was the best location."

Fee really would be laughing now—if Ben had got her away. Or were Solaris henchmen manhandling her even now?

Don't go there. Reason stepped in. In his current mood, his father would delight in telling him all about it if she'd been caught.

A gesture from the Old Man and more of his workers appeared at the lower end of the hollow, carrying bags and tools. Caleb only hoped they had some idea of what they were doing. He moved back a pace. "The rock is still here."

"Barely." His father stared in horror at the brown puddle, flung up his arms and strode forward as if to bodily force the water out of the hollow.

Caleb watched the men digging furiously, trying to make out what they were up to, then realised and rushed forward to grab at his father.

"Unless you want to get drowned in the backwash, get back up onto the bank. Talk about overkill. Heavy duty blast charges? What do those fools think they're doing—busting down a metropolis-sized dam wall?"

"From the reports I've been hearing, yes."

Caleb kept on towing his father up the bank to safety.

The men had finished and looked about to set their charges. Caleb seriously thought about saying nothing to them. Not an option, unfortunately. "Tell your men to stand back. The rock stratum around here is full of silt. They'll end up smothered if they stay there."

His father said a word into his comtab, but gave no sign of thanks. His personal stooges remained on guard either side of him. Below, there was a mighty whoosh of dirt and a huge sloshing sound as the infant lake threw a very adult tantrum, the tidal wash roaring down the crude channel created by the Solaris explosives.

Their precious Council Rock was rocked a full metre off its base and left lurching askew in the rapidly draining centre of the hollow. All that remained of his team's work was a straggly creek filled with a putrid mess gouging a new course straight through the base of the hollow, and a brown, muddy residue staining the sand and grass.

The Old Man couldn't even destroy things aesthetically.

"Satisfied?"

His father glared back. "Not by a long shot."

Caleb's hold on his temper was usually iron hard but the last few days had lacerated it badly. The filthy scar in the hollow finished it. He marched back to the cab, thrusting aside the idiot with the gun who tried to stop him.

"You can drop me off at the base on your way to your next bombing. Some of us have work to do."

The gun was in his face again. Caleb shoved it away. "Call your moron off. Does he really think you would let him shoot a Winter son?"

"Don't be so sure."

"He shoots me, and how long do you think you'd have the loyalty of my mother and brothers? Imagine what a family feud would do to your bottom line profit."

"I've got men tracking the rest of your precious crew. Or you think they're untouchable too?"

Caleb flung up his hands. "Look at the accounts one day. My livestock operation gives us a healthy profit and important contacts. See how long the environmental regulators stay off your back if you shut it down—and I need every single one of my team to make it work. You threaten one of them, and the whole lot disappears. So yes, they're as safe as me."

Caleb was furious by now, so angry he missed the other man coming up behind him.

Then a sharp pain, blackness, and his hands flailing urgently.

"Sorry son. Can't afford to let you go on as you've been doing," said a gruff voice as the darkness took him. His father had really done it.

CHAPTER TWELVE

Fee clung desperately to the saddle as her horse's hooves thundered beneath her. Ben led them in a twisting, frantic race against the grinding of wheels and the roar of engines too close behind.

A hand slapped her horse's flank. "Hold tight."

Never had she obeyed an order so religiously. She was barely in control of the animal, hemmed in on all sides by the rest of the plunging horses, and the cloud of dust thrown up by their horses left a trail too easy to follow.

Next she was flying through the air, plucked in full gallop from the saddle of her horse and clinging madly to the back of the rider in front. Young Ben, on a horse bigger and more agile than her own. Suddenly, she and Ben were peeling away from the rest of the herd, hooves striking hard against the flat plane of rock as they plunged into a winding tunnel hidden beneath a giant's pile of jumbled rocks. She barely dared breathe, expecting any minute to be scraped off against the stony sides.

Just as it felt as if she would be trapped forever in the rock tunnel, they burst out into daylight. Ben twisted the horse's head, setting them racing directly for the rock wall at the far end of the hidden canyon. Another sudden swerve at the last instant possible and they pitched into darkness, broken only by twisting shards of light striking through cracks in the ceiling above.

It was the clue she needed. She had studied the geotech plans of the area and knew that eons ago water had plundered its way through a limestone wash south of the main camp area. From above, the plain appeared flat, broken only by the occasional patch of blackness where the land gave way in a deep hole, but below ground a maze of fenestrated alleyways gouged through the substrate right up to a broken ridge of weather-worn hills. A maze impenetrable by any without specific coordinates to guide them.

Ben seemed to know the tortuous tunnels like his back yard at home.

Finally, to her enormous relief, he pulled their horses to a halt and lifted her off.

"Shh." He laid a soothing hand over the horse's muzzle and led them farther into the dark, one hand holding her as he led them into the heart of the dense rocks, finding his way by touch as much as sight in the dimly lit passage. Just when it felt like they would be lost in darkness forever, they broke free into a huge, vaulted chamber lit by a series of holes high in the walls. Bright, blessed rays of living sunshine.

"We should be safe here, but keep as quiet as possible."

"And the others?"

"Safer than if you were with them."

Well, that was honest.

Thankfully, he didn't wait for an answer but turned to tend his horse. A small spring splashed into a basin of water in one corner. Ben filled the bucket set on one side, offering it to the lathering horse. He kept it fully saddled, not even loosening the girth straps as she had seen Caleb do when they halted on the trail.

She looked around, straining to see in the speckled light. Dark ovals hinting at rooms lead off the central cave but other than that, there was nothing remarkable, nothing suggesting this place was any more than a convenient hideaway.

"So what now?" she said when he'd finished with the horse.

"We wait for the all clear."

"And if we were followed?"

Ben shook his head. "Unlikely. We know this part of the plain better than anyone. Those Solaris office types will be thoroughly lost by now."

"Even Ser Winter? He owns this land."

The young man's head came up at that. "He doesn't, if you mean the Old Man. Range rights only, and that's different from ownership. It's why we can build the lake site out here. No one owns it."

Sol Winter reminded her too much of her father. "Anyone told him that?"

The strain left the young man's face and he chuckled. "Only Caleb, and you can guess how that went down."

She had to laugh with him. Yet the last she had seen of Caleb Winter, he was walking down the steps to meet his father's men, just before Ben rushed her out of camp.

"Caleb knows of this place?"

That stopped Ben. "He set it up and *will not* tell of it."

"Sol Winter is his father."

"And that's about all they have in common when it comes to the land."

There was a rattling of rocks above and Fee almost stopped breathing. No need for the warning hand signal from Ben.

They waited nervously, then a rattle of hooves and one of the riders she recognised from earlier. He slid to a halt and leaped off his horse.

"Caleb's been taken."

The plains folk had been arguing for hours. The rest of the riders had piled into their hidden retreat not long after the messenger arrived. Fee leaned tiredly against the back wall, feeling every one of her bruises and the after effects of that mad escape.

"What about the Solaris men?" Fee had asked, only to be waved off. The riders had got them thoroughly lost, as predicted by Ben. They weren't the cause of the heated debate.

"How do you know he's a prisoner?" Fee had also asked. Caleb Winter had walked down those steps readily enough. She didn't ask twice, the anger of their rebuttals silencing her—but not her thoughts.

More riders shoved through the door, led by the eco-engineer Kal. He marched up to Bob as the team comms specialist peered intently at his screen, ignoring the general uproar.

"What news?"

"They've taken him to the Homestead. We'd be hard put to get him out of there now, not quiet-like anyway."

"Who says?" said a foolish shout.

Fee tugged at Ben and urged him out of the crowd. "This has gone far enough," she said when she got him clear, and was relieved to see the trouble in his face. "Is there a secure room where I can put a call through to Central?

"Yes," then added slowly, as if loath to tell, "there's a fully shielded comms room in back. It's the store for the local backup gear, for emergency use only."

"Take me to it."

"Sorry, out of bounds."

"To a ranking Survey eco-engineer?"

Ben looked like she'd struck him but she had no choice. If she didn't put a stop to this soon, the whole mob of them would be barrelling down on the Winter compound, hell bent on releasing their leader by any means necessary. Having to pull rank on a nice kid like Ben was the least of her concerns. Finally, he nodded.

"This way."

They slipped out the back door of the cave, leaving the rest to their ongoing wrangle. He led her down an unlit back corridor, forcing her to find her way by the touch of his hand on her arm. He slapped a mark on the wall and light flooded through a door from a small room, one holding a full complement of Survey emergency gear. She fell on the com unit with glee, and a moment later had the connection she needed.

"Fox? Fioruisghe here."

"And Caleb?"

"That's what I'm calling about."

Just once, Fee would love to know what her boss was thinking. His voice was flat, uninformative, and as she told him what had happened, half of her suspected he wasn't at all surprised at the turn of events.

"Plan B is in operation, I take it?"

"Yes," she said, but couldn't hide the hesitation in her voice.

"You *have* been briefed on it?" Fox's voice was no longer so flat.

"Ah, not exactly."

Silence.

"So who, precisely, has taken charge of operations there?"

Fee looked blankly at Ben. It had never occurred to her to ask. He mouthed "Kal", but not loud enough to be heard. The boy had a very well developed ear for trouble.

"Kal Mendip, one of the other eco-engineers," she said to Fox.

"And you?"

What did he mean? "I'm only here for the technical side of the project."

Suddenly she was glad the boss was half a continent away. There was a quality to his silence that had her feeling as nervous as Ben looked.

"What part of your orders led you to believe you are there in a technical capacity only, Sera den Coille?"

"But … I assumed. This is not my land."

"It's your *planet*. Put this Kal on the line."

She looked at Ben, who pointed out to the main room.

"Can we call you back, Sir? He's in another room."

Another ominous silence. "Security status, den Coille. How safe are you?"

She glanced at Ben, and he gave a quick thumbs up.

"All secure, sir. We're in a safe haven."

"The caves?"

Again Ben nodded.

"Yes, sir," she said.

"Fine. You have five minutes to call me back, or I'm sending in a full Survey guard unit."

Which would really blow this thing sky high. "Understood," she said, and hastily shut down the unit before he could reply.

Ben led her back to the main room at a jog, and together they elbowed and pushed their way up to Bob.

Fee shoved herself in front of him, breaking his connection. "What the …"

"Central wants you to call in now—on my code."

Ben broke in before Bob could refuse. "Better do as she says. This comes from the top."

Not quite, but Fox was the regional operations head. Bob must have seen something in both their faces and abruptly passed the sensor unit over. She keyed in her prints and personal access code, then entered Fox's coordinates.

A crackle of sound. "Is that you, den Coille? Took you long enough."

They still had more than a minute to spare, but she wasn't about to tell the boss that. From the startled glances suddenly swinging their way and the sudden, deathly quiet, the plainsmen around them recognised his voice.

"Den Coille, put Mendip on."

The other eco-engineer shoved forward, the first signs of uncertainly on his face. "Kal Mendip here, Sir—acting Liaison Officer."

"And self-appointed leader, I hear, despite the presence of Officer den Coille. Who, along with Officer Winter were the only ones fully briefed and charged with this operation."

"But … that's…"

Fox had always been able to reduce his officers to stutters. He'd done it to her often enough.

"I understand Officer den Coille has not yet been briefed on Plan B?"

"No sir. That is, she has been …"

"Injured? I am aware of that, but not that the damage was to her head."

"No, sir."

"Then brief her immediately. Might I remind you that the Survey chain of command is set by Central, not field staff?"

"Yes, sir." There was a definite glower on the man's face, and Fee's heart sank.

"I expect a full report, den Coille, once you have been briefed and Winter is released."

"Well, yes, about that, sir—," she began.

"It's in progress."

"Yes, sir." You did not argue with that particular tone in Fox's voice. But did he really believe Caleb's friends would sit back and do nothing to rescue him?

"Winter's release is in progress, and he will be back at camp by evening," Fox repeated. "Do not interfere. This mess is bad enough already."

With that, he cut the connection and left Fee as the centre of attention. A very large part of her wished the floor would rise up and swallow her whole.

She squared her shoulders and turned to Kal. "So, Plan B?"

For an unnerving moment, she though he would refuse. A grunt, and he thrust his com unit forward to link with hers and switched open a file. "It's all there."

She began to scroll through. It didn't take long. The plan was so audacious, it just might work. "I need to review this properly. Is there a quiet room somewhere?"

"Ben will show you," said Kal.

There was too much shuffling of troops around her, too much unspilled tension in the air. "About Caleb—you all heard Fox?"

A few, soft Yes's, but nothing resounding, and far too much muttering underneath. What she wouldn't give for the sound common sense of old Jim or Marabeth. Unexpectedly, it was Kal who backed her and came to her rescue. "We stand down and let the Survey do its work," he ordered. "Get some rest. You're going to need it."

Fee stepped back. "Thank you," she said softly to him.

He shrugged. "We're Survey first."

He nodded to Ben, and Fee had no option but to follow the young man into a side room.

Trust your fellow Survey only. It had been hammered into her so often in training.

Nobody had said what to do when *you* were the enemy outsider.

The room held a couple of large, comfortable chairs, and a bed. For a weak moment, she stared at the bed longingly, but instead settled into the chair and turned to the files.

An hour later and she was even more stunned by the audacity of the scheme. Plan B wasn't just an idea or a set of data; Plan B was a whole new lake. That was what all the activity had been about last night. The sudden blasts and rumble of heavy equipment. She studied the chosen site, pulling up the weather and geotech profiles.

It would work—was probably always part of the longer term vision for this area, but to do it in one night? Caleb Winter had a seriously top-notch team here.

She had worked on other Survey projects away from her mountains before, but none that felt this important—and none where she had felt so ill-informed or missing so much of what she needed to know.

Enough.

She slammed the file shut and marched back into the other room. The plains team lay variously sprawled over the rock floor, catching up on much needed sleep after their marathon night effort, but all heads lifted abruptly at the sound of her footsteps. Kal eyed her from his place against the wall. "You've read the file?"

"And am duly impressed. I need to see this lake for myself."

One of the men shot up. "After this morning, that site will be crawling with Solaris staff."

"But—we've got Survey people there." She swung back on Kal.

"Caleb knows what to say—and who to say it to. Jeb's right; you can't go anywhere near site B. The mood Old Man Winter is in, he doesn't need to find a den Coille helping build that lake. You want to start a Plains-Mountain war?"

Ben stepped up. "I can get her close enough without being seen."

"No." Putting him at risk was not an option. Yet surprisingly, Kal looked at the young man as if considering it.

"No," she said again, as loud as she could without shrieking.

"If anyone other than Caleb could do it, it would be Ben," said Bob beside her.

She stared. Even after the last few hours and a sleepless night, there was the barest trace of fluff on the young zoologist's chin.

Ben gave a half hitch of his shoulders. "I've been scrabbling around this country since I was a nipper."

"There's more to the boy than he looks," said Bob. "Mind, it depends on you. It's a fair hike in."

Bob and Kal stared pointedly at her; or rather the arm she still held awkwardly.

"No worries," said Ben." I can take her up a back gulley. It's a bit easier, and the Solaris men won't know that way."

Kal was silent, studying the young man. Fee dared say nothing. She needed to see this new lake, needed it to answer the many questions ricocheting around inside her head, but to put a bare cadet at risk? She studied Ben's face again, seeing the youthful exuberance, but then saw the rest. This boy would deliver what he promised. She gave Kal one, long, slow nod.

Which was how, many hours later, she ended up crouching in the lee of a bluff, halfway up a shale-covered hillside, baking under the hot sun and questioning her sanity. If this was easier, what was the other route like? They had driven the first part, but after that the countryside changed. The only way farther in was by foot.

A scrape of rocks and Ben leaped down beside her, a thoroughly questionable grin on his face.

"All clear. Follow me and keep close to the side of the slip. The entrance is just round this corner."

She peered round and saw nothing. Only a mishmash of scrubby bushes and sun baked rocks. Were there no trees in this blasted land?

"It's a bit of a tight fit, but that won't be a problem for you," said Ben breezily.

He was right. They pushed through the scrub, scratching her arms on the vicious spines hidden beneath the grey leaves. The opening was barely visible, a tightly coiled breach of the rock face they had to slide around sideways. It opened up into a narrow passageway along a natural rupture in the granite blocks thrusting up from the plains, a steep climb that left her panting and greedy for water. After that, the route was easy enough, along a pathway between overhanging rocks and so narrow and winding there was little chance of being seen from above.

Suddenly, Ben flung up a hand and dropped belly down, flat to the ground. Up front, a small patch of sky showed through thick tufts of native grass. Together, they wriggled forward and pushed right to the heart of the grass.

His hand clamped down hard on her shoulder. Just in time. One more push, and she would have tumbled over the dizzying drop right in front of her nose. She shoved her head down to the dirt, clamping her mouth against her arm to silence her horrified gasp.

When her head cleared, she slowly lifted it to peer out. A strained grin at Ben. He'd done it, brought her to a perfect spy hole, hidden by the tall grasses and looking right down into the hollow below. She recognised some of Caleb's team working along the banks of the growing bowl of water, and scooting nervous glances at the strangers in heavy vehicles scrutinising everything they did. Gone were the diggers and the heavy equipment that lumbered through the night. Not even a sign of them. She turned to Ben, unable to talk, hands spread as if unable to take in what had been accomplished here. It looked as if they'd been working on it for weeks. They had even added the first of the plantings on the far banks.

Bringing her training to the fore, she surveyed the site. It was a natural hollow, the shape well-suited to a dam. But not as good as the original site; it would only ever be a shallow stock water reservoir. This dam was no threat to the Solaris empire. It could never be a lake big enough to irrigate the plains or affect the local weather patterns.

More vehicles pulled up, more trucks bearing the logo of Winter Solaris. Ben passed her a set of viewing glasses and she zoomed in on the new group. Then gasped as a man opened the cab of the leading truck, and out climbed Old Man Winter himself. With him, his son. Caleb Winter. Walking freely on his own. No guard, no sign at all of any restraint.

She wriggled backwards fast, uncaring of how many scrapes she collected. Wanting only to be out of there. As soon as she was sure she was out of sight from below, she stood up and half ran, half stumbled back down the passage way. Footsteps followed behind. She ignored them, but they kept coming. She swung round to face Ben.

"We're all Survey together? Old Man Winter must not see me? Or is it that Caleb Winter didn't want me to meet his father and find out what he's really up to here?"

She stalked off, too angry to say more. That she had been made a fool of, that she understood.

Ben tried to stop her.

"Spare me. As soon as I get within secure hailing range, I'm out of here. I want no part of whatever games you're playing."

"We're not," tried Ben.

He was so young, but she was beyond letting that make a difference. "And Caleb Winter is the soul of honesty?"

She shoved hard at the young man, too furious to care. Then set off again, rushing down the passage and stabbing at the com unit on her wrist as she squeezed out the cleft in the rock face. She was free, but still she ran, her thumb playing recklessly over the surface of her com.

No answer; not yet. Too close still to the Solaris trucks. The plains Survey's security screens blocked her. She slithered down the slope, desperate to get clear of this place.

"Sera den Coille. Fee. You'll hurt yourself."

She'd already done that, slipping on the loose rock and banging her arm, but she wasn't about to let the plainsman know.

His hand came down on her shoulder, still trying to stop her. She shook him off, using her childhood training in the constantly flexing trees of home to twist around and send him flying, crashing into the stony ground.

She refused to feel bad about it.

"Stop, wait. What's got into you?"

"You lied to me. All of you lied."

The boy had looked shocked before, but now his face flushed bright red and he scowled ferociously.

"Plan B? Of course we did. How could we know you wouldn't go blabbing about it to the wrong people?"

"To head office you mean? Is that what your real boss said?"

"Wha …?"

"Sol Winter of Solaris. Caleb Winter's father. The man he just walked *freely* out of that cab with."

"You're mad."

"Mad? You bet. Stupid, no, not any more. Your crew might have fooled the Survey into sending me here, but no longer. If this is some elaborate plot against the den Coille's—leave me out of it."

She set off down the slope again, jabbing viciously at her comtab and swearing every time she got no answer.

She was carrying water and was pretty sure she remembered the way back to the skimmer. Tears streaking down her face and jaw set, she started out across country. The skimmer was there, somewhere. Once she found it, she was done here.

CHAPTER THIRTEEN

Shards of pain ricocheted through Caleb's skull, hammer strokes of agony driving through his head with each thudding pulse of his heart. He prised open his eyes, lost for a minute, then realised where he was and the agony compounded.

His old bedroom in his family home; a room he hadn't called his own for years. A room that echoed with calls to a loyalty he could no longer honour, rebukes from every beloved toy, each childhood treasure carefully preserved on shelf and cupboard. His old reader lurching as haphazardly askew as he'd left it on his departure to college, the bed quilt made by his grandmother especially for him as a child, his school medals hanging polished on the wall.

All kept frozen in time by his parents to remind him who he was.

He tried to sit up, winced as a sharp pain struck his head. He lifted his hand, exploring the back of his head and winced again as he found the tender spot. His father's pet thug really had belted him in the head.

What in hell had the Old Man found out?

He rolled upwards, slower this time, and waited till the dizziness passed. The sun blazed through his window, making him swear out loud. From the angle of it, hours must have passed. Who knew what was happening at the camp by now?

He lurched up, clutching chair, shelves, wall, anything solid to help him to the door. Hands on the pad, wrenching the too slow mechanism open and he was through, to find a guard blocking his escape. He swung his arm back, and another guard grabbed him from the other side.

"Leave him."

His brother Ethan, coming round the corner. The men released Caleb, but he still swung his fist at them. It hit with a resounding "thud". Maybe not as hard as he would have liked, but it felt good. The sound of the angry roars erupting from the morons holding him felt better.

His brother glared at the men to stand down. They dropped him flat, forcing him to grab for the wall or he'd have fallen over right in front of his tormentors. At least he was standing free.

"Thanks."

"We're still brothers. No one thumps a Winter—you taught me that."

Caleb grimaced. His own words, said many years ago in a schoolyard brawl. Their peers had quickly learned the truth of it, and left the three Winter boys alone. "The Old Man in his study?"

Ethan nodded. "Mother too, running security."

So it was to be kept civilised, which didn't mean he should imagine she supported him. "What's she wearing?"

A trace of a black grin from Ethan "The full pearl regalia."

No sympathy, not today. "You wouldn't consider helping me out the back door?"

"Not today, *brother*." Then, as if he could hold it no longer. "The Council Rock. Do you despise us that much?"

Caleb knew exactly how his brother felt, but 'orders from Survey Central' wasn't going to cut it today. He shrugged. "It was the best option for what we needed."

His brother's reply was to open the door to his father's study. Hell, he wasn't ready for this. Dizzying flashes of light still racketed in front of his eyes and he dared not move too fast. Another half hour would have helped.

No, it wouldn't. Half a year would make no difference to the coming discussion.

"You're awake." His father, standing behind his desk and growling. Caleb squinted. His mother sat beside him, and yes, she was wearing the full set of necklace and earrings. No doubt on her wrist and hands would be the rings and bracelets. He daren't look down to see for fear of falling over.

"No thanks to your men."

The lump on the back of his head left him with little inclination for polite courtesies, and the rant of outraged paternity was going to happen whatever he said. Only by concentrating on the dark wall behind the Old Man could he keep at bay the nausea from the flashes of iridescence.

When silence fell, he guessed his father must be finished.

The Old Man's face was bleaker than at the start. "Have you nothing to say?

Caleb didn't answer, concentrating too hard on staying upright.

"Why?" said his mother. "You owe us that at least."

He swallowed, calling on every particle of bloody minded grit he possessed. "The stock need an irrigation dam and that hollow is the most suitable."

"You destroyed the hollow to provide drinking water for *livestock*—animals we can do without?" His father.

"They provide a necessary emergency food supply and an alternative income stream, and they keep the government off your back."

"That's as maybe. There was no need to flood the Council hollow." His mother again. "It will be restored, and you will find an alternative."

He would have liked to merely nod in answer but daren't risk moving his head. "Agreed. My people had already started enlarging a wash hole over by the south branch for another dam. We'll use that instead."

His father bought it, just. Maybe he'd blown out the worst of his rage.

Or maybe not. "Agreed—if this site is as you've said. We leave in five minutes."

"You don't believe me?"

"Not anymore." What that cost his father, he had no idea. It was the Old Man who had taught Caleb the poker face trick.

His mother frowned, narrowing her eyes as her gaze swept over him. "No. He is going back to bed, now."

Caleb badly wanted to do exactly that, but he had no intention of staying here a minute longer than necessary. Especially not under the care of a mother who knew him too well. "Give me ten minutes and I'll be with you."

He would too, if it killed him.

Somehow he made it out to his father's truck and through the bumpy ride out to the second lake site. They lifted off hard, hugged the contours so tightly Caleb felt each bumpy hollow in the thrumming of pain beats in his head, and landed with a whump that forced him to ask for a stop so he could stumble out of the cab and give in to the constantly threatening nausea.

"Not a word to your mother," was his father's response to the spasms racking his gut.

It was a relief when they pulled up and he could climb out onto solid ground. His father stumped over to the lake edge, took note of the new diggings, the plantings, the soil that looked as settled as if turned over weeks ago rather than during the furious frenzy of the previous night. Even the bushes showed the odd sprout of new growth, as if having passed through transplant shock already and begun to settle into their new home.

He walked down and stopped beside his father, the water lapping at his toes. The hollow they'd used for the dam was a natural soak hole, a place where water could be found by digging in the driest of years; surrounded by sandstone cliffs on three sides with the red dirt beach sloping down beneath his feet. Bare, barren and starkly beautiful.

One day, the plantings and the wind break shrubs would shade a clear pond that people would class as a *pretty spot*. Fee would like it, he guessed.

"It should rise another metre, once the ground water soaks through, but that's about it."

Some of his team were nearby, down by the shore, but he didn't risk looking up to see if there was any signal from them. Not with the glare of the sun in his eyes and the sick feeling still in his gut. A quick lift of his hand had to be enough. None of them were stupid.

His father put up a hand to shade his eyes, staring out at the shallow pan of water. Caleb's landscaper and botanist were classified geniuses, as far as Caleb was concerned, and he hoped they'd managed to grab a few hours' sleep after the hurried planting and filling of the new lake.

"Seen enough?" he said.

A grunt. "Yeah."

"Drop me off at camp. Unless you plan to hold me hostage?"

For long minutes, the Old Man looked to be considering it, till he turned to walk back to the ground skimmer. Caleb let out the breath he'd been holding and followed.

"We'll go by the Council Rock first, then to the doctor's."

Caleb stopped and stared. "Are you serious? The doctor?"

"Your mother's orders," muttered the man he could never quite repudiate, "for that bump on your head."

Maybe that was remorse in the Old Man's face and maybe not. He was beyond caring. "The doctor? No."

With which he marched over to the truck and climbed in.

At least his father took it slower this time, pacing the trip to match the pounding in his head, and when they got to the Council Rock, he said nothing when Caleb refused to leave the vehicle to go with him to inspect the destruction in the muddy basin.

The Old Man climbed back in.

"Satisfied?" said Caleb.

"For now."

"And the stock lake at the south wash?"

"Can stay."

It was the nearest to a concession he'd get from the Old Man. Ethan agreed with him that this area was useless for solar arrays—too prone to scouring wind patterns—but the Old Man was another matter. Maybe he'd actually been listening to them. Though what would he do when the cloud cover changed was another matter.

His father drove, his men banished to one of the backup vehicles, and he was relieved to see them set off in the direction of the camp. Hopefully to deliver him home. So maybe the day hadn't been a total disaster.

His father climbed out first, holding the door while Caleb made his painful way out.

"Send your mother a copy of the medic's report."

Caleb grunted. Not until the last of the vehicles roared out of camp did he give in to the sick pounding in head and gut, crumbling to the ground.

Old Jim got to him first. He could tell by the smell of worn leather that clung to him always; followed by the warm flour and spices of Marabeth.

He came to slowly, letting his senses confirm his safety before lifting his eyelids. The dry grit of dust coated each breath and he felt the beat of his heart measure the pulse of the earth.

Still alive and able to function. It would have to do. He opened his eyes.

Jim's strong hand came down and as so often before, it was his brawny shoulder he leaned on as he levered himself up.

"So what has your Da done to you this day?"

"Not the Old Man. One of his flunkies. A bang on the skull is all."

"Ah well, thick as it is, nought to worry about then."

But Jim kept firm hold of him and Marabeth stood on his other side.

"Get me Suze."

Jim's mouth dropped open at the medic's name.

"Promised the Old Man I'd get checked out," Caleb said by way of explanation as Jim helped him onto his bed while Marabeth put through the call.

From the speed she got to his rooms, he guessed Suze had seen him arrive home. He could have done without the next ten minutes, retching badly when she felt the back of his head and he needed Jim's strong arm again to help him to sit up. A scan, complete with all the annoying routine of a medical examination. At the end, the older woman leaned back, her mouth tight. He lifted an eyebrow.

"If you were anyone else, I'd tell you to rest and take it easy." Suze had known him since he was a kid, knew how likely that was. She sighed. "At least they hit you on the head. Thickest part of you." She packed up her bag, and took the dask Marabeth handed her. "Up to you now," she said to the cook. Both women exchanged a smile he'd seen too many times before. "Try to get him to rest, will you?"

Marabeth saw the medic out shortly after. She came back in, hands on her hips, and studied him as he leaned back against his headboard, unsure how long he could stay upright.

"A hot bath and a good feed." It was her stock remedy, claimed to fix anything. If only it was that simple.

Yet bathed, rested and seated much later with a bowl of warm broth filling his stomach, he could almost have believed it was that simple. Then he asked a question.

"The den Coille woman, Fee, where is she?" and the silence told how lacking in simplicity it all was. "She is back?"

Marabeth busied herself at the stove and Jim sat, legs stretched out before him and eyes set on the window.

"You might as well spit it out."

Jim set down his feet, and leaned forward. "She was watching from the cliffs when you stopped at the south lake."

There was an ominous note in Jim's voice and an anxious look from Marabeth.

"I seem to be missing something here."

"When you climbed out with your Da." Jim paused, knotting his work scarred hands together. "It didn't look so good."

Caleb stared at him, mind blank. Till the meaning of the words hit in a cold spike right through his gut. "She saw me climb unrestrained from a Solaris truck?" Jim nodded, and he cursed. "It was either climb out into fresh air, or stay and puke my guts out."

"Guessed it was something like that."

"So where is she now?"

It was Marabeth's turn. She left off fiddling round at the stove and came back to sit beside him. He had known these two since he was a small boy, and had rarely seen either look at him as seriously. Something was very wrong.

"Where is she?"

"Ben's monitoring her."

"I repeat, where is she?"

Jim paused, crossed his legs and leaned back into the chair with a long hmmph. "Well now, as Ben tells it, she took one look at you climbing out of that skimmer and jumped to all the wrong conclusions."

"She thinks I'm working for my father—yes, I got that."

"No. Not just you. The whole crew of us."

And he'd thought this day wasn't turning out too bad? "So what did she do?"

"Swung round and marched off."

"And Ben?"

Marabeth reached out a hand to hover just over Jim's. The older man finally looked up from his study of the table. "Nothing—leastways, not yet."

He rarely feared anything but right now, a sharp edged terror slammed into him. "You mean . . .?"

"She marched out into the South March, and was walking still, last we heard," said Jim.

Marabeth jumped in. "Ben's keeping a close watch on her."

"He's with her?"

The cook twisted her hands. "Not exactly."

"How, not exactly?"

Marabeth refused to meet his eye and Old Jim shuffled. "He tried to, but she wouldn't have a bar of it," said Jim. "He's back aways, keeping her under his eye."

He opened his mouth, forced down one breath, then another before he was able to speak. "Let me get this straight? A mountain girl with no idea of our land is marching out into one of the driest, most dangerous washes on the plains, and all of you *let* her?"

Jim reddened. "It seemed best. Leave her be to blow off her steam, then we can ship her back on the morrow, away from trouble."

Caleb's fist banged on the desk." She's Survey, and you heard Central. She's needed for this project. We do not let her go, or let her be, or whatever else you want to call letting her head off into danger." He banged open a cupboard and grabbed out the painkillers. Swallowed a couple and shoved the rest in his pocket.

"Anyone wants me, I'll be in the South March."

He opened the door of his skimmer but a hand clamped down on his shoulder. "You're not driving in that condition, son," and Jim settled himself into the driver's seat.

"Long as you know I'm heading for the South March?"

"I'm not your Da." With which Jim slammed the skimmer into action and set out rather more bumpily than was good for Caleb's head. He said nothing, sheer horror riding him hard. He had to get to Fee.

A call came through.

"Boss." Ben's voice, urgent and tense. "You need to get out here, quick. There's a blow up coming."

Jim poured on the juice and Caleb let out a string of oaths that had the old man grinning. "You learned more than book stuff at that college of yours."

Caleb ignored him. Jim could think what he liked, as long as he kept up the acceleration. A sandstorm, that was a *blow up* out here. Unless Ben and Fee got under cover, they were in real trouble.

"You have transponders on you?" Survey transponder signals could get through weather that beat the best civilian gear.

"Yeah, for me," said Ben. "Fee; far as I know."

She's not stupid. She wouldn't throw it away, no matter how angry or how much she mistrusted him. "Can't you get any more out of this thing, Jim?"

Already in the sky Caleb could see the ominous thickening that heralded a big blow. Out on the March, the cloud was moving fast.

"We'll be in the middle of it soon," signalled Ben.

"You safely under shelter?"

"Tucked tight in a hole in the cliff face, boss."

"And Fee?"

A scary pause, then a slow answer. "Last I saw, she was heading for a pile of rocks at the foot of the hillside."

"Not in a shelter?"

"No," said Ben, "but that pile will block the worst of it. She has some protection."

"Unlike us," said Jim. "Time we got under shelter too, boss."

"Step on it," was Caleb's only reply. Ahead of him, too close now, a thick, boiling wall of dust and sand rolled inexorably onwards. "Set up the receivers."

The relief in him as first one, then two beeps sounded loudly in the cab was immeasurable. Ben was where he expected, buried deep in one of the holes on the honeycombed side of the cliff face. Water and wind had gouged a maze of caverns through the low hills, creating a series of holes known to be safe in a blow. The March itself was a dry, flat plain open to the worst of the scouring winds at one end and surrounded on the others by a jagged bank of hills that funnelled and twisted the wind to a tearing fury. When a big blow hit the March, all the locals, man and animal, knew to take shelter or perish. But a Mountain raised girl? What would she know?

They drove into the nearest of the pocked hills, Jim steering the skimmer into a long, open cave that would protect them till the sky cleared. It was the only real option in a blow.

Caleb pulled out the survival pack on the back seat and pushed it over to Jim. "Get into the west chamber. You'll be safe there."

Jim began to follow orders, but heard that last bit and glared angrily. "Don't you mean *we*?"

Caleb shook his head. "Fee's in danger. She's Survey, she's needed—and she was entrusted to me."

Jim's hand on the stick eased not a jot. "Not at the risk of your life." The stockman eased the skimmer neatly into the west branch of the cave system and locked the doors to the cab. Caleb merely leaned across and thumbed the master switch. This was Winter territory, and a Winter thumbprint overrode the controls on any machine, even a Survey cab. He opened the door, threw out the survival kit and lifted a locator tag for Jim to follow, sending it after the kit.

Jim grabbed his arm. "Ain't letting you head off on some fool errand."

"You don't get a say in this."

The old man opened his mouth. Caleb reached across and shoved him neatly out the door. It was soft sand below, he would not be hurt. Caleb locked the door and was in the driving seat and backing out before Jim could scrabble up. The old man would be safe here, but he still sent through a delayed call for a pick up in case he couldn't do it later.

Yeah, and why would that be?

Ignoring the voice, he set the controls to Track, following the insistent beep of Fee's transponder—a woman who knew little of the dangers of this land, an outsider soon to be exposed to the full force of the storm's fury, at the mercy of those roiling banks of dirty brown.

She was still walking, but thankfully hard up against the hill face. He checked the readouts. There were two safe holes close by her—if she knew they were there. Plus she had a survival tent in her kit bag. It was compulsory for any traveller venturing onto the plains, and Ben had confirmed she'd taken a complete kit when she marched off.

Did she know what was in it, or how to use it?

He gunned the vehicle, heading straight for the furious tide of sand. Her beep had paused, no sign of moving towards the safe holes. So she didn't know how to read the local codes in the plasguide bag. He switched up his gearing and changed to crawler mode, then smashed full on into the whirlpool of garbage that was the storm front.

He'd helped design these vehicles, with triple propulsion, ground skimming for normal use and thick wheels and caterpillar tread when needed. Their engine filters were the most efficient the Survey made, which meant they exceeded anything else available. Today, they kept it going for another couple of kilometres.

He jiggled the systems, flushed vents and cursed in every tongue he knew. It made no difference: the truck choked to a halt.

He checked the readouts, calculated, swore again, and grabbed the full survival suit in the emergency locker. Hoisting his own emergency kit onto his back, he took a slug of clean, grit-free water, pulled on a protective coverall with face mask and breathing rig, before he overrode the door controls. A membrane slid in behind him, protecting the interior of the cab from the whirling dust, but did nothing to help him get where he needed. For that, all he had were two ground sticks clamped to his hands, each with claws to bury into the grit and anchor him against the furious wind.

Then he stepped from the shelter of the cab and the full force hit him.

He'd stopped close to where the hill face reared up from the plain in a jumble of scoured boulders and broken shards of rock. There were places there to hide, so many safe shelters, but he set his head against them.

What he was aiming on doing, it was singularly ludicrous; a foolhardy attempt to rescue a virtual stranger. He checked the readout on his wrist com again. Mark four: survivable for another hour, if he was lucky. And Fee den Coille, poorly protected and untrained? Far less than that.

He dug in his left stick, felt the claws reach into the dirt and grip tight, painfully lifted the right and dug it in, anchoring it in front of him. Then used that to drag himself forward, before hauling out the left to plunge it down and secure his next anchoring point. Over and over, crawling tediously over the broken surface of the March plain, guided only by an insistent pulse of sound and an insane belief in survival.

Suddenly the pulse on his readout changed. She was moving, away from any safe hole. He dug his sticks deep into the ground and surged forward.

CHAPTER FOURTEEN

Her feet hurt, her mouth tasted of grit and on top of it all, the harsh scrape of a coming storm buffeted her face. A scarily dry and unforgiving wind, blowing her hair one way then another, the strands a vicious whip that lashed her cheek and obscured her eyes.

She grabbed onto her hair, shoving it out of the way and stared up at the darkening sky ahead of her. She had been born to water, to a land blanketed in forest and bathed in mist. This desiccating wind was like nothing she was used to, and that looming cloudbank spelt danger. That was no light gust of annoying currents that would pass quickly.

Her only assurance; the weight of the emergency kit on her shoulder. The one, invariable rule of a Survey field op's life. Never leave base without your emergency pack.

She had been marching roughly parallel to a row of pock-marked hills and thought she had a good idea where the skimmer was parked. No point trying to return by Ben's route. The tract of hills beside her was a mess of hidden passages, holes, clefts and hiding spots, a trap for outsiders like her, even with a com unit. No, she had marched off into the desert instead, trusting blindly she could recognise the shape of the rocks they had parked behind, and determined to beat Ben to their vehicle.

He was following her. She couldn't see or hear him, he was too good for that, but a prickle at the base of her neck said he wasn't far off.

She just had to trust his intentions weren't malicious.

That young kid a baby-faced assassin?

She had trusted Caleb Winter, and look where that had got her.

She stumbled over a rock, abruptly putting a stop to her brooding. In the sky above, the clouds turned a dirty yellow and she suddenly remembered a holo-image from a college lecture.

That was a true sandstorm, big, violent and coming down fast.

She turned and ran for the hills, eyes scanning constantly for any kind of safe hole as her fingers tapped madly on her comtab.

Nothing, no sound, no answering call sign. She kept running. There, a dark slash ahead of her that must be a gap in the rocks. She glanced again at her com unit. Still no signal. The storm, cutting it out.

Now she was in trouble.

The base of the hills loomed, and she was scrabbling up, fingers clawing into dirt in her frantic race to safety. The grit-laden wind lashed her face, hands, any exposed skin. She ducked her head, screwing her eyes tight against the onslaught. A couple of metres more.

She thrust into the crack, the barest of openings, wedging herself around a rock into the space hidden behind.

Blessed stillness. She dropped her head to her knees and breathed slowly as her heart knocked against her ribs in a cannonade of panic.

Slowly, slowly, in and out. Concentrate on your surroundings. Survey basic training had been tough, but now she thanked the heavens for every bawling out and painful muscle, and counted down each tenet of the survival litany drilled mercilessly into her.

Where are you?

In a sliver of free space between two huge boulders. Around her, a jumble of rocks piled one on the other with a tonne weight of solid rock above her head. It might feel like a tomb, but those rocks were wedged solid. The result of a long past landslide, they weren't going anywhere, not even under the buffeting from the storm piling down on them.

Small rivulets of dirt puffed out where the winds clawed at any chink in the breaches. Hopefully they would get no worse. No, don't think that. Outside, the noise rose to a crescendo as the full force hit. Too late to go anywhere else.

Again she made herself breath slowly: in, out. *Fear is your friend; panic your enemy.* One of her instructors' many maxims, but the one they had drilled deepest. Breathe through it, she could hear them barking.

In and out, counting each precious lungful, slowly, not too deeply, not in this dry, killing air.

Next on the schedule: *check your kit bag.*

Extra water, a big canteen full. She opened it, but allowed herself one mouthful only. No knowing how long she would be stuck here.

She recognised some of the rest of the kit's contents. Food sachets. First aid—the full Survey mobile pack. You could do field surgery with it, said a grimly amused part of her. Another packet that opened to reveal sheets of some filmy material. She turned it over, trying to figure it out, letting her fingers wander over strange clasps. Finally it came to her. Tent. This was a tent. Nothing like the wet weather slicks they used at home, but she guessed it filled the same function. No good to her now, not against the hurricane winds battering her refuge.

Another drift of dirt fell on her shoulder, and she brushed it away.

You're safe. A bit of dirt hurt no one.

There was a suit of some kind, a protective coverall by the looks of it. Now that could be useful, remembering the stinging of wind borne chips against her cheek. She shook it out and wriggled into the thing, praying not to tear it against the rocks in the tiny space available.

The material was far tougher than she'd expected, and the suit had a face mask with breathing tube and some kind of temperature regulator. She could feel her skin relaxing into the cooling atmosphere.

You are safe here.

Maybe if she said it often enough, she might believe it. The shriek of the wind outside said otherwise.

Another drift of dust, enough to make her duck her head. They were coming faster now, a constant film clogging up her nostrils.

Another clump of dirt, more dust, then a whole cascade of sand, piling up between her and the narrow, shrinking entrance way.

Don't panic.

Forget that, said her terrified brain. She grabbed the kit bag, zipped up her coveralls and shoved through the pile of dirt.

The shrieking power of the storm hit her, the wind tearing round the corner of the rocks and pulling mercilessly at her as the enveloping dust choked her throat. She pulled the hood on, the tough fabric of the mask keeping enough of the clouds out to let her breathe—just.

The coverall came into its own now, protecting her skin from the grasping winds. She stuck her face cautiously round the corner into the full force of the wind's fury. A large bush barrelled past, bowling over and over in the turbulent gusts. That would be her, if she attempted the open plain.

She pulled back, crawling farther into the gap left between the rock fall and the slope of the hill.

It didn't stop the wind, didn't stop the exhausting tug of storm driven gusts and debris, but by clinging to the rocks, she could hold her position. That was all. The wind was too strong now for anything else. No twisting round, no releasing her grip on the rocks to extract the water and supplies from the kit bag. It stayed safely on her shoulder but was no use to her at all.

Already she felt a drying thirst, her tongue swelling. That brief mouthful was long gone, and her tongue traced over cracking lips.

Do not panic.

Her fingers dug into the sharp edged rocks, scrabbling deeper to anchor her to whatever shelter she could find on the outside of the pile.

Not inside them, not under them, never again.

She ached all over as the wind tugged at her, urged her to give in. Let it take her where it would.

She clung tighter.

You can't fool me, said the demon in the wind. I will have you.

Her right hand clutched convulsively at the rough indentations in the rock, grasping onto whatever hand hold she could find, and she dug her heels into the fractional clefts below her, wedging them against the opposing face.

The true worth of the coverall came to her aid, moulding to her body and refusing to billow out and give the wind an anchoring sail.

Would it be enough?

She listened desperately for any change in the howling of the gale, and found nothing to reassure her. Could feel her arms, her feet weakening.

Could feel them giving way, and could do nothing. Could feel her body slipping away from the safety of the rocks.

"Fee?"

A man's body, big and solid, suddenly enfolding her, and a gruff voice in her ear.

"I have you safe."

It was the best sound she had ever heard.

Until something slithered over her and she panicked.

"Shh. Keep still. It's a tethering net to hold us in place till I get the tent up."

"A tent, in this?"

"Wait and see."

One of his hands gripped onto his sticks as with the other he flung open the strange slick of material from her kit. Eyes squinting through the grit, she just made out where it landed. A small hollow between the rock pile and the hillside. Barely flat and with just enough space for two bodies.

The tent shuddered into shape, tether pegs borrowing into the rocky soil. She looked at it doubtfully. Those pegs were very thin, and the fabric too light, surely.

"It's stronger than it looks," said Caleb.

"Maybe. How do we get to it?" The wind was in full fury now and she had to listen hard to pick out his words.

He held out a hand. "The net will hold you against me and it's less than a metre away. I can do that safely. Trust me."

Two simple words. Why they should make a difference after what she had seen earlier, she couldn't say, but they did. She let go of the rock, put her hand in his and pushed away from her refuge.

Less than a metre, he said. It might have been an eternity. The net snapped tight, fastening her to his side and surely stopping him from walking. If it did, he gave no sign, lifting his arms easily over her head and using his two sticks to manoeuvre across the vortex.

How they made it safely to his tent, she could never say. He stroked a hand against a seam, the tent opened and they ducked into the tiny interior.

No room to stand or sit up under the low roof. They crawled fully in, letting the door seal close behind them as he released the net. She hauled off her hood, gulping in the clear, filtered air. He laid down his sticks, shoved back his own hood and pulled her tight against his body.

She should be frightened. The interior of the tent was smaller than her previous refuge under the rocks, but here was no massive pile of rocks threatening to collapse on top of her. There was light, an eerie glow seeping through the fabric walls, and a large body curling protectively around her as they lay on the floor together.

She lifted her head and mouthed "Thank you." Then met his eyes, and found an answer to that part of her that knew his voice and relaxed at his touch. He smiled, his mouth skewed as if he too recognised the inevitability of this moment. His hand tilted her head up and his mouth descended to meet hers.

Cocooned from all outside responsibilities, it didn't matter that it was too noisy for talk, to speak the small nothings that broke down restraints. No more need for that, not between them, not in this place. Coveralls shed in the tight, twisting space, his body rose over hers, and she welcomed him in, and there was an inevitability to that too. Beyond time, beyond thought, they grabbed at life in the face of nature's deadly challenge.

Afterwards, she lay replete in his arms and said nothing, relieved when he did the same. What this man made her feel was too new, too sudden. Nor could she put it into words. Other ones came to her instead. *In the face of death, live for the moment.* A truth from her oldest relative. For now, Fee would enjoy this man's touch, the strength of his body lying close to her. But after that—no, the complications were just too overwhelming to consider. She would seize this moment to the full, but there would be no after.

It took hours, well into the next morning, before the storm receded. They made love once more, fierce and passionate as if grabbing at a disappearing instant. Not long after that, the sound began to die away; the roaring bellow sinking to a constant susurration. The light changed, brightened, a clear wash of colour replacing the eerie glow. Life returning to normal, and she became conscious of exactly how she was lying, and with whom.

She struggled to sit up, banging her head against the tent ceiling, and ducking down again as she frantically sought her coverall.

Caleb Winter propped himself up on his elbow and watched her struggle.

"You can't go yet. The wind's too strong." His voice might be dead flat, but he stared at her chest as she yanked the coverall closed. Then looked up, and his eyes caught hers. "This . . . was not wise."

Wise? "No," was all she could manage.

"You regret it?"

"Don't you?"

Did she imagine that hint of bitterness in his eyes? "I'm a man and a Winter. Regret good sex?"

She spluttered. Time to change the conversation. "Whatever." A sickening thought hit her. Was this whole *incident* part of his plan? Ben's innocence, his antagonism towards his father. All a charade?

What was really going on here?

"We are going to forget this ever happened. I was sent here to do a job, and if you thought to distract me with—this— forget that also. This thing *did not* happen."

He jerked up at that. "This *thing*? We had sex, sweetheart. More accurately, we made love—together—mutually consenting. *That's* what happened. And if you think I planned on getting you lost in a storm that nearly killed you," he reached for his clothes, angrily jerking them on, "you are insane."

She backed away, ripping open the door seam and nearly choking on the cloud of dust swirling outside. A hand slapped past her to close the seam again, and thrust a water bottle in her hand.

"I told you it's too early to leave."

She gulped down the water and refused to give in to the stinging in her eyes. It was dust, she was tired. She *did not* cry, not ever.

"Oh, hell." His arms reached out to gather her in. Too worn out to fight, she let herself relax into the refuge offered. Just for a minute, just enough to regain control. But soon she made herself struggle for release, and his arms dropped immediately.

She eased back, keeping as much distance from him as possible, and lay back down. It was a small space, but she made sure not a single part of her touched him. "I saw you getting out of your father's vehicle."

"So Ben said."

"Then you will understand why I wonder what's going on here."

His mouth tightened. "Believe what you will." She glared and he shrugged slightly. "My father was calling the shots. He already suspects I'm up to something here and didn't need any more ammunition. You should understand that."

She had to nod, her own family in mind.

There was a grim cast to his mouth. "I'm Survey first, just like you."

Maybe, but there were still too many hidden secrets in those eyes and closed face. Could she trust him? "I will do what I was sent here to do, but any sign of using me to further the empire building of Winter Solaris and I'm out of here."

A sharp edged flash in his eyes.

"As for the…"

"The sex?"

"Yes, that," she agreed hastily. "It was a mistake. Fear of the storm."

He said nothing, but lay there, studying her, judging her.

The com unit crackled into life.

"Boss? You okay?" said a voice.

Caleb Winter never took his gaze off her, even as he spoke to Ben's disembodied voice. "I'm fine."

"And Fee, did you find her?

"Yes," said Caleb. "I found her. She is safe."

From the absence of sound outside, the wind had died completely. Inside, the silence echoed that absence. She shuffled towards the door seam. "It must be all right to leave now?"

He nodded, and she thrust open the seam, escaping out of the tent.

Escape: that's exactly what it felt like, but as she emerged and saw the changes in the valley floor, the sick feeling in her gut told her Caleb Winter was not all she had escaped.

There had been plants on the plain before the storm. Sparse, barely clinging to life, but there had been plants.

Now, dust and sand covered everything. The rocks she had clung to so desperately were swept bare on the exposed faces and dirt plugged the crevices. She looked for the narrow passage leading to her refuge—gone, buried under a heavy drift.

She would not have survived, not if Caleb hadn't found her.

A step and a voice. She turned and he, too, was staring out at the land.

"Not too bad. A few months, and it will be back to normal." She could only gape at him, and that straight mouth of his tilted upwards. "I've seen worse."

The words had to be said, though they near choked her. "I owe you a debt of gratitude. Thank you for protecting me through the storm." His mouth tilted higher, and she saw the amusement in his eyes as he recognised the precision of her thank you.

As for what had happened between them during the storm? He would keep it private—for some reason, she was absolutely sure of that—but it was a complication.

A complication. That's all you call it? Who're you fooling?

Her inner voice wasn't always right.

Yeah, you keep telling yourself that.

The com unit crackled to life. Saved by the beep.

"Boss, you need pick up?"

Caleb released her gaze and bent to talk into the com unit. "Shouldn't think so, long as my skimmer's still working. Keep this channel open in case, and get yourself checked out when you get back to base. No stupid heroics. There's been enough of that already. We have work to do."

He switched off and surveyed her, from the crown of her madly thatched hair to the battered toes of her boots. His mouth twitched as she couldn't resist dragging at her hair to try to bring it into some sort of order, but all he said was, "You up to a walk? My vehicle's not far away."

He reached down to collapse the tent and repack his kit. She tried to help but he shook his head. "I've got it."

Standing uselessly by watching him, never had she felt more completely an outsider.

He looked at her and cursed. She went to step back, but he put his hands on her shoulders, gently pulling her forwards. Then slid them down to take hold of her hands, turning them over to expose the torn, scratched surface of her palms and fingers.

"Leave it to me, just this time."

She snatched her hands back, hiding them in her pockets and refusing to acknowledge the sting of her palms, or her eyes.

He finished quickly, and passed her a walking stick. "It helps in this loose stuff."

Setting out, she trudged in his wake. He was right about the *loose stuff.* The ground was covered in soft, slipping sand and churned-up dirt. After her first stumble, he took hold of her arm, catching her into his side whenever she missed a step.

It would have been nice, if it hadn't been so impersonal.

Good sex, that's all you are, and felt pathetic at the rush of pride in the added adjective. Good sex, not just any old sex.

Sex that would not be repeated, not with a man whose agenda she had about as much faith in as she did this land that was the lifeblood of him.

A land they were both pledged to change.

CHAPTER FIFTEEN

Caleb's vehicle was covered with a pile of silt. He toggled his com unit, and minutes later, the machine broke out of its prison of dirt. It meant they would be back to proper home comforts much quicker than she'd expected, yet the trick of it irritated Fee. One more clever plains adaptation that proved how little suited she was to this place.

"Very efficient."

He grinned, and it widened even farther when she stumped over and thumped into the cab without another word.

"Back to camp," he said once they were on their way.

"After we take a look at this Plan B lake."

"No need for that. The second dam's only there as a distraction.

"Maybe, but the Survey sent me here for a reason." She stared resolutely straight ahead.

He slammed the machine into overdrive, shoving her back into her seat, but did change course. Hopefully to the lake B site, but she was in no mood to ask. Trying to remember the local map didn't help either, not given the changes in the land. Before, it had been burnt orange and ochre, colours that sang with the dramatic beauty she was learning to see in this land. Now, it was a uniform, muddy yellow and the piled-up masses of sand from the storm hid any recognisable landmark, leaving her thoroughly disoriented.

Caleb Winter was no happier when they pulled up at the new lake, striding across the dirt to the water's edge. She refused to scurry after him, choosing instead to stop at the top of the bank and slowly scan the basin now filling with water before strolling down to stand beside him.

She eyed the brown wavelets lapping at her feet, still whipped by the tail end of the wind's fury. Then twisted around to measure the distance to the sharp lip that must be the final high water mark.

"How deep in the middle?"

"Comes up to my knee at the moment."

She did some quick calculations. "This will still hold a considerable body of water; more than adequate for irrigation and fostering vegetation change in the surrounds."

He shrugged. "Not enough for a microclimate change."

"No," she lifted a hand to shade her eyes, peering across to the far side, "but enough to boost the effectiveness of Lake A if you make a couple of changes. Can you bring up the topography of this area?"

He scowled but pulled up the file on his com unit, waiting till the screen shimmered to life in the air between them. He had set it to holo-display. A three-dimensional chart of the land between this lake and the original Lake A formed on the ground. She walked around it, considering.

Finally, she put her finger on a section of flat land, midway between the two. "Call up the soil types."

He obeyed but didn't so much as glance at the graphics forming above the holo-map. "Sand and loam, overlaid with a layer of sediment from ancient floodings."

"So could be cropping land?"

He nodded. "From the files the Survey sent through, that's their third-stage plan for this area."

She walked around the holo-map once more. Considering options.

"What would a cash crop far sooner mean to the locals? If we joined the two lakes."

He stared at her fingers, running circles over the river flats of a more fertile past. Eons ago, there had been true topsoil here, but the wind had dealt to that.

Yet with shelter belts planted on the nor' west side and the natural protection of the surrounding hills on the other sides…

He looked up at her, his foul mood banished. "It might just work."

Fee pulled her finger through the holo-map, rearranging it as she went. "If we pull up a creek here, and here. Most of the channels will run underground, but not all, and people believe a lot more in water they can see."

He nodded slowly. Keeping his father out of it would be a problem, but apart from that…"It would bring the locals around, the ones whose children have to leave because there's nothing for them here except cleaning solar arrays or mechanic's work."

It would break his father's stranglehold. Or was that part of the Survey's plan all along? And if so, what about this girl; what was her role in it? What had her briefings said before she came here?

"You've got a point," he said gruffly. "We'll put it to the others back at camp."

But when he pulled in front of the Admin block, it was to find a man in uniform standing at the top of the steps. A very familiar uniform: the crisp tunic of the Federal Guard.

He slammed to a stop, belatedly apologising to the woman beside him and silently cursing at her wince as her hands grabbed hold of the webbing. "Sorry."

He doubted she heard him, her eyes fixed on the man, and a look on her face as wary as the clench in his gut. Very wise, when the Survey called in the big guns.

He took his time securing everything. Fee didn't move either.

"Ready?"

"No," she said, but her hand moved to the door, forcing him to follow.

Together, they pulled out kit bags and approached the man waiting for them.

It wasn't until they were on the top step and equal with the visitor that Caleb spoke. "Marshall."

"Winter, den Coille."

Fee stepped up beside him. "Ser Marshall. Welcome to the plains. How may we help you?"

The man's gazed flicked at Caleb but he answered Fee's more formal tone with the required forms of respect. "You have been summoned to Survey Central. I have a flyer waiting."

Caleb stepped sideways to pass the man. "Not possible."

Fee grabbed at his arm. Anyone else he would have shaken off. It had been a long day and right now, he wanted nothing more than to throw this clod off his step, talk to his troops, before heading to his quarters to clean up and get horizontal.

It was Fee who stepped up. "We cannot leave the project at present."

"My orders are set."

Caleb recognised that look. The man wasn't being deliberately obstreperous. His orders really were set, and set solid.

A sudden spurt of anger at Central, which he thrust back. It would achieve nothing. "Let me call Fox."

But their boss was no help either, and he saw his own frustration mirrored on Fee's face.

He switched off the unit, strode back to the waiting soldier. "We'll be ready in an hour."

He grabbed Fee's arm and marched her inside to start packing. Her boots beat an angry tattoo on the floor. "We'll never get these lakes done."

They made the deadline for the flight, but it was close. So much to be set in motion, work to be delegated, so much to finish off and so little time. He'd already known that he and Fee worked well together, and this day proved it. She had to be as bruised and sore from the storm, as exhausted as he. And as thrown by what had happened between them in that tent.

Forget it, she'd said.

If she thought he would forget making love to her—not going to happen. Except that he still had no idea how what she felt about it. Hoped yes, but knew—no. That they were going to be lovers had been fixed, right from the moment he first saw her. That physically her desire matched his, he had suspected for some time and had it confirmed in that tent.

It was what went with it that had him pitched six ways to never. What she felt; what he felt.

No time to work it out now. The Marshall was waiting on the steps of the flyer, face tight and hand already set on the door rails. Caleb picked up Fee's bag and loaded their luggage into the hold.

"Ready?"

"Not in this lifetime," she said, squared her shoulders and stepped on board.

He followed her, taking the seat opposite hers. "Did you have time to do anything about your idea for the new dam?"

"I left the bare sketch of it with Kal. He's going to work with Adam and Gerard to flesh it out."

"Have you told Fox?"

She glanced towards the cockpit, where the Marshall was settling in beside the pilot. They were in lift off mode and unlikely to hear anything, though the cabin was sure to be under audio surveillance.

"Not yet. It can wait till we get to Central and find out what this is all about."

He sent her a tight smile of approval at the bare answer. She was on guard too.

The flyer lifted then levelled off, setting a course north. There were a few hours of flying time to Central. Time to catch up on some badly needed sleep. He would need all his wits about him once they landed. With luck he might even get rid of the pounding in his head. He settled carefully back against the seat rest, turning slightly to avoid the tender swelling hidden by the hair at the back of his head. Fee was strapping in, her face pensive but looking like the fight was coming back to her. For the next few hours, she was safe. No need for him to keep watch.

He closed his eyes, shutting out the woman, the cabin and all the other piled up problems waiting to explode in his face.

Fee wriggled around in her seat, trying to find a comfortable spot, and glared at the man across from her. Asleep—just like that—as if nothing was wrong. She chewed on her lip, tucked her feet underneath her, and cursed her lack of stature. This flyer was designed for giants, or plains folk, and she was small by mountain standards, let alone by the norm found on the plains.

She peered through the window but there was only the odd wisp of cloud and the plains spread out below like a vast brown map. Too distant to seem real. Last night had been real, and what she felt about it threatened to tear apart everything she had always assumed about her life.

Work. That was the answer. Much better than brooding. First: lock down her data securely before they hit Central. Like most field ops, she didn't fully trust head office. The only data senior staff would get from her were the files she was absolutely forced to surrender, and she'd make damn sure she knew why they wanted them first.

She slumped back against the headrest. It would be nice to have someone on her side for a change, someone not working their own agenda, and yet again thought back to that tent and the man across the aisle.

There had been no hidden agenda; not during that storm. They had made love because both of them wanted to, because death knocked on the door and life was precious.

She squirmed again, disturbed now by her thoughts, not the seat that was too big, too hard. Last night happened because she wanted Caleb Winter too much to refuse him.

"Deal with it," he'd said to her back on her balcony at home. Deal with whatever this was growing between them. Problem was, she was no nearer to knowing how to do that now than she had been that night.

She pulled up her notes, tried to concentrate, gave up in far too short a time and stared out the window instead.

If only she had the slightest idea what she'd got herself into.

It was a relief when the landscape began to change and the pretence of working could be discarded. She peered out the window, watching the first signs of the massive city of Urbis appear: a cluster of houses, a road, a major power plant thrusting upwards from a tract of estuarine wilderness.

The city was on the northern edge of the continent. Rivers stopped their furious race to oblivion here, stretching out their trunks into a cone of branching twiglets, as if reluctant to disappear into the unifying water of the sea.

Their ancestors had built their first settlement close to the coast and beside the major branch of a river that came from far up in the hinterland. An ideal place to act as a base for the expanding colonisation of a new world. But that was many hundreds of years ago. Arcadia was long settled, Urbis now the capital city of a populous and economically stable world, and it had grown in size to match its importance. Today, the city spread across the estuaries of three mighty river systems.

Not an ideal geo-setting for a megalopolis, yet the pattern was set and the engineers, architects and planners had to make the best of it. A final year project for every trainee eco-engineer was coming up with another adaptive mechanism for the city. An aid for keeping the city viable in the face of floods or the liquefaction that inevitably attended any earth tremor disturbing the shifting gravels and sands on which the city was built, or to protect the precious fertile soils of the river flood pans in the face of burgeoning urban spread.

She remembered the look on her supervisor's face when she'd said: "Just move the city."

"Think you're the first one to come up with that, den Coille? Get thinking."

She leaned forward to get a better look through the window. There: a tower set on a clawed network of flying buttresses with legs delving right down to the solid bedrock underlying the treacherous upper layers, and above it, spiralling streets of paths, gardens, shops and homes. An artificial tree supporting an entire suburb. That had been her project and she still felt an inordinate surge of pride at the finished product. So few student projects ever came to fruition.

Opposite her, Caleb Winter stretched, yawned, then unbuckled and stood, coming to lean over her to see what she was looking at.

He was too damn close. She refused to show the effect he had on her by moving backwards.

His head tilted toward the suburb. "Yours?"

She nodded. "What about you?"

"A bit harder to see." A slight smile of amusement touched his face as he called her bluff. Of course Caleb Winter would have been good enough to have a project accepted. But he surprised her. "It's trees. Windbreak plantings on the incoming branches to stop the more destructive gales."

She remembered those winds too well. Roaring up from the south, where the mighty central plain sucked all moisture from the air. Days of choking dust and exacerbated tempers.

"Another ten years, and they should be big enough to cut down the velocity of the winds. Seemed the least I could do, given that it's the changes from settlement of the plains that's driving up the strength of the big blows."

His words matched the niggling thought in the back of her head. "We're a trial. Our regions get to be the fall guys for Central's new approach, because it helps Urbis. That's their main objective."

"To protect the city, yes. Improving the lives of minor provincial regions; not so much."

A dry smile touched his lips. The man wasn't stupid. She looked at him through new eyes. Just maybe?

"Why do you think we're here?" she asked.

One brow cocked up. "Apart from explaining how a relatively simple project has careered from one disaster to another?"

"Yeah, that. There's more though."

His mouth straightened, a grim line, and he nodded his agreement. "Yes." He glanced forward to the pilot's cabin, as if in warning. No more to be said, not now. But at some stage, she and Caleb Winter were going to have a good long talk.

The landing at Survey Central was routine. Too much so, setting her nerves on edge. They passed through security with a minimum of fuss; no second pauses, no long litanies of clerical interrogation or last minute need for decontamination of field equipment.

They were either particularly high in favour, or in so much trouble that Central wanted them processed and free to be disciplined in the quickest time possible. She had a sinking feeling it was the latter.

Fox was waiting for them in the main briefing room. A small man, unprepossessing in appearance, but she'd long ago learned his looks were no guide to the man.

"Take a seat."

Her heart sank. She recognised that tone of voice. Caleb slouched into the second chair, legs stretched forward. He'd no intention of letting Fox have it all his own way, obviously.

Not that Fox gave any sign of it. He switched his screens to group display, shimmering into life in front of each of them but doing nothing to impede their view of each other. "The current progress report. It appears less than adequate."

Ten minutes later, they were in no doubt of the meaning of his words.

"You were caught in a dust storm in the South March. Winter, frequency of such storms?"

Caleb still slouched and his voiced was dead flat. "Increasing by a factor of 3.65."

"Den Coille, rate of precipitation over the western mountains?"

"Becoming more episodic, Sir. Average rate is increasing at an acceptable rate, but the variation in volume per unit time is widening. More heavy downpours with an increasing risk of catastrophic erosion."

In plain language, which Fox didn't need, the total amount of rain wasn't up by much, but when it fell, it came down in bucket loads that scoured away the soil, despite the tree cover. They needed trees with a wide canopy and deep seeking network of tap roots, trees that sank deep into the soil and stayed there. Not the simple buttresses and shallow roots of the festia trees that dominated her home area now, too readily bowled over by any rough weather.

"In summary, the situation in both your home zones is becoming increasingly unstable?"

She nodded. Caleb grunted.

"Yet this project, this bridgehead project you were charged with, the exact state of this critical project is—what?"

She said nothing and Caleb crossed his arms. No need to labour the point.

It didn't impress Fox. "You have an explanation?"

In the face of Caleb's continued silence, Fee launched into a rambling précis of the events that had held back their work: her accident, her father's reaction, Caleb's father's interference, the new backup plan.

"And you call that acceptable?"

Just once, she wished Fox would lose his temper.

"Den Coille, where exactly do your family think you are at the moment?"

"I left a note to say I was heading off on a research trip."

"To where?"

She shrugged. "They know to contact the Survey if there's an emergency."

"So they have no reason to think you have been kidnapped by Winter Solaris, to force Den Coille cooperation?"

Caleb's feet struck the floor.

"Of course not," she said at the same time.

"So why is your father hammering on the door of Federal security, demanding they rescue you from the Winters?"

It wasn't possible. "My mother …"

"Seems to have been singularly disinclined to talk sense into anyone on this occasion."

"She believes it too?"

Fox said nothing, which she had to assume was his way of saying 'Yes'.

"They're insane."

"One might think so, if they had not recently had a visit from the eldest son and heir of the Winter family, who used the occasion to thoroughly pry into den Coille's home base."

Caleb thrust forward. "I was scoping out the area for phase two—and I was damn discreet."

"So discreet that den Coille saw fit to lock you up. From which you escaped, taking his daughter with you."

Fox might have been discussing the weather, so flat was his voice, but Fee wasn't stupid. The only part she couldn't figure out was whether he was utterly furious, or hellishly pleased. She was getting a bad feeling. Just what was going on here?

"Why should my family assume I've been kidnapped? The Winters have nothing to gain from holding me."

"Nothing—except that your family is the largest grower of festia on the west coast, with plantations up and down the mountain chain. Plantations that depend on a high rainfall and a consistent market for their foodstuffs. Goods that, let me remind you, are manufactured in plants currently driven largely by Solaris energy, but which could equally be driven by hydro plants.

"Only if Father pulls out some trees and dams land currently under plantations."

Caleb thrust forward. "Which won't happen, not quickly enough to affect Solaris, so it's all theoretical."

Fox cocked an eyebrow and Fee felt like shrinking. "Not that long," she said. The plans have already been drawn up for it."

Caleb swung round on her. "You know this, how?"

"I drew them up for him a few months ago."

"Those gullies on your side—they're as unstable as hell!"

She gulped, and wished she could make her voice sound stronger, more sure. "Most, but there are some that would stand it."

"Those dams were vetoed, den Coille," said Fox. "The gullies in question contain the last surviving remnants of the full forest flora and fauna."

"It was a cover." She caught at her hands to stop their twisting dance of nerves. "How else could we explain what we were up to when the Survey asked us to scope out the area?"

As impossible as knowing what the Survey planned now.

Fox sat back, tenting his fingers together and switching his gaze slowly from one to the other of them. "There seems little more to say at present. We will talk again tomorrow. In the meantime, it would help if you refrained from doing anything particularly stupid." He stood, and an aide entered the room. "Failing that, keep your heads down. Unless you enjoy being noticed by management."

A shiver traced Fee's spine. There was an edge to Fox's voice she'd never heard before, almost as if he was warning them. It was gone as quickly as glimpsed, and their sardonic boss was back.

"Report to medical, both of you, then Parthas here will show you to your quarters once they release you."

After which, the man walked out of the room before they could say anything else. Getting in the last word as usual.

The aide led them down the tunnels to the medical wing of headquarters. The smell hit Fee before the noise, and neither was welcome. She'd spent too much time in medical over the years and would only come in now if forced to it. Given the high risk factor for eco-engineering work, most field ops were the same. So why wasn't Caleb protesting, why did he agree to go first?

They reached the waiting room, and he palmed the clinic door. "See you when I'm finished."

Fee made no attempt to take one of the chairs nearby. "This medical. They checking anything intimate?"

His mouth quirked up at that. "No. Not unless you're offering."

She gave him the obligatory grin and shake of her head, but wasn't fooled. He did not want her in there.

Tough. "Let's go."

Inside, a team was waiting for them. Fox's doing, she guessed. The doctor ran a hand loosely over the back of Caleb's head. It could have been a lover's caress, except for the concentration on the woman's face and the unmistakeable wince from Caleb as she touched the back of his head.

"Who hit you there?"

He winced again at the sharpness of her voice, but Fee couldn't help it. "Who, and when?" she demanded again.

"My father's man."

"The day they came to camp?"

He went to give his usual nod, but stopped mid movement.

"And now? How bad is that headache?"

Caleb didn't answer, but the doctor tilted his head up and stared into those shadowed, Winter eyes. "Off the scale, at a guess?"

Caleb didn't deny it, and Fee suddenly felt sick. "So at the new lake site, when you climbed down from your father's truck?"

"Climbed out freely without being forced to? It was get out, or stay inside and puke my guts out."

"Oh." All her assumptions, turned face about and trashed again. She swivelled, almost galloped out of the room and waited outside for the nurse to finish dressing his head before quietly returning for her own check up. When would her world stand still again?

CHAPTER SIXTEEN

It was a single room. One bed—one large bed—two people.

The man opening the door waited for them to enter as if nothing was wrong. She studied his face. Yes, he was definitely waiting for them both to enter the room. She let Caleb walk in, but remained in the doorway. After a night and day stuck in the medical wards, alternating between being poked and prodded by a parade of medicos and endless hours of enforced bed rest with far too much time to think, she really didn't need a room mix-up as well. "See you at dinner," she said to Caleb, and turned to the steward, "If you would show me to my quarters, please."

"Here, Sera."

"You are mistaken."

He glanced at his com-unit. "No. Den Coille and Winter. Couple. Arrival 11th of Cycle 6. No mistake."

The man scanned the bags on the table at the end of the bed. Caleb's bag and hers. Caleb watched the man work.

"When was this booking made?" The steward showed him the com. "Four days ago. Before the storm. You might as well come in," he said to Fee.

She wasn't ready to agree but the steward had sidled out the door and down the corridor before she could stop him, leaving her no other choice.

The bag on the bed, the one sitting side by side with the carryall she had seen Caleb thrust into their transporter as they left; that bag was unmistakably hers. There was the scratch from a too-hasty tug through a door on a trip two years ago.

She stalked across the room, stopping at the wide window looking out onto the grey streets and blocks of apartments. This whole building was Survey accommodation. There was no need for any doubling up. She swivelled round and glared at Caleb, who was calmly opening his bag and transferring the necessary contents to the cupboard.

"We have to sort this out."

He looked up. "You can try, but there won't be another room."

"I am not sharing a room with you."

"You can, and will. You think this was an administrative hiccup?"

She shook her head and peered at his face again, scrutinising it more carefully. He was a hard man to read, but she was learning. That slight tightening about his mouth, the carefully measured step to the cupboard and back as he unpacked.

He was furious.

Yet he carried on as if nothing was wrong, as if this whole situation was acceptable, opening the closet and hanging in place the warm jacket he'd brought against the colder winds of Urbis. He kept working, tidying away pieces in his night drawer, checking out the light and heat controls, working slowly around the room and familiarising himself with its features.

Checking for sensors.

Of course.

"We'll see," she said, as if not yet giving in but going with it for now. Then began to copy him, unclasping her bag, setting aside her bracelet, sliding her fingers along each drawer and piece of furniture.

He gave a brief nod of approval, stowing his bag beside hers in the bottom of the closet and tilting his head towards the small balcony. She followed him out, huddling against the nip in the air and breathing in the traces of snow and fresh trees sifting in over the stink of the street.

He glanced around, walking right over to the railing. She looked out at the view, letting her gaze slide around the doorway, the railings, the overhang. There, there and there, the giveaway roughness of a sensor. But standing at the railing, facing out into the cold wind, they should be safe from eavesdroppers. She leaned over the rails beside him, watching the traffic zip past.

When he spoke, it was in a low rumble, as much felt as heard. "What does the Survey gain by a union between Winter and den Coille?"

She nearly gave herself away in her shock. "Union—you mean?"

"You and me. Winter and den Coille, becoming family."

Her and Caleb? "It would never work." Her hands gripped the rails. "They must be mad."

"You think?"

There it was; that edge in his voice.

But after the storm, and the night in his tent, was there any doubt? Fee and Caleb; that worked more than all right.

But Fioruisghe ingh Bram an Scathach den Coille, daughter of the mountains, and Caleb Winter, eldest son of Winter

Solaris and a confirmed plainsman? They weren't talking mutually enjoyable fling here. If Caleb was right, the Survey had something far more permanent in mind.

She couldn't meet his eyes, not now, and switched back to studying the building across from them. An itinerant sun beam was pricking at the left corner, denying the flat grey and the gloomy cold of the city street. She shook her head slightly. "If they want any hope of saving Arcadia, the Survey has to break the power of the corporates. Has to force them to put their profit making second to the planet's needs. Uniting den Coille and Winter Solaris does the opposite. Imagine it. Together they would be one very strong conglomerate with full economic control over our sector."

She stared at the cars hovering in the streets, held up by a snarled knot of impatient traffic at the far corner. She had seen Caleb with his family, seen the tension and the hurt that lay under it. "Why with you?" she said.

"My father's heir, I guess."

"Except you're not, not really."

"Nor do I want to be. But my father… he…" He fell silent, as if struck by something.

"Where would we live, anyway?" she carried on. "You love your plains and I need trees." Then stopped too. "Who would lead the combined corporate," she whispered, and looked at Caleb.

He was as serious as she had ever seen him. "Exactly."

She thought of her father, negotiating away full control of his business but gave up. Wouldn't happen, ever. "They would tear each other apart."

Caleb nodded grimly. "Where would we live is only the start of it. Whose name would our children bear, where do we go for birthdays, feast days, which mother gets precedence? Which clan would we belong to?"

It did not bear contemplating. "Those bastards. It will destroy Den Coille and Solaris." Let alone what it would do to their families. She felt sick. That the Survey, her Survey, would do this to her.

Caleb lifted a strand of her hair that had come loose from her travelling braid, tucking it with finger tip lightness back into place. "They're playing for big odds. There's nothing they would not do."

"Sometimes—they ask too much."

"Yes—and yet, I have never refused them."

A grey cab hooted savagely at the small zinger that suddenly cut up in front of it, twisting and rupturing the banked up traffic into agitated chaos and she clenched her fists on the rail.

There was no answer to that.

After a time they drifted back inside and, by unspoken consent, opted for the communal dining hall rather than eating in their room.

The tables were starting to fill up, many of the faces familiar. She chose a seat by an old friend from training days, introduced Caleb, then friends of his wandered across and within a short time they were the centre of a group of visiting field staff.

On the surface, it was like any other visit to Central. A time for the simple pleasure of catching up on the gossip: who was with whom, the new children born to old friends, the hard times and the good out in the field. And that old favourite game of field staff—who could tell the most outrageous tale of Central interferences and botch ups. The laughter rang loudly, belly deep and edged with the dry hysteria of seasoned troops. Tonight, though, she picked up an undercurrent. Fear and a growing sense of desperation. There was a viciousness to the head office taunts she'd never heard before.

In a big family like hers, you learned the importance of idle chat. How to discover the hidden threads under the chatter. She'd had enough practice at home, navigating the cross weave of family and business to achieve her goals. Tonight, the goal was different, but the game the same.

"What dragged you away from your precious trees?" asked her friend Sharrah.

Fee frowned as if in vague complaint. "A summons from Fox. Something about the current project."

She told Sharrah of the making of the lakes and working with Caleb. That brought a lifted eyebrow and a twinkle of appreciation as her friend studied the tall man sitting beside Fee, deep in talk with another field op.

"Nice work for some."

Fee had never been able to control her blushes. "It's business."

She switched the subject and after another of those looks of hers at Caleb, Sharrah allowed the change. She soon had Fee reduced to uncontrolled shrieks that had her clutching her stomach. Sharrah had a wicked turn of wit and her latest job was in a forest similar to Fee's home but totally unlike the windswept coastal plains of Sharrah's home. The woman could dissect a place's foibles quicker than anyone Fee knew.

"My speciality is coastal marine zones. What am I doing marooned up a tree, swatting bugs and trying to explain stuff to locals? As if they would listen to a word I said anyway."

There it was again; that shade of desperation. "It's bad?"

Sharrah sighed. "Getting worse."

"In what way?"

Fee was shocked to see the glitter of tears in her old friend's face. She put on her best 'I'm all sympathy' mask and prepared to listen. Then noticed that Caleb was doing the same, and from the stream of talk from his neighbour, very successfully.

There was talk of clubbing. The only alternative, the problem of that single room.

A man clapped Caleb on the shoulder. "C'mon, mate. About time you took a break from work. The old town has missed you."

This particular friend of Caleb's was now a Central office boffin. Too valuable a source to pass up. Caleb looked at her and she agreed, but wondered what she'd got herself into as his friend gave a whoop and draped an arm around both their shoulders.

"Does this girl have any idea who she's going out with?"

"I'm a colleague only," said Fee automatically.

"Friend," corrected Caleb, "for now."

Which was no help at all.

By club three—or was it four—Fee had stopped worrying. She also discovered that Caleb could dance, rather well as it happened, as his body naturally moved with hers.

By club five, she'd moved on to blissful unconcern and was raising her voice in song.

Caleb stopped his own singing and peered down at her. "You do know you can't sing?"

"And you can." Beautifully, in fact, a low, smooth baritone rumbling through her.

By club six, she was warbling along with him again, the crowd had thinned and even their oldest friends were making noises about finishing the evening. Fee glanced down at the drink in her hand. It was pink and green.

"These are good," she decided.

Caleb's face was somewhere above her. She leaned back against the arm that held her, and discovered something else. "You have a nice smile. When you're not being—you."

"Thank you. Yours—is dangerous."

She lifted her glass to take another sip. He was still smiling at her, and she thought she might come to rather like it.

"You're going to pay for that in the morning. What is that stuff?"

She studied the glass. "Don't know, but it's good."

"Time we got you home, I think." He gently took the glass from her hand and hauled her up from her seat. She tugged, and turned to face the others seated near them. Her mother had made sure all her family knew the importance of good manners, that she did remember. "G'night all."

Caleb chuckled. "They're all strangers. We're the last to leave. C'mon, Sleepy Beauty."

"Not sleepy."

"Not a good idea to tell me that."

That, she really couldn't figure out. Then gave up and decided to just enjoy the very large, very warm body holding her tight. He unlocked their door, bowing with a flourish for her to enter, and waved a small card triumphantly in her face.

She frowned.

"That blonde girl's address?"

"No, my little mountain beauty. Even better—a sensor disruptor." He slapped the card against the wall and punched in a code. "The Survey's sensors can't get through these, according to my source."

She looked at the innocuous card. "You sure about that?"

Caleb grinned. "Had it from a friend right in the heart of the geek squad. The Survey has been trying to crack them since they started appearing on the streets."

It all sounded too easy.

"No frowns. You're so beautiful when you smile."

Her mouth dropped open and she gawped up at him. Maybe she did need another drink. He gave her that smile again, and this time she was absolutely sure. She also realised that she liked Caleb Winter's smile very much. His head dipped, and his lips caught hers and that she really liked. Within a very short space of time, he'd kissed her into deciding that it really didn't matter if the card worked. Nothing outside mattered, and certainly not what might happen after tonight.

He opened the bedroom door, carrying her while kissing her into oblivion, and whispered in her ear, "This is between us. I will not let the Survey force us into anything."

Then they were beyond discussion.

Next morning was another matter. She woke to a single, weak strand of sunlight playing on her face and a strong arm holding her. She stretched, feeling the delight of the night in newly awakened muscles, and a smile tickled her lips. Fee and Caleb; yes, they were very good together.

She turned, and saw his warm eyes turned on her, and an answering smile bringing his face to life.

"Good morning, Sera den Coille."

"And a fine one to you, Ser Winter."

They must look like a pair of loonies, grinning idiotically at each other. But then she tried sitting up, and didn't know whether to clutch her head or her stomach. "What was in that stuff I was drinking last night?"

He grinned. No sympathy at all. She lifted her pillow in threat, at which he too sat up and the malicious side of her took great pleasure in his wince.

He grimaced. "They usually keep something in the bathroom cabinets."

She fell back, praying for the room to stay in one place as he swung his legs over the edge of the bed, creating a thoroughly disturbing wave of motion.

"Medicate, clean and eat. That usually works best."

Did he have to sound so positive?

She waited for Caleb to take the bathroom before levering herself out of bed.

It took two stim tabs and a full heat cleansing to bring her near to human again. Breakfast was a silent meal but not because there was nothing to be said. Once done, she shoved back her chair.

"Some dask? She pulled out two cups, poured them both and picked hers up, the bitter, familiar smell both desperately needed and acridly nauseating to her abused insides. "I need fresh air," she muttered.

It was even more miserable outside than on the previous day. She huddled into the warmth of her jacket, hands cupped around the hot cup, letting her head recover. To anyone seeing the pair of them out here, in weather that any sensible Urbanite knew to avoid, they looked like a pair of out-of-towners taking in the view. Urbis was the largest city on Arcadia and it was some view, she admitted—if you liked cities. She stared at the towers and man-made mountains of habitation, letting her eyes track the traffic busily sifting through the buildings around them. They were in the privacy layer here, above the allowed routes and therefore free from interruption, but she still felt hemmed in. A huge urban clutter, filled with people and things. Pressing in on her, demanding she surrender.

Caleb leaned on the rail beside her, gazing out at the view as well, but she could feel the tension in his muscles when his arm touched her, and he dropped his head down close to hers before speaking.

"You remember much of last night's talk?"

She tilted her head towards him. "I wasn't that far gone." A snort of disbelief she sensibly ignored. "It's bad out there, and getting worse."

No humour from him now. "You picked it up too?"

"What?"

She needed to hear him say the word.

"Fear."

Yes. The word she couldn't say but it had overlaid every piece of idle chatter and acerbic quip. "Your friend from up high?"

"Full of it. More than the front line. Rank and file Central staff are the most scared. As if they know something, and it's not good."

She gripped the mug tighter, tipped it up and swallowed it down, welcoming the burn of hot liquid in her throat. Then slammed it onto the small table and hugged herself hard. "I need more information."

Caleb looked like she felt; too suddenly, stone cold sober. "You think we'll get it?"

She nodded slowly. "If this is important enough, yes. I think we will get anything we care to demand—except freedom."

She kicked against the parapet, frustration and rage boiling inside her. A ping on her com-unit, and one on Caleb's.

His mouth stretched in a grim caricature of a smile.

"Seems you're right."

She looked down. Fox: *My office, one hour.*

Sometimes, being right was not a gift.

CHAPTER SEVENTEEN

At Fox's office, Fee reached for the door buzzer, but Caleb caught her hand.

"He knows we're here."

He slapped his palm against the pad and walked in before the door had fully opened.

She wished she could do the same, shoving her anger outwards. How could the Survey think them compatible? They might know about last night, but that proved nothing.

And the night in the tent?

Chemistry. Physical attraction, that's all it was. The man had tried to intimidate her since the day they had met, and made no secret that he resented her intrusion into his world.

While you made quite sure he couldn't stay in yours when you used him to authenticate a scam disease outbreak in the target gully. The scam had been needed to keep her father away from their project site, but it didn't change the facts. She had lied to her family.

So she was no better than Caleb. But that was no basis for *marriage.*

What about the survival of their world?

Fox made no move to rise, despite their eruption into his office. He sat back, that same closed look on his face as always, as Fee took one chair and Caleb grabbed the other, switched it round to straddle it, arms flung over the back rest as he leaned forward in challenge.

Fee could have told him not to bother, except that Caleb knew their boss as well as her.

"You have contacted your teams?"

Fee nodded. "Just before coming over."

"The projects?"

"Would go better if both of us were there to do our job—Sir," snapped Caleb.

"My family?" asked Fee.

"You haven't spoken to them?"

She shuffled under that bland look of query. "It seemed best to leave it to the Survey." It was a more diplomatic answer than: *Not likely, not when I have no idea what you and the Survey are up to—Sir.* No, that would not have gone down at all well.

A smile hovered on their boss' face. "I hear you both had a pleasurable evening."

Caleb crashed up, swinging the chair the right way around and slammed it down again. He leaned over the desk, more furious than Fee had ever seen him.

"Cards on the table, *Sir.* Why is the Survey so hell bent on getting the two of us together?'

For a minute, Fee thought Fox was going to deny it. Something nasty clogged the back of her mouth. "All those years ago, back at college. We were deliberately targeted?"

Fox stared back, no change in his face. "Were you fast tracked through your degrees? No. They are bona fide reflections of your abilities and knowledge."

Caleb growled. "We're good at what we do, Fee. Don't let anyone tell you different."

Good of him to say it. But a tiny seed of doubt had been planted and she couldn't stop it growing.

Caleb glared at Fox. "Were we targeted?"

"The eldest son of Sol Winter and a daughter of Bram den Coille? Of course you were. This is no game."

"And the plan to disrupt both corporates by having us marry, with all the conflict that would cause?"

Fee let Caleb do the talking, her brain and tongue frozen. How good was she? What was the truth of what she'd believed about her place in the Survey?

All the while, Fox kept silent, watching them. *Studying us as if we're lab rats.* At the end, he leaned back, folding both hands over his stomach.

"So when was this latest version of the plan dreamt up?" said Caleb.

"The plan to alter your home regions? Some time ago. As you've no doubt guessed, your regions are important for a number of reasons."

Caleb grunted, voicing Fee's thought. It matched what they had discussed already. The growing imbalance of the plains and mountain climates was starting to threaten Urbis.

"Having you two lead it? You're both top in your fields. Your project work alone earned you your current seniority. But did we think it an absolute gift to have eco-engineers with your family background willing to work for us? Of course we did. You think the Survey can afford to ignore any possible advantage?"

Fee shuffled and even Caleb eased back. Fox was actually going to be open with them.

"An Alliance inspection team came to Arcadia last year. A routine audit of the developmental progress of this world, they said."

Fee was absolutely still now. Alliance. The distant, rarely seen ruling body of all the human worlds. The Alliance had paid for the eco-engineering of this world all those generations ago, and still enforced the ecological regime governing development of the member worlds. They held the final authority when anything threatened the whole body of human settled planets, and a stream of refugees from a failed planet definitely fit their brief.

There was a slight tic in Fox's eye. A rare sign of tension that made her feel no better.

"The outcome of the audit was not favourable," he said.

"What do you mean?"

"You both know the situation here is worsening?"

Fee nodded. Caleb growled. "Yeah, it has to be stopped."

"Exactly," said Fox. "It has to be stopped. The Alliance authorities have given us a deadline. Two years to show significant change and prove the Arcadian government can take charge to reverse the degradation, or …"

She waited, breath stilled. Caleb tensed.

"Or?"

"They will forcibly evacuate this planet, bring in their own eco-engineers to restore the balance and re-settle Arcadia with new immigrants. No Arcadian would be allowed back."

"Can they do that?"

Caleb grunted. "Their fleets swamp anything we could put up."

Fox agreed. "They can, and have."

"So we make it public; get the rest of Arcadia on side to help us fix things."

Caleb went still and the tic on Fox's face worsened. "We tried that, years ago," he said.

"It didn't work at that time, agreed, but it might now."

"Policy has examined all options and the matter has been fully discussed with government."

"They don't believe the Alliance will do it," guessed Fee.

An abrupt dip of his head was Fox's only answer, but his silence said it all.

"But who was at that meeting, and how much did they know?" said Caleb now.

She'd never seen Fox so stiff, so much the face of bureaucracy. "Appropriate officials from the Survey and government."

"So not a single eco-engineer? No one with any idea what the facts mean." His fist crashed down on the table. She envied him, wished she had the power in her arm to smash it to pieces. The Alliance didn't bluff.

"The decision has been made," said Fox.

Was there an alternative? Fee still had no idea when they finally got to walk out of Fox's office. A week. That was all he gave them. A week to decide their answer. So far she'd been able to ignore the question, but Fox had put an end to that.

Caleb marched beside her, head hunched, with not a word to her all the way from headquarters to their room. She had made love with this man last night but had no idea what he was thinking now.

Marriage. Economic union with the Winters—that's what the Survey was asking of them. Maybe if she kept it at that level, she could *deal* with it.

Deal with it. The same words Caleb had used back on the balcony of her home, but there had been nothing passionless in him that night.

Admit it, you're attracted to each other.

A tame way to describe what lay between them. Last night and the night in the desert—attraction was far too bland, too clinical a label. Yet if this marriage must happen, their mutual *attraction* was a good thing. Wasn't it?

Beyond that, they worked well together. She was good at what she did and so was he, but together, they were better. No false modesty there. She had enough successful projects on her file to know when a partnership worked well. Projects paid for by her work for Den Coille: the water scheme, the hydro dam projects, and others. Unfinished plans only when she could get her father to accept that was all she could do, but too many others had extended the range of festia on the western slopes. They had disguised her true goals from her family, got her family to agree to release her for Survey work, but did that justify what she'd done? Worsening the environmental situation even as she fought hard to conclude projects elsewhere to save it?

She had sold her soul so many times for the Survey. Why did this feel like once too many?

They rode in silence up to their room level. She looked sideways at Caleb and discovered he was likewise studying her. For long minutes they held each other's gaze, but it seemed he was no more ready to speak than she.

They walked into their room, and she went immediately to her bag, taking precious time in the small routines of stowing her gloves and removing the coat she'd worn outdoors.

Caleb roamed the apartment, jacket flung over the nearest seat, and looking anywhere but at her.

The worst of their new reality suddenly hit her. "What if we have children?"

"If?" He stopped the relentless pacing to glare at her, then flung himself into a chair. "The Survey is counting on it."

"But…" She gulped, forced herself to sit. "I've bartered my conscience enough times in the past."

"But to sell your own children as political weapons?"

She was beginning to learn to read him. That deliberately insolent pose, the slight tightening about his mouth, the bitter edge to his voice. He felt as sick as she did.

"Why do we do this, if not for our children and their children? And no matter what we do, there's a storm coming."

"Yeah, the mistakes have gone too far. We can only stop the worst of it. But our children should have seen a better world."

"Should?" Now it was her turn to pace the room. "You think that's an option? Go through with this charade but stay childless?"

Grief enveloped her, shocking in its intensity. An image came suddenly of a young man, tall and lean with all the bright joy of adolescence. Hair tawny in the sun, and with that sparc walk of the man opposite, yet touched with the lilting flexibility of the mountains. A boy with his father's bones and her dark eyes laughing at her like her brothers had when she was little and told to hide their latest escapade.

That boy was never to be born?

"No."

"You have a better idea?"

No, but it changed nothing. It was elemental, a denial that came from so deep inside her she could not gainsay it. "No," she repeated.

"You want a child? With me?"

She couldn't acknowledge it out loud. Could only dip her head ever so slightly.

"How would you keep it safe? Keep them safe?"

The cold edge to his voice slashed through any romantic dream, yet she could not take back her denial. "*If* we marry," she said.

He looked at her as if she had some brain cells missing. This from the man who couldn't get enough of her last night. "You actually believe we have a choice?"

"Fox promised. A week, he said."

He waved that away. "Not Fox. I meant this screwed up home of ours. Arcadia. It's too far gone."

He spoke as if to a child—or someone paralysed by shock. It might be true, but it was also an insult. She picked up a cushion and hurled it at the grey drizzle seen through the outside window. "Does it never stop raining here?"

"You like rain."

"Don't humour me. I like *my* rain, mist on green trees and flowers. Not constant grey drizzle on miserable blocks of buildings."

Caleb watched her give in to the fit of temper.

A child? She would bring a child into this mess? He would give the Survey almost anything, but not his child's future.

His father had tried to do that with his sons, and looked to be succeeding with Ethan and Si. But not with him, and nor would the Survey with a child of his.

Not even if this woman was the mother? Grief ate into the fine bones of her face and he felt the echoing blow of it inside him. Grief for the loss of a purely imaginary child? That was not practical, not sensible, not *rational*.

He reached out and pulled her in close before thought or reason could stop him, one hand stroking down and down her back.

"We will find our way through this."

How, he had no idea. All he did know was where they must go. Where there was a chance this would all make sense. "We're going home."

That night, he let her prepare for bed first, ready to take the couch. She climbed in, turned down his side of the quilt and waited for him to join her, dark eyes steady.

He let go the breath he hadn't realised he was holding.

They came together in silence, and in silence they lay till long after. Eventually, her soft breathing told him that sleep had claimed her, and not long after, he also succumbed. All he knew when he woke was that sleep had robbed him of hours that would never return, hours when he could have looked his fill of her, like now. She had become embedded in him so quickly, yet he was still no closer to understanding her. Why did she want a child so badly? Why, when she knew it would be no more than a tool to their Survey bosses?

Fee looked out at the mountains and took a deep breath. Then more. Deep, soul-filling breaths of the air of home.

Their flyer came in low, skimming down the eastern side of the ranges, all the time keeping to a non-threatening slow sweep. Her father's techs were becoming disturbingly skilled and increasingly trigger-happy, and their flight path stayed well away from any sensitive area even though the Survey flyer was modified to mimic the signature of local craft.

She still scanned the slopes below for trouble, not realising how tightly her hands were clenched till Caleb prised one off the armrests of her chair and forced her to take a drink. She gulped it down to appease him, spluttering as a fiery burn hit the back of her throat.

"What in hell is that?"

"Mother's ruin, we call it. Helps to relax you."

"Thank you," she managed to croak, "but I am fine."

"Suit yourself." He took back the cup and downed the noisome brew in one cheery swallow. She refused to acknowledge the twitch of his lips, and turned back to scanning the land below.

They were coming over the brow of the North gully, over the site of her team's project. She gasped. So much change, so much achieved by her team without her.

Caleb leaned forward and peered down.

"Impressive."

It certainly was. The festia were gone, and near the waterfall a series of puddle-shaped clearings showed signs of levelling and replanting. In a few weeks, the first tender shoots of meadow grasses would show up as emerald green splashes. Farther up, the replanting of trees had begun. Spindly and small yet, but alive, the baby trees thrust their heads upwards through a jumble of twigs, discarded festia wood and burgeoning undergrowth.

It was raw hillside, a scabbed breach of the once-heavy forest cover, yet already a pattern was emerging, new intersections of plant, animal, air and soil in the reformed zone. A promise of what must come into being over the whole western side of the ranges if balance was to be restored.

Eyes never leaving the ground, she called to the pilot, "Put us down above the falls, in that fallow section just above the top proto-meadow."

A chuckle from Caleb. "She means the flat bit by the round rock, just above the top patch of dirt."

"Thanks, mate," said the pilot. "Eco-speak isn't in the flyboy manual."

Fee briefly glared at Caleb then switched back to soak in the view of the gulley. The ground was coming up fast and excitement bubbled through her.

They touched dirt and she thrust off her belts and scrambled out, just as her team came surging out from the undergrowth. Seamach was in front and she hurled herself at him, laughing and pounding him on his back.

"You guys. It's wonderful."

She couldn't stop the tears. After the last week, all the intrigue and political games, to see this was extraordinary. *This* was what she was.

"It's beautiful."

Seamach laughed. "If you think that, the plains have robbed you of your eyes and nose."

"All right. *Will* be beautiful." She was choking back tears, and felt a now familiar arm curl around her shoulders, then release her.

"Looking good," was Caleb's gruff comment to Seamach.

Seamach stared, a question in his eyes. She shook her head. "Later," he said, the tone of voice making quite clear he meant to find out what was going on. She gave a short nod of her head and turned to greet the others before walking down to the first meadow, the team beside her bringing her up to date on their work.

Once there, she crouched down and let her fingers trail through the newly turned earth. "You managed to get all the seed types?"

"Uh huh. Brought them in as bird feed for that menagerie of Fridha's."

She stretched up and tried to imagine the final meadow. She had seen the holo-simulation of it but holos weren't the same as the real thing. A wave of grasses and flowering herbs, a balanced mix of cool temperate, high rainfall meadow plants was the formal description, but what that would look and feel like was hard to picture. It was too new to her forest world. Too new, too many changes turning her world upside down. Suddenly overwhelmed, she took off down the slope, too overcome to take care for the rough ground and hidden traps. Branches and newly-turned clods waiting to trip the unwary. She stumbled but ignored the pain, desperate to reach the new planting.

Another fall, and this time a large hand lifted her up. "Slow down before you break something—again," Caleb growled.

She muttered a "Thank you", brushed off her legs and twitched away from his imprisoning hands. He dropped his arms and stepped back.

"I need to feel the trees." As an apology, it wasn't much but it was all she could give him. She slowed her steps and watched the ground. He matched her, pace by pace, but made no attempt to hold her again.

Finally she was at the new plantings and could run the silky fronds of the tiny seedlings through her fingers. Trees, her trees would come back. This one was a baullnia, the leaves just unfurling, the single trunk that would grow to a mighty, multi-crowned spread less than a finger width still. But the promise was there and if she shut her eyes and concentrated on the feel of the leaf, she could see it. See what would be, not the raw scar of what was.

Caleb gave her ten minutes. He had seen the shock, felt the grief in her. He too, knew what it was to face the truth of what they did. One day soon, water would cover the dry plains of his birth. Yet they had hard choices to make and two Survey teams to lead; teams hurting as much as they were. He stepped in close, one booted foot almost touching the tree she knelt beside.

"Planting's going well here. Time to move to the next phase."

Seamach had come down the hill, the rest of her team close behind. No chance of hiding the effect of his words on Fee. Luckily no one carried weapons these days, though the garden fork Kebhyn carried looked distinctly threatening. He waited, tense and ready for one wrong move. What happened next was up to Fee.

She slowly straightened, her back to her team. Took a deep breath, that stunned look forced back behind a bland mask. If he hadn't seen the open grief, he would never have guessed her true feelings.

He knew the effort it cost to shove that half-smile on her face, before turning to face her team. "You have done wonders here. Caleb's right. We're ready to begin Phase Two."

For long minutes, the outcome lay in the balance. She stood firm and stared her team down. Till Seamach gave a nod, and the others followed.

"The control room is just over the brow," he said.

Fee nodded back. "Good. Time for dask, followed by a strategy meeting." She turned to the silent girl standing at the back. "Caerthida, don't suppose you've been baking?"

"Yes. It is useful stress release," said the woman, only to be jostled by another, similar looking girl. The zoologist Fridha, if Caleb remembered rightly, a cousin of the literal minded Caerthida but not in the least as socially impaired.

"Course she has. Soon as we heard you were on your way," said Fridha. "And Joseph has a pile of your favourite fruit waiting. Kebhyn even gave up some of those new tubers he's been developing for wet climates."

Fee laughed beside him, and it sounded genuine. "So lunch first, then a meeting."

It broke the tension, and the rest jostled in, all talking as they headed up. He followed silently behind, watching each one of them in turn.

Seamach dropped back to walk beside him. "You had a good reason for what you just did to our Fioruisghe, plainsman?" A heavy arm fell across Caleb's shoulder and he wasn't stupid enough to think it benign. Not when the rough fingers found the critical points on his neck. Basic self defence was part of all Survey ops' training. This man was beyond basic, an expert who could easily incapacitate him in a split instant.

"You ever hurt her like that again and you answer to me," the man said.

They stayed in the gulley two hectic days, he and Fee having to cram in as much as they could. The mantra drummed into them in training was proven over and over. *Specialists in none; master of all.* It was the unique strength of an eco-engineer: providing the overall guidance to bring a project to completion. Pulling together all the disparate strands of work by their team's specialists to bring about change. Despite the tension and Seamach's ever-watchful presence, he discovered again how well he and Fee worked together. It wasn't merely that their particular skills were complementary. It was the instinctive understanding, the unspoken way they each picked up the other's intent and moved it forward.

He had worked with other eco-engineers but never quite like this. By the end of the second day, the ease of their working partnership had spread to the rest of the team. They even pulled him into their discussions, as if forgetting he was not of the mountains.

But never Seamach. The big man was jovial, hearty even, yet Caleb did not forget the feel of those steely fingers on the back of his neck.

Don't hurt her, or you answer to me.

Except hurting Fee was exactly what Caleb must do.

CHAPTER EIGHTEEN

The Survey ship arrived to take them on to the plains. Caleb stepped forward, urgent to escape this wet place. Then halted, shaken by the bitter reality of his first, undeniable response. If he and Fee married, where could they live? His home was on the plains; his heart's blood came from there. Not here in this place where the sun must fight to break through the banked-up clouds and moisture oozed from every surface.

They waited for the ship to land in a cleared patch that barely held back the forest. Dank, engulfing, a constant odour of dead leaves and wet mud. A warning to any underestimating the power of the trees.

Fee stared at the trees too, but her face told a different story. Love, longing and grief lodged in those dark eyes of hers. This was her home; her body that of someone about to step into exile with little hope of return.

He stood to one side as Fee said goodbye to each member of her team. Cheery hugs and false promises of "See you soon". Next the usually restrained Caerthida stepped forward and hugged Fee hard, tears in her eyes. Fee hugged her back.

She was going to break. He saw it in the tight lines of her shoulders and the tension in that beautiful body. He stepped forward, sweeping a hand around her shoulders and shoving on a smile as false as her words to her team.

"Don't worry. It won't be for long. I'll keep her safe." He thrust out a hand, forcing Caerthida to release Fee as she shook hands with him. The distaste on the geologist's face was clear, but she said nothing.

She wouldn't, of course. Caerthida was Survey, as was all the team. Underneath their mountain ways, they shared the same knowledge and loyalty as him. The Survey had to win this fight or their world would be lost.

Seamach was the last to farewell Fee. A hearty hug as he frogmarched her into the flyer.

"Go teach those plainsmen to make water," he said gruffly.

Caleb was about to follow when the big security man's hand on his shoulder stopped him.

"Remember, plainsman," he said softly.

Caleb halted, watching the slim backside in front of him. He nodded curtly at Seamach. "I hear you." Then shook off the hand and stepped into the flyer.

Fee looked out the window as the forest disappeared beneath her. Each lost tree, each fold of hill disappearing from sight tore her in two. She clung to the view out the window, greedy for every last minute of home. The flyer lifted, climbing the slopes well away from den Coille flight paths. Too soon, they were over the ridge lines and beginning the descent to the plains.

She kept her eyes on the view, not ready to talk to Caleb. Seamach had said something to him as he stepped into the flyer.

She didn't know what, but knowing the two men, it wasn't hard to guess the subject.

Caleb's problem for now.

To distract herself, she took to studying the plant life on the slopes below, noting the differences from her western side of the ranges. Hiding in the protection of the deep gullies, patches of baullnia flourished along with the odd festia, but they were rare. The change in climate was too abrupt from west to east, the ridge line above an absolute divide. What water remained in the clouds fell on the eastern slopes in fiery torrents that scoured hillsides as the cold clouds hit the furnace blasts from the plains. The slopes below carried the toll. Shingle slides covered whole mountainsides; the only vegetation, rugged grasses and tough shrubs.

For the upper slopes, that was normal; the inherent ecosystem that had always held sway there. Not so the lower ones. Caleb's holo-maps had shown the truth. Historically, they had been covered with forests similar to those on the western side. Not as lush, the species slightly different, but certainly not these barren slopes of scruffy grasses and prickly thorns amid the scars of gravel deluges.

Some had been caused by settlers clearing the slopes, but the violent weather patterns now prevailing had finished them off.

Weather patterns that were spilling over to her home on the western slopes.

They levelled out as they headed over the plains and she took a deep breath, turned and met the gaze of her—*colleague,* was the safest she could come up with.

"How long till we make the lake site?"

He stared back, hooding his eyes and stretching out those long legs. "An hour till B; half an hour more to A."

She crossed her arms defensively and caught a quick twist of his lips, as abruptly gone. Irritation, anger, pain? And she'd thought she was beginning to be able to read him? He frowned and the man who had woken her to delight in the morning was banished. The plainsman was back.

"My father and his men haven't been told we are coming." he said.

She nodded curtly.

"And your father?"

"My team can keep secrets," she told him.

This time, it was definitely a twitch of irritation. "Is he still threatening the plains with action if he can't find you? I'm not on Seamach's *need-to-know* list."

"Not for now." The Survey had told her family she'd been called away on urgent business. Seamach reckoned Da wasn't stupid enough to believe them, but for now he was waiting. "He still has his men on standby."

"Should I warn my father?'

"Only if you want all-out war." She saw the suspicion bloom in his eyes. "I am den Coille, yes, but I'm Survey first."

"And will not let them hurt your family."

"No." She clenched her fists, her nails cutting into her palms. "But my definition of hurt is not the same as my family's."

He choked, and to her astonishment, bent over and gave himself up to a deep belly laugh. It was raw, harsh and honest. Finally the hacks of mirth slowed to deep breaths, morphing into a slow chuckle, and for the first time he fully met her gaze.

"That, Sera den Coille, is the best description of this mess I've heard yet."

Her lover was back, and for an instant Fee allowed herself to hope. She lifted her shoulders cheekily and smiled. "So fill me in on progress. You know all about my site."

"Because I asked," he said dryly

She squirmed, the moment too suddenly lost. A big hand fell on her knee, gentling her to be still. "That wasn't criticism. It was an invitation."

"Didn't feel like it."

"Sometimes, Sera den Coille …"

"And if you call me that again…"

He looked down at her, one brow lifting. "I can never figure out if you're spoiled, or hard done by. Something must have made you so damn prickly."

She tried to pull her leg away, but his hand clamped down, fingers smoothing over the mound of her knee. She glanced down at it, frowning, and up to meet his eyes.

"You do know how many brothers I have, not forgetting my sister? Spoiling wasn't on offer when we were little."

"Maybe, but you are well loved. I've felt your brothers' eyes between my shoulder blades." Okay, so that she could not deny. "As for your mother and father, I'm not sure which is the more dangerous. That prison cell did not feel like a welcome."

Guilt slapped at her, and she felt the blush rise in her cheeks. "I got you out of there."

"For which, *Sera* den Coille, I am heartily grateful."

She lifted her hand to thump him for that one, and he caught it effortlessly, chuckling anew. "Stop spitting at me and come over here."

Before she could stop him, he'd unclipped her harness, lifted her over and settled her in the seat beside his, clipped the belts tight again and pulled her gently into his side.

She did not complain, all her fight and fear suddenly gone. What had he said? An hour to the first lake site. That was one hour before they had to worry, one hour before they would be watched, one hour before she had to decide anything. She set her head on his shoulder.

"So show me what's so special about this dried-up land of yours."

By the time they made it to Site B, she was laughing too hard to fear anything. Each blade of grass and empty creek bed harboured a story of the man beside her and his misbegotten youth. She almost felt sorry for Sol and Helena Winter.

As the lake site came into view, she reached for the window, eager for that first glimpse.

Piles of dirt, the beetle-like scurrying of people moving below, and—the undeniable sparkle of water.

She lurched forward, and banged her head on the window. "Ouch."

Caleb chuckled and hauled her back to safety.

"It's so full!" She thrust a finger against the window. "I've seen your updates, but this. What your team has done here!"

Landing was a chaos of back slaps, shouts of hello and crowding around Caleb. She hung back, reluctant to spoil the moment, but Caleb grabbed her hand and dragged her into the melee. Together, they were shown how far the team had come, how those rough and sketchy plans she and Caleb had drawn up to enhance the dam were coming to fullness, and the changes the team had made. She stepped over to look at a channel leading into a small side pond, and listened to the hydrologist explain how they planned to use the pool and plantings around it as a trial filter for the runoff from the mineral-laden hills.

"For when the rains get regular here," the man said. She looked up in surprise at the eagerness in his voice. "My boy loves to grow things. With a bit more rain hereabouts he could become a crop farmer. Maybe some of those new shrubs young Matty is developing, or those grains of his made to suit this area."

"You don't mind the changes?"

"Not if it gives my family more choices for a life here. Always thought I would have to lose that boy of mine to the wetter lands up north. Now, who knows?"

There was a huge smile on the man's face.

"This is very clever," she said, one arm taking in the channel and the pond, "and it will look so pretty."

The man positively glowed under her praise. She watched him move away. He had really valued what she thought of his work.

Maybe, just maybe, there *was* a place for her on the plains.

They stayed an hour before heading on to the main site under full communication silence.

"Take the southern approach," Caleb ordered the pilot. "Patch through to Bob for the coordinates. It's the least watched by Solaris bots," he explained

"Are we ready to start filling again?"

He nodded slowly. "Soon as it becomes possible. The Old Man's too suspicious for us to risk it yet."

"A big hole in the ground doesn't look suspicious?"

Caleb touched a hand to her cheek and grinned. "Not when it looks like flood banks and a barrier to keep the stock from destroying Council Rock creek."

"He bought that?"

"Partly. It will do till something bigger takes his attention."

The dryness in his voice said it all. She clutched her fingers, tracing the bare skin where a ring would sit. "Oh."

His hand dropped away. "Yes, that. Or a visit from your father."

She squared her shoulders and forced herself to look up

"And the Survey?"

"Has its lawyers on standby to slap a protection order on as soon as the water gets above the three metre mark deep. This is technically public reserve land, even if Winters have run it for more years than anyone can remember."

There was a big flaw in that argument; Sol Winter. She pictured the man, the hard resolve in his eyes echoed in his son sitting opposite.

"The courts are a long way from here."

"Maybe, but hopefully they'll hold him long enough to start the planting and spread the word among the locals."

"That they can have a future where they choose what they want to do? They don't have to be trapped into working on a Solaris solar farm."

That struck home, too personal to a Winter son. A flash of anger in his eyes and a chill as his face closed over, taking on the mask of professionalism. The man was having to betray his father, his brothers, his mother; his family's whole way of life. *As are you.*

The words had to be said though. If they didn't make the change now, someone else was going to make it for them. The

Alliance wasn't about to pander to the likes of Sol Winter—or Bram den Coille.

An old phrase came to mind. *Gird your loins*—and that, my girl, suits this situation exactly. In more ways than one. A particularly luscious memory of their nights in the big city suddenly came to mind and she had to fight the urge to grin smugly. It lit her insides and gave her back her courage. Those nights in the city had been a shared pleasure, in full and equal partnership.

There are two professionals here, Mr Caleb Winter, and I bet my grades were as good as yours. The Survey grabbed me even though I'm a younger daughter. While you—the oldest and strongest willed of the Winter sons? You were always a target.

What she did was plaster on her sweetest, most patronising smile. "Time to fill me in on what's been happening here. The real word from your people, not the official version in the reports you sent to Central."

It set him back, she was pleased to see. Did he think he could shut her down so easily? Though she had to give him points for a quick recovery, as for the rest of the trip he blandly outlined what his people had told him so far.

It sounded good, almost too good. As they neared the main lake site, she leaned against the window, eager to see the truth of his words.

The first bank came up. A curving line of natural seeming hillocks rising from the dry desert land in a smudge of rock and new grasses. They lifted higher, moved out over the new earthworks.

There was the Council Rock, displaced still by the catastrophic action of the Solaris men and lurching drunkenly in mid-stream in accusatory disarray. But for the rest of it, she was too close to see the full extent, to understand the whole.

"Take us higher, please."

Caleb signalled to the pilot and they lifted upwards. The sky had that unending clarity she associated with the desert. No misty drizzle to hide the emerging lines below.

"That's it." She waved at the pilot to stop, and they hovered overhead. Now the curving lines made sense.

The earthworks roughly followed the creek bed, but with her eco-engineer's eye, Fee recognised the illusion. These were embankments, built to hold in rising waters. The plains were not exactly flat and from up here she could see how the new banks worked to enhance the natural folds and hollows, enclosing a large, meandering depression in the middle.

She had seen the figures, seen the schemata and the cross-sectional plans, but only now did it all come to life. It was almost complete, the channelling earthworks in the bed only needed.

"Your rock will lie deeper than ever." Then gasped at her lack of tact, and looked around guiltily. Was that a twitch of his mouth? A fleeting crack in that irritating mask of his?

She looked closely at the dry ground and the new piles of rock and dirt. "What your team has done here, it's amazing. But stop banks for flood protection? How did you get your father to buy that one?"

The first crack, a real smile on that austere face, and maybe the man she had made love to had not totally vanished. "Haven't you read your background files? Floods here are rare, but can spread for kilometres. These banks fool my father and his men because they look the same as the banks already built around many of our dry rivers."

Which just proved that you can't beat local knowledge. She had seen that part of the report, including images of similar flood protection schemes, but to see it in place was another matter. Yet Sol Winter was not a man easily fooled, even by this.

"No one asked why there's no gap in the banks for the creek's outflow?"

The man who had played games with her in that city bed was definitely back. A smug grin and laughing eyes. "But there is. Look north."

She did as ordered, craning her neck to follow the lines of the creek bed to where the faint line of it disappeared in to the dry soil, and saw a shallow cleft in the surrounding hillocks. "One small explosion could seal that easily."

Caleb's grin widened. "Exactly, and will do so if the rising waters threaten the lands lying beyond it."

"Your father bought that one too?"

"It happens to be true."

She crossed her arms. "So you're fine with this now? No qualms about burying your council rock under metres of water?"

Just like that, the grin vanished and the mask was back. "There is no other choice."

"And us?"

But they were landing, and surrounded by his team, all wanting to talk or show him the latest site plans and diggings.

The eco-engineer Kal was in charge, his earlier attitude unchanged and some of what he reported had Fee decidedly worried. After the third time she asked him a question and he replied to Caleb, pointedly ignoring her and staring well above her head, she thrust herself to the front and glared at Kal.

"Caleb isn't the one who knows about water usage. *I* am. Kindly tell me exactly what flow patterns you have in place here. I set guiding structures into the plans, and from what I can see, they've been completely ignored."

"Dunno what she's talking about," he said to Caleb.

It was the final insult. "Of course you don't. It's not your area of expertise. But it is *mine*. Thanks to the ham-fisted blunderings of Solaris when it blew up the last lake, as soon as we start filling the water is going to pour into this lake far faster than we planned. A rush that will scour out the underside of those banks of yours quick smart, and you'll really have a flood on your hands."

She swung round on Caleb. "Did you know about this?"

He studied her face, then his plains eco-engineer's. "Kal told me you cleared the changes," he said to her. "They were a problem for us. Too artificial and no reason to be there for flood protection. My father is not stupid."

She flushed, but was not pacified. "I never thought he was, but those channels are essential to control the rate and direction of filling. I wouldn't have put them in if they weren't important."

For long moments it hung in the balance as he stared at her. Until, still holding her gaze, he said. "You heard the lady, Kal."

He began to walk off but after a couple of paces stopped and turned slowly back. "That's the last lie you tell me, Kal. Do it again, and you're on the first transporter out of here."

Then he was walking away; slow, deliberate and at a pace, she belatedly realised, that she didn't have to look like a hopping idiot to keep up with. A deep breath, a swallow of ruffled pride, and she paced as deliberately beside him.

"That going to be a problem?" she said with a slight tilt back to where the other eco-engineer stood glaring at her.

"Yep," Caleb Winter said, a bite in his quiet voice. "Believe it or not, the man is good at what he does."

She hadn't doubted that; the whole team was. "And?"

"He's a third cousin by marriage to me, and related to most of the others."

"Oh."

It was a factor she hadn't built in, that the plains team were family in the truest sense. It shouldn't have surprised her. Half her own team were some kind of distant cousin either to her or to friends of hers. But they were on a deadline. Fox had given them a week only to make a decision.

"Won't make any announcement from us easy."

"No," said Caleb Winter in that abrupt manner of his.

Silence fell, awkward and loaded, as they walked across to the site control centre.

"Maybe if we wait till just before filling to build the channels. That would cut down the risk," she finally said.

Caleb kept walking but turned to give her that slow regard of his. "It'll help. Doesn't change that he lied."

No. Nothing would change that. Caleb Winter was not a man who trusted readily. That he believed her over Kal—it meant a lot. But it also broke something with the rest of his team.

What would he decide; how much was he prepared to lose to save Arcadia?

And you?

She plodded gloomily beside Caleb.

CHAPTER NINETEEN

Ben was the first of the crew to spot them as they came over the rise into the main camp and climbed out of the skimmer. "Hey, it's the boss and our mountain lady. Had enough of skiving off in the big city and come back to do some real work?"

Old Jim came out of the main hall behind him and scuffed the young zoologist on the head. "There's a reason they don't send young fools like you up to Central. No telling what you'd say."

Adam, the hydrogeologist, came up on his other side and ruffled the young man's hair. "Nah, he'd be too busy getting lost in all those big city night spots. Just like the boss here. Enjoy yourself, mate?"

Beside her, Caleb's mouth twitched but he shook his head. "All business this time."

"Yeah?" Adam switched his gaze to her, obviously sceptical, and she made to move away from Caleb. He stopped that by the simple expedient of catching hold of her hand. Not hard, just firm enough to make it plain to the team that something beyond work was going on here.

"All business," Caleb said again.

Adam lifted an expressive eyebrow, but fortunately left it at that. "Good to see you back, Fee. Finally someone who can tell these lug heads how wrong they are." He jostled Ben aside and flung an arm good naturedly around Fee's shoulders. "Come on, leave the boss to sort out this bunch."

Caleb gave her an almost imperceptible nod and dropped her hand so she gave in and walked away. Behind them, all was quiet for at least ten paces, and then a hubbub of noise broke out.

"Don't look back," said Adam, all cheeriness banished. "You and the boss got some explaining to do, and it's best he do it on his own."

She would have stumbled but his hands tightened on her shoulder. "Keep walking."

It wasn't till they were out of sight of the others and into the hut holding the holo-projector that she dared tug away from Adam. She had always liked the hydrogeologist, the nearest of the non-eco staff to her own specialisation, and appreciated his sense of fair play.

She had trusted the man. Till now.

"You have any actual work reason for dragging me in here?"

"Yeah, but first, what in hell is going on with you and the boss?

She came from too big a family to give in to attempts to strong arm her. "Not your business."

"A den Coille matching up with the eldest Winter son? It's my business, all right, and that of every member of this team. You any idea of the ructions this will cause? Ructions this project doesn't need, not with what's gone down so far."

She shook his words off. "Wait till next week. We'll tell the team everything then, and that's a promise—and it really is business."

He stared at her for a minute longer. "This going to cause trouble?"

She shrugged. "Can't promise anything—but the Survey is in charge."

A look of surprising sympathy settled on the man's face. He studied her closely, seemingly finding what he sought, and gave a small lift of his shoulders as if shaking off that problem for now and stepped over to the holo-field. He switched it on, scrolling through the development scans up to the present state of the lake, then overlaid the planned structure in bright green fluoro lines.

"As for that other reason—look at the lake's progress."

She forced herself to release the tension in her shoulders. The holo-image covered the area of a large dining table, with the current lake site displayed in minute dimensional detail, right down to the slide of rocks placed artlessly near the opening gap and poised to close it when ready.

"The guidance channels in the lake bed?" she guessed.

"The *missing* channels, yeah. The ones you insisted were in place before we blow that aquifer. The ones that had me thinking you knew what you were doing."

He hit the controls, raising the structure up and bringing in the view of the complex series of underground openings and porous soils holding the water coming off the western ranges. The artesian reservoirs were the main water source for this region. Ensuring the continuity of that precious resource was a bedrock principle of the lake's design.

She looked over the holo-field, noting where Adam had pulled up red lines marking the areas of significant risk.

"I've already told Caleb and Kal we can't start filling without them."

Adam grimaced. "Went down well?"

"Not as you'd notice."

"And?"

"I compromised. We can leave off digging the channels until filling is due to commence."

Adam's fist slammed into the side wall. "I should have known not to expect a backbone from a mountain-born. Thanks a bloody million."

"What the…?"

He jabbed a finger on one of the control panels. "You checked the weather reports lately?"

Did he think her some untrained amateur? "A bit of rain up in the hills. Too far from here to worry about."

"You reckon?" He punched the holo-field controls again, expanding the zone and bringing in the full extent of the aquifer, right up to the base of the hills. She look at the meteorology screen he'd activated, a swirl of blues and reds, then at the aquifer, tracing channels and doing calculations in her head. Calculations she should have done one hell of a lot sooner.

"Oh…"

"Yeah, that."

There was only one choice. "Get the diggers out there, now."

He made no move to obey. She thrust her chin at him. "Tell them, and remind them they work for the Survey, not Solaris. They start now, or they are gone."

Then she was racing across the compound.

Caleb was still in the middle of the group of team members and from the look on his face, had lost patience with their grilling. It didn't stop the leaden silence falling as she joined them.

Unfortunately, she had no time to pander to prickly sensitivities.

"I've told Adam to get the diggers started on those channels straight away." Which dealt effectively with the silence, as a chorus of shouts broke out.

"You what?"

"Who in hell you think you are, lady?"

"Who's running this show, Caleb?"

All the time, the tall plainsman's eyes had never left her face, and he chopped his hands swiftly down in command.

"*We* are. Fee and me. End of discussion." He ignored the angry shouts and fixed all his attention on her. "Why?"

"There's a storm coming up in the ranges. That water is coming down the aquifer channels and will bust open the Solaris blocks on the west side. Without those lake bed structures, there will be a catastrophic breach of the walls on the north-east face as the water hits it."

"Hey, my family's home lies that way."

The shouts had died down, but started up again. Only this time, no one objected to her presence.

"You sure about this?" said Caleb.

"Ask Adam, if you don't believe me. He's the hydrogeologist."

"All right, said Caleb, taking command in that inbuilt manner of his. "Bob, call the evacuation of the village. Jim, get the stock out of the way." He turned to Fee next. "How long?"

"Six hours, worst case scenario. Depends on how much water comes down."

"You heard her. Chaba," he turned to the senior engineer, "can we get those channels dug in time?"

"It'll be close, but hey…" The woman swung round, calling out names and barking orders into her com unit as she hurried across the compound.

The next hours were a whirlwind of tension and action. She and Caleb were based in the holo-room where they could track everything going on. Chaba had press-ganged every digger, ground truck or vehicle of any kind into action, and thrust shovels at anyone left standing. The only exceptions came when Marabeth intervened to grab a couple of decent cooks to help out in the kitchen.

"Them bodies will need feeding if you mean to work them without a break," she said.

It was the only exception Chaba tolerated. The engineer turned out to be a cool-headed task master, running her team with a fierce will that none dared stand against. She was constantly on the move, switching locations between the holo-room and the lake site, com unit never stopping as she barked more orders and listened to progress reports.

Inside the holo-room with Fee stayed only Caleb, Bob at the com, with Chaba bursting in from time to time. A mini tornado rushing in to seize hold of a screen to zero in on a particular section, mouth a curse and hurry out again.

Bob liaised with the villagers, coordinating the evacuations with the police and fire chief and handling it all with the ease of a well-oiled procedure. She watched him switch channels and pass on a stream of orders in the same calm way he always worked.

"Everyone seems to know exactly what to do."

Caleb nodded, his mouth tight. "Flood and fire; our two biggest enemies here. Drought gives you time to act, but for the two big F's—no time. Those we practice for."

A new voice came on the com. Bob leaned back and pointed at Caleb.

"The Old Man," was all he said, getting up from the chair.

It was a terse conversation. Fee didn't have to hear the other end to get the gist. The rigid line of Caleb's back said it all. She went in search of Marabeth.

She was back with a tray of hot drinks and Marabeth's special savoury pies just as Caleb signed off. White lines bracketed his mouth and a barely hidden grief lurked in the depths of his eyes. Silently she passed him his drink and pie, then the same to Bob and took the third mug for herself, withdrawing to the far side of the room. Caleb's fist was clamped to his mug as he ate. He munched slowly, staring all the while at the com screen, and it was not till the pie was gone that he slowly rose from the chair and gave back the com controls to Bob. He walked over and propped himself against the wall beside her.

She raised an eyebrow.

"They'll let us run emergency control," he said.

"But they're watching?"

"Oh yeah."

She stared into her drink, what was left of it. "So living on the plains is out?"

He shrugged, as if to say *who knows*. "The Survey is up for one hell of a reaction," was all he said.

Chaba burst in, her raised voice preceding her. "Boss, tell that SOB I don't give a God damn about his plants. Those banks blow, and there won't be any pretty plants for kilometres around here."

Chaba slammed the zoom on her screenshot, zeroing in on the view of the lake edges. Rows of struggling tussock grasses stood in front of the oncoming diggers and a single figure waving his arms in challenge at the machine, at the same time huddling protectively over the baby shoots. Fee giggled. Nervous tension, maybe, but she couldn't help it.

It was Frank, the team botanist, even more fanatically devoted to his charges than her own team's Kebhyn.

Caleb scowled at her, not entirely managing to suppress that telltale twitch of his lips, and toggled on his com unit.

"Frank, get out of there now. You want to save plants, save the ones that have a chance."

The man ignored him, frantically digging up the small grasses and shoving them into the bag slung over his shoulder as the diggers approached.

Chaba flung her hands in the air. "Do something, Boss, before the fool gets himself killed."

Since the diggers were slowly coming to a halt, there was no chance of that. Fee stifled another fit of giggles, and tried hard to ignore the glare from Caleb as he spoke into his com.

"Jim, get security onto him. He goes, peaceful or not, any way you can if necessary."

Fee watched in fascination as two big men ran in and tackled the older botanist to the ground, only to have the man bounce back up again as soon as they released him, clearly screeching his head off as he grabbed protectively at his satchel of seedlings. One man seized hold of him while the other took the bag, and they marched him off, still struggling to get loose.

Finally one of the guards pulled out a stunner and gave him a zap, and they picked him up and flung him onto the deck of the nearest utility, not forgetting the precious bag of grasses.

"'Bout time," muttered Caleb. He raised his voice and spoke to the guard via his com. "Mark, lock him up till we're finished."

She should *not* find this funny. It was bitter, and sad, and tragic, but she had to grin at the one-sided struggle. Caleb took one look at her, and was afflicted with another twitch of those barely controlled lips. "He's harmless."

"I know. You have to feel sorry for him." The smile came back to her face. "Sort of." In the face of so much panic, one man's worry over a bunch of baby plants somehow restored her faith.

Caleb crossed his arms. "Now that's fixed..." Fee smartly wiped the grin from her face, bringing the nearest she had seen to a smile to Caleb's face since they had arrived.

"As for you," he said softly. "That week Fox gave us? Forget it. We decide tonight, before this whole thing blows up in our faces."

Their teams would have to know about this, but only after *what* they had to know was decided, said the look on his face. A decision that must be made on the run, in the middle of too many other insanely pressured decisions.

Once the sun began to set and she was safe from being seen by surveillance detectors, Fee hitched a ride out to the lake site, needing to see for herself how they were going. The diggers had been busy and the channels were almost done.

Chaba's fellow engineer and Marabeth's son Jareth was standing at the top of one of the banks, scanning the site. Fee climbed up beside him, and was grateful to see that ready smile of his. She had saved his life once, but with everything that had happened since, was no longer sure of her welcome. His smile widened even farther when he caught sight of what she carried.

"Your mother is convinced you're famished out here," she said.

His hand was already diving into the bag and pulling out a still warm pie. "Thanks," he mumbled between mouthfuls. Then stopped, shamefaced. "The others?"

"Don't worry. Marabeth's offsiders have replenished the supply lines and are taking some out to the drivers."

"That's all right, then," and he shoved down another of the biggest mouthfuls she had seen. She passed him the hot drink, and he gulped that down too. All the while the engineer was eating, his eyes skimmed the activity below, until he suddenly thrust the leftovers at her and leaped down the bank, shouting into his com unit.

"Not that deep. Not there. Look at the plans, why don't you?"

Chaba's project management style was contagious, it seemed.

Fee scanned the lake bed, assessing trench depths, angles and what work remained. Were they going to make it in time?

A buzz on her com unit and Caleb's face came on, asking that very question.

"It will be tight," was all she could give him.

He cursed, quickly and harshly. "So cut some corners. The rains have started early, and heavier than expected."

"On to it," and she went to switch off.

"No—there's more."

More trouble? What else could go wrong?

"We have visitors coming, first thing tomorrow." Aah, that kind of trouble. "Don't leave the lake site," he ordered now. "I'll be there as soon as I can."

Then he cut her off, leaving her frowning at her wrist and with a sinking feeling in her stomach. She thrust it away as Jareth bounded up the slope.

"Get Chaba on your com," she said. "We're cutting some corners."

Ten minutes later, the chief engineer had arrived and she, Jareth and Fee were frowning over the new scheme. It would do—just. At some later stage, they were going to have to make some modifications.

Underwater, and with robot extractors? Twice as tricky, and three times the cost, but there was no option. Not if they were going to save those banks tonight.

"Go for it," she said finally, and was relieved to hear no argument from the engineers.

She stayed where she was, nervously switching her com screen between visualisations of the aquifer filling rate and the countdown in the lake bed. Chaba came up to stand beside her, a string of orders ricocheting from the engineer's red hot com.

Almost.

A warning siren screamed in her ear.

"Get those diggers out now," she yelled at Chaba.

They had two heavy flyers on standby. A rumble through her boots, and they lifted off at maximum speed. Down below, a roar of engines and clouds of dust signalled the rapid retreat of the lighter, more mobile ground skimmers.

She watched the aquifer chart. It was filling, so quickly. Far quicker than she expected.

"Chaba?"

"We'll do it," the other woman said. But whether that was reassurance or only a desperate wish, Fee had no idea.

The heavy flyers were lifting fast, drivers still in the digger cabs as they used every last moment to dig out the best channels possible. Anxiously, she studied the lake bed.

Then Chaba passed her a set of scanners.

"Look west, just south of the intake area."

Fee swung the scanners round, zeroing in on the area Chaba pointed to. Was the dirt of the lake bed darker there? She zoomed in closer, set the moisture scans. Yes, there, the tell-tale spreading shadow of an area of seepage. Quickly, she zoomed up the viewer function of the scanners, sending the image sequence to her com and bringing it up on screen to transpose the expected lake filling pattern over top. It was unmistakable.

"That bed's about to blow!"

Out on the lake, only one digger remained, still toiling away while waiting for its lift.

"Get that driver off there," she yelled desperately.

Using the two heavy lifters was out of the question. Both still carried diggers swaying beneath them. No matter how fast, the water would take the driver of the last digger before they could make it back.

Chaba toggled her com unit. "There's only one flyer can do it. A personal one, coming in fast." The woman stared out at the lake bed, hands clenched tight on the scanner.

Fee looked at her com screen, watching in horror the growing stain, saw it darken as the water concentration in the soil increased. She knew to a micron the density of the soil cover on that part of the bed. It was where Solaris had blown open the aquifer channels, shattering the surface of the original creek bed to let the precious water drain away into the labyrinth of chambers and porous strata lying below the hollow.

That area was now only a pile of loose rocks, clay and sand. No strength, no structure, a chaotic mass of debris that would offer little resistance to the water pounding against it.

A spray of dirty white spurted upwards. "It's going," she yelled.

Chaba looked up. "Here's the flyer." A small craft, flying too fast and dropping down to skim the waves.

"Hold on, Bennie," Chaba whispered.

"What!" Fee grabbed the scanner again, zooming onto the threatened digger. Horrified, she recognised the dark head. Young Ben. "What's he doing out there? He's an animal expert, not machinery."

"His dad was in charge of the Solaris maintenance division. Ben has been playing on diggers and other machinery since he started walking—when he wasn't watching bugs or birds. He's one of our best drivers. Just didn't want to make it his life, he told his folks."

"No." Her fingers clung to the scanner, and Chaba had to tug hard to break her hold.

"Sorry, I need them."

A sudden roar hit the air, and the water pouring from the ranges exploded through the puny crust, powering towards Ben's digger in a mighty wave.

The flyer was overhead. "He's too late," gasped Fee.

"Watch."

A figure flung itself out of the doorway, falling to the ground. Another figure she recognised too well. "That's Caleb," she screamed, and began to run.

Chaba's arm swept out, throwing her to the ground.

"He'll kill himself," screamed Fee, desperate to get free.

"No, he knows what he's doing. He's wired to the flyer. Watch."

All but sobbing, Fee huddled on the ground, desperately watching the lake bed.

The tall figure plummeted down, swinging towards the digger. Ben stood on the cab top, hands up as if pleading for life.

A mighty roar, and a wave of water rushing towards them, ignoring the painstakingly built lake bed channels and intent on swallowing up the puny humans in its path.

Caleb swung towards Ben. The water raced on. Fee shut her eyes, tears rolling down her face.

They were gone. She couldn't say his name. Could not name him and make it final.

A shriek in her ear. "Look, Fee. Look."

She opened her eyes, saw the vicious swirls of water, the power of the wave finally broken by the underlying channels. The cab of the digger poked through the brown foam, and she searched for any sign, a head, any body part that would tell her where Caleb and Ben floated.

"Look up," said Chaba, and grabbed her head, forcing her to look skywards.

Dangling beneath the flyer, suspended precariously above the grasping waves, hung two dark shapes. The smaller head was Ben; the other, upside down but unmistakeable. Caleb, alive.

They were safe.

CHAPTER TWENTY

Amid the flurry of backslaps and congratulations, a small fury stormed towards Caleb. A fist ploughed into his belly, and he doubled over. "Oof."

"You could have been killed!"

For a wisp of a girl, she sure packed a wallop. Chaba hurried up, a lift of her shoulders as if to say she'd tried to stop Fee, and a decided gleam of laughter in her eyes.

"She shut her eyes when you grabbed Ben," the engineer said by way of explanation.

Holding onto his gut, he carefully straightened up and caught Fee's arm before she could slug him again. "I knew what I was doing."

Her cheeks were bright red but it was the terror lurking in her eyes that silenced him.

"No worries, Fee. He's done it millions of times before," chimed in the ever ebullient Ben, already forgetting his near brush with death. Whether the boy was blind, or just plain stupid, Caleb couldn't decide, but at least it diverted the attack from him. Fee swung round and jabbed Ben in the chest.

"Playing hero and staying till the end. What did you think you were doing?"

"Knew the boss would get there."

Fee sputtered, took a breath. "Did you even see that wave? The size of a house and barrelling straight down on you."

Her small fist clenched and he thought she was going to slug Ben good and proper. But she flung up her hands instead and began walking away. Straight for the dirty swirling waters filling the lake bed.

"Hell!" He rushed after her, forcibly halting her headlong march and turned her back, only then seeing the tears. Her face was white, her mouth open but no sound came out. Nothing except the heavy tracts of weeping, scarring both cheeks.

Shock. She's in shock, said the trained part of him. His arms ignored the rational, pulling her close and holding her tight. After a long moment when he barely breathed, something seemed to give way in her. She flung her arms around his body and her fingers dug tightly into his sweater, as if burrowing for refuge.

Another long wait, and she lifted her head. "You could have been killed."

That was the moment he truly understood what the Survey asked of them, and what he could lose. A precious, unexpected gift that was but a hair's touch away from fulfilment, but could have been half a world. How could it survive what the Survey demanded of them? He lifted his hand to cradle her face. "It's an old game we play here. Snatching live targets from the air. I've been champion the last five years."

She scrubbed at her eyes and twisted back into his shoulder.

"It wasn't as dangerous as it looked," he said softly.

"You could have drowned."

He didn't deny it. "I was Ben's best chance."

Something shifted in her face, a flicker of terror forced down hard, and he watched in fascination as she took in his words and rebuilt her courage. A slight shake, as if to dislodge the stranglehold of fear, a brusque nod of her head as she accepted his word, and his colleague Fioruisghe den Coille was back.

He preferred the Fee of their nights in the City but some wishes could not be granted. "Come on, we've still got the clean up."

She nodded abruptly. "I'm not sorry I thumped you," she said, and he allowed the lie.

It was another two hours before he was free again. He went looking for her, and cursed the delay when he finally found her. Still strong, still working as hard as any of them, but the dark smudges under her eyes and the white lines bracketing her mouth told of the effort needed just to stay on her feet.

If only he could say *Leave that. Go to bed.*

Not possible, not for them tonight.

She slowly straightened as he shoved his hands in his pockets and came to a stop, bracing himself. "We've got visitors."

"Your father's people? Thought they were due tomorrow?"

He shook his head. "Too early, as usual. It's the Old Man himself, with my mother riding shotgun."

"Not literally, I hope."

Truth to tell, he wouldn't put it past his mother. "Not today," he said, hoping it was true.

She looked ready to fall over. "So much for talking."

"There's more," he said. They're not the only ones on their way."

Now it was she who shook her head. "The Survey? They don't need to be here for this."

Actually, they did.

Unfortunately, he couldn't see them making it in time, not in big enough numbers. "It's your father," he told her, " with most of your brothers and a whole phalanx of den Coille supporters—and our scans show their flyers are armed." She blanched and he swore, grabbing her before she fell. "Do your family normally carry arms when they make house calls?"

"No." Her voice was a bare whisper. "But my father, he's never trusted Solaris. Armed flyers mean his personal guard. They are all trained soldiers with full strike capability."

"He must know you're here." His hands clamped down and she flinched. He released her immediately, but then took gentle hold again, unable to let go of her. "We're in for a bloodbath. My father's men are all ex-military as well." He took a deep breath. "That talk? It's now, and it's short. Will you marry me— tonight?"

It wasn't particularly romantic, but there was nothing romantic about this marriage. Not now.

"How soon can you get the Survey proxy on line?" There was no smile, no joy on her face. Nothing they both should have been entitled to feel. It made no difference.

"I made the call on the way here. Apparently their lawyers had the contracts drawn up weeks ago. They used contact DNA from our apartment on that last trip for the compatibility tests. No issues were found and they're waiting for us online now."

He studied her face, not sure what answer he hoped for. Smears of mud snaked down her cheeks from the night's work and her tears, and her exhaustion was plain to see.

She was so beautiful.

Fee searched his face, hunting for any sign of denial. Marry now, when she felt like an entire building had collapsed on top of her?

She shoved ineffectually at her hair, then grimaced at the dirt on her hands and knew there would be yet another smear on her face. She was grubby, badly in need of a wash and change of clothes.

Married like this?

"Take me back to camp, and give me half an hour to clean up." That she could control, if nothing else. She was not going to be married looking like something dragged up from the lake bottom.

She should *not* be getting married like this, full stop. Unfortunately, two opposing and very angry corporate families said otherwise. You cannot make war on family, and marriage makes family. The oldest law of Arcadia's colonisers.

Even when family are your worst enemy.

Half an hour was little enough time, but Fee was ready long before the end of it. Staring at herself in the mirror, all she could say was that she was clean and her clothes were tidy.

There was a knock on the door. Caleb, she supposed, and plodded over. She opened the door—and fell on the neck of the woman on the other side.

"Marabeth!"

The older woman patted her shoulder. "A wedding in camp, and I have to find out from gossiping kitchen boys. Now, you just stop that fashing, my girl. You're going to have a proper wedding, and so I've told Mr Doom and Disaster Winter."

Fee gulped, swallowing her tears. "There's no time. It has to be done quickly."

"There's always time," said the steely eyed cook. "You sit yourself down in that chair while we take care of everything. Ladies!"

Soon, it seemed every woman working on the lake site was squeezed into her tiny room.

"We haven't time for this," she tried again.

Marabeth just waved a hand at her, and thrust her down by her shoulders when she tried to stand up, all the while keeping up a running debate with Viv, the team veterinarian. A woman who always looked too irritatingly glamorous for someone who spent their life mucking around with livestock. Fee now discovered how much time, effort and sheer pain went into looking like that.

"Ouch," she squealed, as the woman braided the strands at the side of her head and ruthlessly pinned them back to her scalp.

Her hair had always verged on the uncontrollable, and the dry static of the plains made it worse than usual. From the amount of muttering and tugging, Viv thought the same.

"Urk." That one was genuinely eye-watering.

"Don't be a baby."

"You might as well stop. My hair is unfixable. "She reached up to try to smooth the stubborn waves down, only to have her hand batted away.

"Your hair is gorgeous. In a minute, if you just sit still, it will be fabulously gorgeous. Stop moving."

"We haven't got time for this," she said yet again. "You don't know what's coming.'"

"We know exactly," said Marabeth grimly, "and if you think anyone will be fooled by a vid-cast of a hole in the corner affair with a grubby, abused looking bride and a worn out groom, then you are as stupid as your husband-to-be."

To which Fee could say nothing.

More women poured in. Next she knew, her clothes were dragged off and flicked to one side with a disgusted grunt by the terrifying Viv. Something flowing and silky was thrust over her head.

"Look up," snapped Viv when Fee tried to see what was happening. "You'll mess your hair."

Someone was behind her, pulling and prodding at the gown, followed by a sound of shears and the buzz of a hand held sewing machine. She hoped the person wielding it knew how close her skin was to the sealing beams.

More long minutes, the gown was carefully extricated, and she was standing in the middle of a crowd of women wearing very little and too bemused to worry.

"Sit," said Viv, and Fee obeyed.

A woman attacked her face. Fee knew about cosmetics. As her father's daughter, her presence at formal functions was unavoidable, and she had learned the skills needed to *present a good front* as her older sister used to say. The quick dabs of her own toilette were nothing like this, though. The woman's lips pursed. A brush here, a tight squint of concentration as Fee held her eyes as wide and as still as she could, considering a stranger was wielding a small blunt instrument very close to the pupil of her eye.

"Right, up with you."

Fee stood and Viv stepped back, scanned her from head to toe, then gave an abrupt nod. The dress was carefully eased back over her head. She lifted her arms, turned when ordered.

Finally, silence.

A sigh from Marabeth, and the first smile she had seen from Viv. The woman's face softened and glowed. "The mirror," she ordered quietly.

A full length mirror appeared. Fee tried to look.

"Shut your eyes," said Viv gently.

Fee hardly dared breathe.

"Now open them."

"Oooh!"

Was that her? The woman in the mirror had her dark hair, her height, her eye colour.

Fabulously gorgeous, Viv had promised.

"I look beautiful."

It was as if she had given a signal. All the women began to laugh together.

"Of course you do," said the indomitable Viv. "You are a bride—and now, you look like one."

Fee stared again at the woman in the mirror. Her hair flowed from an intricate cap of braiding threaded with baby flowers. A long dress of creamy white, softly fitted to her small waist then floating out in a sweep of intricately embroidered florets that celebrated the curves of the slim body beneath. A tiny corsage of flowers was tucked into the sash at her waist, matching the buds threading her hair.

"Where?" She touched the fragile petals. They were real. "It's so dry here."

Another girl stepped forward. "We have a greenhouse. The flowers are my hobby. One day, we will grow them in the open."

If the lake works, and the next and all the others after that.

"But the dress? How could you find something so fine, at such short notice?"

Marabeth cleared her throat. "It was my daughter's."

Fee began to pull at the fastenings. "No, it's too much to ask of her."

"Stop that," snapped Viv.

Fee ignored her. "I can't take this, Marabeth. Please, thank your daughter—but this is *her* special dress."

There was a strange silence. No one would look directly at her, except Marabeth.

"She passed away three years ago," said the cook. "She got caught in a wind storm like the one you were in. But this one came up too fast, and was stronger than any before. "

"There was no time to send out a warning, or for her to make it to shelter," said Viv quietly. "We've never had a storm like it." A frown on that glamorous face, a stark look of loss. "She was my best friend."

Marabeth took Fee by both hands, tears in her eyes, and Fee felt the echo in her own eyes. "She never got to wear this dress," she whispered. "She loved her Josh so much. It was made to be worn by a bride. Please, wear it in her honour—and make sure no other young woman has to face a storm like that. It's why I joined this project."

Fee squeezed Marabeth's hands in pledge. "I will not forget her."

She turned slowly, looked at herself in the mirror, and lifted her voice. "Thank you, all of you. I look so—beautiful."

It was the only word that fit. She was, stunningly so.

Except that exquisite creature in the glass? It was not her.

Beside her, the cook straightened, a soft smile on her face. Then the older woman stepped up, squared her chin, and gave one resounding clap of her hands. "Now it's time," exclaimed Marabeth, and flung the doors wide.

Caleb checked the watch on his com yet again. Jim saw it and poked him in the side with an elbow. "Don't panic. She'll be here. Marabeth's in charge."

He supposed that should reassure him, but Marabeth was apt to work to her own priorities. Did she fully understand the danger they were in?

"You'll not be married in those rags," she had said, "and nor will Sera den Coille. Go get yourself properly fixed up."

She had commandeered Jim as her proxy general, and Adam as well. "He has the best dress sense of you men." Not that she meant it as a compliment, not from the look she cast the hydrogeologist. Best of a bad bunch, said that look.

That had been an hour ago, and he'd been ready for at least half an hour. How long did it take a woman to dress?

There was a hush, a silence that flowed up the room to surround him, and he slowly turned.

She was beautiful.

He had thought so the very first time he saw her, standing on that dusty road, and when she grimly agreed to marry him with the marks of toil and exhaustion stark on her face an hour ago.

But now?

"Close your mouth," said Jim.

The com came on and the service started. He closed his mouth but Jim still wore that wide grin, and he suspected his own face looked like that of a stunned fish.

The Survey adjudicator appeared in the holo-field. The Chief Justice, no less, about as top brass as they came. Next; the security screen. Retina, DNA, voice pattern, CNS scan; the full set. The Survey was taking no chance anyone could question the legality of this marriage, and he came back to ground with a thud.

A sideways glimpse of Fee, the real Fee, before they both stared straight ahead. Beneath that stunning cosmetic veneer, she looked as sick as he felt. He reached out a hand, her fingers clutched his and he took a firm hold back, enclosing her small hand within his own. It was only then that the wound-up coil inside him relaxed.

The ceremony flew by for Fee, her only anchor on reality Caleb's hand firm on her own. She put her fingers on the scan plate, gave her promises when told, spoke the old, most formal of words binding her to the man beside her and her family to his family. It was insane—or horrifyingly sane, she couldn't decide which. This was a union of House den Coille with House Winter; and where Caleb and Fee came into it, she was hard put to say.

Suddenly she remembered those shared nights in the City, and the day in the desert when they had sheltered from the storm. Houses den Coille and Winter might rule the minds of others here, but it was a strong body and images of the love-making of one man that was at the heart of this ritual. She, Fee, was marrying Caleb the man, not Caleb Winter, eldest son of Winter Solaris, and that was what she would fight for.

Whatever the Survey was planning.

Then it was over, and laughter and cheers broke out behind them. It was full night now, getting late, and all of them, all their fellow Survey staff, had been working as long and hard as she and Caleb. All must be as exhausted, all as wary of what was to come.

Yet when she and Caleb turned to face them, all she could see was smiles.

"Open the doors," cried Marabeth

A banquet, a veritable feast, filled the tables. Laden with food and cheery with garlands. A bridal table took pride of place at the top end of the hall, decked out in paper love knots and festooned in garlands of real plants. She had thought the plains flora ugly, dull in colour and harsh of texture, but displayed here by someone who obviously loved these hardy plants, their rare beauty shone through.

"How?"

Ben strolled up, grinning. "We pulled out all the special supplies, everyone made something, and us *useless young ones* got to put it all together."

The look of triumph on his face was infectious and she grinned back.

"Thank you." Such small words, poor offering that could never cover what she felt. "But the lake, everyone. You're all still so busy with—other stuff," she finished lamely.

Caleb chuckled. "Polishing up weapons and preparing camouflages are well enough. This is our best defence—and it will be our only wedding," he added softly, as if making a promise, a very personal one.

The party was soon in full swing. There was laughter, good food and that edge of exhilaration that came from tension too long held.

Caleb rose to give a speech of thanks but the noise barely subsided, augmented by various suggestions that brought an unforced smile to his face and had her giggling, flushed with embarrassment.

It was at that moment that the outside doors crashed open. Grim-faced men poured in, armed to the hilt. Leading them was Sol Winter. Absolute silence fell.

Caleb bowed. "Father, how timely. Welcome to our wedding."

The silence turned disastrous and Sol Winter's glare turned on her in one potent moment of recognition before switching back to the man at her side.

"Wedding! To a den Coille. Never going to happen."

"It has," said Caleb coolly. He turned on the large com unit on the wall, displaying the legal record and passed over a copy of the certificate, duly authorising the marriage of Fioruisghe ingh Bram an Scathach den Coille to Caleb Winter of Solaris, and certified by the Chief Justice and a number of senior Survey officials, including their own Fox. "The original has been duly notarised and is lodged in the City High Court. It's unbreakable."

Sol Winter stared at the screen then at the page in his hand as if at poisonous vermin. "You any idea what you've done here, boy?"

"Yes."

It was all Caleb gave his father. Sol Winter might name him boy, but it was a man tried and tested who answered him. His hand found hers under cover of the table, and she laced her fingers tightly in his.

Sol Winter glared at her in loathing. "Mountain spawn," he spat. "You think to steal my lands through this farce?"

"You will speak to my *wife* with respect," said Caleb.

Fee kept silent. So much depended on what happened next, on whether Sol Winter bought their bluff. The Survey troops were on their way, an elite troop of soldiers posing as bodyguards up till now, until tonight forced them to show the department's true capability. But would they arrive in time.

Did Sol Winter have any idea what was at stake here? If he did, they were lost.

Caleb swept out an arm, taking in all of the invaders. Men bristling with arms and standing ready to use them, control fingers twitching. "I assume this is your honour guard, come to join our celebration? They appear to have left behind their wedding gear."

Sol Winter glanced at the paper in his hand again. "They know exactly why they're here. Them, and the full squadron on hold above you. As for you, *boy*, what are you up to? Scaring the village with talk of floods."

"Think again, Father. Your men's amateur explosives damaged the aquifer outlets. Without my team, that village and thousands of hectares would be under water by now."

His father's eyes went coal black and he scrunched up the marriage paper in his hand, flinging it to the floor. "Partying while peoples' lives are at stake."

"Were," Caleb corrected. "Go outside, check the stop banks, then come back and join us in thanks. And send that squadron home."

"That squadron will stand down when I decide they can," growled Winter Senior, "and that is not yet. Not by a long shot."

Caleb's clenched down on hers, a small squeeze of reassurance before releasing her, to cross his arms and glare at his father. He shifted slightly, his shoulder pressing against hers and her sudden sense of loss disappeared.

"You are welcome as a guest at our wedding feast," Caleb said coldly. "Your men are not.

"Wedding," spat Old Man Winter. "You didn't think to let your family know beforehand. Your mother, your brothers. Or do you expect me to do your dirty work for you there too? Hey boys, Caleb got himself hitched to that girl from the mountains."

"I was hoping to spare my wife a scene such as this."

There was silence, father and son staring each other down.

It was a confrontation that had to come some day, but why today?

Across from her, Bob signalled urgently, using secret Survey hand signs. *More visitors incoming.*

She dared not sign back, fearful of breaking the tension between the two men. The best she could manage was a query of eyebrows.

"Den Coille," Bob signed back, "and…"

The doors crashed open yet again and men in the forest green of her father's troops poured into the room. She gasped, suddenly understanding Bob's "and…" A second group followed, more den Coille troops, but in their middle, arms held tight by their guards, stood three people. The tension in the room shot up to a whole new level.

"Helena, Ethan, Silas. What in hell is the meaning of this?"

It was Solaris men who grabbed Sol Winter, holding him back hard as all the den Coille weapons suddenly fixed their sights on him. Helena Winter shook off the men holding her, her sons bristling beside her, bruises clear on their faces.

Then her father strode into the room, and the only saving grace Fee could find in the whole rotten situation was the absence of her own mother and the rest of her siblings. Bad enough that two of her brothers formed part of the guard, both glaring at her with a what-have-you-done-now look.

"Winter," said the head of Den Coille, "that is my daughter you have there. Release her. No one steals a den Coille and gets away with it."

"No one has stolen me, father." She gestured to the screen displaying the full, official record of their marriage. "You're just in time for the celebrations." She lifted a hand and took Caleb's arm in full view of all in the hall. "You have met my new husband, Caleb Winter of Solaris. I expect you would like to greet him properly and congratulate us. "

Bram den Coille looked as if hit by a mallet. He shoved past his troops and the Winter family, not stopping till he'd ploughed through all the Solaris troops to stand right in front of her.

"Your what?"

"My husband. Caleb Winter is now my husband."

She would swear that was an actual growl from her father. He appeared to have forgotten he was surrounded by Solaris men as he turned to glare at Sol Winter.

"This is your doing. You've always wanted our lands."

"Nothing to do with me. Blame your daughter and that viper son of mine," Winter thrust a finger at them, "and don't think to break it, not that contract. Know any lawyer willing to go up against the Chief Justice?"

Fee held out a hand to Bob, who wordlessly produced another copy of the marriage contract for her father.

It was as if the room held its collective breath. Bram den Coille scowled, reading the clauses, then flipped it over to see the names and authorisations of the adjudicator and approving witnesses. The scowl grew blacker. Disappointment, rage, bafflement, betrayal. All mingled in that strong, beloved face.

Her father might have never understood her, but it had never occurred to her that he would stop loving her.

"Hold on," said a soft voice beside her.

She swallowed, fighting for control. "As you can see, it's legal, Father."

All that did was infuriate him. He crunched the paper in his fist, before deliberately turning his back on her.

"Satisfied?" he growled at Sol Winter, thrusting the scrunched paper into the man's face. "You sent that boy in to spy on us, and this is the result. What else did he take from us?"

"Take! That girl lured him there, getting herself shook up badly enough he was obliged to see her home." Sol Winter thrust forward, a breath away from the fuming Bram den Coille. "Should have known not to trust the mountains to return the courtesy."

"Trust!"

Who shoved first? Fee doubted either man knew. But shove they did, two fit and hardy men in their middle years, both lost to sense and filled with a storm of anger.

Another unmistakable sound. Every weapon in the hall suddenly slamming into full firing hold, aiming directly at the troops opposite.

She caught the look Caleb threw Bob.

Minutes away, he signalled back.

Discreet hand signs filled the room, but no one was foolish enough to think either set of invading troops would miss a move against them by Caleb's team.

Her father stood isolated from his men, surrounded by armed Solaris troops, too many with weapons aimed directly at him and most probably set to kill. Fee didn't know whether to laugh or cry at the scale of the mess. Then realised her father knew exactly what he was doing. The plains troops were powerless, unable to fire at him in case they hit Sol Winter.

The two men grappled for a hold in a nightmarish display of physical force. Her father might be in his middle years, but he was not a man who chose to run his empire from an office. He was fitter and stronger than his lean mountain build suggested. A match for Sol Winter, equally strong, and so far neither could make headway.

"Turn the lights off—anything," she whispered to Caleb.

"And risk them firing blindly?

"Who would be so stupid?"

She looked at the men and women of den Coille and Solaris. Grim-faced, fingers ready, watching intently the battle of wits and muscle in the middle of the room. Troops who had too much at stake to readily stand down.

Breathe, just breathe, she told herself.

Nearly here, signed Bob.

A den Coille trooper suddenly realised what Bob was doing with the earpiece and finger controls of his com unit. A weapon crashed down and Bob slithered to the floor.

Suddenly the weapons of both sets of troops changed direction.

Caleb's hand tightened on hers, and she could feel the tension in him, a mirror to her own. They were both well-trained, but those weapons were now pointed straight at them.

By the wall, Bob sprawled on the ground. Unconscious? She focussed on his chest and saw the slight rise that told of life.

One worry down, but he needed medical help and soon.

She watched the two men in the middle. Her father was fit but Sol Winter had the advantage in height and build.

Was that a hitch in her father's step, a weakening of his hold on the other man's arm?

"Get ready," muttered Caleb. "Go low."

Breathe, Fee. Breathe.

The doors crashed yet again as even more troops barged into the room, this time dressed in black.

Breathe!

The Survey cavalry had arrived. Then a shockwave of recognition raced around the room. That black armour and distinctive logo were not the Survey's.

The Federal Police!

CHAPTER TWENTY-ONE

The police fanned out, taking aim at every single person in the room as their leader stepped forward. His black field kit was broken only by the logo on his chest and the triple lines of gold stripe on his shoulders announcing his rank; Supreme Field Commander of the Federal Police of Arcadia.

Marco an Fallon was known and feared across the planet—and utterly incorruptible. Flanked by a squadron of Federal troops in full battle armour, he marched towards the two men standing stiff and watchful in the centre of the room.

"Sol Winter, Bram den Coille. We have a report that you are in violation of Penal code, Primary 61A. Please advise."

A sudden chill fell on the whole room and Caleb swore softly. "When the Survey plays dirty, they go all the way."

Penal code 61A, one of the fundamental laws set up by the first colonists on Arcadia, ironically designed by settlers intent on increasing their wealth and influence without the risk of armed conflicts that had beset so many other worlds. A legal marriage irrevocably bound the families of any couple, and any aggression or conflict between them was prohibited on pain of seizure of all the assets of both parties.

If found guilty, the Federal government could take everything belonging to the den Coille and Winter families, or anyone associated with them.

The Survey had just declared war on the corporates.

"Anyone still think we work for a minor, backroom department?" muttered Fee.

In the middle of the room, the heads of den Coille and Winter Solaris stood shoulder to shoulder, suddenly united against their newly discovered, joint enemy.

"Commander, this is a *private* matter."

"You have nothing to do with this."

Marco an Fallon paid them no attention. A man who understood the power of silence, he stood at the head of his troops and waited.

Her father broke first, turning to his men and giving a chopped hand sign. "Stand down before someone gets shot." He pointed at Caleb's mother and brothers, still surrounded by den Coille troops. "Winter, your family. No need for our protection now the danger is past, and the police are here to keep us all *safe*."

For the space of a heartbeat, Sol Winter made no move. Then he flung his arm down and his men, too, holstered their weapons. He held out his hand and his wife and sons walked stiffly across, to be engulfed by his troops.

Not one of them looked at her or Caleb. It was as if they no longer existed. She tried to catch the eye of her brothers. Both refused. Only Marco an Fallon paid her and Caleb any attention, and that she could have done without. Not while his men still held their weapons primed and ready for action at the slightest provocation.

The commander swept his gaze slowly over the room, over each and every member of the Den Coille and Solaris guards. Finally, finished his scrutiny, he turned with military precision towards their table.

"Eco-engineers Winter and den Coille. I trust all is well."

"Quite well, thank you," said Caleb.

She couldn't bring herself to speak the lie, and instead nodded slowly.

The commander studied her, as if in judgement. The police answered to the Planetary Council, not the Survey, and the relationship between the two bodies had always been convoluted at best.

"This union was the free choice of both partners?" he now said, looking first at her.

"Yes," she said firmly.

"It was," echoed Caleb.

"Good." He nodded to his men and they holstered their weapons. No one in the room was foolish enough to take that as a sign they were free to do as they pleased. These soldiers were the best in Arcadia, trained and seasoned. The corporate troopers were no match for them.

"A squadron will remain here until the current projects are properly established to the satisfaction of the Survey. The Council is taking back control of all reserve lands in this region, and an environmental auditor will arrive tomorrow."

There was a choke of horror from both their fathers. The commander swung round. "Is that a problem?

"No, no," muttered Sol Winter. Her father shook his head.

A headache beat a tattoo behind her eyes. So many tangled machinations lying under the surface. If she'd wanted to be part of such games, she would have chosen politics, not the Survey.

But she was a den Coille and had been trained by a mother who was a master at managing the affairs of a large and ambitious family.

She plastered a smile on her face and ignored the pinched lines marking the faces of their opposing relatives. "Thank you, Commander. We look forward to working with your assessor. His information will be a useful addition to our databanks. I'm sure you agree, Father? Ser Winter?"

Like a cold day in Hell, but neither man was stupid. Both buckled up their rage and nodded coldly.

An Fallon said nothing at first, only stared at the two men, studying first one then the other.

Her father flung up his hands. "You win, Commander. There will be no trouble from Den Coille."

"Or Solaris," said Sol Winter.

"Thank you." The commander did not drop his stare. "A second squad will remain on alert, as backup. For now, though, we have interrupted this wedding party long enough."

He turned to face Caleb and her. Fee wished she could be anywhere else. In the middle of a burning furnace sounded preferable.

"Eco-engineers, my apologies for the disturbance. The High Council places great importance on family, as you know, and wishes me to convey their congratulations on this happy occasion. They are taking a particular interest in such an— *auspicious* union."

The merest hint of a pause, but Fee felt as if her lungs were seized with ice. Then Caleb stepped forward, to her utter relief at being spared the obligation. "Our thanks, Commander. Please join us for the rest of the celebration. Father, Ser den Coille, you are of course always welcome."

Fee felt sick. Both fathers looked as if seized with the same illness, and firmly refused any desire to stay. An excruciatingly correct bow from her father, a flick of his hand and the Den Coille troops marched out. Not once did he or her brothers look at her.

The plains folk were not so formal. The barest of nods from Sol Winter as he stalked off, his troops following.

Helena Winter did stop. She ran that supremely elegant eye over Fee. She had never felt so insignificant.

Next Helena looked at her son.

There would be no parental repudiation here. No, far worse than that. The woman briefly let her pain show in her face. "I assume you have a reason for this?"

"You have seen my bride, how beautiful she is," said Caleb.

Helena glanced across at Fee and back to her son. "Don't insult me with such games."

Caleb grimaced. "Yes, I have a reason, and it is sufficient."

Helena said nothing more, her eyes alone showing the effect of his words. Back held rigidly straight and making no attempt at unseemly haste, she turned and walked out with her Solaris guards marching in step beside her. Caleb's youngest brother Si brushed past them to follow her and she saw Caleb's hand go out. Too late. Si refused to look back. Then his brother Ethan came up.

"If you wanted Solaris, you only had to ask," he said to his older brother. "Bringing in the Feds is over the top, even for you."

"I don't want Solaris," said Caleb. "That's yours."

"So why try so hard to destroy it? The work of generations of our family?"

"I'm not. I'm *trying* to save the world." Caleb put a mocking edge to the words, a throwaway line, and his brother's hands tightened into a fist before he too swivelled and stalked out.

He looked so much like his older brother, Fee could weep. She looked away from Caleb, giving him his moment of privacy. She knew how he felt. Neither of her brothers had even bothered to ask her reasons.

The Federal police watched the Den Coille and Solaris troops leave, weapons still held ready and bodies poised for action.

Marco an Fallon watched the opposing parties with equal vigilance. "I have troops outside and airborne," he said to them now. Your families will be escorted back to their own territories."

"*This* is Winter territory," said Caleb savagely.

The commander turned that contained look on him. "Not any more."

The outer doors closed on the last of the corporate guards and the Commander signalled his men. Minutes later all the police had marched out as well, the doors clanging shut behind them.

The food still stacked the tables, the flowers bravely defied the fates with their beauty but Fee had never felt less like celebrating. It had been a long day and night.

Old Jim gave a sigh. "I've had about enough excitement," he said. "I'm off to bed."

The others followed, exhaustion settling into their faces now the drama was over. With muted farewells and hollow good wishes, they made their way out.

"You two better do the same," said Bob. "Go to bed, that is. For the questions to come tomorrow."

It wasn't till she had stumbled halfway across the yard and Caleb tugged at her arm as she veered toward her own room that she got Bob's meaning. She stopped, cheeks bright scarlet and shook her head. Left, right. No.

Caleb bent his head as if to kiss her. "There are Fed guards on all four corners of the yard. Tonight, you share my quarters."

He lifted his head and his arm came round her shoulders, exactly like a loving, newlywed husband. It was only the tension in his body that kept her sane, that kept her from screaming out loud.

His door shut behind them and he dropped his arm, swinging abruptly away from her to the far side of the room. She stood where she was, just inside the door, reluctant to make any move suggesting she sought ownership here.

Caleb marched over to a cabinet, yanking it open and pulling out a bottle. "Drink?"

Yes, anything to anaesthetise her mind. She was so tired that a few mouthfuls should be enough. He splashed a healthy shot in a glass, set it on a side table, then threw himself into one of a pair of chairs.

She walked slowly over, taking the long way round his seat, picked up the drink and moved back to the doorway. It was a man's room, all browns and comfort, the only element in common with the beautiful Winter homestead an inexplicable sense of style. Everything in this room belonged here, from the overstuffed chairs to the open reader displaying the work of an unknown poet. She aimlessly tooled it over, found more volumes. Poetry wasn't something she had ever explored. Music had always been her escape.

A rug lay over the back of the empty chair. It could be cold at night in these dry lands. She took stock of the rest of the room. An office desk, a small kitchen unit with hot drinks dispenser, and the bed.

She shoved forward abruptly and came to a perch on the second of the big chairs, lifted her glass and swallowed a deep gulp. Only then did she look him in the face. A bitterly amused smile traced his lips, but his eyes were dark with storms.

She glanced briefly at the bed and took another swallow.

He gave a single, harsh laugh. "Dutch courage?"

She shrugged, trying fruitlessly to pretend this wasn't happening. "You reckon just sharing quarters will fool them?"

He took a swig from the bottle. "With Marco an Fallon on board?"

"Your father may have packed up and gone home."

He gave another crack of laughter. "Will yours?"

"No."

"Don't expect Solaris to either. My guess; both sets of troops will be staying hard against their respective boundaries."

"I'm surprised they know where that is. The foothill country has been Winter grazing lands as long as I remember, while we've always considered the upper slopes of the eastern side of the ranges ours to use."

A grimace this time, another swig from the bottle. "Marco an Fallon will make sure our parents know exactly where the boundary lines are drawn."

"And will be in here first thing in the morning with medical scanners to verify this marriage," she finished glumly, the glow of the alcohol finally settling into her veins. She slumped back in her chair. "We've made love before."

"You think I planned that? Had sex with you as part of some cold blooded scheme?"

If she hadn't felt soiled and small before, she did now. "Sorry," she muttered, and wished she could banish the heat in her cheeks.

He shoved a hand through his hair. "Oh, hell. What we had—I didn't expect it to happen."

"Thanks." She crossed her arms in protection.

"No." He paced across the floor, then swung to face her. "You are very beautiful."

She hunched her shoulders. It didn't sound like a compliment. "I'm pretty enough, I guess. So I've been told." She couldn't deny it; she had never been short of offers, just choosy over which she accepted. Right now, she had a nasty suspicion which of her assets the Survey valued.

"Take that look off your face," snapped Caleb. "You are beautiful, yes. Stop dead in the street, stunningly beautiful. You are also intelligent, brave and a damned good eco-engineer. No one gave you a free pass through college or work."

"Well, thanks."

He shoved another hand through his hair.

It was so wrong, all of this. She watched the tall, lean man in front of her and remembered other times. She knew what lay beneath those clothes. Making love with Caleb Winter had been an unexpected joy. They had just begun their journey of learning to know and respect each other. What might it have become? Too late to wonder now.

He stopped pacing, shoved his hands into his pockets. "I do still want you. Can't see that changing anytime soon. Just—not like this. But …" He took a breath. "You want to come to bed."

She gripped her glass, lifted it and took a deep slug. Waited till the belt of it hit her veins. It didn't help. No wall, no distance could lessen the wrongness of all this.

"Yes, I'll go to bed with you. No, I will not make love with you, not right now, not when we're both tired and pressured. And not when I don't know how many pairs of eyes are out there snooping."

"They can't see in. I scanned the room for surveillance."

She lifted her eyebrows, sceptical about whether that could work against the Federal police. He stared belligerently back.

"Okay, but I am still not having sex with you now. We can sleep on it. Let them all get bored. When—if—it happens, we do it in our own time."

For an instant she thought he would still insist, despite the relief in his eyes. Stubborn man. He began to unzip his tunic, watching for her reaction.

"No." She put up a hand. "You can make me want you, but I will not make love with you right now."

He actually growled back. "I don't sleep in clothes."

"Oh." She felt smaller than ever.

He had stripped off and pulled back the covers before she could bring herself to begin the elaborate unfastening of her glorious gown.

He let her struggle, then swore. "Turn around." Next minute, his hands were on her back, undoing the myriad of decorative buttons. Brisk, workmanlike, exactly what she had asked for. Yet she had to fight to ignore the slow sweep of hands as he undid the ones low on her back or the sensual slide of fingers as he smoothed the dress from her shoulders.

He stopped, snapped "Dim," and the lights cycled down to their lowest setting. "No free shows, not of you."

"If the police are watching."

"You are mine to see only," was his reply.

Her gown was off, his hands caressing. She was beginning to forget why she hadn't wanted to do this now. Till she looked at the drawn shutters, hiding them from the outside world.

"No," she said, her voice a whisper.

For answer, he picked her up, carried her to the bed, and laid her carefully on it. Then they were together, the covers pulled up, and he had curved his big body around hers. "Hush," he said. "Sleep."

"You can do that?" She eased into him, feeling the evidence of her disbelief lodged against her, and the swift clench of his muscles in response.

"If it kills me."

She could not stop the chuckles even with their edge of hysteria. There was too much honesty in his words. She eased back from him.

"No." His arms tightened, keeping her still. A held breath, one sounding as if drawn from his depths, "I need to hold you. I need an anchor."

She ceased her movement, knew how he felt after the insanity of the last hours. She closed her hand over his and let her head fall back onto his chest.

She only hoped the Survey knew what they had unleashed.

Surprisingly, sleep must have claimed her soon after. She woke to a tangle of limbs and a strong beam of sunlight coming low through a small gap in the shutters. She lay still, savouring the warmth and a rare feeling of contentment.

Then remembered last night, and why she had been so worn out. She sat up abruptly.

"Oof." Caleb rolled over and she lifted her elbow out of his stomach. He opened a bleary eye. "You're awake."

"Sorry, didn't mean to disturb you."

Both of his eyes opened, blinked, and he peered at the shutters. "Damn sunshine."

He pulled her back down. "I could get used to waking like this. Now, wasn't there something we planned to do this morning?" He nuzzled at her throat, and she lifted her head to ease his way, too delighted at his playfulness to think of the night just past.

Then remembered again. "We can't," she wailed. "Who knows what my Da and yours have been up to while we slept?"

"With the Feds watching them? Precious little," and his arms folded her close. This time, she gave in, unable to ignore the hands driving her crazy.

A hand found her breast, squeezed, lightly brushed her ribs and she giggled, slapping him and wriggling around, which brought her butt square against a very awake part of his body. "You planned that."

He squeezed again, pulling her closer. "Nope, but I'm not complaining."

She stretched backwards, testing. He was so hard and ready for her. "Mmmmm"

At that, he rolled over and up, twisting her beneath him in one smooth move till she lay looking up at a face lit with laughter. She had been half in love with him for weeks, but in that instant Fee knew she was lost.

"Hey, you," she said softly.

That gorgeous smile widened. "Hey you, back." He lowered his head.

He had not kissed her like this before. Slow, subtle. She stilled, her hands tugging his face close as his kiss spoke of a promise and a future.

Then his hands took full possession. The nape of her neck, the curving hollow low down on her back, her swell of breasts, before tracing a tantalising path lower and lower as every private inch of her came to life.

This was so much more than the nights in the City. She was beyond speech. It was a very long time before either of them was capable of saying anything more.

"That was …"

"Amazing, awesome, unbelievable?"

He had collapsed back on the bed and she sprawled over his chest. Now, she propped up her arms and grinned down, loving the unfettered smile he wore. "All of the above," she said, and began to trace lazy, satisfied circles over his body with mouth and fingers. His hand laced through her hair. He gasped, chuckling. "You need to give me a minute here."

"What, not as young as you used to be?" Her fingers kept up their teasing exploration.

Her grabbed her hand, playfully wrestled her over, and soon after proved beyond doubt how wrong she was.

When she woke again, the sun was gone and faint noises of the camp stirring for the evening filtered through from the outside. Fee lay still, savouring the memories of the day.

She was married. To Caleb Winter.

Later, the ramifications of that would rear up in concert against them, but for now it felt—good.

A hammering on the door brought her back to reality. Caleb shot up, glared at the offending noise, swung out of bed and grabbed his discarded trousers. She shoved back the covers.

"Stay put," he ordered, thrusting a hand against the intercom. "Who's there?"

An equally gruff voice snarled back. "Time to get your butts out of there, *Sirs*." It was Marco an Fallon.

"Trouble?"

"There will be soon."

Caleb glanced at her. She held up ten fingers. "Give us ten minutes."

"No more." This time, the strain was clear in the Federal Commander's voice, and Fee scrambled out of bed.

She discovered someone had transferred most of her clothes here, neatly hanging them in the closet shared with Caleb's gear, her personal things tucked into the bag set on the floor below. Later, she would think about that, consider what she felt. For now, she used the quickest cleanser cycle and was out and dressed by the time Caleb had plugged into the secured Survey channel and brought up the latest messages.

She raised an eyebrow at the look on his face.

"Read it—and wait for me before you race out of here."

She took his seat as he slammed the door of the bathroom.

"What the …"

The door opened and a wet Caleb thrust his head out. "Wait *here*."

"But …"

"Door on lock. My voice over ride," he snapped, slamming the bathroom door again. She tried the outer door. *He did not just do that.* Then cursed in every tongue she knew. He had voice-locked the razzing door on her!

He was as quick as she in the cleanser, but she was still pacing across the room by the time he emerged. She barely noticed how good his bathed, buffed and dressed self looked, but did note he had gone for Survey dress formal, the same as her. Like most Survey, she rarely used her uniform and had never seen Caleb in his before.

Today seemed a good day to remind others of who they worked for and the seniority of their rank.

"About time," was what she actually said to him. "My Da…"

"…has imprisoned your team and charged them with subterfuge and commercial espionage. I know. Your screaming at him won't change that."

He took her by the shoulders, gave her a gentle shake, then suddenly bent and caught her lips. A gentle kiss, a kiss of good morning and affection. "That's for last night," he said softly. Then stepped back and straightened up. "Ready?"

For this? To fight her own father for the safety of her closest friends and allies? Not ever. "Yes," she said.

"Unlock," he said, and together they stepped through the opening door.

Marco an Fallon was pacing up and down the hallway, a phalanx of troops behind him. He swung around, snarled "About time," and thrust up a hand in a 'Follow me' gesture.

Fee refused. "Commander," she called out. He swivelled back, glaring angrily.

"My team? Are they safe?"

"For now."

Caleb moved to stand at her shoulder. "And?"

"You think that's all I have to worry about?" An Fallon stared at them both, and she stared as implacably back. His eyebrow twitched. "The Survey legal team is on it. Your people are in protective custody, under house arrest. A Survey team is on the way to secure their release and take control of the project valley."

Caleb gripped her hand. "That's a …

An Fallon cut in "… declaration of war. You think I don't know that, *Sir.* Now will you come with me? You're needed in the control room."

CHAPTER TWENTY-TWO

Organised chaos greeted them in a room filled with police and Survey staff. Fee nearly turned on her heels at all the salutes as they walked in, far harder to face than the jovial catcalls from Caleb's team.

"Look who's finally dragged themselves out."

"'Bout time," muttered Old Jim, and thrust a dask at Caleb.

Marabeth hustled up and hugged her tight. "Ignore them." She shoved a big muffin and dask at her. "You'll be needing sustenance, I daresay." She dug an elbow into Caleb and winked, bringing a flush to his face as red as the one Fee could feel burning up her cheeks.

"That's enough," snapped an Fallon. "Eco-engineers, Sirs, follow me please."

Marabeth's face went as red as Caleb's. "These two are just wed. Leave 'em be."

Caleb lifted an arm around Fee, tucking her shoulder into his as he pulled her close. "It's all right, Marabeth," he said. "We married to stop trouble, and it hasn't gone away yet."

"Stuff!" Marabeth stuck her hands on her hips and snorted. "You two married because you can't keep your hands off each other."

An Fallon's mouth tightened. "Winter, den Coille." The man was clearly running out of patience. Caleb steered her after the commander, but Marabeth had a parting shot.

"You married because you are meant to be married."

An Fallon ignored her and marched them through the outer office to the inner com room, controlled now by his troops. He thrust a hand out, an order for them to come close to the screens.

"We have Eco-engineers Winter and den Coille."

Full size screens shimmered into life and suddenly they were facing Caleb's parents on one side, her own on the other, and between them, a formal, contained projection of Fox. The three screens were angled to put Caleb and her at the apex, as if under judgement.

Fox stared expressionlessly at them, but it was their parents who raked them from top to tail. A part of her wished she was braver, or stupid enough to squirm on the spot. The rest knew to stay rigidly still.

Caleb stood as fiercely upright as she, making no attempt to look at his father. His mother's attention was all for Fox and the den Coille's.

As for Fee's own father, he refused to notice her at all while her mother looked like she had lost some element of herself. This was not the woman who healed her hurts and took her part regardless of the right of it. This was a woman fighting not to break.

Fox stood square in the middle, dressed in uniform and feet planted in full parade ground mode. "The Survey has agreed that both of you will submit to a biological scan to confirm the marriage is a true one. Will that be a problem?"

She had known it was coming, but nothing could prepare her for the shock of it. So soon after the magic, to have what lay between them exposed and reduced to biology and cells? Something sordid slithered over her skin.

Caleb's foot briefly nudged hers, his body bent infinitesimally closer. "We do submit," he said.

She had to force out the nod of consent. "We submit."

"The examiners? They will be independent?" Her mother did not look directly at her, but Fee knew that tone of voice and her heart beat fractionally lighter. Not one of the den Coille children had ever doubted their mother would defend them from all comers—and win the bout. Not till Fee married a plainsman and the Federal Police held her father to account at the point of a weapon. She had thought her mother lost to her, but that special tone said *No*, and she breathed once more.

"Not Survey," said the gruff voice of Sol Winter now, and the cold eyes of Helena Bascombe Winter agreed.

"No, not them." Her father, discovering a threat in common with a sworn enemy.

"The Survey will monitor," added Fox in a voice that brooked no argument.

An Fallon moved into the square. "Central Ministry of Health officials will conduct both examinations, with full monitoring by the Survey and the respective families."

There were too many voices in the room used to being obeyed. She glanced at Caleb and he leaned fractionally closer in support.

Her father glared his opinion of that. "And if the examination is positive, what next? Where does fealty lie? Is my daughter's owed to her family still? As for our new son-in-law!" He almost spat the words out.

Fox's voice cut in. "The matter of fealty has been previously decided by precedent. Both parties of a marital union owe primary fealty to the other partner. Familial fealty must respect that, and do nothing to impede the primary fealty."

He had to be repeating verbatim the words of a Survey legal team.

"So is she den Coille or Winter? She cannot be both."

"Fioruisghe is my wife," said Caleb suddenly. "Any action you take against that, you take against your daughter." He returned her father's cold look with an equally cool but implacable gaze.

"Fioruisghe?"

Her father had a knack for squeezing the truth from his children. It had worked with her in the past. Many years in the past. Was it true, what Caleb said? Politically there was no choice, but personally? Of that, she was unsure, both of him and of her feelings.

She turned her gaze on her father, and it was as Eco-engineer den Coille she answered him. "My marriage is valid. If you seek to destroy that, you act against me," *and against our world, Da. If only you had believed that. Now, it's too late.*

Her father studied her face. She saw the exact moment he realised she had done this to him before—faced him as a professional, not a daughter—and that her professional loyalty was not to him. His face closed over.

She had lost her father.

There was little more to be said after that. Fox remained silent and only the dry orders of Marco an Fallon filled the void.

Instructions on procedure, sounding painstakingly contrived to ameliorate as many hurt sensitivities as possible.

It changed nothing. The Council and the Survey had today openly taken on the corporations, and she and Caleb were their frontline weapons. Those Survey reports of the Alliance's ultimatum better be true.

If only she trusted the Survey. The field workers and the truth of the threat to their world, yes. Survey Central and the agenda of its senior officials, so fond of convoluted political games?

They were separated then, to be joined by the appointed monitors. The screens had been a diplomatic cover, or a security precaution. She guessed the latter, but some at least of their families must be in the same building, as the den Coille and Winter's choice of monitors now joined them. Her last view of Caleb was of him marching out, head held tall in a surrounding posse of police, Winter employees, his team medic representing the Survey and her eldest brother Cumchdach representing den Coille. Cumchdach was his father's son in allegiance and no fool, but there was a core of their mother in him. He would not lie, not openly. Caleb's hand had brushed hers briefly before they were ordered away, and she kept the memory of it with her as the police waved her to follow in the opposite direction.

The phalanx around her was similar. Helena Bascombe Winter appeared as the Winter representative, and Fee swallowed. From the look on Caleb's mother's face, she was definitely not there as an ally.

To add to it, her mother appeared from another door and took her place beside Helena Winter. It didn't surprise Fee; her mother would not have been left out of anything so closely involving her family. Neither woman looked at the other, and Fee groaned silently. Could this day get worse?

It didn't improve in the room that had been turned into an emergency field clinic. Fee had been through enough scans that she merely nodded to the technician, took the proffered shift, and went behind the screen to change. She wondered who had insisted on the covering shift—her family or the Survey.

The reprieve was temporary. After the usual body scan, the dreaded part began. The presiding physician approached her, hands already gloved. The one brought in from the central Health ministry. "Have you had a pre-cervical swab before, Eco-engineer?"

Fee shook her head. "Not for this reason."

The woman had the probe ready and the technician began to fold back the shift, standing between Fee and the onlookers. Helena Winter's voice cut in.

"Our own physician will also examine the girl."

Fee had been staring at the ceiling, trying hard to block out that she was lying in a room of strangers of both sexes as a woman prepared to probe her most private bodily parts. Helena Winter's voice put paid to that, and she twisted her head, shoving away the technician's hand.

"Not a male physician," said her mother's voice, even more sharply.

"You daughter is prudish?" There was a gleam of triumph in Helena Winter's face. Fee grimaced. Prudish? No, not that she could claim. Far too mild a word for what she felt.

Her mother smiled, with that smile that had never signified pleasure. "Mountain ways are clearly more restrained than is the case on the plains," her eyes raked over the sharp-featured little man in the Winter cohort, "and nor does your *physician* have the required training in this area."

It was unanswerable, and Helena Winter knew it. "Next you will ask for the men to be cleared from the room."

"Why, thank you. That would be much appreciated." Her mother glanced at the presiding physician, who spoke to the police troopers, and all the men quietly moved out, taking the sharp-faced Winter physician with them.

"Sera Winter, do you have a female medic available?"

Caleb's mother shook her head, her armour back after the brief setback. "I may not have Sera den Coille's level of expertise," a cursory nod at Fee's mother, "but Winter Solaris does recognise your qualifications," she conceded to the Ministry's physician. "We would have preferred our own confirmation, but since this is not possible we will settle for overseeing the procedure." A thinning of lips, a look of challenge at Fee's mother. "As long as we have an unimpeded view of the process and equal access to the results.

"Eco-engineer, is that acceptable to you?" *Not in a million years.* "It is," she said to Caleb's mother and to her own.

A brief and reassuring smile was her reward from her mother, and a hint of the pain she hid. Fee's mouth would have fallen open if not for Helena Winter. Could her mother support her in this?

Next her shift was opened, a bright flush heated her cheeks as she saw Helena Winter moving to better watch, and Fee switched her gaze back to the ceiling. Whatever was happening here, it was not to her!

Finally it was over and Fee stumbled in her haste to reach the sanctuary of the screen and her own clothes again. A minute later, and her mother was there too.

Fee reached back to find the chair behind her and sat on it, carefully doing up the last closure in her tunic. She watched warily as her mother came close. Would this day's unexpected traps never end?

Yet her mother simply held out her hands, enclosed her in a hug and enveloped her in that special scent that always meant safety.

"My little Fioruisghe."

Fee tried so hard to hold back and almost succeeded. For a brief moment only, she collapsed into her mother's shoulder before forcing herself to struggle out of it.

Her mother let her, standing back and putting a gentle hand under her chin.

"I won't ask if you know what you're doing. But…" Her mother wiped the trace of moisture from Fee's eyes, patting her hair back into place, "I know what happens when a patient's life is out of balance, and our mountains…" Her mother shook her head, as if surprised by her words.

"Take care, daughter," she said softly instead, before returning to the outer room.

There was no time to wonder. The screen was thrust aside and the technician announced the results were ready. If Fee had thought them to be delivered in private, she was wrong. The head of her police guard stepped forward and ordered her to accompany them back to the control room.

Now she was back in the main room, the set up changed to a com room so that all on base could see and hear the findings. Her mother disappeared through a side door and re-appeared in the screens on the walls, and Caleb's troop returned.

He took his place beside her, turning to search her face. "All right?"

She shrugged noncommittally. "It was as expected," and turned to face the front again, wary suddenly of the fierce gleam in his face. If he made one move to hold her, she would crumple completely, and from the brittleness in his face he was as close to exploding.

She felt him watching her, then turning slowly to face their persecutors.

The physicians returned, and she could face this alone no longer. She put one hand out for his, and clutched tight when he grasped it.

Together, they faced the physicians as they each handed a small disc to the commander.

"The examinations were complete and performed to the full required standard?"

"Yes, Commander. We can confirm that the marriage was consummated within the required time frame and both partners are fully fertile. The union is valid, and irreversible by outside parties."

Her skin felt too tight. Even her hair hurt, as if caught in a blast of an ice laden fury. She—no, they—had truly done this, and it was irrevocable.

"That's it," said Caleb's father. "Boy, you've made your choice." His screen blanked out and she felt the shock of it as a faint tremor running from Caleb's suddenly tightened fingers to her own.

Her father thrust back a chair and leaned forward. "Den Coille will abide by the law," he said to the Commander, "to the last *enforceable* letter." That screen went blank too. All that was left was a room filled with the blank stares of the police troops, the disconnected eyes of the medical team and the cold gaze of Fox.

"The Commander has your orders," he said. "The lake must be completed on schedule and the change in forestation patterns of the den Coille mountains set in place as planned."

With that, he blanked his screen off, and the pall in the room lifted. Somewhere near the back, the chattering started and spread in waves to the front but stopped just short of them. Caleb kept hold of her hand and they both looked to the Commander. "What now?" said Caleb.

"You return to your duties." The man was so matter of fact, the last hours might never have been.

She felt again that cold intrusion of the scanning probe. "Just like that? We all go back to work?"

"Yes. A full squad will stay to keep out intruders," which meant hers and Caleb's family, she guessed, "and another is being dispatched to oversee the work of the mountain team, so that there will be no more obstacles in the way of your projects."

He clicked his heel, lifted a hand in salute. "Eco-engineers." He signalled his troops to march out, along with the central medical team.

The door shut behind them and Fee could finally breathe properly. "Obstacles! We break our families' hearts and he labels them mere obstacles."

"At least your family has a heart."

"No." She seized both his hands. "Your mother will not cast you off."

His face was closed tight. "You saw my brothers' faces. They used to look up to me."

She was beginning to know him now, enough to hear the pain under the words, and flung her arms around his big, taut body. "They will come round," she whispered.

Then the crowds were on them, with awkward words of congratulation and support. She forced herself to tolerate it, but was heartily relieved when Caleb flung up a hand. "You heard the Commander. We have work to do, and only a few hours of daylight left."

It was like someone flicked a switch and brought back Normal.

"Okay, boss."

"Fun's over already."

"Slave driver."

Slowly, the team drifted out, back to the tasks interrupted so savagely. Caleb tugged her hand. "Come on, we better see what we've been left with."

She glanced down at her dress tunic. She needed her work boots and gear.

They called briefly into his quarters to change, grabbed the rest of their gear, all in carefully contrived silence, and shortly after stood on the edge of the rapidly filling lake. Brown, foamy wavelets lapped at their feet, the steadily dying remnants of the powerful surge of water that had so nearly obliterated all they had made here and threatened so many plains homes.

She studied the water level, mapped it out against a memory of the plan in her office. "It's near done."

He followed the track of her gaze. "One thing came out right."

Out in the middle, a small tube sticking out of the water showed where Ben had come so close to being taken, and where his bulldozer remained. "Better get the lifters onto that," said Caleb. "We'll need it for the next site."

She nodded. There was nothing more to be said. The rapidly calming surface had covered over the remains of the hideous activity of the previous day, leaving a large lake just as originally planned by their bosses. A few shrubs, some judicious rocks, and in short term it would look as if it had always been there, with no trace of the price paid.

She found his hand, closed hers tight on it. "Your family; they will come round." His face said he believed that as much as she. "They must."

By mutual consent, a whirlwind of deferred work filled their next hours. So many details had been put on hold during their forced trips to her mountain home and the city, all now calling urgently for attention. It was well into the night before they at last tumbled into bed. Together, and too tired to worry about it. It was expected. That's how Fee justified it, and refused to acknowledge how right it felt when he hooked an arm around her and tugged her into his side.

"You okay?" His voice rumbled through her body as his lips grazed her forehead.

"Yeah—no, not really."

His hand traced the orbit of her face. "Remember what you told me. They will come round."

"No, they won't. Not my father, not my brothers and sister. This marriage, it threatens the bedrock of what they are." She thought of the endless plantations of festia, all the family dinners and the roundtable of argument and plans that dominated their lives growing up. Her father loved his business, loved the challenge of pushing the land to its limit and taking the leadership of his people. "He means well, my Da. All he makes comes back to our people."

"But is that what they want? To have only what he gives them?"

She chuckled, hearing the hollow echo. "He believes it is, and all those who agree with him are kept safe."

His spurt of laughter was as empty as her own. "Your brothers and sister?"

"Are good people but have always believed they will take over after my father."

"Mmm. So my father thought once of me." His hand stroked slowly down and came to rest on her backside.

"Your brothers? Will they …?"

"Forgive me? Si, maybe. He's more hurt than angry at the moment. He used to tag along after me and Ethan all the time as kids."

He fell silent.

"And Ethan," she prompted.

For a long time, she thought he wasn't going to answer. Not till his hand opened wide and drew her closer. "He loves the business, really loves it. He's a good man, my brother, and all he has ever wanted is to run Solaris. Not for the money, or the power of the role; just to make the business work as well as he can make it."

"Now?"

He took a deep breath. "I'm his big brother, and I've just betrayed everything he holds dear."

CHAPTER TWENTY-THREE

Some days later, Caleb watched as Fee clumped down to the lake edge, scanner in hand. The geotechs had banged in some pegs to mark the final shoreline, and the waters already lapped at several of them. She stopped just shy of one in danger of being engulfed, checked the readout, then glared at the water.

She was dressed today in the sand-coloured work clothes of the plains, a broad brimmed hat shoved on her head to keep her pale, forest-raised skin safe from the fierce plains' sun. Standing legs apart, one hand on hip and wearing the thick boots of the plains. She hated them, pulling them off as soon as she returned to quarters each night and wriggling her toes in blessed freedom. In her home trees, she'd gone barefoot or worn the flexible, soft-soled shoes of the mountains, ideal for a life spent in ever-moving branches.

She'd tried to get away with wearing her own shoes here once, he remembered, chuckling. A few sharp-edged stones and one scuttle across a hot patch of sand had cured that.

She stomped back up the slope, aiming directly for him, and he quickly hid his grin. That pout of temper was so damned sexy.

"I told Adam his flow boundaries were wrong. The final shoreline is going to be a full half-metre above what he predicted. We'll need to strengthen that bank on the west side.

"Jareth's over that way now."

"Good, he can sort it."

"He can," he agreed, and waited.

"Can I have your flyer? It'll get there quicker." He handed her his pass, and she reached up for his kiss, before stumping off.

Whenever she left him now, she did that as naturally as breathing, and every time the shock of it lit up every cell in his body. He watched her till she was out of sight, enjoying the sway of her sassy little body, before opening his com channel.

"Jareth, Fee's on her way over to you." He smiled unsympathetically at the reply. "Yeah, just sort it."

"You only want an easier night, boss," grumbled the young engineer.

Too right, mate. Too right. He broke the connection, and strode off to his next job.

He dug in deep with the planter probe, feeling the satisfying tug of the earth resisting his invasion and the pull of muscles working hard. He hoisted the last clump of dirt out of the way, picked up the waiting sapling and placed it in the hole. A shovelling of dirt, a splosh of water, and one more plant stood ready to hold the line against the scouring winds of the plains. He stretched up, easing out the kinks of unaccustomed exertion after the frustrations of the days in the city. They were nearly done, a line of shrubs, trees and grasses forming a barrier around the lake shoreline. He bent again, picked up the spade and set another sapling into the line. He and Frank, the team botanist, had pored over plans and drawings of this planting, checking wind patterns and water courses until there could be little possibility of error. Yet he still liked helping out with the physical planting, testing the plans against the reality of dirt and topography.

He crouched over, readying another sapling for its home in the dry sand. A hand traced the leaf margin, dove grey and smoky green as were many of the desert plants. Not like those of Fee's home. He propped the sapling into its hole, lost in a memory of deep velvet eyes with that luminescent trace of green so dark as to seem black. The colour of a mountain spring hidden deep in the bush or water pouring in a torrent over the dark slate of rapids, with that hint of iridescence glimpsed once in her forest on a water bird lifting in flight. She had a tunic from home, a thin sliver of forest green shimmering in exotic invitation over her lithe curves. Maybe he'd suggest she wear it tonight. After dinner, when they were alone once more.

"We got company."

It was Bob. He'd been too lost in dreams to hear him. He let go of the plant and stomped in the dirt roughly round it. "Where's the Feds? That's their problem."

Bob shook his head. "It's Ethan."

Now that was unexpected. He rocked back on his heels, and stared up at the comms specialist. "Here?"

Bob hooked a thumb over his shoulder and in the direction of the compound. "In your office."

"The Feds?"

"Couldn't hide him from them. They got the place ringed tight. One's in there with him now."

Just what he needed; his brother riled up more than he was already. "Thanks," he said and caught an answering wry grin from Bob.

Nor was his temper helped by the officious trooper guarding the entrance to his office.

"That's my office."

The man merely waved a weapon in his direction. "Spread your arms, Ser Winter. Please."

The man wasn't going to budge. Frisked, just so he could walk into his own office to talk to his own brother. Caleb could try to take him, except things were enough of a mess already. He spread his arms against the wall, legs astride, and let the man do his job. "You do this to my brother?"

"At the gate and before he got through here."

"But it was okay to leave him alone in an office with all my files?"

The man finished his sweep and pocketed his scanner. "Our people can't hack your files so it's unlikely any plains business exec could manage it."

The lake has to be finished. Maybe if he repeated it enough, he might just be able to hold off popping this oaf. He'd come here to talk to his brother, just talk, not barge in with a temper geared to explode in both their faces. The man finished his scan and knocked on the door.

"Eco-engineer Winter to see you."

So Ethan had locked the door on the man. Good. It made it easier to smile at his brother when the door opened, despite the scowl on Ethan's face. One up to the Winters.

"Ethan, how can I help you?" He put out a hand of welcome, and slammed and palm locked the door behind him before the Fed could see his brother's clenched fist of rejection.

Ethan had always been the most reasonable of the Winter brothers. Pig-headed, their father had labelled Caleb—true—and Si had pulled the laughing idiot trick so often his father actually believed it. But Ethan was born a master of compromise, always able to pick that difficult middle path between what their father demanded and what Ethan wanted to do. Downright devious, Caleb had once called him. That was after a teenage Ethan had somehow persuaded their father to lend him his latest, upmarket flyer to take a girl to a school dance.

There was no laughing today.

"You can tell me what you're up to," said his brother.

He was relieved Fee was far away and fully occupied. "My job."

"Destroying Solaris?"

"Trying to save it, and every other company on Arcadia."

Like hell, said the look on his brother's face. "You are so full of bullshit."

If only he was in the mood for this. Holding tight to his temper, Caleb walked across and sat down behind his desk, hands gripping the arms of his chair as he counted slowly in his head. It didn't help.

"Take a seat and try to be civilised."

Ethan glared at him but did fling himself into the chair on the other side. "So tell me why the Feds and the Survey have taken over our home lands, and why you made it possible."

What to say to that. Deny it? Not when it was true. "It was necessary."

Ethan shot out of the chair and slammed both fists on the desk. "Destroying us was *necessary*?"

Caleb rubbed a tired hand over his face. He shoved back his chair, needing space, and looked his brother straight in the face. No sign of reasonable there now.

"Our father is destroying Solaris well enough on his own. The Survey had no choice but to step in when Solaris began destroying the rest of the world."

"You better explain that. We're the biggest company, employing most of the people in this region. Break Solaris and they starve. You take the solar arrays away and that land is dead. No one can live here without the money we bring in."

"Not as it is now. It will take us years to change that. But that land is not dead, and before Solaris stripped it and covered it over, it supported a fully functioning ecosystem. Now, the desert is spreading. Solaris is destroying the plains, not the Survey."

Ethan threw himself back in the chair and grunted. "You back on that again. Scrawny bushes and dry grasses won't feed anyone."

"No, but food-bearing shrubs and water for irrigation will help." Caleb leaned forward, praying he could find that old bond with his brother. "How many times have you tried to get the Old Man to use a different solar generation system?"

"Like those roofscapes of yours, you mean?"

"For a start."

"Is that your plan—break Solaris and set up in opposition?"

Caleb's chair crashed back and he was around the desk and hauling his brother out of his chair before he could stop himself.

"Go on, do it," snarled Ethan.

What in hell. He caught himself, carefully opened his hands and let Ethan drop back into the chair. Then he stepped back and sat on the desk edge. "When you try, you can wind me up faster than Si."

He looked at his brother, and Ethan returned the stare, looking as sick with anger as Caleb felt. Till suddenly, in that weird way of their childhood, they both broke into laughter, just like every other time Ethan had done this to him. Only this time, black shoals of pain lay beneath it.

Ethan's mouth twisted. "It's a knack."

"Yeah." Caleb sighed, took a deep breath and held out his hand to his brother. Ethan studied it, and for the longest of moments Caleb thought he'd lost him. Then he took it, hauled himself out of that chair and before Caleb could block it, had slugged him on the chin.

"Hey!"

"Ouch." Ethan was shaking his fist. "That chin of yours is a hard as ever—but you deserved that."

Fair enough, he probably did. A real grin warmed his face.

Ethan sat down again and Caleb hauled over the spare chair, setting it down in front of his desk. He sat down, leaned back and crossed his legs, facing his brother. At least Ethan was listening, but the first hint of anything less than the truth would shatter any accord between them.

"You're truly not trying to destroy Solaris?" said his brother.

"Me, no. The Survey, not so sure. My bosses don't always give me the big picture." Caleb took a deep breath. "This is one battle the Old Man can't win."

Ethan grimaced. "The Feds?"

"Them, and the whole government arsenal. This is a fight they can't afford to lose."

Ethan still had his *I'm listening* look on his face, but he wasn't convinced, not yet.

"That ecological stuff of mine is true."

"Yeah?"

"Yes." How to put this and make his brother understand. "Any chance you can get the Old Man to change? To cut his profit margin?"

Ethan snorted.

"That's what the Survey thinks too. There are three less-damaging solar power systems he could be using, other than mine, but none would make him as much money."

"Give us one good reason to change."

Could he? The Alliance ultimatum was on a 'need to know' only. He balled his fists and thrust his hands into his pockets. "He has to change if he wants to salvage any kind of business—and that's all I can tell you," he added as Ethan opened his mouth to object.

Silence. Caleb knew that look on his brother's face. He was considering it, which was something he guessed. When Ethan looked up and studied his face, Caleb met his look, as wide open as possible.

Ethan leaned forward, elbows on knees and clasped his hands, breaking eye contact. "Very well, you have good reason for your actions and you can't tell me because of Survey rules." He glanced up. "This minor environmental monitoring agency you work for? Advisory and guidance—that's what you and the rest of your pack always said."

Caleb shrugged. "It's a bit more," he conceded.

Ethan snorted again, a caustic gust of disbelief. "You're head of a whole team of environmental saboteurs and have a full squad of the toughest troops on the planet backing you. Resource consent permits sure as hell didn't pay for that."

There was nothing Caleb could say. The Survey was out of the shadows now, and was not going back. Given the deadline set by the Alliance, brute power was their only option.

Ethan sat back, and this time his clear green eyes challenged him head on. "So where does your new mountain wife sit in all this?"

"As my wife," he shot back, "and wipe that stupid grin off your face."

"Yeah, well. The parents think this marriage of yours is a forced contrivance of the Survey, and that examination was jacked up by them."

"It was real. The results are final. Fioruisghe den Coille is my wife, and staying that way." Why it was so important for his brother to believe that, he couldn't say, only knew it had nothing to do with the lake or the Survey.

"And you are both going to live here, on the plains?"

Of course it would be Ethan who asked him that. Caleb broke off eye contact, leaned back and looked up at the ceiling, before he could bring himself to sit up and meet his brother's gaze again.

"Aaah," his most percipient brother said.

Caleb lifted an eyebrow.

"Nothing," the grin on Ethan's face was the first real one he'd shown, "but Si will be pleased to hear you haven'tgot everything worked out. He's way past mad at you, and blames your wife for it. Thinks you're about to leave the plains for good, after spending half our childhood thumping into us how amazing this land is"

"Yeah."

"So how do you like trees and mud? I hear that's all they got over the other side of the ranges."

He glared at Ethan. "You're getting worse than Si."

"And?"

"I can't breathe over there," he finally admitted, "and Fee's the same here. She showers as much as the rest of the team put together, and her office is choked with plants from home."

He hadn't talked about this with anyone. Not even Fee—especially not Fee. She was gorgeous, funny, so gutsy and just a quirk of that mouth of hers could make him desperate with want. But she did not belong here, while her beloved trees left him gagging for clear skies and long horizons.

"I don't know if we can live in the same place," he admitted to the brother who had not forgiven him and probably still opposed him, "and it's tearing us up."

A chair crashed. "Trying to make me feel sorry for you? That's low, even for you, *brother*."

Ethan slammed to the door, glared at him till Caleb rose and unlocked it for him.

"The marriage is real," said Caleb.

"And the Survey had nothing to do with it." Ethan stopped in the doorway and Caleb had to wave back the guard. His brother looked him up and down.

"Stay away from Solaris lands."

"Not possible."

Ethan stood there as if made of brittle stone about to disintegrate. Or did he think that only because that's how *he* felt.

"Goodbye," said his brother. Then he was gone.

Fee knocked on Caleb's office door. The dinner hour had come and gone, and still he hadn't emerged. No reply, and the light was off. She banged harder on the door, and when that didn't work, tugged on the catch.

It was unlocked. It slid open and she half fell into the room. Caleb sat at his desk, silhouetted against the window and still as a dead tree stump on a moonless night. She paused, suddenly afraid, then braced herself and hit the lights. He looked up at her with a face as closed to her as the land that gave him life. This man was her husband. The Survey might have forced them into it, but he was still the man who had saved her life in the desert and laughed with her in the reaches of the night.

"I hear you had a visitor?"

His eyes looked at her but gave no sign he heard or saw.

"Your brother Ethan?'

He nodded slowly.

"So what did he want?"

It was like watching a frozen cascade thaw, slowly, drip by drip, as his eyes came back from a far distance. "To talk," he said.

"About what?"

He lifted his gaze, stared at a point above her, and his hands deliberately released their grip on the arms of the chair. "Family matters."

Did he seriously expect her to accept that? She leaned forward and thrust her face into his. "What family matters?"

He waved a hand as if to ward her off. "That's between my brother and me."

"Don't give me that." Fee stalked around the side of the desk and shoved at Caleb. "You're not the only one with an unhappy family. Or who's had to put the Survey first."

Finally, a spark. Anger glinting in those dead eyes. "So when do you hand over that valley your team's replanting to the Survey, and watch your family's faces as you kick them in the teeth?"

"You already watched that. The day we got married."

He thrust out of his chair and it crashed to the ground behind him.

He was so tall, so angry.

"Or are you losing your backbone already?" she said to him.

"You know I won't hurt you, ever, or you wouldn't dare say that."

A like anger roared through her. "So which comes first: Arcadia, your family, or us?"

Utter silence fell. The question came from some place inside she hadn't known existed. Horrified, she opened her mouth as Caleb yanked her into his arms, and his mouth descended.

The kiss overwhelmed her. He was wide open; so angry, so fired up, that he kept nothing in reserve. It released all constraints in her, the only reality his mouth, tongue and hard, hard body.

When they finally broke apart, long moments later, he rested his head on hers and whispered in a voice of strangled hope: "There is no choosing. The Survey made sure of that."

He stepped back, and was once more Eco-engineer Winters. "I've called a meeting of the team in the main hall. Time to update them."

He opened the door, waited for her to pass through. But then touched her on the shoulder. Not a hold, just the imprint of palm and finger. It stopped her cold. The look on his face held her there.

"Once, the answer would have been easy," he said. "Now?" She put her hand over his, and his palm spread, held her as if fearful to let her go. "Don't let me betray you as well. Don't ask me to choose."

He released her again as abruptly, striding forward. Leaving her to follow.

The hall was full when she arrived. All the team were there, even those who had left the field at the same time as she. An order had gone out to everyone, it seemed—except her.

She looked at him, and he returned it. "I don't give you orders."

"So when were you going to tell me about this meeting—or don't you want me here?"

That wasn't all she was asking, and they both knew it.

"Check your com unit," he said.

She glanced down, but it wasn't in its usual place on her wrist. "Oh." She scrabbled in her pockets, found the small disc buried under some pebbles and lab test strips. "I took it off when I was taking lake edge samples."

She activated the unit, checked the shimmering readout displayed over her hand. "You asked me to come see you."

"To *request* that you talk to the team with me. The Survey made us partners on the work here."

And in life, he should have added, was about to add, she was almost certain. Whether he stopped because he was unsure how she felt, or because of his own ambivalence, she no longer knew.

But she did know how she felt about this man.

CHAPTER TWENTY-FOUR

Fee watched as Caleb stepped up onto a chair and Jim yelled at the crowd to pipe down. Caleb might go along with the fiction they were both co-leaders of this project, but these were his people. She stood quietly to one side, watching the faces of the crowd as much as she listened to Caleb's words.

"As you've no doubt heard," he said, to general laughter at his dry tone, "the Survey has openly taken control of this project. You are all now officially Survey employees, instead of a rag-tag bunch of less than competent stockmen."

"Hey, speak for yourself," yelled a voice at the back.

"At least I can stay on a horse, Rab."

The mirth now was genuine, but strain still lurked on too many faces.

"And the Old Man?" called another.

"Is right royally pissed," said Caleb, "but can't do anything about it. Solaris so much as sneezes over the wrong side of the reserve's line, and the Feds will put them in full lockdown." He turned to her, and held out a hand for her to step up. Someone shoved a chair forward and Caleb helped her clamber up onto it. She still felt like an interloper.

"The same goes for den Coille," she said too quietly, and had to repeat it. A polite silence met her. "They have to. Neither my father nor Sol Winter is stupid. They will not attack a family concern legally bound to them by marriage."

Not unless they find out that the Survey is hell bent on their destruction.

"So we carry on as usual?" asked Bob of Caleb. "Is that why you called us here?"

Caleb's quick eye flick said he'd heard Bob but he looked out across the room, taking in the whole crowd as he answered, the sudden grimness of his face quelling all comment.

"No."

Simple, abrupt, clear as crystal. "We're on a full war footing. The Survey doesn't trust either family and, as of today, we trust no one not in this room right now—except other, proven Survey field staff."

"That include her?" said someone. She flushed scarlet and Caleb turned a thunderous stare on the man.

"Yes, it includes her. Especially it includes her, and every single member of her Mountain team. They have put as much on the line as anyone here." He raised his voice so it carried loudly to the far corners of the room. "Anyone got a problem with that can leave now."

She held her breath.

No one left, but there was nothing friendly in the silence.

She stepped down and eased back into the shadows as Caleb continued. "However, we make this decision for ourselves only, not for children or families who can be hurt by them. If staying here puts your family at risk, go now with our respect and thanks. The Survey will wipe your names from the record and keep your loved ones safe."

This time, there was a low rumble of voices, a few gentle shoves and arms flung across shoulders. Slowly, reluctantly, a small group silently left the hall.

"Ben, you too," said Caleb quietly, looking directly at the young, red-faced zoologist in the front row.

"Go on, boy."

"It's best," said the sympathetic voices.

Fee moved quietly over to Bob and nudged him in the side.

"The boy is the eldest of a family of five," said Bob. "His father worked for Solaris and died in a work accident a couple of years ago. His mother's a first grade teacher, with teacher's wages. Without the Solaris payout and Ben's wages, the family will starve."

"But…"

"Argh, don't worry. Caleb's already got the Survey to fix the boy up with a job in the city with a Survey shell company. It's better pay, and Old Man Winter will never know he's Survey."

"He'll suspect. Like he would anyone who worked for Caleb."

"Yeah, but he needs proof to do anything about it. Not even Old Man Winter can risk upsetting too many plains families."

Something still bothered her. She scanned the faces of the rest of the room, saw how closely they watched the exit of their colleagues and the nerves on their faces.

"The others left behind? Their families?"

"Don't work directly for Solaris." Bob watched them too. "But, yeah, they're at risk. No one in these parts likes getting offside with Sol Winter."

The last of the group left the hall and an ominous silence fell. As one, they all looked to Caleb standing high above them.

"We've talked about this often enough," he said. "You all know what to do. We have a job to do, and that's what we will do—but stay sharp. The Feds guarding here don't know this country like we do—or like Solaris does."

How he did it, she couldn't fathom, but the mood in the room changed, became the everyday, the workable. *We can do this*, said their faces as they filed out. Many came up and talked with Caleb before heading out. When the last had left, she walked over to stand beside him.

"You are your father's son."

He raised an eyebrow. She ignored it.

"They're all ready to jump through fire, just because you told them to."

"They may have to," was his grim reply, the brave front dropped. "You did the same to your team."

She shook her head. "I don't have your knack for command."

"Yeah? The whole bunch of them weren't ready to skewer me if I so much as looked at you wrong?"

"That's family," she said.

He held out an arm, and she let him pull her in against his side. "Your methods may be different—less direct—but they're just as effective. You have mountain folk pulling out trees."

"And you have plainsmen planting them."

The truth in a nutshell. The magnitude of what they must do suddenly hit home, stunning her to a halt. He sensed it, became as abruptly still as she, then drew her round to face him and brought his forehead to gently touch hers.

"You really think we can do this?" she whispered.

"I don't know." Words she suspected he could say to no one else. "But together, we're going to give it a damn good try. If not, and we fail …"

That was the essence of it. There was no *if not*. Not if they wanted to save their home world.

"So we carry on, build the lake—and the next one. Replant my mountain slopes…"

"…Watch our families, watch the Survey—and hope like hell we're not on our own in this."

Their kiss was a promise, a vow and a desperate plea, and when they made love that night, it was as if on the last night before a battle. To Fee, the exquisite care he took of her and the passion of his release had the cadence of a farewell. Of giving her a memory to last through the lonely years ahead if the worst happened.

It was a worry that came to her often in the next weeks. Everything was too quiet. The Feds patrolled the camp and surrounding lands, keeping the peace to let the Survey do its work.

Yet, despite all, the first lake was taking shape. Fee tracked water courses, traced flow paths down hidden chambers, and monitored the air as bit by bit, the harsh sky above the plains began to soften under the gentle assault of vapour droplets percolating up from the lake. At day's end they would all gather in the hall, coming together to share in the details of the day's progress over the evening meal; the small triumphs, the laughter and tears of frustration, and occasionally the news from outside.

Very occasionally, thanks to the Feds. It was as if they were on an island surrounded by predator infested waters. Only here the water was the dying land of the Solaris solar arrays on one side and the steep, festia covered slopes controlled by Den Coille on the other.

Fee sat in the hall one night, gazing through the windows and up at the harsh lines of the rocky summit of those mountains. A hand played idly with the sleeve of Caleb's tunic as he sprawled beside her. A clattering of dishes formed an easy background noise from the trio rostered for kitchen duty, and a group played an old tune in the far corner, weaving an intricate tale of deception and whimsical tomfoolery, with light hearted carillons of strings playing rivulets of sound over the clear voice of the engineer, Chaba.

Fee leaned contentedly against Caleb, one ear on the music, the other on the slow rumble of his voice as he talked over the last plantings with Kal Mendip, the eco-engineer most specialised in plant-soil interactions. The night before, Caleb had showed her the pattern behind the plantings, using her bottles and creams as trees and purloining a pair of silky underwear to act as the lake. Only when he starting laying a trail of powder to show the wind patterns did she stop laughing and grab for her things. Which only ended up with her in a tangled heap of limbs and smothered shrieks on the floor, as Caleb switched focus from the plans for the lake to some very earthy plans for her body.

Laughter bubbled up inside her at the memory. On a night like this, she could easily ignore the patrolling troops outside who kept them safe, and the increasing chorus of demanding messages from Central head office. Her eyes traced the fabric of the mountains, from the moonlight touching the tops down to the dark smudges showing where the snow line finished in winter. Only patches of trees survived in the gullies on this side of the ranges; the land baked dry and the slopes dominated by ground hugging scrub and rocky washes of shale. Few festia grew there, nothing like the thick plantations and lush rain forests of her west mountain home.

She nudged Caleb, his talk with Kal having petered out as both listened to the music. "Remind me again who owns the mountain land on this side of the ranges."

He glanced down in surprise. "Technically the state, but in real terms? Your family, I thought."

She considered it, and shook her head. "We did try planting it once but the climate is wrong. Too cold right up on the peaks, too dry lower down, and irrigation was out because of the terrain."

His hand played through her hair. "They're no good to Solaris for the same reasons. Much cheaper to build solar arrays out here on the flats than on those rocky slopes. I think the Old Man considered it once—I was a kid still—but there was no money in it."

She leaned back, giving his hands the freedom of her face and neck, and thought it through. He took full advantage, his voice the careless murmur of a fully distracted man. "No one wants them, I guess."

"Meaning," she said, "they're free for us to use."

His hands paused then resumed the considered path of a man still more interested in the findings of his fingers. "To do what? That land is all right for summer grazing or wind generation, but that's about all."

"Trees," she said dreamily. "Lots of trees, all up those slopes. Trees to bring back the balance. It won't stop the storms and other problems on the western slopes, but it might ease the dryness on this side—and show the people of the western slopes what can be done."

Caleb's fingers kept up their drugging cadence through her hair. "Mmm, maybe," was all he said, as his fingers searched out and found the spot at the base of her neck he had discovered one night, a spot that responded now to his touch by sending warm rivulets of desire surging through her veins. All notions of trees were banished, and not long after, he tugged her to her feet and they hurriedly murmured their goodnights.

A mere tracery of thought lingered as she glimpsed the far slopes out the window again. Tomorrow, she would go up there, but for tonight…"

The sun breaking through the shutters woke Fee the next morning. She stretched lazily, revelling in the feel of joyously used and thoroughly satisfied muscles. A lingering memory of happiness from the night just gone.

Arms up high then out, hands seeking right to the edge of the bed, but Caleb was long gone. Only his scent remained, a warm earthy smell of sun-baked plains. She lifted her head and peered at the tracks of sunlight. Strong, bright yellow. She had slept in.

She ought to be down at the lake edge, taking the first of the day's transpiration rate readings.

One day would make little difference—and there were enough others to do her work. Caleb must have left her to sleep in, making her a present of the morning.

A giggle of delight filled her and she stretched out her toes in tingling anticipation. She was taking a holiday. Today was hers, and tonight would be Caleb's. She squirmed deliciously, plotting exactly how to thank him. The green dress, she decided, the thin, silky one from home, worn without an under tunic.

For now, the sun tugged insistently at her senses and she flung back the covers to cleanse and dress for the day. A sparkle of excitement fluttered through her. No workman plains clothes today. No, today she pulled down her mountain clothes.

Until she remembered the heat of the plains that must be endured first, and pulled out her knapsack to thrust her forest tunic, leggings and soft boots inside, stomping into her plains' work gear and stupid big boots. Just for now, she promised.

She stepped towards the door of Caleb's rooms, but suddenly switched direction and made for the window facing the back alleyway. If she took the front door and started heading out of camp, she would have a Fed clinging to her shoulder all day. Not going to happen. This day belonged to her, not some bumptious, over-protective Fed trooper. If her own family couldn't find her unless she let them in their home forest, no Solaris plains spy was going to catch her. The tree cover on this side of the ranges was still dense enough to hide her.

Half an hour later, she was heading out of camp, very pleased with herself. She hadn't lost her ability to slip sideways through peoples' attention. A half wave here, a hurried purposeful stride there and she was gone before anyone registered her passing. Act normal; that was the trick of it.

She made first for the lake site, a route so commonplace that the Feds on guard at the camp perimeter barely gave her a glance, and followed the road they trusted until out of sight. On the far side of a knob, in a blind spot between two rocky outthrusts, she pulled her skimmer off the roadway and hauled out the one man flyer she had stowed in the freight compartment. Small, light and agile enough that if she kept low to the rising hillocks that blended into the foothills, she should escape the Feds' surveillance network.

For a time anyway. She had no illusions about their vigilance. This was a holiday, but soon they would catch her up and it would end.

So she meant to enjoy to the full the short time she had, pushing her small flyer to its limit. Two hours later, she slipped into the cover of the trees. The flyer slid neatly into a cleft in the bank and she stripped off the despised town clothes, replacing them with the dark forest green of her mountain tunic and leggings. Toe off the thick boots and pull on the supple leather of her mountain shoes.

Feeling more like herself for the first time in weeks, Fee set her foot into the nearest knothole and grabbed a low hanging branch, hoisting herself up into the tree. All round her, the rich tangy scent of sap and bruised leaves filled the air. Arm over arm, feet easily found the best footing and soon she was swaying in the upper canopy, her body revelling in the familiar rhythm of the branches. The feel of it was not quite the same as home; the air sapped of water, the trees reaching only to the rise of the next ridge, and below lay the orange and yellow spread of the plains as grass disappeared into a cloudless sky rather than rivers racing into the spray tinged tips of treacherous seas. But it was enough for today. It would have to be, though the need for her own trees was like a physical pain some days.

She would return home one day. Quite how, was unclear, but some day it would happen. That she had to believe.

For the next few hours, she revelled in her freedom, twisting from tree to tree, dipping down to the shrubs, discovering to her delight a small hidden spring falling in a diamond crusted spray over the sharp edged rocks lining the gully bottom. She explored that snaking hollow from the top edge where the trees diminished into small, whip-like striplings, down to the few mighty giants still left standing where the gulley poured into the plains. A fragment of what she was sure had once been here. This land was too empty, too much of it like her home slopes to have always been so bereft of tree cover. Up higher, where the soil fertility dwindled and the howling dry winds of the plains held rule, yes. There, the tough mountain scrub and grasses must rule. But these lower slopes—no, they should harbour trees. Not the festia of her side, it would never be wet enough here. But baullnia, and farsee, and the beautiful dappled leaves and pale splotched trunks of the beith should flourish. Would flourish, she vowed.

Finally she climbed up to a hillock in the centre, two hands planted on the bole of the solitary tree crowning the ridge, and stared up the valley. Her adventure was coming to an end. There was no sign yet of the Feds but there soon would be, furious at her escape and bent on imprisoning her again. She had no sympathy for them.

A wrinkle of something in the distance caught her eye. They were coming for her. She stood on a branch, triumphant, watching the speck enlarge, then finally began her descent. She would walk to meet them, not be dragged ignominiously from her trees.

The sound of their flyer was a discordant whine among the sighs of the trees as she made her final jump to the ground, landing lightly in a roll and bending over to brush off the leaf dirt. Her bag sat where she had left it, propped in a fork of an adjacent tree.

She briefly thought about changing back to her plains work gear but discarded it. Today, she was who she was. If the Feds and the plains folk didn't like that—and Caleb?

She lifted the bag up, shouldered the weight of it, and stepped through the gap in the encroaching shrubbery at the tree margin.

Something hit her on the head. Blackness and the muffling, engulfing feeling of a shroud dropping over her. Then she was sinking into oblivion, a sense of falling, of being hoisted, gagging helplessly.

A voice said "Hello, Sis."

Then she knew nothing.

CHAPTER TWENTY-FIVE

Her head ached and a bright light stung her eyes. Fee came hazily to awareness. A hum of noise, the light shining in her face again, and she scrunched her eyes shut.

The light wavered, assaulted her full on.

"Come on, Sis."

She knew that voice and the panic inside her eased. She reached up and bashed at the hand holding that annoying beam on her face. Then struggled up, opened her eyes and glared at her oldest brother.

"Cumchdach mac Bram an Scathach den Coille, have you lost your mind?"

She shut her eyes again. Maybe if she tried hard enough, this whole debacle would turn into a nightmare she could wake from.

The pounding at the base of her skull gave the lie to that and she reluctantly opened her eyes again. It truly was her eldest brother scowling down at her, and behind him, the rest of the unholy gang. Every single one of her four brothers, crowding around her and looking both thoroughly pleased with themselves and angry as hell—at her, she assumed.

She was no longer afraid, not for herself.

Cautiously, she eased up from the bare boards of the bunk they'd laid her on, and only then recognised where they'd brought her. Their old hut, built as a retreat by her father and taken over by his brood as first a clubhouse then later a precious escape for the siblings from the demands of being a den Coille.

Positioned safely within den Coille home lands but well away from the settled trees of their home branches, giving them all a touch of the freedom they needed. It was high on the forested slopes of the ranges, not far from one of the passes crossing over to the east. An ideal spot for this idiocy.

"How long have I been out?" she grumbled, glaring at each of her brothers in turn. "Do you morons have any idea what you've done?"

That brought scowls aplenty, but not a single shred of regret.

"Seolta, was this your idea?" Her second brother, dark-haired, dark-eyed and most like her wily father in spirit. Cumchdach might be the natural leader of the brothers, largest in build and strongest of muscle and heart, but it was Seolta who drove them.

She looked at the two youngest: staunch Ceart, ever loyal and steadfast in pursuit of the well-being of the family, and the youngest of them all, bright-eyed Aigherach. Still not yet out of his teens, the only one in the family younger than her. This was probably all some exciting game to him.

She pinned her gaze on Seolta again. "You could have at least kept Aigherach out of this."

"I made them bring me," her youngest brother said, thrusting forward. "We've been waiting here for days. Knew you couldn't stay away from trees too long, and someone had to stop you destroying den Coille."

"Me, destroy? You have no idea."

"So how about you spell it out, little sister," said Seolta coolly. "All we have done is rescue our dearly beloved Fioruisghe from a forced alliance with our enemy and eternal exile."

That had her jumping up, then wishing she hadn't as the pain in her head burst into a million throbbing shards. "You think? No, what you've done is deliberately break a whole parcel of laws and set yourself against the Federal government in the process. Kidnap of a government official going about her fully authorised and Federally backed duties, assault of said government official," she touched the back of her head and winced at the size of the bump there, "illegal entry into a federally controlled reserve, obstruction of a legal marital union. Shall I go on?"

"Tell that to Da," said Cumchdach.

"He knows about this?"

Silence.

"Mind if I tell him?' She reached out for the com-unit, only to have Seolta shove her back down.

"Hey," said Aigherach. "That's Fioruisghe."

Fee made a quick sideways roll, reaching for Seolta and seized him in a lighting fast hold. One of the many things taught her by the Survey about which her family knew nothing. She thrust him down onto the bunk, an arm across his throat and her fingers pinching a crucial nerve point that rendered him immobile.

"You have overstepped yourself this time, *brother.*" She lifted her hands and freed him. He jumped up, scowling blackly and for once losing his damnable cool. Being bested by your baby sister did that to a man, but she didn't feel sorry for one minute.

The only pity was she couldn't take on the whole lot of them, and win. Or rather, couldn't do it without badly hurting them, and she wasn't ready for that yet.

"Are you going to call Da?" she demanded of her oldest brother. "Or even better, let me go before this thing gets a powerful sight worse?"

He looked at Seolta then at her. One slow nod, and a curt order to the others to leave her alone. "You're not going anywhere."

She sat down on the nearest chair. It had been worth a try. A glance out the far window. Mid afternoon, she decided, so still some time before the Feds would realise she was gone and take action.

Cumchdach made the call. In the other room, out of her hearing. He stalked back in a few minutes later.

"We're taking her home."

She moved swiftly, falling into a defensive stance. "Not going to happen."

"It is—if you value the safety of your team." Seolta brought up a holo on his unit, shimmering drunkenly in the air in front of her before coalescing into stark, crystal clear images.

All her team from the valley—standing on a top ridge, outlined against the grey, western sky and surrounded by den Coille troops. The weapons pointing at them looked very real. Where were their Federal guards?

"You threaten our own people!"

"Ours? That seems to be in question."

Seolta had that insufferably smug look on his face. *Get out of that one, Sis,* it said , and there was no point in denying her team's allegiance. "They are still den Coille. From this area."

"And their first loyalty is to…?" said Cumdharch.

Must be to the Survey. "The Survey looks after its own," she warned. Unlike den Coille, she added to herself, but her brothers caught the look on her face. Cumdharch and Ceart had the grace to flush. Aigherach looked about to do something stupid, except that Ceart wrapped a big arm around him.

"The Feds?"

"Called away urgently. Something about a developing situation in the southern range. They still trust den Coille."

Seolta again, that look on his face more smug than ever. She so wished Samhchair was here. Second in age, her sister had always been the calming influence in the family.

"Samhchair?"

"Wanted no part of this," said Cumdhach.

"But didn't stop us," said Seolta.

Another knife added to their battery. She looked again at the holo image. Her team stood resolute, grouped in the defence formation of their common training: Seamach standing guard in the front and Joseph controlling the rear.

"You won't hurt them," she said.

"You certain of that?" said Seolta.

She met his eye, holding it as if totally sure of her convictions.

He smiled nastily. "The Survey will believe them at risk, and that's all that counts. As for the reality, they're safe as long as both they and you cooperate."

Her brother met her gaze, holding it with equal determination. In many ways, he knew her best of all of them, had always suspected her role as the den Coille eco-engineer and her commitment to the family's wealth. His was total. She saw the steel in him now, scarcely hidden behind the taunting exterior. There were only two people in the world Seolta deferred to—their father and Cumchdach.

"Brother, don't do this," she said to him now. "Let me and my team go. Any other course plays directly into the Survey's hands, and they are playing in deadly earnest on this one."

"Can you tell us why?" said Cumdhach.

She could only hold her face still and answer flatly, "I am not authorised to do that—but the stakes are the highest."

Seolta snorted. "Yes, the Survey and government want control of the den Coille lands. We've always known that."

There was nothing more she could say. Seolta's words held too much truth. How much, not even she was certain.

"The reasons are good," she protested lamely.

Not one of her brothers moved. She had to break through, had to stop this now. *Don't let them fight too hard, don't let me hurt them.*

Then Ceart moved to set himself against the doorframe. The biggest, strongest and best fighter of them all, not even Survey training would guarantee she'd prevail against him.

And if she did, and made it outside, what next? If she could make it to the trees, she would easily escape her brothers, but they knew that as well as she and by the way Seolta and Aigherach stood, they had a fall back plan to stop her.

Fighting family had some unique problems. They knew each other too well.

It was why you should never do it.

She gave up her defensive crouch and let her shoulder slump. "This will be the end of den Coille," she said, in a last, half-hearted protest. "At least let my team go."

"No. They're too useful as hostages," said Seolta.

Pain washed over Cumchdach's face. "It's for Da to say."

The sound of a forest skimmer broke the moment, hovering overhead, as a troop of den Coille men burst in. One grabbed her hands and brought them close to bind them.

"You don't need to do that to her," said Aigherach.

Cumchdach looked at her, a question in his eyes, and she was forced to deny him. One abrupt shake of her head, and she held out her hands firmly in front of her.

"Your choice," he said, and watched her with a face masked of all emotion as the man pulled her bindings tight and held a weapon against her while he marched her out of the room.

Even Aigherach kept silent, finally learning the truth of what must come. She had hurt her brothers today, hurt them badly with her rejection and yet couldn't regret it. Could only mourn.

The stakes were high. She had said that to Cumchdach, but not even he could guess how high. After this day, she only prayed she never learned the Survey had played her false.

There was no chance for escape before they boarded the skimmer and once inside, she was shoved onto a bench seat, right against the window and with too many bodies hemming her in to do more than slump against the bulkhead. She stared out at the green leaves and grey skies. All she had wanted was a few hours to herself in the trees she loved. Now, she had brought disaster on them all.

It was a few hours back to den Coille headquarters, but with no sign of rescue by the halfway point, Fee was losing her feeble hope. No sign came to show her absence had been noticed and remarked on, but a small part of her had still waited.

Now, staring at the gathering clouds above, she relinquished that sliver of hope.

The increasing blackness of the skies matched her mood exactly. Rain was no stranger to these slopes. Then she noticed the trees below them, and the whirling dance of the leaves as the rising winds caught them. She looked at the sky again, craning her eyes westward. Dark clouds roiling madly, the ominous leading edge of a major storm front.

"Cumchdach, put the hammer down on this thing. Or set us down, now!"

She leaped up, forgetting her bindings and the big men around her. Seolta shoved her rudely back.

"Stop your tricks, Fioruisghe."

"No trick. Look at the sky. There's bad weather coming, very soon, and it's going to be nasty."

Her brother stared hard at her, then reached over to look out the window. Around them, others did the same.

"Fee knows weather," said Ceart in his slow voice.

"This is no trick," she pleaded. "You need to warn everyone at home."

"How bad?" said Cumchdach from his seat across the aisle.

"A deluge, and gale force winds. Those clouds are thick with water and ready to spill."

"Seolta?"

At Cumchdach's order, Seolta took her chin in his hand and stared intently into her face. *Please believe me*, she thought. He could read her best of all.

Finally he released her. "She means it," he said.

Cumchdach was unbuckling as he called out to the pilot on his com. "How long to base?"

He strode up the aisle to the pilot station and seconds later she felt the fierce surge of the engines at full throttle.

"Can we make it home?" said Seolta. Fee looked at the clouds, assessing the wind speed and direction from the tree movement below. "Take the long gully route. It should bypass the worst of it to give us a bit of time."

Seolta passed it through his com, "And warn them at home," he added. Then turned back to her. "Evacuation?"

The city had long practiced for this; a mass evacuation if a heavy soaking destabilised the land beneath the trees. She thought over the city as she had last seen it, reviewing the drainage and building plans.

"Hopefully not, but they should be ready."

A gust of wind buffeted her.

"Hold on," called the pilot over the comm.

Fee braced. "Who's flying?"

Seolta braced beside her, and shoved out an arm to hold her in place. "Finbar. He'll get us through."

If anyone could, it was their old childhood friend, and the best pilot Fee knew. She checked outside. They were low over the ridge, following her suggested route. But the winds tore into the branches below and the first heavy rain drops slammed into the leaves.

They would be cutting it fine.

A whoosh of the engines, bucking against the fury of the storm, as the elements unleashed their furies. Fee checked the conditions out the window again.

What the … She jumped up, swearing as the bindings cut into her wrist, and stared in horror at the land below. "Who authorised that—and get these things off me." She wheeled on Cumchdach, thrusting past her stupid guards before they could stop her. "Which idiot ordered clearance of the plant cover on that top slope?"

Cumchdach slowly pulled out his knife as she thrust her bound hands at him. "You going to do something stupid?"

"Aarrgh." She was almost too angry for speech. "A million buckets of water are about to come down on us and you worry about what one kid sister can do to you?" She shoved her bound wrists right against the knife, and he slowly sawed off the strapping, leaving her to shake off the last tag. Free. She stormed up the aisle to the pilot's room.

"Hey, you can't go in there." Cumchdach reached out to grab her and she swung and thrust a fist right under his rib cage, where it would hurt the most, the vision of that bleak slope driving her hard. She'd had that entire slope above the home trees covered with a carefully planned canopy of mixed trees and criss-crossed with a meticulously thought-out pattern of drainage channels. Now, all that remained was a desecrated panorama of raw tree stumps, ravaged channels and brand new plantings of the omnipotent festia.

Cumchdach fought off an explosion of gagging coughs to straighten up and reach for her again.

"Let her go, brother," said Seolta's sharp voice. "Fioruisghe, what do you know?"

She ignored the demand, heading for the pilot again. "Stand aside, Ceart. I need that com in there."

"Or," said her steadiest of brothers.

"That hillside," she jabbed her finger at the window. "Nothing is holding that land down. It will soak up this rain like a crumbling sponge…If it gives way…" She could not say the worlds out loud. "Just let me pass."

Ceart's face was white. He shoved open the door to the control cabin. "Give her the com."

The pilot looked at her, looked back at her brother, and waved her towards the com bank. She punched in the emergency channel drummed into every den Coille child.

"Evacuate. Evacuate. Class 1 Emergency. Get your families out of there."

A crackly voice and a well-loved face suddenly blocked the screen. "Cancel that," her father growled. "Fioruisghe ingh Scathach, you are no longer free to use this channel."

She gave back a scowl as fierce as his. "You want me to trigger a full Federal emergency?"

"And which of those fool brothers let you loose?"

"They had to. You are about to have the whole top fields pouring down the south gulley and right into a very big chunk of the city. What *fool* cleared that slope?"

"This fool. That's good growing land. It will make us a tidy profit."

"You think I planned that planting and drainage for my own amusement?"

"Who knows why you did things? I don't—not any more."

"Can it, Da." She waved a hand, too upset to bother arguing. "You have to get out. Get our people out of there. If you don't …" She choked, struggling for words. "It will be carnage, Da. Please, call the evacuation."

He was not going to listen. Never had she failed so badly. She turned back to her brother. "Say something. He has to listen." She scrubbed hastily at the tear that threatened. She never cried!

Ceart moved up, stood beside her. "She speaks truth, Da."

Then Cumchdach on her other side, with Aigherach beside him. "She believes what she's saying. Whether she knows enough to make the call…" He shrugged. "Who knows what the Survey has taught her."

Another body behind her. The dark presence of Seolta. "Listen to her, Da. Fee does know about this, and I would know if she was lying. Call the evacuation."

She held her breath. A long, endless moment as her father gave her that hard stare that had reduced her worst moments of childhood into worthless spouts of immature bravado. This time, she could not let him win.

Slowly, still holding her eye, he lifted his wrist, spoke deliberately into his com unit.

"Class 1 emergency. Evacuate. Plan priority A3C. Begin now."

CHAPTER TWENTY-SIX

Organised chaos reigned in the main flyer port of Manascraoch, filled with people hurrying one way only. A swirl of transporters lining up for passengers, men lifting bags, women hastening children on, parents with babies wrapped in their arms. All pushing, shoving, making a show of queuing for the line up of large freighters waiting to lift them away from danger.

Her brothers surrounded her as they stood in the opened hatch. To imprison or protect? Cumchdach's face said imprison, and the grim distrust on Seolta's face made clear his feelings. *Make one wrong move, little sister, and you will be locked up tighter than a file of den Coille final accounts.*

She would so like to oblige, but that top field sat too clearly in her head. It was raining hard now, great sploshes crashing to the ground and soaking quickly into the soft carpet of humus on the forest floor.

Ceart took her arm and ran with her across the landing pad to the dry refuge of the control building. She burst through the door, head down, and rammed into a solid, and very human wall.

Her father had sent his best troops to welcome her home.

"Thank you, Sers. We will take Sera den Coille from here."

"No, you won't," said Aigherach, bursting through his brothers.

"Your father's orders, Ser," the leader said, and Seolta pulled at Aigherach. She almost felt sorry for her little brother.

"Of course," said Cumchdach, "but we will accompany you," said her more astute brother.

They marched down the corridor, heading to the bowels of the city. There was no time for this. Outside, the rest of Manascraoch's inhabitants hurried to fill the freighters. That was where the troops were needed. Not here, not taking her from the work she needed to do.

"Where are we going?" she demanded.

No answer. The men gripped her arms and hustled her down corridors and walkways, into a room she finally recognised. Her father's business office. She had never entered it by this door before.

They waited. For what? And waited too long, till finally a clump of footsteps broke the silence. Her clever, imperious and beloved father erupted into the room.

"Boys, you're needed to help with the evacuation. You know what to do."

For an instant it seemed her brothers would refuse. "She will be safe?" said Cumchdach.

"She is my daughter still."

Cumchdach gave way first, and the rest followed him. Aigherach looked about to argue, till Seolta thumped him on the arm, and dragged him along. Ceart silently nodded, a brusque fist raised in support, but he also left her. She was alone, with her father and his troopers.

"Where does the danger come from?" said her father.

She tried to shake off the trooper's hold. "Down the south gulley," she said, copying his cool tone. "We're in the direct flood path here. Any mud flow will take out this part of the city, plus the rest of the south-western quadrant."

"Captain, you heard my daughter. Tell the engineers and set your squads."

That got rid of half the troop, but she was still held firm by the rest.

"We need to get out of here, now," she said.

"In good time. After you tell me why you have set yourself against your family."

"You're really going to do this now?"

"We have time."

"No, Da, we don't." The rain was drumming heavily down, the battery of it piercing deep into this enclosed room. "Take me to my team. We have work to do."

"No."

The finality of that single word sent a shaft of fear through her. "What have you done with them?"

"They are where all traitors go. Where my troop think you should go." Her father had always been a master of the timed pause. "The Trunk cells."

She had to grab at the nearest trooper to stop herself collapsing. "Release them, now. Those cells are right in the path of the mud flow."

"If there is a mud slide."

"You doubt me?"

"After what you did, daughter? Marrying a Winter?"

"Yes, I married Caleb Winter. I work for the Survey and the wealth of den Coille is *not* my priority. You would let my team die for that?"

She'd had enough. A quick side step, a knee here, a jab there, a twist and she had two weapons from the troopers' belts. A stunned silence as she aimed them at the Sergeant of the troop and her father. "I look after my own, Father. Tell them to stand down."

He looked coolly back at her, but she knew her father. Enough to recognise the anger and the shock hiding behind his eyes.

"You won't hurt me," he said.

"You think? A Surveyor, and a Winter now. Stand down, Sergeant."

The man was going to be a hero. By all the roots! She met the trooper's gaze full on, but he still went to move. She shot his knee, then switched to sweep her aim over the remaining troopers.

"I'm a fully trained Survey field op. That means, gentlemen, that I can cut every one of you down before you move a micron, and I can choose to hit you precisely where it will hurt most. Nor have I any interest in whether you have future offspring."

"Fioruisghe!"

"That includes you, Da. If you force me, I will incapacitate you. Unlock the cells, now."

"And the sergeant bleeding to death in front of you?"

"Don't insult me, Da. I shattered his kneecap, not a major blood vessel. His men can carry him out of here as soon as you release those cells and I'm safe away."

He growled, and thumped a fist on the desk.

"I am your daughter, Da, and just as pig-headed as you."

Finally, he gave in, and punched the control panel on his desk.

She let out her breath in relief. "Thank you—and Da, a piece of advice. Call the Survey in, now, before they come in anyway. The world is changing."

She had no time to wait for an answer. She was out of the room, running hard down the fully deserted corridor. Da was not stupid. Only he and his troopers had stayed in the vulnerable area. But as she ran, her ears strained to hear any faint rumbling.

She had seen the effects of mudslides before. A Survey team had been sent in to help clean up a hillside engulfing a small isolated settlement. The local Survey op was with her when they found the first body. A small child, still as in sleep but with a look on her face that Fee had never forgotten. No child should die in such terror.

"I tried. I tried to tell them," the local agent had said, over and over, as he tenderly wiped the cloying mud from nose and mouth in a vain attempt to make the small body presentable for her parents. Their bodies were found an hour later, and Fee had forcibly marched the man out of there. He was almost catatonic with grief.

"You warned them," she had said, but knew it made no difference. She was not going to live with such guilt, not today, and she ran faster than ever.

One more corner, another row of faceless doorways before an open door yawned in front of her. The cells, built right under the base roots of the baullnia at the south-western edge of the city. It was the last bastion of mixed tree cover on the city's perimeter before the festia plantations took over. Above her was only an empty gulley leading to that newly raw hillside waiting for planting, a too steep slope made of little more than lightly bound soil and decaying humus overlaying a hard clay pan. Without her carefully planned drainage channels and tree cover, the plummeting rain was free to take the path of least resistance. Down to the base of that spongy soil cover, then whoosh along the impermeable clay pan in a huge river of mud, water and debris that would bring anything in its path hammering down on the settlement.

How much, that was the unknown. That, and when.

She rushed in, frantically checking cells, each and every one of the small, gloomy box rooms. Empty. Free of her team. They were gone, already escaped. Her father had kept his word. Out of the cell block again, heart racing and feet pounding as she ran along the route they must have taken to escape the mud.

No sign of her team. Until suddenly, a dropped tunic she recognised as belonging to Kebhyn, a discarded sash from Sorcha. She ran faster now, after them, and for her own escape to safety. Everyone else here had gone, the empty cells promised that, and the lack of pursuit said her father and his troopers were safe away as well. She was almost out, almost beyond the flow path. No sign of her team. Has they made it? They must. How much mud would come down?

A faster spurt. Then she heard it. The first low rumble. An open door, nearly free. How much was coming? That noise, a loud crack, the eerie whoosh of the wet sludge rushing closer, crashing into and destroying anything in its path. She was in the trees now. Others had run this way. Broken branches and myriad footprints told of their flight.

Nearly safe, and no more sign of her team. They must have got away.

The roar was on her.

Boom. Sloosh. A high wall of mud, barrelling down.

It was here.

It had been a long, frustrating morning. Caleb wanted nothing more than quiet, a lunch with no interruptions and Fee's face across the table. With her, there was no need to pretend he had all the answers. If he tried, she'd quickly call his bluff or burst out laughing.

He put a foot on the step of their new, shared quarters, and stopped mid tread. When had her presence become so essential? He shook it off. She was his wife; of course he enjoyed her company.

A wife you were forced to marry, said the voice lurking at the back of his skull. He shoved it back and carried on up the steps.

What had she been doing today? She'd looked so peaceful, sleeping in their bed this morning, that he had let her be and told the team to cover her jobs today. The workload was hard on all of them, under ferocious pressure to get the lake finished and prove its worth before the fragile constraint of Solaris splintered into killing shards. But it was hardest on Fee. This was not her home and his team didn't fully trust her. Worse, she read every nuance of that attitude yet could never show a single sign of what it did to her. It was a talent, her ability to read people, and she often picked up on tensions in the team before he did.

So that was why he enjoyed their evenings. The puzzle was solved, and again he shoved down the insistent voice that said he was missing something. Well, maybe not everything. Fee was just plain gorgeous, and wanted him every bit as much as he wanted her. A grin warmed him as he opened the door and called out, "Fee, I'm home," slung his bag on a hook and slipped off his shoes.

He was halfway down the hall before the silence of the place registered. No answering shout of "In here." No exotic but amazing smells from their small kitchen. He opened all the doors, refusing to acknowledge his disappointment. She was either still busy or had decided they were eating in the common room.

They made sure to make regular appearances there; mealtimes were the best place to pick up on the mood of the team and catch up on progress. Yet Fee was an astounding cook, taking the plains' fare and twisting it with mountain touches, and he had come to treasure their quiet meals together. Just the two of them.

He checked his com unit for her message. It had become a habit for them to send one if either must change plans.

Nothing, and his disappointment deepened.

He put through a call to Marabeth. "Fee mention where she was going today?"

"Haven't seen her," the cook said, with the harried voice of one interrupted during a busy time of day. He tried the eco-engineers and the others working with her. After the last, "Haven't seen her all morning," the disappointment changed. Now it was worry. He called the Feds.

"Haven't seen her all day, and her usual skimmer's still in the garage. Thought she was staying home?"

"No, she didn't. Find her." He snapped off the connection and began to hunt in earnest.

Their room was tidy. No sign of struggle or disturbance, everything still where Fee would have left it. No intruder could copy that so exactly, so she must have left freely. That was something, he guessed. He opened the wardrobe, trawled through her clothes. From one end of the rack, and back again before he realised what was missing. Her mountain clothes—the ones best suited to trees—and remembered her talk of the evening before.

"Damn her." He punched in a call to the garage. "Did Fee take a vehicle out today?"

"Yeah—aren't you with her?"

"No, I am not."

"Oh. She said you'd asked her to pick it up, that you were meeting her at the perimeter."

His worry escalated. Now it was fear, a tight knot sitting hard in his belly. Why would his wife leave camp secretly? What was her target? The trees on this side of the ranges, or her home. She'd finally decided to throw her lot in with her family?

No, not possible. But the alternative? With her family meant she was safe.

"Trace that flyer. I want to know exactly where it is now."

He was at the garage before his com came to life again. "Found it, boss. Up on the lower slopes, dead east of here. Scanning closer now for the precise coordinates."

"And Fee?"

Silence. Then a careful: "No occupants apparent. Not on a distant heat scan."

He was running now, signalling to the tech and pointing to the fastest flyer on the block. *Fire it up.*

The Feds arrived as he took off, an angry crackle erupting over his com. "Get the fix from the comms office," he snapped back.

"Return to base, Eco-engineer." The chief guardsman, suffering from a delusion that Caleb took orders. "This could be a trap."

"Could be—and could be my wife is hurt up there. Follow, Chief, but do not stop me."

He slapped off the send function and ignored the tirade of ever more frustrated demands. If this was a trap, Fee was the bait.

"Come on, machine." He slammed it into boost drive, taking a high profile and careless of the stream of invective coming from the chasing Feds.

"Bob, finished that location scan?"

"Not yet. Wait." A nerve tearing silence. "Got her,' said a triumphant voice. "In a gulley, three degrees north of your path. Patching the coordinates through to your system now."

"Thanks. Now get those Feds off my back."

"No can do, boss. Not with you flying at that altitude and making yourself a big, fat target. Don't suppose you would drop down to a safer level?"

Caleb didn't bother to answer that one. Up here was faster, end of story. He switched the display and clung to the signal, getting stronger and stronger.

"Any life scans?"

"Not yet," said Bob's stiff voice.

"She has *not* gone over, not of her own free will." Whether he was convincing himself or Bob, he refused to consider. "Come on, machine." But he already had it on full.

Finally, finally, he was on top of the signal and could drop down. Land, unstrap, unlock the hatch. Just in time, his good sense took over and made him switch to a localised scan before opening it. He had to force himself to wait till the full scan was complete, and the readout showed 'clear of threat'. The hardest wait of his life.

Finally, an even tone signalling safety, and he could open the hatch. He was out, hurrying down the steps and towards her light flyer.

Bob was right. No sign of life. Caleb yanked open the canopy. No one; no dead body, no sign of life at all.

Branches snapping and the roar of engines announced the Feds' landing as Caleb rifled through the cabin. So little sign of her. A left over lunch basket, her recorder set on the dashboard, samples spread on a flat panel, separated by type but not yet bagged and preserved.

The Feds burst through the door. "Ser Winter, you will come back with us to the secure perimeter. Now. We will find your wife and bring her home to you."

Caleb ignored them and thrust a hand towards the unfinished samples. "Someone has taken her."

"If that is so, Ser, we will find her," the man said soothingly, "but first we must get you back to the security of base camp."

Caleb had never liked being handled. "In case I defect too?"

"No, no, Ser, of course not. We will find Sera den Coille also. No doubt she is lying safe somewhere. A routine patrol passed over here earlier and found nothing of concern."

They wouldn't. Not without knowing this land. Caleb stepped out of the flyer and waited for the Feds to follow. He watched their leader set foot on the ground and figured he had about two minutes before they started pulling their guns. He began to hunt again, pacing hastily over the flat area Fee had set down in.

They pulled their weapons just before the two minute mark.

"We have to leave, now, Ser Winter."

One more step. A faint smear on a rock at his foot, the colour a rusty brown. "Shine your scanner on this."

"If we do, you will agree to come with us?"

"We'll see," he said.

The Fed pulled out his scanner and entered a code. Their forensics programme was as good as the Survey's for this sort of work—and he doubted they would let him use his com unit scanner anyway.

The man ran the unit over the rock, peering at the readout. "It is positive for Sera den Coille," he said, his voice neutral, refusing to name the substance. Not that Caleb needed the reader's confirmation. Dried blood was hard to mistake.

"You still think she wasn't taken away by force?"

"Our data base contains all routine den Coille entries. Given the circumstances, the result may be questionable."

"The Survey's isn't." Caleb no longer cared if the man tried to stop him. He coded in his unit, ran a scan over the rock and bent over the surrounding ground as the picture of Fee appeared in his screen. "Positive for her," he snapped, "and there are tracks of four others here."

The guardsman stood unmoved. "No sign of a struggle?" The scathing tone showed the man's growing annoyance.

Caleb worked hard to keep his temper. "No, but one of the four is carrying an extra weight, and none of the footprints match someone of Fee's build. "He thrust the com unit at the chief. "See for yourself."

"I am not trained to interpret such data, as you know, Ser."

"Then patch it through to someone you trust who is."

For a minute it looked like the man would refuse. Just to be difficult, Caleb was sure. Finally he took the proffered unit, set it against his scanner and initiated the upload. Caleb waited impatiently as the chief walked to the edge of the clearing, talking on his unit. The rest of the troop stayed on guard, guns pointed right at Caleb and looking too ready to do a whole lot more.

Then the chief returned, and handed back his unit. "Headquarters confirms your analysis, and Survey Central has agreed to give us a full scan via your unit."

He snatched at his comm, hurriedly linked into central and coded in his authority for release. "Thank you, Ser Winter," said the voice in his ear. "We're linking into your base now. Where do you think agent den Coille would have gone?"

He thought, and reviewed the image of trees as he came in to land. "She would have gone to the head of the gulley and worked her way back down."

All Caleb wanted to do was storm through the trees, but had to rein in the impulse. The scanner would find hidden tracks better than him, and he had a fair idea Fee wouldn't have walked at ground level in any case. Up in the fragile branches was her preferred option.

Had she fallen?

He paced over to the landing site, wearing a frown and kicking uselessly at fallen sticks.

A crackle in his ear. "Boss, they've found flyer traces. Just over the gulley ridge line and through a gap in the rocks."

"Show me how to get there." He activated the vid screen on his unit, bringing up a visual to one side of his eyes. A pathway set in glowing lines, winding in and out of the trees above him. He couldn't run faster, damn it, not in this terrain. He was halfway there when Bob's voice came back on.

"No point, boss. No signs of life at the site. But the footprints and heat traces show she was taken."

He seized on the word. "You sure?"

"Uh huh. No trace of her footprints and the heat residues show a large body carrying a smaller one. Also…"

"What?"

"There's no sign of struggle. She wasn't fighting them."

"Unconscious?" Or hurt. Or willing. No, that was the one thing he refused to believe. Not with the sick sense of urgency in his gut driving him on, the sense that *knew* she was in danger. "Origin of the flyer?"

And knew the answer before Bob replied. "Den Coille's, Manascraoch."

He swung round, back to his flyer and the Feds, and strode up to their chief. "We're going in to Manascraoch, and we're going now."

The Fed pilot stepped out of the cockpit as Caleb barrelled his way forward. "Sorry but no can do, Eco-engineer. No one is flying over that mountain ridge. Bad weather's brewing and all flights are grounded.

One look at the man's face showed the truth of his words.

"Bob, call the Survey and find out if that flyer from here is still in the air. Get them to scan all craft heading into Manascraoch."

Another wait. There had been too many this day. He cursed the hours of blissfully unconcerned work with no contact with Fee when he'd stupidly assumed she was sleeping or as busy as he.

"Boss, the report says one local flyer just landed at Manascraoch port. Just in time, I'd say. The storm front is hitting that area hard. No flying in or out of there now—and you better take cover. The tail end of it will whip over the tops."

"Will do." Caleb cut him off and looked to the skies. The black edge of roiling thunderclouds rearing over the mountains from the west matched Bob's words. His flyer wouldn't stand a chance in the air, and the Feds' pilot wasn't about to try his bigger and sturdier craft either.

He was stuck here, while Fee was over there. Enduring what, held by whom?

"I'm going to eviscerate Bram den Coille when I get hold of him."

The poker backed guards chief frowned at him. "You have no real proof he has taken Sera den Coille against her will."

Caleb pointed at the stained rock, and thrust the scanner at the man. "Yes, I do."

The chief refused to back down. "If you are correct, Ser, we will arrest Ser den Coille. Once we have proof of kidnapping. If you are not, if Sera den Coille has returned to her family of her own free will, any action against a den Coille will be viewed as criminal assault. Do I make myself clear?"

Caleb wished he could smash something. "Perfectly. So what about the lake project? You are aware of its importance?"

"The project has an A1 rating," the chief replied, his voice blankly neutral. "The government would appreciate it if Sera den Coille returned to work. It will not compel her to."

"You would let a corporate win?"

"If there is no legal basis for any alternative," said the man coldly.

"Despite knowing what this world faces?"

The man nodded stiffly. "We have been made aware of the Survey's concerns."

And don't believe them any more than most of the rest of the population. Caleb growled his frustration and stumped off to lock down his flyer. "Bob, get a rescue team ready. Set to go the minute there's a break in that storm front."

The next hours were hell. All Caleb could do was sit tight in his flyer. He had locked the supports into the ground and was safe enough, but every battering pummel of weather outside only emphasised his helplessness.

Den Coille had taken his *wife*. That hurt his pride. They had taken Fee—and that hurt some quite different part of him, took on an importance he was not ready to accept. Not yet. They worked well together. She was sexy as hell, bright and smart and understood him as no one else. He enjoyed being with her.

But no one must hurt her. For that, they would answer to him, whatever his proud, prickly, stupidly independent-minded wife thought of the matter.

Too many hours later, Caleb crested the top of the mountain range, followed a hair's breadth behind by the Feds. So long waiting, not knowing what was happening on the other side.

A crackle on his unit. "We're ten minutes behind you."

The rescue team. Bob had been as good as his word, and had assembled the team in record time, then sent them out to wait as close to the mountains as the storm allowed. The trailing end of it still lashed the high western slopes but as he dropped down below it Caleb saw too many signs of damage left behind.

"You have medical and engineering supplies?" he asked the team leader.

"Of course," said Kal in his usual clipped off voice. The man might lack empathy but he was tough and capable.

At last Caleb was on final approach to Manascraoch. The usual "hail and identify" call was suspiciously abrupt, but it was the storm signs below that stopped his heart. A full third of the city had been washed away or buried under an enormous carpet of brown oozing mud. Half the hillside must have come down.

"Den Coille—Caleb Winter on hail. Where's my wife?"

CHAPTER TWENTY-SEVEN

Fee grabbed the nearest tree and flung herself up into the branches. Trees were safe, trees were home. She was uphill from the mudflow. Far enough? Who could know? She scrambled as high as she could manage, clung tight and stared at the roaring hell coming towards her.

So much mud. It poured down in a crescendo of snapping trees, grinding of rocks, smashing of buildings as the mud flow tore into everything in its path.

No sounds of people screaming. Had they all made it out? Then the torrent was on her and terror drowned out all concern for others.

She was above it. Her heart pounded from her hurried race up the hillside, as well as from sheer horror. But she was still alive, though her tree shook from the earth's barrage. She risked a peek down. The base was still free, still above the flow path, no mud scouring away its roots' deep hold onto the ground below. More and more mud coming, pouring down the mountain even as the first wave surged past her.

She was high enough. So far. She clung tight, wedging herself firmly into a Vee in the branches. The rain came in a full torrent now, powering down in heavy sploshes of icy cold water as the wind pulled away at her meagre refuge, doing its damndest to drag her out of her sanctuary.

On and on. Wind and rain pounding down. She was totally drenched, and cold, so cold. A sudden jerk, a quick grab at a branch. Sleep was her enemy. Remember!

Still the rain fell, still the mud poured down the hillside. Now burrowing a track into the slopes above her tree, the mound around its base turning into an island stronghold. For how long? So much had come down that the whole face of the hill above the city must have been washed away.

It beckoned her, an evil, sucking mess of dark brown death. One slip, one careless snooze making her relax her hold on her perch and she was gone. Falling, drowning in that siren call of eddying, squelching, bellowing sludge.

"Caleb, I need you so badly now."

A head bang, another shudder, and she jerked back from the precipice of sleep yet again.

It was a matter of time only. She leaned closer into the trunk, wedging as tightly as possible into the junction of tree and branch. Then dragged her soaked hair out of her eyes to glance down.

The mud level; was it higher? Did it lap now at the base of her tree?

A matter of time.

"Winter, that you? Bram den Coille's voice was shaky and stunned over the com unit.

"Fee. Where is she?"

"Too late. She was headed for the south east section. It's all gone now," said Fee's father.

"Her com unit? She had it on her?"

"No."

Another voice came on. Younger this time. "Cumchdach den Coille here. She has no com unit. We took it off her at the start. She went after her team, into that section that got washed away."

His brain was cold, too much to take in, but he had to force it to work. Fee needed him. "Exactly where was she heading? Patch the coordinates through to me."

"Done—and Winter," said Fee's brother, "if she is lost, you and the Survey will pay. One day, somehow, you will pay for my sister's life."

The voice cut off abruptly. Caleb shoved his flyer to full power, followed the talisman of the glowing red route on his screen.

One day? He was paying right now.

He slammed his craft into hover right over the route marker. Below, that was where she was making for. He looked down, brought up full visuals. There was absolutely nothing left there. No buildings, no people. No tiny, quick-fire figure dressed in forest green. Just an endless carpet of deadly mud. It oozed slowly downward, all sign of houses, offices, the businesses once flourishing here, now gone.

He set the scan wider, flying over the mud in a desperate grid pattern, eyes peeled and all sensors on maximum alert. Where would she have gone if she knew what was coming?

Upwards. Up that steeply sloping hillside above.

The mud flowed inexorably on, creeping farther and farther up the slopes as the last of the rain petered out into a drizzle.

He swung to the left, to the nearest bit of high ground.

"Maximum scan. Full visual and audio."

The audio was a mistake. The gloop of the mud, the cracks of trees and buildings filled the cabin. He kept it on anyway. Maybe, just maybe, one small human voice would rise above the clarion call of disaster.

Tracking, tracking.

Finally, there, in a tree right on the edge of the sea of mud. A small figure on the infra red scan, just warm enough to be human and wedged tightly into a branch of the tree. He gentled the engines, terrified of causing a downdraft, and sank slowly towards the tree.

Was it her?

The figure began to topple, but jerked back just in time. It was enough. He would know that utterly feminine shape anywhere.

Her life scans barely registered, her body temperature dangerously low.

"Emergency extraction procedures. Target entered: live, full care."

Slowly, so carefully, he hovered as close as he dared as his flyer let out the rescue net. Down, down, till it rested along side of her.

"Don't fight it, sweetheart," he whispered, directing the strands sideways, feeding in her target shape.

The netting settled on her, wrapped her closely. She jumped, pushed it back, then stopped. The net was standard Survey rescue gear. All ops trained regularly in its use.

"That's it, love. Let it take you."

And slowly, terrifyingly slowly, the net safely cradling and holding her, he began to pull her up.

At last, an eternity later, the cable with its precious burden was inside his craft. He snapped the doors shut, shot up high, away from the deadly mud, and set his flyer to hover far over a ridge line free of the tearing winds.

Then he ran, yanking free of his harness to race back to the cargo bay.

A dark shape, lying still on the floor, curled up in the soft strands of netting. He ran a scan as he crouched down, his fingers seeking the curve of her neck.

She was alive.

Just. Her eyes were shut, and her whole body was drenched and shivering.

He hailed den Coille again. "I've got her. Is your hospital still working?"

Caleb had never felt so helpless. Fee lay submerged in a tub of warm fluids, unmoving, the only evidence of her continued existence the steady whoosh of the ventilator and the constant blip of her heart beats.

A woman stood beside him. Fee's mother, Dr Scathach den Coille. In control, her voice even, but a white pallor marred her face and her mouth was clenched tight shut.

"She will recover?" he said.

"Yes. Her vitals are holding."

"How long?"

Fee's mother gripped her hands together. "Her body temperature was dangerously low. We will keep her unconscious and in the fluid bath for another twelve hours."

"Oh."

The Feds were landing outside. He ought to go meet them, help with the chaos in the city. The woman beside him was a doctor; she must be needed to help with the victims of the muddy horror. Neither of them made a move.

"How many?" he said, his eyes never leaving Fee's motionless body.

"Injured?"

He shook his head. "Dead."

"None. Not this time. Fioruisghe warned us in time. We practice evac procedures regularly." She was quiet a moment. "There was another mudslide once, a long time ago in a another city."

He knew about that. It was a standard part of the second year curriculum. Then something struck him, and he turned a look of query at Dr den Coille.

"Yes. I grew up in Cothromaich. I was barely in my teens the year the mud came. My family, we were lucky, but so many others…"

He had no need to ask more. The mountain city of Cothromaich had balanced on a tree-covered bluff. The views over the deep river valley below and out to sea had drawn visitors from all over the planet. Or did, until the day the rains undermined the cliff base and half the city tumbled into the valley, taking so many with it.

The mountain death. That was what his lecturers called mud flows.

"No deaths today. Good." The machines whirred and Fee's chest rose and fell, rose and fell.

"She is alive," said her mother.

He held a breath, let it out slowly. "Yes, but why was she here at all?"

"That, you will have to ask her father."

He turned slowly to meet Dr den Coille's gaze. "The Feds have just landed. They are the ones who'll be asking that question."

"I know." Her hands twisted harder together. "I have to go soon. I'm needed out there." She beckoned the nurse over. "She's in good hands. She is safe here."

Maybe—but he was not leaving till the Feds or his own people took over.

Dr den Coille's mouth tightened further. She glanced at her timer and listened to the incoming message. A brief reply, then she had a word with the nurse monitoring the care stations. "I'm needed in the emergency room," she said, but hesitated, till suddenly she lifted her head to meet his eyes full on, her face utterly serious. "In medicine, balance is important. A body must be in equilibrium to be healthy." She looked at her daughter.

"I have six children, young man. All of them precious to me." She put out a hand to stroke the cabinet holding Fee. "Our world has lost its balance. You and Fioruisghe, your work—"

She broke off, as if she had said too much. "Take care of my daughter," she whispered, and walked briskly out.

A call came over his unit. The Fed guard. "Ser Winter?"

He clicked back, giving his location.

"Are you secure?"

Was he safe? He had checked the room when he came in, knew it could be locked both from the inside and out. Yes, he could be trapped here, but outside were streams of injured, cold, lost people.

"Yes, for now," he said. "Tell my team to hurry. The hospital is untouched, but they are needed. And find Fee's team. I'm guessing she was looking for them when she was caught out."

"Will do."

"As for the rest of the den Coille's…"

"We will find them, and take whatever action is required," interrupted the guardsman.

We'll see about that, thought Caleb. "I want a full security unit on this room."

"On our way."

The next few hours were a mess of activity. Despite his deepest needs, Caleb had to leave Fee in the care of the nurses and Fed guards. There was so much damage outside.

No deaths, not yet. That was a miracle, but there was plenty of tragedy to go around.

Fee's team had been in the part of the city washed away. The cells, he heard whispered, but not to his face. That would have been too disloyal. Fee had been trying to rescue her mountain team—and her father had let her try. Maybe he hadn't believed her warning, but he'd still put her at risk. Caleb would not forget it.

Thankfully they found her team. The guards had released them as soon as the evac order sounded, it turned out. So Fee had risked her life for no reason. His own team arrived and he took them to meet up with Fee's people.

Kal strode up as Seamach, Fee's security man, stepped forward.

He pointed at both in turn. "Seamach, security; Kal, eco-engineer."

Kal shoved out a hand. Seamach raked him up and down, then put out his own hand. One quick clasp, all that was needed.

Survey first. The two teams had both worked in many different situations and were similarly trained. They soon meshed into an effective unit that took charge of the rescue operation.

Find people still trapped, stabilise the mud flow, get rid of debris causing immediate danger. Standard operating procedure in disasters. They knew what they were doing, and the locals recognised it. Caleb set to with the others. Someone gave him food; he gulped it back. Hours later, another someone thrust a hot drink in his hand.

"You can do no more." It was Fee's plant man. He looked as drained as Caleb felt. "Fee's due to wake soon."

Caleb looked blearily at his unit. "Right." He commed his offsider. "Kal, you all right there?"

Seamach came up. He and Kal had formed a joint command. "We're fine here, lad, and it's Fee who needs you now. Dr Scathach signalled to say she's bringing Fee out of her sleep phase."

Fee slowly emerged from her bath. She was warm again, was her first thought, blessedly warm and toasted. She was also wet, but no longer from the relentless pounding of freezing cold rain. Her throat burned, as if something had been thrust down it, and there was a distinct odour to the room. Antiseptic, unnatural. Hospital.

Faces came next. Her mother's, worried, wearing a forced calm. Caleb's. Angry, worn out and anxious.

"I'm fine," she croaked, struggling to sit up. Until she realised how little she was wearing and took in the manic look on her mother's face. It was one thing to know your daughter was married to a man you considered an enemy; it was quite a different matter to be brought face to face with the reality of it—or rather skin to skin.

That Caleb showed no sign of picking up on her mother's embarrassment only showed how worried he was. "You sure?"

he growled. "One day, we're going to talk about your bloody-minded quest to get hurt, repeatedly and often."

She ignored that as unimportant. "The city; how bad?"

A glare only, but she knew she was merely putting off a lecture, and that only because she still looked too pathetic. A growl of frustration, then he answered her worry. "A third gone. No deaths, but around four thousand injured or homeless."

She struggled to sit up again. Damn this weakness. "We have to get out there. They need our help."

Her mother's hand clamped down on her shoulder. "You have done quite enough already, young lady."

"I have to find my team."

"All safe, and too busy working with Kal's team to make sick bed visits right now," said Caleb. "The guards let them out as soon as the first evac alarm went off."

Maybe it was stupid to feel redundant; yet it didn't stop her. "Thank the trees that someone used their heads," she said politely. Then looked properly at him for the first time. "When did you last sleep? You look awful."

The faintest of smiles, and a shrug.

"How long before the new Survey team arrives?" she asked next.

"They came in a few hours ago."

"So why are you and our teams still working?"

"Someone has to."

Not good enough. "Mam?" she said.

Her mother was checking her charts and looking at her readouts. Fee began to climb out of the water bath.

"Sit right back down," said her mother, "and you see she does, young den Winter."

Caleb nodded, but her mother still waited till Fee had settled back into the water before leaving.

"And you needn't tower over me as well," Fee grumbled to her husband.

Surprisingly, he pulled over a chair and sat down, leaning his elbows on the side of the tub. His eyes studied her with a definite glint.

She slapped a hand over her chest.

"Spoilsport."

"Our teams," she reminded him. "Why are they still out there working?"

"Makes good PR." His fingers splashed into the water, tracing her breast before gently closing her mouth shut. "The city has watched mountain and plains team working together to save their families and their possessions. The Survey is the hero of the day out there right now."

"For doing our job?"

"Part of our job. They'll see the other side of it soon enough. Starting from a positive impression won't hurt, and having both teams work together has been good for our people too. Reminds them they are Survey first."

She had to agree, despite herself. Having the hard work of the Survey reduced to such a mercenary purpose didn't rest well with her, but it was necessary.

So much more venality to come; so much to be lost to the greater cause.

"Kiss me, please," she said.

The Feds were knocking on the outer door before her mother agreed to her release from the tank. She took full advantage of the interval of peace, and allowed Caleb and her Mam to coddle her shamelessly. But it could only be an interlude, a short-lived respite from what must come.

She was dressed and set to leave. A last hug for her mother. She clung tight, inhaling all she could of the unique mix of hospitals, warmth and flowers that always signalled home for all her family before she slowly disengaged and took her mother's face in her hands, drinking it in and planting the memory of it deep in her mind.

"You're frightening me, daughter." A teasing smile that could not quite cover the tension in those beloved green eyes.

"I do love you and Da. Even my brothers and sister. Please remember that," Fee whispered. "Whatever happens."

She released her mother and took her place beside Caleb.

There was a tear on her mother's face. "I told your husband; the balance of our world is failing. Remember, you are my daughter always."

The Feds banged on the door again and this time they didn't wait to be invited in.

"Eco-engineer den Coille and Winter. We need you in the main hall."

Her mother stepped forward. "Chief, my husband?"

He said nothing, gesturing for Caleb and Fee to follow. But just before he closed the door, he turned back to her mother.

"Your family is in the main hall, Dr den Coille. You may accompany us there."

Her mother's face blanched and she barely nodded her reply. Fee couldn't meet her eyes, and was so proud of her mother as she followed them, surrounded by guards. The miracle was that her mother was not a prisoner, was free to go. An option the woman who had raised them all would never accept.

Caleb's hand came out, tucked her arm into his and gave it a squeeze.

In the main hall, the Feds waited. Still, silent, standing in ranks as if an entire section of the city outside wasn't sliding down the hillside in a slurry of mud and human hopes. At the other end of the hall, blocked off from all the exits, sat her father and brothers. They sprawled in chairs, surrounding the one table left there and usually used to dump mugs on. This was their space, their city, and their unworried poses shouted that to the world. Except that their only audience was the Feds, and now Mam, her and Caleb—none of whom were fooled. Her family were prisoners, and she was the key.

"Eco-engineers." The chief of the Federal police squad waved her to the back of the room, towards her father. Her mother followed, and took her place beside her father as the guards moved into a phalanx surrounding them all.

Her father had always seemed so tall to her. Yet he was dwarfed by Caleb and the city Feds. Not that any sign of it showed on his face. "You are recovered?" he said.

She couldn't speak. Not yet. Seolta shot out a hand and shoved a rising Aigherach back into his seat.

"Eco-engineer den Coille," said the chief guard. "One question only. Did you return home of your own free will, or were you brought here by force?"

A deep breath. A clutch of Caleb's hand. Then she released him. This was something only she could do.

"The latter."

It was the nearest she could come to voicing the accusation, desperately seeking refuge in cool formality.

"By whom?"

Her eyes locked with her father's, were held in thrall. "My understanding is that it was at my father's order."

Ceart and Seolta both grabbed hold of Aigherach this time. Cumchdach sat stonily, staring directly at the Fed officer.

"Thank you," the man said. The guards moved to surround her father, blocking in her brothers, and holding them all in stasis.

The chief nodded in dismissal. "Your doctor has released you, Sera den Coille. You are free to return to the lake project."

"But… we're needed here!"

"No." It was Caleb who grabbed her hand and pulled her away. "We need to leave, now."

She couldn't even say goodbye. Not to her mother, face carefully devoid of expression. Not to her father, staring at her coldly and leaving her in no doubt he understood exactly the consequences of her denunciation. Nor to her brothers, the bitter charge of betrayal clear in their eyes.

Seolta stood, and every weapon suddenly swung on him. "Fioruisghe. The evac alarm. How did you know that top field would come down?"

Thankfully he stood dead still. Fee pulled her arm out of Caleb's. "When they felled the trees, they also destroyed the drainage channels. Those trees and channels were designed specifically to stop landslips from that slope. Without them, given the rain that was coming, the mud flow was inevitable."

"You told us those were watering channels; that the plantings were for an assignment for your final exams."

Then Cumchdach thrust up, slammed his hand on the table, and the tension in the room rocketed up to a whole new level. "You knew that slope was a danger—and you never told us?"

"It was Survey business. Confidential."

"Not good enough, Sister."

A guardsman stepped in, shoved his weapon against Cumchdach. "Back down," said the squad leader. "Ser den Coille, we will shoot your son if he does not sit."

Her father waved down her brother. For such a long moment, she watched as Cumchdach refused and the guard's finger tightened. Until finally he sat, watching her, always watching her.

"Get her out of here, Winter," said her father.

Caleb took her arm again, and she made it out of the hall somehow. The door shut and her legs gave way. Caleb grabbed her, propped her up against him. "You will walk out of here. You must," he whispered in her ear.

"He was right. I should have told them. They are my family."

"And you just broke them. We both know the Survey has to break the corporates if they're to stop the environmental destruction of Arcadia."

"You and I; we handed them our families on a plate."

"Yes." The flat statement calmed her. He could have denied it, but Caleb was stronger than that. "We destroyed our families, the heads of this sector's two biggest corporations. But our fathers made it possible."

"We are Survey."

He gripped her arm. "We are Survey. There is no other choice."

It didn't make her feel better.

CHAPTER TWENTY-EIGHT

"There she is!"

Caleb grabbed her back inside and slammed the door shut. "What in hell!"

A glimpse only, but that had been enough for her. Angry faces, arms raised, the rattle of stones against the door as Caleb shoved it back in the face of the mob. "What the…! Didn't we just save this lots' skins?"

"And I betrayed them. Family matters here. "

"How in hell did word of your father's capture get out so quickly?"

Even as he spoke, the guards came pelting out of the hall to surround them, the chief ordering men into place and waving her and Caleb back. "We've left your family locked into the hall. It'll hold them for now." Though not for long, said the look on the chief of guards' face, and Fee had to agree. Unfortunately, her family's freedom wasn't going to satisfy that mob out there. They were after blood: Survey blood.

"What next?"

"We've sent word to our headquarters and the Survey. Your teams are being pulled out and will take off soon. So far, no one's gone after them."

"And us?" said Caleb as he pulled her close.

The chief turned to her. "Is there another way out of here?"

"Not one that won't be watched. There is a side fire exit, but they all know about it. This is a public hall. Everyone uses it. We used to play in the back corridors as children."

"So the only way out is through that mob?"

"What about the roof?" said Caleb.

Fee shook her head. "Overlooked by too many other buildings. We're on the lower branch levels here."

The chief stepped back and spoke with his men, then called up his com unit. Caleb pulled Fee back into a small, easily defended alcove off the main foyer, and the rest of the troops got busy piling up furniture against the door as blows hammered on it from the outside.

The chief came back. "I've been informed that the Survey has a ship on patrol near here. They can be here the soonest." He looked suspiciously at them. "A coincidence?"

Caleb gave him the bland look that had once so infuriated Fee. "Routine procedure. The Survey monitors any environmental disaster in case backup is needed by the local rescue units."

"Yet they didn't see fit to come down to help?"

"No point. Not with a full Survey rescue unit on hand." He held out his hand for permission to access his com unit and the chief nodded. A minute later he had his report back, and sent it through to the chief. "All the Survey staff on the ground are safely away, including both Fee's and my teams, and a full Survey squadron is on its way for us."

"Squadron? The Federal Alliance polices this world, not the Survey."

Caleb shrugged. "There's too many places the Survey isn't welcome. It's always maintained a security force to protect our people. They're liaising with your central comms team now. "

A call came in on the chief's unit. Very shortly after, the man signed off, mouth grimly set. "Seems the Survey is taking over this operation. Our unit will stay only till they've secured the entryway."

Fee and Caleb didn't argue, readily ceding the illusion of authority to the guards. It cost them little, and they needed these men still. The noise outside rose to a crescendo of unleashed fury.

"How long?" she whispered

"Half an hour."

She couldn't stop the clench of fear. Caleb pulled her close "You will be safe," he promised.

The chief said nothing, not willing to promise so much, she guessed. But Fee believed the strength in Caleb's face. She nodded slowly. "Yes, we will."

A cough, and the chief stepped impatiently forward. "Maybe, but a few chairs and stuff against that outer door isn't going to hold off that crowd. Sera den Coille, you know this place. Any ideas?"

"The back room. It's defensible and inconspicuous—they'll have to take time looking for us."

A small store room under the main stage area, it was the only room she could think of that had two doors to open to force entry. It wouldn't stop intruders but it would slow them down."

Caleb took one glance at the enclosed, windowless room, looked at her as if she'd lost all sense and signalled the incoming Survey ship.

"They're too far away still," he said in disgust.

"This room is the best option going," she insisted.

He said nothing to her, swivelling to give a string of rapid fire orders to the Fed guards, before belatedly remembering the chief and making a half hearted attempt to get man's agreement.

It was irrelevant. His orders stood, and the troop split into two. One half of the squad to guard the main entrance doors and buy time; the other half to protect the small storeroom door.

Caleb demanded and was handed a weapon. She refused to touch one. The whole situation was explosive enough already.

"Everyone in place?"

The chief nodded. "Inside, and lock the door," he ordered them.

"He doesn't mean? No." But the man did, and Caleb grabbed her and shoved her inside the room. Then slammed the door and locked it behind them.

The weak light showed a few dusty shelves with boxes of unknown contents and some old crates piled up against the back wall. He pulled down two, pushed one towards her and sat on the other, leaning his back against the wall.

"The Feds. That mob will pummel them."

A tight faced look from Caleb, a slight shrug and a brief nod.

"No one is dying for me!"

"Don't." Caleb's voice was as angry as she'd heard it. "It's their decision. The only one we've left them. You think I like sitting in here while brave men risk their lives for us?"

No, she did not think that. Not from the tense set of his shoulders.

"Their job is to protect us and keep the peace; our job is to save the planet. Sit still and wait. The Survey will be here to take charge soon enough."

It was the bitterness in his voice that kept her silent. She sat, and waited.

An hour had gone by. The mob had breached the outer door and the second squad outside their door was hunkered down ready to repel them.

"They're landing," said Caleb.

She checked her com unit, saw the display of blips of the ship's troopers landing in fighting array in the plaza outside. She must brush fear aside.

A crash outside and the zing of weapons firing.

Off her pallet and hunker down behind it. Caleb copied her, shoving his in front of her.

She shoved forward, beside him. "We go out together."

He shoved her right back. "Stay behind me, and don't argue." The white lines on his face echoed the strain inside her. She reached out a hand, found his.

"If we don't get out of this, "she whispered, "you need to know I think I'm in love with you."

Silence. Too late for regrets.

He never took his eyes off the door, did not look at her. "Woman, you have some timing." He turned, a fleeting glance at her, before returning to his watch on the door.

What she saw in his eyes in that short instance set her heart thudding.

"We will get out of this," he said. "I will not let anything happen to you. And—what you said. It's mutual."

That was all. Crouching behind a ratty old box, minutes away from possible death, a gurgle of laughter played in her chest. He had not given her the words, maybe never could, but it was enough. She leaned into his hand, lifted it and touched his knuckles softly with her lips, then placed his hand back on the weapon.

"Together," she promised.

Another crash, so close this time, and the shouts of injured men right outside the door.

It opened, the chief appeared in the gap, a bloody gash marring one side of his face. "We go, now," he said, a brusque jerk of his hand for them to follow.

One deep swallow, all she dared give to quell her nerves, and they stood together. Outside the door, bodies lay on the ground. They were dressed in greens and browns; the colours of the forest.

"They're stunned, not dead," said the chief bluntly. His men surrounded them, a wall of protection. "The Survey ship is in the second courtyard. They've cleared a path."

That meant the side door. They ran down the hallway, up a flight of stairs and towards the door. A roar of sound met them. So much for her faint hope the mob had missed this exit.

The guards stopped just before the doorway, and the chief spoke into his com unit. He pointed to the doors, and two men separated out, taking up positions either side. "The Survey is holding the exit. It's only a short walk, a matter of fifty metres. Ready?"

No, never. But she nodded as Caleb gave a quick grunt.

Suddenly they were outside. The mob knew them instantly and a cacophony of jeering yells greeted their appearance. Only a too thin line of heavily armed guards kept back the mass of jostling bodies to hold open a narrow pathway of space leading to the ship. They must walk that?

She stepped out. Caleb kept her between him and the chief. He held on to her, half dragging her with him as they walked briskly forward.

Don't show them fear. Her father had said that to her once. She had gone with him to negotiate the purchase of land from a family fallen on hard times. Her father had paid them a fair price, she remembered, but it had made no change to the hate in the eyes of the man made landless. The dispossessed never forgave those who took their lives away.

That same hate vibrated in the air, came from the mouths and fists of the men and women held back by force of arms only. People who had lost much today, and knew already from the kind of ship squatting in that courtyard how much more was to go.

Freedom—an indefinable term, one of her lecturers had tried to tell her. Rubbish. She looked in the faces of the people who had once been family and friends, and knew freedom was a word easily defined, unless you were the one taking it from another. Then it became conveniently intangible.

She stumbled, and felt Caleb grasp her tighter. One small sign of weakness, with an immediate response. A clod of earth sailing through the air from the back of the crowd. One clod only; but enough to break wide open the fear holding the crowd back. A hail of sticks, earth, stones, whatever came to hand soared towards them. Not people, not yet. A barricade of troops held firm in a protective net around them. A net drawing ever tighter.

The path to the ship disappeared; troops falling under the pressing mass of bodies like leaves in a deluge. This was it. Caleb's arm came round her, his other flailing madly at any who came too close. The phwhish of shots firing.

"Above their heads," screamed the chief. "Shoot to stun, not kill."

One dead body; one badly injured mountain born. That's all it would take to release a lethal mayhem.

A fist met her arm. The Feds battled gamely on, circling in a last stand.

"Save yourselves," she whispered. "We're not that important."

"Yes, you are," said Caleb.

Close work now. A chaos of fists, shots and butting bodies. She stumbled. Falling again.

Then a sudden lurching sideways of every organ in her body. A pressure blast, thudding her into oblivion. She knew nothing more.

A hand shaking her, rough and insistent.

"Go away."

"Wake up, Sera."

They shook her again, prodding stupidly at her. "Open your eyes."

A voice, chittering in her ear. The woman would not leave her alone. Fee tried harder, her head throbbing.

Slowly, she managed to ease her eyes open. A white room, a smell sharp and antiseptic but no safe waft of Mam's flowers.

Hospital, said the tired remnants of memory. She had spent too much time over the years in hospital rooms.

"What?" Her voice shouldn't sound like that. Thready, barely there. "Water."

A hand came near, another one under her head, and blessedly cool drops trickled down her throat.

"What?" she tried again, forcing her eyes to open wider.

A head bent into view. A woman, the owner of the voice she guessed. "You were caught in the pulse wave."

Pulse wave? "They're not legal! Who?"

"Don't worry. The Survey set it and the Feds agreed. It was the only option. How much do you remember?"

She had to work at that. "A store room. A mob—Caleb!"

The woman held her down.

"No, let me go. Where is he?"

"Sera, you will hurt yourself."

She struggled harder, grabbing at the stupid line of tubing tying her to the chattering machines. "Where is he?"

"Right here, Sera. On the bed beside you."

She turned her head. A man lay still, unmoving, and it was as if the pulse wave shattered her anew. "No."

"He's fine, Sera." The woman's hand shoved her back down on the bed again. "He's sleeping. He'll wake soon."

The woman's voice soothed, her hands gentle and patient but Fee didn't believe a word of it until she saw Caleb's body move. She snatched at the sensor patches covering her, shoved back the gentle soothing, flapping hands and scrambled across to him. Not till she held his hand, not till his eyes recognised her did she relax.

"Who in hell authorised a pulse wave?" was his first demand when he got enough control to struggle up and fling off the annoying medical leads.

"It was the only option to rescue you from the mob," said the nurse.

It did nothing to appease Caleb. "The civilians, the Fed guards with us? Will they recover?"

"Of course, Ser."

"My family?" she dared to ask.

"Safe in protective custody," said the woman, and that was all. Why did she suddenly feel so cold?

A doctor bustled in, identified by her logo and the relieved deference of the nurse.

"The mob? What are the stats?" demanded Caleb.

"No casualties, Sers," said the woman.

"Lucky," Caleb muttered.

Fee knew how he felt. A pulse wave. The technology was still new, and the results unpredictable. The intended effect was to knock out anyone within the set radius. An easy and effective way of quelling a riot such as the one that nearly caught them, but the risk of injury or death to the victims was high; the use of the wave allowed only under warrant from the supreme planetary court.

They were missing something here. How did the Survey get permission to use such a weapon, and why did their rescue ship just happen to have a wave generator on board?

Caleb's hand clenched on hers, and his eyes sent a warning. He was starting to add things up too, but no questions tonight; not to medical staff employed by the Survey.

A month later and she still had no answers. Or none that eased her growing disquiet. All was superficially back to normal. She stood at the lake edge, taking the daily measurements and checking her soundings of incoming and outgoing water flows.

They had decided to keep the subterranean channels open, treating them as inlet and outlet rivers. Which they were, in function at least, if nothing like the fast running, quicksilver torrents of her mountain home.

Home. The word was enough to start her choking up. Would she ever return, and where were her family now? She ruthlessly rubbed away the tear, then realised her hands were covered in the sticky clay forming the new lake bed. She pulled up a corner of her tunic and scrubbed hard, wishing the lake had settled enough to see her reflection in it, but the muddy, ochre wavelets gave nothing back. Hopefully she'd cleaned the mess off her face.

A foot step behind her, one she knew well. A hand fell on her shoulder and she leaned back into Caleb's solid body, the familiar sun-baked, work heated smell of him engulfing her in comfort.

"You're back." She pulled his arm around her, letting him take her weight and force her niggling worries back into their corner by his presence. "How'd it go?"

He leaned his chin on her head and she felt the slight shift of his shoulders. "About as well as expected."

"Your father still holding out?"

"Mmm. Trying to."

Caleb had been out to his family farm, in yet one more attempt to break down the wall of hostility.

"He does know he can't win?"

A dry chuckle, bitter and flat, then silence. In truth, Sol Winter had already lost the battle. The Survey controlled all the lands at the base of the mountain and had forced a full environmental audit on the Winter Solaris solar arrays.

"Is the audit result in yet?" she asked Caleb. Was that why this visit had failed?

"It's not finished yet."

She turned round at that, rotating in his arms to keep their solid protection around her, and stared up at him. "That audit should have been finished a full week ago. What's the hold up?"

His mouth twitched sideways, as if to say *you have to ask*?

She did. "Your father's stopping them?"

"Trying to," he said. "He can do little but delay them. Not when each auditor has a full squad of Feds with them."

But the man was inventive enough to use whatever minor impediment came to hand. One day, the threat of a windstorm blowing up that kept the audit team kicking their heels indoors while glaring out at the clear, cloudless skies of the plains. Another day, a faulty water canister that forced the team back to base early, having run out of water. Annoying and life threatening in this region. Sol Winter was playing a very dangerous game.

"I wish…"

He tilted up her chin, stopping her avoiding his gaze. "What?"

All those niggling worries suddenly flew back into her head. "Something feels wrong in all this." She shook her head. "Not the environmental situation—that's real enough."

He gave that slow nod of his. "Too many other field staff are seeing the same problems as us. Arcadia is out of kilter. We fix it, or we suffer."

"Mmmm. But the Survey? Their role in it all?" She took a deep breath, looked at him straight. "How much do you trust head office?"

His face was as grim as she'd seen it. "I don't. But I do believe the science—we're in trouble. Just not sure how bad."

That was all they said about it that day, but Fee couldn't stop it turning over and over in her head. She began haunting the populist chat channels, looking for patterns, dissent, anything. The official news channels didn't help. Everything was fine; the den Coille arrests were due to simple infringements of environmental controls. The family was fully cooperating with the authorities and business would be unaffected. The Survey had put in staff to assist the management of Den Coille until the situation was clarified.

If only she knew the truth of it but all her attempts to contact her family, to find out where they were and what was happening at home, were blocked. By den Coille, or by head office? The too polite voice of the comms server could belong to either, but she was getting a very bad feeling. Her family *must* be safe, it was too hard to live with herself if she suspected otherwise, but where were they?

By day, she threw herself into her work. She had examined the plans for the lake and the projections enough times to know they were valid. They must reverse the increasing differential between the mountain and plains climate, or there would be more landslides like the one that had destroyed so much of her home, and the desert Sol Winter valued so highly would spread right up to the edge of the mountains, baking the centre of the continent in a drought that would kill off all hope of a normal lifestyle or any other alternative to the barren stretches of mechanical solar arrays spreading out across the parched lands.

But who else benefited by the lake schemes?

She stared into the dark, twisting over in bed in a fruitless attempt to find rest.

"You planning to stop squirming around any time soon?" said an amused voice in her ear.

"Sorry," she muttered, and tried, really hard, to lie still. It was impossible, but she forced herself to slowly ease her way over next time she hunted for a spot in the bed that just might be comfortable enough to allow sleep.

Her elbow collided with Caleb's stomach. "Oomph. You really do need to get some sleep, love."

"I know. Sorry," and was awarded with a light chuckle.

"You're such a bad liar," he said. "Come here. I can't solve whatever it is that's bothering you tonight, but sharing it might help."

She twisted back towards him, gratefully burying herself into his chest to find that sense of relaxation it always gave her to touch him, skin to skin. "You already do," she said.

"Ah. Survey head office," he said, as if that explained all. And it did.

"You don't trust them either—you told me so."

"No, but tossing all night and missing sleep won't solve anything."

"So what will?" She thumped him on his arm, a gentle thrust that had him grabbing her arm and giving another of those light chuckles, and pulling her closer. To slowly stroke her, down her back, stroke after stroke until the peace and sensuality of it soothed her, and shoved back the sharp dagger bites of worry.

Peace. Sleep. A touch of his mouth on her head, whispered words and strong but gentle hands on her skin.

A loud bang on the window, and she was suddenly wide awake again. A sharp rattle of knocks, insistent and not stopping. She flung back the covers and grabbed her robe as Caleb leaped from the bed, shoved his trousers on and flung back the window. He grabbed the man standing there and hauled him into their room.

"Aigherach!" She ran to her little brother, tugging at Caleb to release him and running her hands over him to check for injury. "What's happened? Why are you here? "

He shoved off her hands and glared at her. "For help. I had nowhere else to go," he said, making no effort to hide his anger at that. "You got us into this mess. You're part of the mighty Survey. You get them freed."

Caleb pushed him down into a chair. "Start at the start."

"Freed!" said Fee. She switched the light on, and gasped at what the glare of light revealed. Aigherach was covered in scabs, his hair drenched in sweat, filthy from head to toe and shivering hard. "No more questions. Not till you're clean, warm and fed."

"No time," he said, shivering harder and leaning forward, fists clenched tight together.

"Make time." Caleb said. "This way," and he picked her baby brother up, and half-carried, half-marched him into the bathroom. "Food, hot and quick," he flung at her before the door slammed in her face.

Her hands obeyed as her mind still reeled with shock. She opened their chiller. Soup to reheat, toast, a hot drink. That would do it. She was on automatic, heating, stirring, slicing and spreading even as her brain whirled and tried to make sense of it. No sooner was she done than Caleb walked Aigherach back in, clean and dressed in one of his old tops and pants, cuffs rolled up to stop her much smaller brother tripping. Cleaning up made no change to the bruises, the shocked pain on his face. Caleb gave her a brief glance, shook his head as her mouth opened, and steered the boy into a seat.

"Eat first, then talk," he ordered.

For an instant, she thought Aigherach would refuse, but Caleb solved the problem by pushing a spoon of hot soup into his mouth as soon as Aigherach opened it to argue.

It was hot, too hot for that treatment, and between choking, and glaring at her husband, Aigherach was too busy to argue. All he could do was nod his head, pick up the spoon and, slowly at first then ever more greedily, he ploughed into the simple meal.

Whatever it was, it was bad. Aigherach would argue at the drop of a twig, and usually rushed carelessly into anything. That Caleb could so easily cow him into obeying worried her more than the bruises and shock on his face.

Finally he began to slow, began to lose that grey, stark pallor. "Now you can talk," said Caleb. He took the other chair, as Fee pulled out hers and sat down, eyes fixed on her brother.

"What happened?" she demanded now.

Aigherach put down his spoon, set aside the last piece of toast, placing it deliberately on the plate as if to protect it. "They've arrested them all. Locked up the whole family like criminals and stripped control of den Coille from Da." His voice was flat, as if speaking old news, news so obvious, yet so awful, the telling of it could only be done in a far away voice separate from body and mind.

"Who?"said Caleb.

"The Survey. Your Survey," said Aigherach. "They've taken everything."

"You mean they've taken over the admin of the region? The reports said Da and the family were cooperating. That means they had agreed to work with the Survey. Doesn't it?" she pleaded.

"No. Taken over, period. They own our home, our lands, everything."

Still she tried. "They've only taken over the running of the festia plantations so they can restore the natural balance. That's all."

Aigherach thrust back his chair. "I should have known it was a waste coming here. You're just like the rest of them."

Caleb stood with him, put out an arm and shoved the younger and much smaller man down again. "From the start. Tell us exactly what happened."

Aigherach tried to stand again, but Caleb was every bit as strong as he looked, and his fingers gripped tight on her brother's shoulder. Fee could see the bite of it in his face, but Aigherach refused to acknowledge defeat or pain.

"From the beginning," Caleb repeated.

CHAPTER TWENTY-NINE

It didn't take long. The facts were simple enough, easily listed.

"We were rescuing our sister. That's what we told the Feds. There's no way the Survey could make that kidnap charge stick, and all the lawyers knew it."

So naive, but she had tried to warned her brothers.

"We were all in Da's office. The negotiators, the lawyers, all of us including Mam and Samhchair. That was when they came."

"Who?"

"Federal troops. With Survey security forces."

Fee listened to her brother in growing horror. Her whole family—father, brothers, her strong, calm mother and her gentle elder sister—surrounded by troops and arrested. Stripped of all power, title and holdings, then taken away. To where, Aigherach had no idea.

"How did you get away?" said Caleb. Fee could not speak.

"I was at the back. Fed up with it all—too much talk and none of it making sense. When the doors opened, Seolta took one look at them and ordered me to use the back trapway. The soldiers were so busy rounding up the rest, I slipped away in the confusion."

Fee clutched herself in relief. "So you didn't see what happened after that. They're probably all fine, and it's some misunderstanding."

"No. I was in the tunnels, and saw it all."

Fee shoved a fist against her mouth. Long ago, some overly suspicious ancestor had built tunnels into the walls of the den Coille offices. They had played in them as children, but they were dark, dusty and dangerous now, having never been maintained. But they also had peepholes, hidden spy holes looking into all the offices. She put out a hand, needing suddenly to touch her brother, know he was whole and here safe. He shook it off and looked at her with horror in his eyes.

"They hit Mam. She tried to stop them taking the seals from Da's desk, and they hit her. Da was struggling, but four men held him, and Ceart punched his guards but they threw a stun field over him. Then they took them. They tried to make Samhchair tell where I was too, but she wouldn't."

That was no surprise to Fee. Her sister was the most peaceful and gentle of them all, but had a solid core of unassailable strength.

"They said it didn't matter; I was only a boy, and couldn't do anything. They dragged them all out the back door. No crowds, no one to help them. There was a flyer outside, and it took them. All of them."

He dropped his head on the desk. "Took me a week to get here. Had to hide out till I could slip out of the city, go across country. Steal a flyer. A whole week." He lifted his head again and glared at her. "You got us into this. You can fix it. Find them and get them freed."

She shook her head. This was beyond insane. "Why would the Survey do this?"

"Power," said Caleb, in a grim voice beside her, the quiet control of it belying the black edge. "Control of Den Coille's wealth and resources."

"But that won't help the planet's problems."

"No, it won't." He gripped her hand, squeezed it in warning, then turned to her brother. "Fee's team, the mountain Survey field team; where are they now?"

Aigherach shrugged and looked sulky. "Don't know, don't care."

"So they're part of the Survey group running Den Coille?"

He gave a quick sideways twist of his head. "No. Never seen these new people. Your team, guess they're doing what they were always doing. Not seen them since the takeover."

A cold feeling invaded Fee's gut. "What if?"

"I'll send a team across to find them," promised Caleb. "Your team knows that land, and they are far more capable than any outsider. They will be safe somewhere. As for us …"

There was a sudden banging on the door of their quarters. Caleb rose, and put up a hand as Aigherach shoved back his chair. "Stay here. Back in the corner."

Caleb switched off the dining area light, leaving Fee and her brother hidden in the dark, and walked out to the entry area of their rooms. Fee slipped quietly to the corner of the door, out of sight but able to see the doorway. Right now, that bad feeling of hers was at maximum. Caleb saw her, but merely waved her to fade back into the shadows, then opened the door just a crack.

"Silas!"

That one snapped word was enough. Caleb grabbed his brother, pulled him inside, and slammed the door shut, locking the outer door after him. "What in hell are you doing here?"

But Silas had barged in too far, and had seen Aigherach. "Den Coille. Here!"

"Sit down, and be quiet," said Caleb.

Silas shook off his hold. "I should have known not to come here. You're one of them, just like Father said."

Caleb looked ready to argue, but too late. Aigherach was barrelling out of his corner, aimed straight at Silas Winter.

Caleb was bigger, stronger and better trained, but still it took Fee's help and all her training to bring the two young men to a standstill, and all the while she strained nervously for the sound of battle between them to carry outside. Who outside was safe? She had trusted the Survey, had thought the field staff were like family—until now.

Caleb finally managed to strong arm both young men into chairs on opposite sides of the table. Fee knew an insane urge to laugh. Both were battered and hurting, too proud to admit it, and sulky as hell.

"Out with it," Caleb ordered his younger brother now. "What's got you riled up?"

"You get them freed. You and that Survey; you leave us alone."

Caleb took a deep breath. "Start from the beginning," he ordered for the second time that evening.

"Father, mother, Ethan. You get them released, now."

"Released from what, exactly. Or whom?"

"Your Survey. They came this afternoon, nabbed the three of them and took them away in a flyer. Then told everyone they were running Solaris now."

"They can't do that," said Caleb as if explaining civics to a junior grade schoolroom. "Father is cooperating and hasn't broken any laws."

"They can, they did. Said he was 'infringing his environmental consents and endangering the planetary well being'."

"Well, yes, he is. But that's not against the law, not yet."

Silas went to rise, but was shoved back down. "Fat lot you know. It is now, so your Survey say. Greedy pack of …"

"Right, I get your message. The Survey has taken the rest of the family," he glanced at Fee, a black anger at the back of his eyes that she doubted the two boys could see, "and you *just managed* to escape?"

"Yeah. That's right. Ethan told me to hightail it out of there. I took the dune route. No northerner's going to catch me going through there. Even with trackers they'd get lost in seconds."

"An area of sand dunes just north of the homestead." explained Caleb to Fee. "The metallic deposits in the sand play havoc with any guidance beams. Well done, Si."

He pulled both boys into the main sitting area, pointed them to the two chairs and settled onto the couch with Fee. She could feel the tension in the arm he flung over her shoulders.

"So we have the two most powerful families in this region taken under guard to who knows where. And yet both youngest sons just happen to escape to warn us of what happened. Smell something very off, love?" he said to Fee while keeping his gaze fixed very firmly on the two young men so studiously avoiding each other.

She did; very, very off. A stink of politics and manipulation. "The Feds are still working with the Survey," she pointed out.

Caleb nodded agreement. He went back to his study of the two young men. Silas Winter, tech genius from all accounts and Aigherach, the beloved youngest, passionate, headstrong and anything-but-stupid member of her own family. They were of an age—similar education, both bright fire in temperament, though she suspected Silas was a bit less naive. And both just happened to evade capture by a department with years of cunning, guile and experience in subterfuge behind it. Successive governments had repeatedly failed to bring in the changes needed to save Arcadia from humanity's blind avarice, forever blocked by corporate interests. It didn't make the problem go away, so governments had instead ordered the Survey to work behind the scenes, hiding their real objectives even as they strove to quietly move the planet forwards. Always believing that one day, the time would come when they were in a position to force change.

Now was that time, it seemed. The situation was too urgent; Arcadia couldn't wait any longer, and the off-planet, all powerful Alliance had stepped in with that deadline.

Or was that the full truth?

She looked at Caleb, squeezed his hand to get him to turn around and look at her, and saw the same fears hidden in his eyes. He gave her another of those quick nods, those hasty bobs of assurance that were anything but.

"Stay here, keep them out of sight and start packing," he said. "I'll ready the team."

"How can you know they're safe?" It wasn't the boys she referred to, and saw the recognition of it in his face.

"I grew up with most of this team. Not a lot of people can live out here. The ones who do—you can't hide your true colours on the open plains. The land will find you out." He turned to their brothers. "Stay put, don't be stupid, and no fighting. If there is a single hair harmed on Fee's head when I get back, you will answer to me."

Next moment, he was gone, and Fee was left staring hopelessly at two scared and angry young men who had suddenly discovered they couldn't do anything about that anger. Not now Caleb had pointed out the danger their actions had put her in.

"Hot drink for anyone?" she chirped brainlessly as she leaped off the couch and retreated to the kitchen.

Caleb wanted to smash someone, anyone. And wished he knew who his target should be. Right now he didn't trust the head office suits one jot. Whatever they were up to, he doubted it had very much to do with saving Arcadia. It was past time their deskbound chiefs were reminded of the proper work of the Survey. But first he had to get Fee and their brothers to safety and secure his team. He strode towards Jim's quarters.

"You know what Fee and I have to do," he said to his senior staff: Bob, Kal, and the ever dependable Jim, with Marabeth providing her own unique brand of old-fashioned common sense.

"Take to the hills," said Kal, putting on a slow drawl.

"Don't worry, boss," said Jim, "I'll keep these idiots in line. All heads down till you two find out what's going on up in them fancy offices in Urbis, and keep the lakes project going. That about sum it up?"

Yeah, it did. There were a whole lot more details to it than that, but his team had always had an emergency plan. What they were doing threatened too many big corporations, not just his family but others as well. Except none of them had expected the threat to come from their own department.

Caleb had always been wary of head office, never letting them know quite all that his team were capable of, and now that caution paid off. To their managers, the plains country was data in a landscape file, figures on paper only, not real dirt and grit. They didn't know this land. Not like his team; people who had seen its sunrises since the day they were born. As far as anyone from the city would know, Fee and he would vanish off the face of the planet.

"We've a couple more to hide, and they can't come with Fee and me. We'll need a small team to take them under cover."

Kal began to protest, but Jim only asked who. If the old wrangler was surprised at the names, he gave no sign of it. Unlike Kal who wasted a good ten minutes telling him how wrong he was to trust either Aigherach den Coille or Silas Winter.

"Maybe, but nowhere else is safe for them, and Fee and I will be busy."

Kal nodded reluctantly. Caleb called Bob aside and walked a few paces away to stop any more protests from his deputy eco-engineer.

"Bob, I need you to contact as many field teams as possible. Set up a meeting with each—real time, real place—but only with those you can still trust. Any hint of head office interference, and back out of the call straight away."

"Right. Going to tell us the rest of it?"

"It's in your file now. Send it out then gather the troops in the main court. We'll talk to them before we leave." Bob nodded. "And Bob, keep an eye on Kal for me. He's a sound man, but he wants to be leader too badly. Never a healthy sign."

Bob gave a light chuckle. "And you'd give up the boss job so easily?"

Caleb grinned, acknowledging the hit. "But I'm good at it."

A half hour later, and all laughter deserted him. He stood on the porch of the main hall, facing a crowded courtyard filled with every member of his lakes team. Men and women he had worked beside, fought for in the City, argued and laughed with over so many trials. Now, he must tell them he was running away.

"You all know the drill. Heads down, keep up the work, avoid trouble and you know nothing."

"Where you going to be?" shouted a voice from the back.

He reached for Fee, pulled her to stand beside him, and silence cut like a knife through the crowd. "We will be in the city, fixing this mess."

He knew the man who had called out. One of the botanical group. A gardener, in other words a man of peace, and now Caleb was asking him to become a frontline rebel. He should be planting trees at the lake edge and planning the future cropping rotations on the land between the lakes.

Fee moved up closer, to stand shoulder to shoulder with him. Or head to shoulder, her small frame barely making the top of his arm, but it made no difference. She stood as strong, as determined as if she towered over every person here. She closed in, bumping his arm, and he discreetly pulled her hand into his. A promise; between the two of them, they could do this. He braced his shoulders, and waved forward the two young men in the doorway behind him, proud of the way Silas faced his people. Aigherach stood resolute, head high and side by side with Silas. They would do, these two.

"You heard what happened. How the den Coille and Winter families have been taken into custody by Survey head office troops. And you know as well as me that these two men only made it out because the Survey let them go, to force Fee and me into showing our hands. That the next target is going to be us. So I'm asking you to take these young men under your protection, as the brothers they are. Jim and Kal will assign a team to take them out country and hide them from the Survey till we can sort this mess out. We will keep them safe."

There was silence, a lot of head nodding, a lot of fear. Bob had already sent out the full communication with the whole story and what he and Fee suspected was going on. Too little of what he said was news, but harsh reality always sounded worse when spoken out loud.

One voice rose in dissent. "Winters have run this area like it's their own personal kingdom. Den Coille, the same from what I hear. Why shouldn't we let the Survey chuck them out? Isn't that what we've been working for? You want to bring back your daddy so you can take over after him?'

It shocked Caleb to his core, even though he'd known to expect something like it. "You think I want my father's power? That I've used all of you as a way of taking over from him, and getting the Survey to do my work for me?"

There was a lot of shuffling, barely concealed muttering and a fair few jeers at the speaker.

Caleb put up a hand. "No, he has a right to say what he thinks. What about the rest of you? You think I'm standing up here because I'm a Winter?"

He waited for his bluff to be called. He *was* up here because he was a Winter, handpicked by the Survey as a weapon against his own family. He'd told Fee the Survey had put her here because of her track record and ability as an eco-engineer, but that was only half the truth—for both of them.

The silence stretched out and the tension rose. Then a noise came from behind him, and Marabeth bustled forward, fists thrust against her waist.

"You folk ought to be ashamed of yourselves. Who here got one of Caleb's roof designs on their house? A water extractor better than anything bought in a store? Plantings round their home that's saved their house in more than one windstorm? Who's got a son or daughter with a whole new future because of this here lake he's getting us built? You all grew up with this boy. He's plains, through and through. This is his land and he's worked hard for it." She swivelled on him, and he ducked his head, ten years old again and being told off for stealing fudge from her kitchen. "No one gave you that fancy qualification of yours, my lad, so don't you be telling us otherwise." She glared out at the room. "As for you lot, we got a job to do, and this here boy needs our help. So let's get on with it."

She stepped back, gesturing magnanimously for him to take the stage again. There was a lot of embarrassed coughing in the ranks, faces that looked anywhere but at him, then slowly a chuckle, a ripple of mirth spreading through them.

"You tell him, Marabeth," roared old Jim.

"Those Survey staff over the mountains?" called out Viv. "The ones you said have gone into hiding. If head office has gone loco, how safe are they? And if not, what about us?'

"Fee has given us the coordinates she thinks they made for and a squad of our best trackers is setting out to find them. They're good Survey field staff; they'll be safe somewhere."

"And us. What happens to us when you leave?"

This time, Fee stepped up beside him. He tensed, ready for any hostile reaction, but her face was resolute and brave. She was Survey, had worked beside these people, and they waited for her to speak. "Head office needs this lake," she said. "It gives them a legitimate cover for their other plans here. They can't afford to stop it, and they need you."

"Like they needed your team?" He looked for the caller. It was Jareth. Fee had saved his life once, and it was there in his voice. Not jeering, just worried.

"Yes, but the lake is much farther on than the mountain projects, and the Winter family weren't as foolish as my brothers. They haven't given head office a big fat excuse to take them over by kidnapping anyone. If head office stops the lake, they lose their legal argument against the Winters."

"Which doesn't mean you're totally safe," said Caleb. "It's a different enemy this time, but the offer's the same as against the Winters. Anyone who wants to leave now is free to go, with our respect. Fee and I have to leave—they'll be here soon to take us otherwise—but you have a choice."

He stepped back to let them decide. Not one person moved. Not a single one. He raked his gaze over every one of them, hunting for any sign of dissent. They weren't happy; who could blame them. But they were holding.

A deep breath. "Thank you. One day, we will look back on this. Head office are playing a dirty game, but our work is to restore the balance on Arcadia. Not replace the den Coilles and Winters of the world with self-appointed bosses, even from our own side. We're still Survey. We have a job to do. This planet needs us, needs us to do that job—and we will do it." He stuck a fist in the air, and they roared back as one.

"Survey, the planet."

"And good luck," he added in a quiet voice, before stepping back.

"Time to go," he said to Fee.

In front of them, the transporters rolled in and people began piling stuff in to be taken to a secure hideout: confidential data files, important samples, precious equipment no one wanted touched by clumsy hands. Orderly, brave. He was so damned proud of every one of them. Young Ben came up, not much older than their two brothers, but with a level of experience the other two had not been forced to acquire.

"I thought we sent you home?"

He had, but wasn't surprised to see him back. The boy had a backbone of solid steel. He grinned that cheeky open-mouthed smile of his. "Old Man Winter's out of the way, so I figured I'd nothing to lose by coming back."

Caleb shook his head, but had to smile. He thrust out a hand, shook the boy's hand in welcome and pushed Silas and Aigherach towards him. He was a good choice for this job.

"Go with Ben. He knows these lands like no one else, and will keep you safe," he said to Silas. Aigherach was listening, but refusing to show it.

Fee stepped forward and gave Ben a quick hug. "You let a hair on my idiot brother's head get hurt, and I will personally beat you to a pulp," she said, throwing a playful punch at him.

"Righto, boss lady," said Ben and Caleb could see a thawing on Aigherach's face. He guessed her teasing of Ben was much the same as what she did to her kid brother at home. She gave Aigherach a much tighter hug.

"We will find them," she said to him. "Find them and bring them home. Just give us time. Listen to Ben, follow his instructions. He's good people."

Aigherach looked like a young man pushed too far. His face close to breaking, he hugged his sister back. Caleb gave him full marks for the strength he showed in bringing himself back under control. On top of all he had endured, the boy had probably never seen so much open space before and was no doubt feeling badly exposed in this treeless land. Fee had once told him that's how she'd felt on her first visit here.

"Time to go," said Caleb. He stood with Fee and watched as their two brothers climbed into the last of the transporters. A team of horses followed, but they would take them only so far. Knowing Ben, there would be a good hike at the end of it and by the time the group reached their hideout, both young men would be too worn out to worry about anything other than finding a flat space to fall onto and sleep.

He took Fee's hand and handed her one of the two packs set in the doorway. "You ready?"

"No, but let's go anyway." She shouldered on the pack, began to walk down the steps as he picked up his own pack, and headed off to the skimmers.

"Not that way, love."

She stopped, turned and caught the grin on his face before he could hide it, and groaned. "We're riding!"

Two hours into their escape, the call came through from Bob. Fee watched nervously as Caleb took the call.

"The Feds have arrived," he said.

She couldn't stop her glance upwards. "Are we safe here? Shouldn't we go faster?"

"We're safe enough, and fast riding creates dust."

Her horse jibed, and she clung to the saddle. "Relax," said Caleb. "She can feel your tension."

Easier said than done. They were still far too close to camp. A few minutes by flyer.

"We can't be seen from the air, and no vehicle can drive through here safely."

Maybe, but she was hot, dry, gritty and plain scared. Where were her family; what was the Survey doing to them? Even recognising Caleb was right didn't help. They were in a maze of steep-sided canyons with overhanging cliffs, moving in and out of shadow and harsh sunlight. Without Caleb, she would have been lost within a few metres of entering the broken country.

"They'll know we came this way. Horses leave tracks and have heat silhouettes."

"Everything in here is hot, the metals in these rocks confuse the signals, and we laid enough alternative tracks down to force them to waste time following dead ends."

So that was why they had wandered what she had thought so aimlessly, going one way, then switching back countless times. She opened her mouth to argue, but stopped, recognising it was just nerves. Caleb had been watching her, and silently passed her a canteen. She took a short swallow, mindful of the need to conserve their water, and was ridiculously gratified by his nod of approval. Did he think she had learned nothing in her time here?

"The team. You really think they will be safe?" she asked now.

"You know the truth of that as well as me."

The quick quirk of his mouth took the sting out of his words. The Survey bosses couldn't afford to risk losing Federal support, not yet. Not till they were securely in control.

Which was clearly what they were after. Head Office had seen a power vacuum and was set on grabbing it. Fee had put forward the idea one day, wondering if she was insane. The department had been her life's work since grad school, the scientific evidence behind it too compelling to be ignored. The settlers on Arcadia had changed the planet in too many contradictory ways, causing a plethora of local climatic changes that pulled relentlessly at neighbouring zones and destabilised the balance across the entire planet. It had to be brought back into equilibrium.

But the men and women who ran the Survey? Most were career bureaucrats divorced from the work of field staff and overly focussed on power plays within the closed world of head office. No, them she did not trust, and nor did many of her colleagues. Now the top level suits had shown their hand, and it was not pretty.

CHAPTER THIRTY

A bitter wind cut through the crowd and straight into any carelessly exposed body parts. Fee ducked her face deeper under the protection of her hooded cape, clutching tight to the threadbare comfort it offered. She was indistinguishable from the hordes of similarly shrouded workers shoving ahead of her to board the transit unit to Urbis central. Caleb reached out a hand from under cover of his cape to keep her safe, but gave no other clue they were together. After a month of evading Survey spies, they were adept at the small tricks that kept them hidden. Now they had reached the city, and must find and contact the local Survey field staff. It was a risk, exposing them to possible capture, but it was the only way to find out the truth of what was happening at the top.

It didn't stop her being cold black afraid. To bet everything on trusting their colleagues, on believing that their fellow, frontline field staff were as committed to saving Arcadia as they were? That they'd had no part in the games of their senior managers, games that had forced Fee and Caleb to flee their homes and be hunted across the face of this continent?

Nor could they find any word of their families' fate.

"They are alive."

She had told Caleb that on so many nights. One night, she might even believe it.

The scramble of workers filled the unit to overflowing and she had to battle to grab a handhold as it lurched into motion. Too many stood between her and Caleb—she could just see the back of his head—but he was in the same section, and one glance from him as they moved off said he knew where she stood.

An hour later, and it was time to leave the anonymity of the unit and brave the City streets.

The wind whirled around the corner, grabbing at the wisps of hair escaping her hat and whittling its way underneath her cape. She huddled deeper into the odorous depths, badly missing the warmer climate of home. They had cold weather on the mountains, misty drizzling rain that lasted for days, but her mountain clothes were crafted to shed moisture and trap in the warm air. Here, no matter how many layers of poorly made garments she piled on, the biting northern winds still defeated her. Funny she had never before realised how cold it got here. She had studied in this City, trained with the Survey here.

You had a warm apartment, friends to laugh with, and enough funds to dress and eat well.

Now she must keep her head down and scurry along with the other commuters, avoiding security and police as the crowd spilled out into the streets and hurried to offices and workplaces. Only when she was well away from the station and its sharp-eyed guards did she dare move out from the crush of people and slip into a side street. She still kept her head down and walked briskly, giving the impression she knew exactly where she was going. A woman hurrying to make her work place in time, one only of the millions thronging the city streets.

She did know exactly where she was going. It was a good step from the station, but both had agreed that walking was the safest way to move around the city. Soon, she was in a quarter of the City the well paid members of Federal departments made sure not to frequent. The dirt and poverty of these streets was a natural bulwark and would give them cover for now.

Another brisk half hour walk, and she came to a fast food diner, filled with workers grabbing breakfast before starting the day, or night shift staff grabbing a bite and a drink before braving the trip home. Scratched benches, scuffed seats and that ingrained level of grime that told of a place of low pay and long hours. Above the counter, a scratchy news feed streamed. Fee watched surreptitiously, but nothing came up. Not of Winter, not the plains or mountains, nor of den Coille. Most importantly, no images of her or Caleb. The local news feeds had been full of them in the days after their escape. Dangerous fugitives, bent on disrupting the work of the Survey and the smooth running of the economy. The fate of her family wasn't mentioned, nor any hint of where they were being held. Above all, no questioning of the official line. The Survey's media section had done its job well.

Then the reports faded away, till finally their whole sorry saga became a minor by-line, a small event of no consequence happening some place far away. There had been nothing about them on the news casts for the last week, making life much easier. She should be relieved to be so readily dismissed from the collective conscience.

Still she frowned at the feed. A minor starlet on a drug bust filled the casts now, whole panels of reporters discussing the ins and outs. Yesterday's news; that's what she was.

A hand touched her shoulder and Caleb slid into the seat beside her.

"Gidday love. What's a woman like you doing in a place like this?"

She chuckled and leaned into him. One more day of safety, that's what that silly starlet had given them.

That night, they both took special care, bringing all they had of passion, sensuality and caring to their time together. It might be their last. The mood lasted through breakfast, but reality could not be put off forever.

She leaned forward on the table. "So I look up my old classmates, and you look up your acquaintances in Policy. Simple enough."

"Simple, yes, and the first sign of trouble, you pull out and meet back here."

She nodded.

She'd rarely pulled out of trouble in her life, and he knew it as well as she. But it was too soon to let go of the fiction of a happy outcome. They walked out of the one-room bedsit, staying together till the end of the first block, then separated with no more than a light peck on the cheek. A normal couple heading off to mundane daily tasks. How badly she wanted to run back and grab hold of him, to never let go.

She squared her shoulders and walked on.

First on her list was her old college roommate. Or it was until she saw the hidden guard outside her building. A trim woman in her thirties nursing a drink at a sidewalk table, but she sat too ready to move and her eyes constantly roamed over the town square in front of her. Fee swung round and hurried into the nearest store, emerging seconds later by a side entrance. Time to re-prioritise her list.

It wasn't till she got down to fifth on her new list that she found someone not under watch. An old lab partner in her second year of studies, the man was an acquaintance more than a friend. They had argued and debated their way through that entire year, then lost track of each other. She remembered his passion, his belief in their work, and his talent for critiquing to death any pompous pronouncement from senior college staff. Before they left the plains, Bob had pulled the department's organisational files, and she now traced her old lab partner through it. A second tier job in the strategy department; ideal for her purposes. The exuberant man she remembered would be desperate to escape the confines of office walls on his midday break.

The nearest park was filled with trees and gardens. She waited near the wildest looking section, a copy of a pre-settlement, temperate forest glade. As near to her forest home as she could find. She hid in the upper branches of a small beith tree and sat watch over the main gates. Finally, her quarry appeared.

Tracking him through the trees was easy, too easy. He sat down for lunch, breathing out a long sigh and staring at the grass in front of him, before closing his eyes and leaning his head back to let the small patch of sunlight warm his face. She forced herself to wait, casting all round for any sign he was followed, then dropped silently from the tree into the path and sat on the bench beside him.

"Derek! It is Derek der Fielden?"

He didn't recognise her at first, huddling defensively into his coat and beginning to make plopping sounds of denial. Then came a light in his eyes, a tentative grin, immediately wiped clean and replaced by a hunted look. "Fee den Coille. Long time, no see. What are you doing here?"

So he'd seen the vid-casts. "Enjoying the trees, like you," she said, as if nothing was amiss.

He began to stand, hastily scrabbling his lunch together. "Got to go. Just remembered something. Catch up sometime?"

She tugged at his coat, pulling him off balance and making him sit down again. "Yes, right now. I need your help."

He gave up all pretence of innocence. "No. Too dangerous. Your family broke the law."

"Do you know who they were accused of kidnapping?"

He shook his head, as if it didn't matter.

"Me."

"Oh." He remembered to close his mouth. "But you're a Survey agent. Or were."

"Still am. Not so sure about our bosses though." There; she hadn't imagined it. That fleeting glimpse of agreement on his face. "Out with it. What do you know? Come on, you may have a terrible sense of humour, but you were always one of the good guys."

"You never did do small talk well." He sighed. "What is it you want?"

She dropped her attempt at a smile. "I—we—need your help."

"No. I need to eat, for which I need to work, and you are poison right now."

"At least hear me out. You might eat today, but you, and everyone else, will pay for it tomorrow."

He stayed seated, but that was all the encouragement he gave. She launched into her story regardless. From the start, from when the Survey had set up her meeting with Caleb.

"So you did what they wanted you to do. You got married," he said at the end.

"Yes, and the Survey used it to divide and conquer both our families, just as they planned. Problem is, no one seems to have planned what happened next."

"Head office assumed you would go back to being good, loyal technical servants of the Survey, and not bother your heads with high-up strategies?"

It was an old point between them. The seeming inability of senior managers to understand that highly intelligent, technical staff such as eco-engineers did not confine the use of that intelligence to technical matters only. That field staff were forced by their job to be resourceful, strong-willed and fight for every environmental point gained. So why would they suddenly become compliant patsies just because a senior manager demanded they obey an order without thinking. Management hierarchies meant very little to field staff.

"So the Survey gave up waiting on the corporations to change and took direct control." He lifted his hands. "It's hard on your families but if it means saving our world? Well, tough."

At one time she might have agreed with him. The means justified the end; an easy sentiment, too easy and one she no longer trusted.

They had finally heard from her team a week after they had left the camp. Bob kept communications to a minimum, using an indirect messaging route and limiting transmissions to once every three days. Her team had opted to stay on its own side of the mountain, doing what they could to protect their forests.

But the valley of the chaullnia, the valley they had worked so hard to bring back into balance, was destroyed. The Survey bosses now in power in the mountains had re-planted it in festia trees.

"The science was open to question, they claimed. My team knows every speck of that land, but head office found some unknown lab rat on the other side of the world with a different theory on how to manage my homelands. That's what they used to discredit my team's work. The man had probably never even seen a festia tree."

Derek was looking worried, if not yet convinced. "The Survey can't afford niceties any more. We're on a deadline. Fix the climactic anomalies in five years, or we lose this world."

"Two," she said automatically.

"No, five."

Fee sat up. "Where did you get that figure?"

"The last Alliance audit. Five years to show signs of change, or the Alliance will assume control of all environmental functions here—and probably put most of our corporates out of business. Economically, it will kill this world; too many will be forced to leave to find work. We're looking at the end of our world as we know it."

"The version we got," said Fee bitterly, "was a two year deadline, and the Alliance will compulsorily remove all human settlers from this world if we fail to comply."

"Wha…" Derek's face had the stunned look of someone hit with a dead fish.

"You sure of your info?" she said.

He nodded slowly. "A friend was backup on the last intergalactic audit panel. He sat in on the closing meetings." He opened his mouth, closed it, opened it again like a stranded sea creature gasping for air. "No wonder you agreed to marry Caleb Winter. Quickest way to bring both corporates to a tangled end."

"Yeah." And if there was more to it than that, she wasn't about to tell this man.

He fell silent, absently munching on his roll, then swallowed. "Do you have a file copy of your orders?" She nodded. Keeping a record of everything was the first rule any Survey op learned. "I can look into the records and give you a hard copy of the agreements to compare them with. As long as they can't be traced back to me."

It was more than she'd dared hope for. She hugged him tight, tears welling up.

"Hey, mind the suit. I'm respectable now."

She scrubbed at her eyes, caught the twinkle that spoke of her old lab partner, not totally lost under the veneer of officialdom and chuckled. "Yeah right, and I'm next in line for a promotion."

"Only when the Survey loses its collective mind."

An old taunt, straight from their student days. She grinned again. Maybe there was hope still.

Not long after that, she strolled out of the park. Derek had agreed to meet again in a few days, no Survey spies were in sight and the sun was shining. An extra spring in her step, she hurried for the cross city units, eager to get back to Caleb. Success. A small one, but the first of many she was sure.

Her good mood still bubbled through her when she reached the cheap apartment they'd found. It had a window overlooking the street below, a separate rear entrance and a landlord with no interest in their comings and goings as long as they paid him in untraceable credits. The grungy floor coverings and dingy furnishings mattered little beside those.

A familiar step on the stairs, and she raced to open the door. Caleb had barely reached for the latch when she flung it open and threw herself into his arms.

Next she knew, they were sprawled flat on the floor and her hand was slipping in a red, sticky mess. "You're hurt!"

She hauled him upright, hands racing over him to find where he was bleeding. His leg was soaked in red, his coat no better.

He was so heavy.

"Caleb, wake up. I can't carry you."

She tugged, pulled, hauled him through the door and into the apartment, terrified that she could be making it worse. Finally, she shut the door on the world and eased him onto the floor. A cushion under his head, she grabbed a knife from the kitchen and slashed away his clothes, revealing the full extent of his injuries.

A slash to the thigh, deep and nasty, but the blood welled up dark red. No artery hit, at least. Farther up by his waist, a vicious slice to his side went right down to the bone of his hip. He was still bleeding from it. Towels, cloth, a clean shirt, whatever she could find to keep him from bleeding out. Pressure, hard down on his wound. Hold, till her arms ached and despair threatened. Finally, finally, the sodden mass of cloths began to hold the flood at bay. Blood seeped from his wounds, dangerous still but controllable, and she could leave him long enough to dig out their first aid kit. General Survey issue, it was a mini hospital in a box. She scanned and lasered him, then plastered a liquid gel into the cuts. Tough, and sterile, it set quickly into a clear film that would start the healing process and hold the damaged tissues together for now. As long as he rested, he should recover in time.

If he rested. If he stayed here and waited for whomever had done this.

He was so big. Too big to move into a bed and off the cold floor. The kit included a heating pad, and she eased it under him, carefully rolling him part over, until the pad lay fully under him.

He was as safe as she could make him for the moment.

Next priority, clean up the mess outside and do whatever she could to stop his attackers finding this place.

So much blood in the hallway. Too much for the cheap cleaning unit that came with the apartment. She pulled out her weapon, small enough to be concealed at her waist. Maximum disruption level, and precisely set for the top layer of the floor. She swept it across the hall, watching carefully as the gun destroyed every drop of blood. Down the stairs, out the street, weapon discreetly held under her cape, and burning away the incriminating blood trail of stained footsteps and dark sploshes. How far had he come? So much blood lost.

She let the trail peter out in a small garden many blocks away, too scared to leave him any longer. A few blood spattered leaves smudged against the bark of a tree, a few scrapes over the trunk and any pursuer should think he had stumbled here, then climbed the tree.

Her work done, she ran by every back way possible, back to the dingy apartment.

The door was locked, no sigh of a break in. She broke her security seal in relief, quietly opened the door and stepped inside.

He was gone.

No!

A groan, a weak call from across the room.

On the bed, a long shape huddled, weapon in hand and pointing right at her. Then he recognised her, and let it drop.

"You are one stubborn man."

Her eyes and hands slid down him in panic. No fresh bleeding. She glared at him, and flinched when his hand slowly reached out and touched the wetness on her cheeks.

"Hey, you," he whispered. His eyes fell shut again and he slipped from consciousness.

It was a long night. Like all Survey field staff, Fee had been trained in emergency medical procedures, but what she would have given for the security of a proper hospital ward. Or even better, her mother's calm sense and doctoring. Caleb surfaced fitfully during the worst of what she must do, batting her hand away with no sign he recognised her.

No time for tears. "Stay alive. Stay here with me."

The early hours of the next day knocked against the window before he woke properly. A brave attempt at a smile, the merest upward twist of lips, and his eyes looked at her in recognition.

"Hey, you," she whispered, feeling her mouth stretch wide with joy. "You gave me quite a scare."

"Hey, yourself."

His hand reached out and she grabbed it, cradling it tight against her chest, and leaned over to kiss him: eyes, mouth, cheek, a patter of butterfly touches over his whole face. "I thought I'd lost you."

"No such luck."

She stirred his hair, combing it gently back from his eyes with their dark shadows. "What happened?"

"I…" Then a curse, and he began to struggle up.

"Stop that. I'm no surgeon. It's a patch-up job only on those cuts, and you'll open them up again."

"No, get away while you can."

"And leave you here? They nearly killed you."

He shoved a hand against the bed in a futile attempt to lever himself up. "I don't care. They must not have a chance to kill you. Don't make me watch that."

She gently pushed him back down. "I cleaned up your tracks. We have time yet, not much, but still time."

"They know I'm in the city and they'll be hunting me hard. They don't know you're here. You have to leave."

"No."

She could be stubborn when needed. Right now seemed a good time.

Caleb stared at her, wishing the pounding in his head and the throbbing of his body would stop. He had to make her leave here, get away from him. He'd been so careful, using every trick he knew to cover his tracks on the way to meet his old friend from Policy, but he'd been jumped just before their agreed meeting.

They can't have known how tall he was, how big, or what growing up on the plains made of you. Physical strength and fitness were a matter of survival there, not vanity. From their uniforms they were from Survey Security, but all their fancy military fighting styles were no match for his street skills or readiness to use whatever he could find in defence.

He escaped, but not before they cut him badly—for which he'd made them pay dearly. They wouldn't be following him today, or any day soon. He didn't think he'd killed them, or hoped he hadn't. That wasn't a path he was ready to take, not yet. Still, they'd have backup on his trail all too soon. He had to get Fee out of here.

He looked at her, forcing her to meet his stare head on. "One of us has to stay free if we're to find out what's going on and stop it."

She glared right back. "Both of us will stay free. I am not leaving you."

She was his bodily opposite, so small, so delicate, dark hair and shining brown eyes, but in strength of will they were the same. That straight mouth said she wasn't going anywhere, not alone.

Which left only one option. He nodded grudgingly. "All right. Shoot me with some cetaeven and let's get out of here." If he could actually put one foot in front of the other. He wasn't too sure of that, but if it convinced her he was fit to move, he'd do it. Somehow.

She wasn't fooled, looking at him like he'd run mad, an awful grief that tore at his gut lurking in the shadows of her eyes.

"I can do it." He cast his eye around the room. "That chair. Smash those legs off for a brace for my leg, then wrap a tight bandage over the skin seal on the hip cut. That will hold me till we're out of the city."

She did it, grim mouthed but saying nothing. The cetaeven helped but what he wouldn't give for a swig of something stronger. He levered himself off the bed, leaning far too heavily on her for help. His first steps were less than stellar, but with a bit of concentration and a lot of teeth gritting, he forced his body to obey him.

Fee had bundled up their small cache of possessions, and flung both on her back. He stopped, balanced against the wall, and took his bag from her shoulder.

"You can't support me and carry that."

"You can barely carry anything."

"I can, and I will."

He managed to keep up the pretence for half an hour. Onto a nearby unit, off at the second station, down an alley, and through a series of cabs, units and back ways. Still far too close to their original rooms.

"That next unit," he gasped, feeling the sweat starting on his head. He leaned on her shoulder, trying hard to look like any man out with his lady. On to the unit, stay near the door, surreptitiously watching all exits for intruders.

After three stations, he began to feel more secure, even though the cetaeven was already wearing off, his head throbbed and he had to fight to stay conscious.

"He all right?" said a voice.

"Just had a bit too much to drink," said Fee.

The voice laughed, and moved along.

Caleb leaned back against the squab. Then Fee stiffened beside him. "In the next carriage, the brown-haired man on the left of the credit scanner. We get off at this station."

He could have groaned. They were so nearly free. He shook off the pain, tightened his jacket over the hip bandage, and used the wall to lever himself up.

It was an express stop. A few instants only to get off, and everyone familiar with it was standing by the doors and stepping out as the unit slowed. Fee pulled him free, tugged him forward and held hard to his arm as they barely managed to make the street kerb while a gust of wind behind told of the unit pulling swiftly away. He kept his head down, trusting her to sweep the area for danger.

"I think we lost him," she whispered moments later as they rounded the corner of the building with the crowd.

"No, he had backup," she said straight after. "Next corner, the woman reading the vid-casts."

She pulled him to the side, switching pedestrian stream and melding with the solid mass of bodies heading down the slopes to another connecting unit, at the last minute switching streams again and ducking back under a barrier to join yet another crowd of fast striding commuters .

He was barely keeping his feet now. Walking on automatic and following the tug of her hand. "On a unit. Quickly," he gasped.

"Nearly there," she murmured back.

He clung to her hand, his life line in a blur of throbbing, threatening waves of oblivion. A stumble, a quick tug from her righting him before he fell. She was so fast, her instinctive sensing of movement his lifeline now. Blending with the momentum of the crowd, feeling him wavering before he lost it and gave way. One foot in front of the other, that was all he could bring to their passage. She was so tiny, so light compared to him. Where was that seat, that unit?

"Step up," she hissed. He felt a quiver and knew her strength was failing. His legs refused to answer him. "Come on. There's one of them behind us but they haven't seen us yet. We have to make this unit. Step up!"

"Hurry along there," said an impatient voice behind them.

He had to do this. Step up. He focussed all he had on that small order. Lift that leg, step into the unit, fall into the seat she steered him to. The doors slid shut, a whisper of sound, and the familiar whir of the engine. They were on their way.

"Did we?" he said in the spare trace of voice left to him.

"I think so." She eased closer, discreetly twisting her head and peering out at the station entrance as their unit disappeared into the caverns of the city. "He's still there, still watching the entranceway. We're safe." She sighed, a soft sound of relief, and slid back beside him.

Then he knew no more.

CHAPTER THIRTY-ONE

They were in a forest, and Fee felt that twisted coil in her guts loosen by a notch. It might not be as dense as on her mountain home but the trees soared tall and straight around her and the whisper of a chill wind in the branches above echoed the constant rustling of leaves she had grown up with. Maybe she oughtn't to let the familiarity of it make her feel safe, but it did, and right now she badly needed to feel safe.

Caleb had been unconscious throughout the long trip out of the city, stirring only as the unit slowed. It was the last station. The unit guard was working his way along the carriages, banging on seats and threatening any too drunk to get off with a night in the cells. That meant a booking, with a scan of the public records.

"Come on, Caleb. Wake up."

His head lolled and his face had the sickly cast of someone who had lost too much blood. She jabbed him just above the wound on his hip and he gagged in agony. She poked him again.

"Wake up. We've got to get off this unit—now."

He heard her, though she saw the denial of it on his face just before he dragged his eyes open.

"Leave me," he ground out.

"Not an option. You want me safe, you move now. I won't go without you."

He did it. Somehow that stubborn man forced himself to his feet and walked off that unit. She could feel the shudders of impending collapse wrack him as he leaned on her shoulder, but he still kept upright. There was a flitter stand just outside the station, with the ubiquitous city cabs backed up for public use. They had purloined a store of unmarked resident credits when they first neared the city, and she scanned one in now, releasing a battered, two man cab. It was just big enough to fold him into, stow the bags on the shelf at the back and leave the smallest of spaces for her to squeeze in and take the controls.

She smelt the tang of leaf litter in the air, and set the flitter in the direction the breeze called. Soon, they were in the trees and she began to relax. She knew how to survive in a forest; city streets or open plains offered nothing but danger.

Once safely hidden by the canopy, she built a crude shelter, set into the lee of a bank and looking to any casual passer-by like nothing but a tangle of fallen branches and vines. A carpet of dry leaves and twigs made an insulating base for the floor, and small branches knotted with vines and covered by an insul blanket, a bed for Caleb. He'd stood propped up against a tree while she worked, both knowing that if he sat down he wouldn't get up. Now she shouldered him into the shelter and he dropped onto the bed, rolling onto his back and losing consciousness immediately. She spread the other blanket over him, checking his pulse and fighting back panic at the thready flutter under her fingers. A shot of antimicrobials and an infusion of reagent boosted fluids, with a desperate prayer it would be enough. To think how she had taken for granted the abundance of her mother's clinic.

Another long night followed. Somewhere in the dark stretches, she lost her battle to stay on watch, worn out and exhausted by her struggles. Later on, he moved and the creak of the bed frame woke her. She was lying drooped forward over his leg, hugging tight to the strength of his sound limb and with the eerie light of morning filtering through the branches.

"Argh, sorry, meant to watch you," she mumbled.

"Don't. Stubborn woman."

She sat up, rubbing at her eyes. He looked back at her, his eyes clear and knowing, all trace of illness banished.

"You're better!"

"Yes, thanks to you, though I've no idea how you managed it."

That precious, lazy smile of his. If she wasn't so afraid of setting off the bleeding again, she would have flung her arms around him and hugged him so hard he could never escape from her again.

"You're alive!"

"Yes…"

"You need something? Anything—well, within limits," she amended, remembering where they were.

"Water will do fine."

She could do much better than that. Water first, then a hot drink, and a re-heated meal of fresh roots and stew.

"We have to talk."

She shook her head. "Later, when you're properly rested."

His eyes scanned her, heavy with the shadow of pain, followed by a slow blink of acceptance. Minutes later, they closed again in true sleep. She studied him closely, so fearful of being wrong. No, his colour was fine, his breathing normal and he'd lost that fiery burn to his skin. This was the peaceful sleep of healing, and that tightly coiled knot inside her unwound a curve or two.

She left him soon after for a final check of her perimeter set with their pitifully few surveillance sensors, all they had been able to bring with them. Arriving back, she stopped in the doorway, just stood there and listened, absorbing the even in and out of his chest. Normal sleep sounds.

He was going to be fine.

It was Caleb who woke her next, well into the new day. He was carefully pulling his legs from her grasp as he tried to ease out of bed without disturbing her.

She struggled frantically up.

He stopped moving. "Sorry, didn't mean to wake you."

"You shouldn't be up."

"Have to go outside a minute," he said with what could almost be a blush.

"Not on your own."

"Yes, on my own," he said, quite definitely.

She had cut some branches last night, and wordlessly now offered him one to use for support. He leaned heavily on it as he slowly made his way out of the hide.

A scrabbling of branches, a muttered curse and a heavy thump, thump, scrape. He was back, and she could breath properly again. One look at the stark white of his face and she clamped down on the panicked words hovering on her tongue. He nodded thanks, collapsed back on the bed and closed his eyes.

All she could do was let him be. When he opened his eyes again, she wordlessly passed over a cup of water, one hand behind his neck to help him lift his head to drink. He lay back down and she took the cup.

"So much for me protecting you."

"Hey," she said softly. "We're in this together."

He was such a proud man. She was beginning to know him, and realised how far they had come when he slowly nodded agreement. "Partners."

He had said they must talk, and they did need to, but not till he was stronger. On that she was determined. He went along with it for the afternoon, letting her do all that was needed while he alternately dozed and watched her as she worked. Evening came and Fee allowed herself a glimmer of satisfaction as she tidied up after their meal, while the small, portable heat field turned their crude shelter into a cosy nest. She gathered the dishes back into her pack as Caleb pulled himself upright on the bed. He'd wrapped a blanket about his shoulders and passed the other one to her, propping himself against the earth bank that made the back wall of the hut.

"Now, we talk."

She grimaced, but couldn't find an excuse to put him off any longer. "Our city plan wasn't so great."

A brief shrug, his mouth twisted. "Anyone there who could help us is too closely watched, which leaves the remote field staff."

"We trust them still?"

"We have to. There's no one else."

He eased back, using his hands to carefully lift his injured leg into a better position without breaking open the wounds, then pointed at the stab site.

"This was a mistake. It showed their hand too clearly."

"That they're prepared to break the law and attack a rogue agent who threatens their public image?"

"Yes."

She still felt no better. "Were those thugs out to hurt you, or to kill you?"

He was silent too long before answering, a grim cast to his mouth. "Neither. From what they said, they were supposed to capture me, but no one set them a limit. My guess—killing us has not been ruled out."

"So how is that a mistake? Anyone helping us now is in real danger."

He nodded agreement. "Your mountain team, if they capture them. Our plains team, if they get any hint they're helping us."

"Is that why you appointed Kal as leader? Because everyone knew how he felt about a mountain born woman telling your team what to do?"

"Partly…" He gave another of those shrugs of his that said a thousand words. "Kal is solid. He follows his gut and his family have been on the plains from the start. No outsider will make him do anything to hurt another plainsman. He's also a lot more subtle than he lets on."

"No he's not."

He chuckled. "All right, a little more subtle. But a lot brighter, and he is true. He might want the leadership of the team, but not by putting at risk his family and friends."

She crossed her arms and frowned. "That's just it though; he wouldn't be. Central isn't about to stop the lakes project. In fact, all we've heard says they're strengthening the cropping projects and stopping Solaris' plans for expansion. That will do exactly what we hoped for—start to restore the environmental balance of the plains and broaden the economic base for the locals. The Survey is still doing its job on the plains."

"At the expense of my family."

Of both their families; a silent dagger constantly at their backs. Bob had put out feelers with as many other comms staff as he thought trustworthy, but there was still no word of their fate.

"We don't even know if they're still alive."

"They are," he said firmly. "Ethan and my father, they're too damn stubborn to die, and as for my mother…"

It was true, his mother was downright scary, but Fee couldn't even raise a smile. "We have to do something. The Survey bosses can't be allowed to threaten the future of our whole world just so they can have power today."

"So we put that above our families' safety?"

"No—yes—no. That's not a fair question."

Nothing about this whole mess was fair, but it was the first question any field staff would ask, and both of them knew it. How could they expect their fellow Survey frontliners to put their future and their lives at risk to save big corporate families? Business leaders whose actions up to now had been the opposite of what Arcadia needed. "So we save our families by beating the Survey and getting this planet back in balance."

"If they live that long."

She fell silent, hugging her arms tight around her. Were there no good options?

"Come here," he said softly.

She walked over, crouched by the makeshift bed. "This wasn't made for two."

He rolled over, easing carefully down onto the floor beside her. "This is," and he pulled her close, tucking her against his good side. "We will succeed. We will mobilise the other field ops and beat those Survey bosses."

"As soon as we have a plan."

He had to chuckle. "There is that. We'll think of something—but not right now."

No, not right now. Right now, she had nothing left.

It was in the early hours of the morning, when all best ideas came, that she worked out the answer. She jabbed Caleb.

"The politicians. Where do they stand in this?"

"Uurghh," was his less than promising response.

"You can sleep later. " She poked him again. "Do you know any politicians? Or know anyone who does?"

"Yeah, probably, I guess so." He pulled the blanket up higher on his shoulder. It was too dark to see, but she was sure he'd shut his eyes.

"Wake up."

"You really want to talk about this now," he grumbled. "It's the middle of the night."

"The politicians. That's the key. Who else can curtail the power of a government department?"

"Not a politician," he pointed out triumphantly and burrowed deeper under the cover. "Remember the neutrality of the civil service. Politicians set policy and the civil service carries it out. Protecting Arcadia from being forcibly evacuated is legitimate policy. No politician will deny that. Now go to sleep."

She ignored the last bit. "Policy. Exactly. The government sets the policy, not the department. They must be seen to follow government policy, or heads roll—unless the Survey pits its security forces directly against the Federal government. Reckon head office is ready for that?"

He was silent, but the tension in his body said he was considering it. He shook his head slowly. "Not yet. Not far off it, but not yet."

"Right, so all we have to do is prove to a politician that the Survey bosses have overstepped their authority. That they are carrying out a power grab designed solely to enrich themselves. We do that, and we can force the Feds to take direct control of the department."

"So now you trust politicians?"

A grimace. "No, but there have to be some who still believe they're there to serve the people. Or we make them remember it, by finding a journalist brave enough to speak out. That always prods a politician to action. "

"Maybe." He sounded unconvinced. "Even say you find your politician, where's your evidence. The lake projects are coming along fine. As for your mountain project, only your team can prove that the Survey's new strategy puts whole hillsides at risk of collapse. They have the figures and the local credibility. Except they know they'll be nabbed as soon as they put one foot out of hiding." He rolled onto his back, staring at the leafy branches above them as if seeking the answer to a riddle. His next words were spoken so softly as to be for himself as much as her. "What if we're wrong? How can we be sure what they're doing will fail?

He had a point. They'd skirted around it a few times, but never said it outright.

"We need to run the possible outcomes," she admitted.

His hand traced slowly down her cheek. "You plan to walk straight into Survey central and ask to use their analysers? Want to set a new speed record for being locked up with the key thrown away?"

"There must be a way."

It took them a day of arguing, discussing , plain old all-out battle, but finally they thrashed out a plan—one they could both mostly agree to.

First: find their politicians. Belonging to profit-hungry corporate families had brought few advantages to either of them, but the tedious social meetings of their childhood might finally be of some use.

"My mother had an old friend at college who is now on the justice committee," remembered Caleb. "She laughed when Mother caught me feeding her fat pet with the last bun."

"A girl in my first year dorm went on to study politics, and is now the PR assistant for the far north Regional Councillor. Haven't seen her since college, but I did help her pass first year geography."

Fee was surprised how long their list of useful contacts turned out to be. They ruled out relatives as too obvious and ex-civil employees as too biased, but it still left them with plenty of candidates.

Next, collect evidence. She told Caleb of her friend in Strategy. "It's a long shot, but if he agrees to come forward as a witness at a committee hearing, we have a chance of exposing the head office bosses."

A dry twist of his mouth was Caleb's answer.

The last item was the most important. Rally the Survey field staff to their cause. Those in the city were untouchable—all suspect, all likely to be under watch—but the frontline workers in the regions were another matter. They were the ground troops of the Survey: a readymade standing army with a huge knowledge of their local area and all committed to the Survey's task of saving Arcadia. A deep-seated commitment that was now being used against them by the bosses they trusted. Somehow, Fee and Caleb had to convince their colleagues of that truth. Unfortunately, they also had to convince them they weren't merely trying to use them as well, just like the bosses, but in their case to help free the den Coille and Winter families.

"We can do it."

Fee hoped her voice sounded more convincing than she felt, but caught again that caustic twist of Caleb's mouth.

When their planning ground to a standstill, when success could only be guaranteed by action, not words, both knew it was time to leave.

"You can't travel in your condition," Fee protested.

Caleb ignored her. It might be true, but nor could they stay where they were. They were lucky to have avoided the Survey trackers for so long. Caleb called Bob that night.

"I've got a contact in Cerbus minor," said Bob. It was a village about an hour's flight away.

"Too small; too few people." Fee knew how easily people talked in a small community.

"Nah, they're good. Survey head office staff aren't too popular there since they turned out a local and replaced him with a stiff headed no-hoper from Urbis central."

She looked at Caleb. He sat rigidly on his cot, stick near at hand though he refused to reach for it. It didn't fool her. Not when she'd seen how stiffly he moved when trying to walk more than a few metres from the shelter. His wounds were clean and healing, but he was badly bruised and the muscles barely knitting yet. Whatever his pig-headed pride might claim, he was in no state to travel far.

"Can they send an unmarked flitter?" Their Urbis flitter was too easy to trace.

Yes, they could. Bob was a miracle worker, she decided. Just before she signed out, she asked: "Any word?"

"No. Sorry, Fee."

It was the same question she asked every time she talked to Bob. Any word of her family, or Caleb's. Always, no. It was as if they had disappeared off the face of the planet, and yet there was nothing on the vid-casts. How could the Survey kidnap two leading corporate families, and have no protest at all from the others?

"Not with the threat of the same happening to them." Caleb shrugged, as if to say you know that as well as I do. "It's the not-knowing that makes it so effective."

That need to find their families was also a problem with their fellow Survey, just as they'd known. They set out the next morning to make contact with all the groups on Bob's safe list. But the question of their families' fate always came up, and lying to these people was out of the question. Not when they were demanding their trust.

Field staff had been lied to by head office too often, too many battling in desperation to stop the disaster facing their homelands. For them, removing the den Coilles and Winters from the equation was the first sign they'd seen in far too long of the Survey acting to save their world—and if Fee and Caleb thought otherwise, maybe they should rethink their loyalties before expecting field staff to help them.

As a result, they stayed just long enough in each place for Caleb to be fit to travel to the next on the list. They were safe with field staff, but getting them to help was another matter entirely, as they were told often and bluntly.

"Maybe their methods aren't so great, but it's working. Do you know how long we've been trying to get that company to change their ways?" They were in a coastal community, watching a fleet of fishing vessels unload their catch. The Survey inspector kept track of each load coming off the boat, checked that the company staff sorted out the living creatures and sent the at-risk species back into the Survey tanks for return to the sea. "Not so long ago, we'd have been shot at for insisting they follow the rules. We were forced to break in at night and release as many as possible before the fishing companies sent them to the processors."

"They let you do that?"

Their host shook his head. "It was an agreed standoff. We didn't report them, and they let us release a proportion of the catch. It worked, in a fashion, but the breeding stocks have been badly hit. This new approach from head office has come just in time."

The man didn't even try to sympathise with their family's loss. Fee left that village as downhearted as she'd felt at any time on their mission. Caleb could now keep up with walking for a few hours, but they had found no help at all. This man was too like all the others they had asked for help.

"Don't they realise that what happened to us can happen to any of them?"

"Why should they? The Survey has been playing a stealth game for as long as any of us have been in the business."

She concentrated on putting one foot in front of the other, remembering the few times she had tried to get her family to see sense. "It had to. There was so much at stake. No one in power would back the kind of changes the Survey needs, not when it means committing electoral suicide. All most people see is a cut in profits and income."

"Doesn't change what's happening," said Caleb. "The climate situation is real; just not the timeline the Survey fed us."

"Do we really know that?"

He stopped, pulled her round and forced her to face him. They were walking down a forest path on the way to catch the local unit. Slow, but cheap and sure to be packed. Stay poor, stay low to avoid notice.

There was nothing poor or humble in Caleb's face. "You've seen the data. Do you think that mudslide in Manascraoch was a once-in-a-hundred-year accident of nature? That your mountain people can carry on just as they always have?"

No, she did not think that. Even with the changes from the lakes project, the sodden ocean air that swept across her mountain home would still drop too much of its water on her side of the ranges, drenching the slopes below and leaving the plains empty and parched. They needed her team's forest modifications.

If the mountains were a different height, if her coastal region was wider, if they were at a different latitude. If, if, if.

If she didn't know so much, she'd have nothing to worry about. But she did know it, and could not deny the responsibility that came with that knowledge.

She hunched her shoulders and gave him back his stare with one equally as burdened.

"What time did you say that transporter was leaving?"

They just made it, and Fee watched Caleb collapse into his seat. He refused to let her look at his wounds. "I'm as well trained a medic as you," he'd said the last time she tried.

Maybe, but he was running at his limits. The shadows of exhaustion and pain scored deep into his face.

"This next place. We stop a night."

He looked over at her, then closed his eyes. "If it's safe," he murmured. That lack of protest told her more than any medical checks how close he stood to collapse.

They were on their way to the third continent of Arcadia, or the largest island as the old argument went. The least populated of the three, she doubted they would find much support there and had suggested it largely because its isolation meant a break from the constant fear of discovery. The Survey's agents expected them to tour major climate hot spots, not a backwater paradise.

The agents obviously had no training in eco-engineering and knew nothing of the fragile illusion of toughness that was Feldwesten. Most people lived on the continental margins, particularly the western zone. The interior was drier even than Caleb's plains, marked out by the remnant circle of a once great mountain range that circled the continent, now flattened by time, wind and temperature extremes to a cracked barricade of bare rock. The ecology there remained much as it was at settlement time for very good reason. Any major change would tumble the entire continent into rapid decline, the interior deserts lurking ready to take over the hardy coastal fauna. More than any other continent, Feldwesten could not ignore the risks of unbalanced development.

Leaving the mainland some days later was easier than they'd expected. A minor port, harried officials on a commuter flight to a small, insignificant offshore island. A series of more short hops, then a low-grade long-haul service for the last leg from a port too small for heavy security.

Not so when they got to Feldwesten. Arrival there meant official checks. She hadn't bothered with stupid disguises like hair colour. Far too easy to see through. Luckily, one of their contacts had come through; not to help overthrow the Survey, but to at least keep them safe. With false lenses, fingertip masks and synthetic sweat gas gel in place, she approached the counter. The official barely looked up as the automatic scanner swept across her.

She held her breath as a small beep sounded.

"First trip here?" said the bored voice.

She nodded, trying to look ingenuous. "Visiting a relative." Then added in the most nervous voice she could muster, not hard at the moment. "The megalons? They don't come into the cities, do they?"

The official sneered. "Yeah, course they do. Eat one person a night minimum." Fee made herself sway. "Hey, don't faint on my watch. Only joking. What d'you think we are? Cities here are as safe as anywhere." The woman waved her on through. "Mainlanders," she heard her mutter.

Fee breathed again and grinned inside. That adrenaline spike on the scanner was almost impossible to prevent. The woman might think her a cowardly city dweller, but she could live with that.

She waited for Caleb outside the terminal as they had agreed. No point advertising they were together. Thankfully he followed soon after, face untroubled and with a collected saunter. *No adrenaline spike for him, I bet.*

"Show off," she said as he came up beside her. He laughed and tucked an arm over her shoulder.

"Come on. I know a great seafood place by the harbour. The owner's Survey and a friend of mine."

"A *safe* friend?"

He didn't bother answering that and hailed a public flitter. As if he would take her anywhere dangerous. She leaned against him, and decided they had earned a few days break so she was going to enjoy herself. Thanks to their days of island hopping, he could walk without a limp now and only used a stick on rough terrain. Maybe she was worrying unnecessarily.

"You're paying today," she put an arm around his waist, careful to avoid the injured hip, "and if we find anyone here to back us, you can pay for the next week."

He laughed, snatching a quick kiss. "Agreed. I also know a great hotel, with maxi size beds. Plenty of room to play on."

She felt the heat rush her cheeks. "You're on."

They were both doomed to disappointment. It turned out the owner of the seafood diner, Jacko, was now ex-Survey. "Couldn't work for that bunch any longer," he said. "Not after what they did to the Beod project."

Fee hadn't heard of this one, but saw a faint crease of recognition on Caleb's face. She took a deep breath. "Sit down and have a wine with us. Always good to talk to fellow ex-Survey."

Jacko looked at Caleb in shock. "You left them too?"

Caleb lifted a shoulder. "Not much choice. It's a long story, something like yours."

The owner's story wasn't so long, really. Beod was a bowl in the centre of the hottest part of the desert. Already barren, apart from the unique and extraordinary creatures who survived only there. Fauna and flora protected by layers of legal caveats.

"Yeah, much good they did. Not when the keeper turns poacher," said the man. "Your father would feel right at home.

That whole basin is covered with solar arrays now; the cheap slab ones that kill anything beneath them."

"Easy to put up, cheap to run and maximum output for money in." Fee could just hear Old Man Winter spouting the words.

"So why is the Survey using them," said their new friend with a scowl, "and pulling out any field staff who know what those arrays will do? Plus they replaced all the local people with mainland technicians. We've lost half a dozen species from the Beod already."

Fee took a careful sip of wine. "Did you get any kind of explanation?"

Jacko looked at her suspiciously, then at Caleb's arm draped easily over her chair, and his face relaxed. "Something about the feds pulling their funding, so they needed to prioritise their activities. 'Sacrifices must be made to achieve the overall outcome', was the last bit of mummery I heard."

"So here you are now." Suddenly Caleb stiffened. "You got a back way out?" he said quietly.

Jacko's eyes followed Caleb's. "Two men, southeast quadrant?"

"Yeah."

The man stood. "This way."

He lead them through the back of the tables, discreetly keeping diners and large potted greenery between them and the intruders, to slip through a screened door into the kitchen where a woman stacking dishes into a washer barely stopped her work as they rushed by.

Once out, they were in a maze of back entrances and grubby alleys. Through another shop, past open mouthed customers and staff who called out cheerfully, "Who you annoyed this time, Jacko?"

They emerged into a busy thoroughfare, then up a flight of steps and through a battered door. Their new friend banged once, and slipped a key into the lock. "This is my son's place. Don't mind the mess. He's out of town for a few days, so you're safe here for now."

It was as battered as their rooms in the city, and the stramash of clothes on the floors were so like Aigherach's rooms that Fee could have cried.

"Stay down, get some rest. We'll talk tonight. All right, mates?" The man clapped her on the shoulder and gave Caleb a friendly shove. It banged him against the table edge and he crumpled over, face white and gagging. Fee jumped to his side.

"Hey, sorry." Jacko grabbed at his other side.

"He was attacked in the city," said Fee. "Help me get him into a chair."

Caleb struggled up, barely able to speak, waving his hand impatiently. "S'all right," he gasped, clamping a hand to his side.

They ignored him. Fee dragged off his shirt, shutting her ears to his protests, and carefully peeled off the bandage covering the stab wound on his hip. It might be healing, but was still an angry red, covered in scabs and surrounded by mottled green and black bruising.

Jacko winced. "Who in hell you annoyed?"

"Head office," said Fee.

"Head—you mean, Survey head office? You sure?"

Caleb leaned back, eyes closed, before slowly opening them. Fee could have howled at the pain dimming that bright gaze. "Yes, I'm sure," he said. "I recognised them from the security detail on the ship that got us out of Fee's hall."

This was news to her. "But—they *helped* us that day."

"We were still useful then." His voice had that hollow sound she had come to dread. His eyes closed over again.

Jacko sat down opposite, his face equally grim. "Right. Time for the full story. Who exactly are you running from, and what in hell are those shysters in Urbis up to now?"

CHAPTER THIRTY-TWO

It was the start. Like the breaching of a dam, help cascaded in from that day. Jacko might have been ex-Survey but he still had his contacts and Survey field staff stuck together against all comers, including head office. Too many place names in Feldweston clung to projects that had left them feeling betrayed and disillusioned. Within days, Fee and Caleb had met or talked to every field group on the continent.

Then Feldweston proved itself. Isolated, empty compared to the other continents, its people had long ago learned that survival lay in their own hands. That what worked was more important than any theory, no matter how fine-sounding.

Now, head office had attacked one of its own. Caleb's injuries spoke louder than any argument could.

"How those new bosses got their positions in the first place," said one woman to Fee. They were in the merest blip of a settlement, one store and a scatter of houses set right on the edge of the barren interior. The kind of place where you either lived with nature or went under. "All any of them know is to say the right words to the one above them. They know nothing about what we really do out here."

Fee had to agree. As far as she could work out, head office cared little for what field staff thought, unless it threatened their power base. She said nothing though. The anger in the room was boiling over already.

Caleb stepped up onto the stage, making no effort to hide his limp. Silence crashed into the room.

"Folks, Survey. Family all. Thank you for coming. You've all heard our story. Too many of you have one like it of your own. Tonight, right here, we start to fix that."

A huge cheer roared through the room.

There was more to be said, much to be discussed, but that roar stayed in Fee's head. Feldweston would play its part.

Now to bring in the rest.

They left the continent in a scruffy fishing boat, nondescript enough to sail below official notice, to meet up with a Survey flyer on the far side of a small offshore island. The flyer's manifest said research vessel, its programmed voyage set for a routine research trip down to the southern oceans. No reason for anyone to question the periodic stops as the flyer landed to take samples, pausing long enough to sample the water in each area before taking off again, or a stoppage to take on fresh fish for dinner.

Jacko was captain and sole crew today, his borrowed clothes reeking of fish and a battered old hat shoved down on his head. When his small boat bumped up against the sleek exterior of the flyer, he knocked on the hatch, and dragged forward a bin of fish to pass up through the open doorway.

Nothing out of the ordinary to be seen. The hatch opened outwards, a wide shield to keep the sun off the chilled fish, and hide the two extra passengers ready to scramble up into the flyer. Jacko gave her a quick hug. "Keep safe, little sister." Next he turned to Caleb, put out a hand, and farewelled him with the solemn handshake of men bent on a purpose. "Feldweston Survey will be there when needed. Just send the word."

Caleb nodded his thanks with a quick, hard clap on the man's shoulder. "We know. We owe you."

A hurried dash into the flyer as Jacko finished loading the fish, indulged in a brisk debate with the flyer's master about price and the worthiness or otherwise of various antecedents until both agreed they had found the least insulting figure and shook hands on it, then Jacko poled off and the little boat bobbed away.

From her seat by the window, Fee watched it dwindle to a safe distance from the wake of the flyer's launch. A hand rose in farewell and she felt a tug as they lifted up from the sea. She looked back to see the staunch speck chugging back towards an island where blue waves lapped at clean white sand. "Someday, we'll come back here," she promised. "When the tide turns again."

Their return to the larger continent was markedly different from the desperate misery of their escape. Passed from field group to field group, they slept this time in real beds and in rooms with proper amenities. Caleb's injuries finally healed properly, though she suspected he would always bear the livid scars marking his leg and hip.

"I earned them," he said to her one night when she tracked a finger along the purple line, "and they are evidence. Medical records don't have the same weight."

That was true, though she had come to recognise that minute pause before he opened his jacket to a new witness. Caleb Winter was no exhibitionist, but he was a pragmatist. If it helped, he would strip a thousand times, and for every salacious spectator there were an equal number of committed field ops who'd been waiting for such a spark to set them off.

But while they now had their own people behind them, it wasn't enough. They still needed proof. The kind of proof that would force the public out of its smug complacency and have them screaming their anger in the streets. Then they needed a way to let them know about it. Fee haunted the vid-casts and delved through the most obscure of reports hinting at climate trouble.

"How can they just ignore what's happening? Don't they realise that once-in-a-hundred-year storm, or the flowers that won't grow any more, or the creeping frequency of dry years are not normal? Does *no one* listen to the warnings out there?"

Caleb looked up from his screens. "People see what they want to see."

"No, they see what makes them feel safe, but reporters are supposed to ask questions."

He reached forward, running a hand down her arm to clasp her hand. "There's no money in doomsayers. Vids must sell, and happiness sells better." He looked down and studied his fingers interlocking with hers. "You'll find something. Keep looking."

"Thank you," she said softly. She lifted their joined hands, touched his fingers with her lips, then took a deep breath and placed his hands back where they ought to be. Searching the records for proof. "Find anything yet?"

He pulled her head back down, gave her a quick kiss, and released her slowly. A short smile of assurance and he was back to his screens.

Suddenly, he leaned forward, fingers playing rapidly on the controls. "Maybe," he said. He paused the feed. "Look at this newscast."

She traced down, squinting in puzzlement. "The court records of some place called Modogradum? Never heard of it."

He pulled open another screen and set the locator to scan over the holo-map. "Here—halfway between the plains border and the city margins."

She looked at the matching data entry. "There's nothing there but a way station and some trucking diners. Surprised they even have a court."

His finger jabbed at the figures on his screen, rippling through the words. "They don't. This is the monthly circuit judge's court. Look here under 'Minor commercial misdemeanours'. Just after the Lone Circle Diner overcharging a transit customer for a meal."

She followed his finger, linked it into her own database and pulled up the report.

"Open the link," he said.

She did, bringing up the images of the accused, then gasped. "That's…"

"…My father, with Ethan beside him. Charged with 'Various matters of over-utilisation of allocated resources'."

She read it through again, brought up all the related vid-casts. It *was* them. "They're alive!"

"Yeah. A bit the worse for wear," he eyed the gaunt lines on his father's face and the signs of bruising on Ethan's, "but undoubtedly alive, which means the rest are too."

"Your mother, Mama and Da, Samhchair and Ceart, Cumchdach, even Seolta."

She set to feverishly, searching through every database she dared without risking exposure. Beside her, Caleb was equally busy.

She shrieked. "Here, look. For 'Public Disarray'. It's Ceart, looking like he's been in a street brawl." She pulled up her locator. "Jurgum. Another nobody town in the borderlands.

"And here's your Seolta, alongside my Mother. An interesting pair, both charged with 'Misleading commerce'."

Fee looked at the vid of the very brief trial. Neither defendant got to speak, despite rising repeatedly, and both were sentenced to imprisonment plus a fine. Fee ran the figures in her head. "That's everything he owns, lost to the State—or the Survey, I assume. Seolta is furious." She grinned even wider and threw her arms around Caleb. "He's still fit enough to be furious."

His mouth came down on hers, fierce and exultant. "They're all alive." His smile was as wide as hers. "We are going to win this thing."

More searching, a fizzing buzz of certainty growing in her. Finally, finally, another hint. A dimly outlined image in a bulk charge of public misconduct. Cumchdach? "The height is his."

Caleb looked over her shoulder and ran the figures again, comparing Cumchdach's details with that of the unknown defendant. "Not definitive, but yes, it could be him."

It was the nearest they got to the rest. No sign of her mother or sister, no sign of her father anywhere, which was worrying.

"Could be they're still working on him," said Caleb. "He will turn up, and all the others."

She chewed on her lip, and half smiled. "Yes, I think they will."

Caleb shoved back from his screens and powered them down. "Any more searching will merely set off a red light for the Survey. Time to move on."

He was right. She forced her fingers closed, fisting them tight to prevent them trying one more keyword, one more possible link, and stood, shoulders squared and turned to their bags. A simple backpack each, all their possessions at present. "Where to next?"

Caleb eyes sparkled. "Someplace warm," he said, "with a bar, a pool and a very big bed. We deserve a celebration."

The laughter lurking on his lips was irresistible. *That* for frustration, and a froth of happiness bubbled up inside her. "Yes, we do." Picking up her pack to move on yet again suddenly seemed no chore at all.

The door slammed open and their latest host erupted into the room.

"A transmission for you, from Plains Camp comms." He passed the encrypted file to Caleb, who set it in his unit and waited for his screens to settle into view. What now?

A crash of his chair and a wild oath. He swung away from her, but not before she glimpsed his face, and her heart seized shut. She looked towards the local man, but he said nothing.

Caleb's back was to her, the lines of it rigid. "What's happened?" she said.

His voice was flat, scarily flat. "It's from Bob. He's heard from the team hiding our brothers." He paused, still keeping his back to her, his face hidden. "It seems Aigherach lost faith in our promise to look for his family. He slipped away from the team. Except he doesn't know our land, not like the plainsmen who were trying to look after him. The Survey security troops found him soon after."

"Is he…?"

Then, then he turned around, and his face was worse than any words. Grief etched deep into sun baked lines. "No, they caught him without killing him. But not before my team tried to rescue him. Survey security didn't bother with stunners. Not for ordinary field staffers."

"Just tell me. Who?"

"Ben. They shot Ben. He was trying to rescue your brother and they shot him dead like some wild animal."

Fee couldn't breathe. Memories of a sweet, clever and joyous young man. The team zoologist had loved the plains with all of his heart. Not Ben.

"Your brother…he's like you, hates open spaces. He headed for the nearest patch of scrub. They were hiding in it."

"He's only seventeen," she whispered.

"Ben was twenty-three."

She felt sick. Aigherach must have been scared senseless to have tried anything so foolhardy, but that Ben's life should be the price of that was beyond understanding. "They shot one of our own!"

"No, they shot one of mine." With that, he was gone; out the door and gone without once looking back.

Caleb walked, just walked. Where made no difference, not to the guilt riding him. A cold wind slashed the skin on his face, but he barely noticed. It was of a parcel with everything else. Back on their home continent for the first time in weeks, the first shadows of winter etched the skies in the seaside port. They'd chosen it because it was big enough to hide them but small enough to keep them safe. Too small to hide their enemy.

Safe. Like Ben, like all the other men and women who trusted him to keep them free of the danger that stalked his heels. All the safeguards they'd used; the infrequent com links, shifting locations, changing everything in a random, unpredictable fashion. All the hard, tiresome, wearying whole of it. Gone, snuffed into ashes by one scared boy, too blinded by his fear and need for his own kind to trust the plainsmen guarding him.

But it wasn't Caleb who'd paid the price of his poor judgement. No. It was Ben, young, eager, Ben Crane. Beloved only son of a dead Solaris maintenance technician and Caleb's old first grade teacher, Sera Crane. How could he face her, tell her the news? Except he wouldn't have to. Someone else would have done that for him. Caleb Winter, wanted by Survey security and the Feds, spelled only trouble for the Crane family. The only good news in the whole sorry mess was that Silas was safe. One positive in a whole mess of snarled-up bad.

There was a stone in his path and he kicked it away, listening to the solid thunk against the wooden wall of a shop.

"Hey." A man shook his fist from the shop doorway.

He lifted a hand in apology, and walked faster. Away—from the memory of Ben, away from duty, from trouble and disaster.

From Fee.

A splatter of rain, and the day was complete. Before long, a grey drizzle soaked him through, a cold, grey blanket to match the void filling him.

They still had a job to do; he would have to go back to the house, but not yet.

Fee's brother, Aigherach. Only seventeen, she had said, and Ben was only twenty-three. But Ben was a son of hardship and the Plains, and knew that survival demanded hard work and an intimate knowledge of the dangers surrounding you.

How could he have known that one of those dangers was the impetuous stupidity of a scared young man, when that young man had been vouched for by someone he trusted? By his leader, Caleb, and his *wife*. Fioruisghe ingh Bram an Scathach den Coille.

The full name made it easier. Fioruisghe den Coille was a stranger.

But no, it had changed since her marriage to him. She was now Fioruisghe ingh Coille beann Caleb den Winter: Fioruisghe daughter of clan Coille, wife of Caleb of clan Winter.

Or Fee Coille-Winter, that was her married name in his family. She was no outsider, no stranger, not the brave, tiny, and utterly beguiling woman he had married. The wife he could no more deny now than he could set aside the guilt slashing through him.

If he'd never met Fee, never visited the mountains, never encouraged his people to work with them, Ben would still be alive. That wasn't Fee's fault, it wasn't his or Ben's.

But it was fact.

He'd walked in a complete circle, he suddenly realised. The plain wooden facade of the local Survey office loomed up through the misty rain. Their sanctuary for the night. The underground network of field offices was still their best refuge, helping them to travel undetected from one post to the next. And so far there had been no sign at all of head office looking there for them there; proof of how out of touch the bosses were with the frontline staff or with the immensity of the dangers facing their world.

Not that field staff were about to enlighten them. Especially not now that head office had killed one of their own. Ben's death was the game breaker they'd needed. One he would exploit, no matter how much he hated it, and a bitter taste churned up from his gut.

Further, he would exploit it, though it meant he must keep working with Fee. His wife, and the woman he loved.

He stopped dead in the street, frozen in mid step. *The woman he loved.* He'd never admitted it before, not in words. Nor could he now deny the truth of it, and his guilt slammed up a whole lot more notches. He loved the woman whose brother had caused Ben's death.

He didn't know the boy Aigherach. The youngest of the den Coille brothers by a number of years and no doubt spoiled rotten.

No, that was unfair. No point blaming a boy for being scared silly when his whole world had been turned upside down. Yet because of this boy, because everything he believed in and had worked so hard for said he must, he would have to keep Fee beside him, day after day, loving her, yet seeing no way to move past this thing that now stood between them.

She stood at the top of the steps of the office, watching him as he walked towards her. Her face was closed tight in a way he'd never seen before. Her beautiful face that was always alive with how she felt. It was one of the first things he'd noticed about her on that long ago day when they'd first met. So nervous, so ill at ease and defensive, but never still. Like one of her mountain trees constantly moving in unseen breezes. The sheer courage and determination on her face had taken his breath away.

The determination was still there, in the rigid set of her face, and it still took his breath away, but what she felt, what she thought; that he couldn't read. He squared his shoulders and set his foot on the steps.

She clasped her hands together. "They're setting up a com session of all the main groups. They want us to speak to them."

"So this has finally woken them up?"

He couldn't say Ben's name, but caught her almost imperceptible flinch.

"They know they can't wait any longer."

"I'll change and join you."

She said nothing, though he knew from the furrow on her brow that she'd taken in his drowned state. He walked past her before she could say anything more.

He was back swiftly, but kept his hands firmly by his side as he walked with her into the office. All through the call he was conscious of her sitting beside him, of her forced tone of bland assurance. They were both such skilled actors.

They. Still he thought of their work in terms of *they*, of both of them working together. A necessity for their mission, but further, it had become ingrained in him. Or had been until the untimely death of a young man ripped to shreds any hope of their naive dreams and gouged a mindlessly wide chasm between them.

The delegate from the second continent held the channel as they settled in. "We know we can get enough of our people unseen into the capital beforehand, enough to make a crowd that can't be ignored." He'd worked with the woman before and knew her to be as sound as red dirt, and impossible to turn once set on a course. But then realised what it was they were planning.

A mass rally of frontline Survey in the central plaza in Urbis

He and Fee had shared the thought of it, but never yet fixed on a plan. Now it was going to happen, tempers raised too high by the news of Ben. An action based more on emotion than cold hard fact. It could work, but…

"How are you going to explain having so many staff suddenly missing from their posts?"

"We don't," she said with a scarily confident smile. "Head office has no idea if there are real people at work, unless some task is missed. They work on reports and records only. If our teams work double shifts to finish all the essential work, we can set up an automated feed to keep on sending those reports through while we're gone. We'll leave a skeleton staff to keep everything ticking over; enough to make it look like real people are still out there. It won't work for too long, but will be more than adequate for a short period."

Except that any action was likely to take rather longer than her *short period*. Nor was it clear what was planned once they got all these frontliners into the capital. Such a demonstration would make great viewing, but they needed more than a ten second thrill for a vid-cast audience to beat Head Office.

Beside him, Fee leaned forward. "Who's liaising with the media?"

No answer.

"What about a news release?"

"Too risky. We can't show our hand before everything's in place," said the representative from the far eastern coast of this continent. The man had a point, but someone better give the vid reporters a heads up of a big story or their grand demonstration wouldn't even get its ten second flash. He risked a glance at Fee and she gave him back a tight lipped, brusque nod. So they'd have to organise the media coverage, which meant they would have to talk about Ben.

No, not yet. He'd deal with the media; Fee could find a way to get the Federal troops on side. That would keep her away from him.

The call session broke up some time later; too much later. So much talk and little real action, as far as Caleb could see, but they had made one step forward. The front line was now united and determined to act.

As soon as the others signed off, he got out of that room before Fee could say anything. Marched straight out and made for a hill he'd seen from their rooms. It was a small town, and in no time he'd left the houses and was climbing the bare, windswept slopes. At the top, he stopped, took great gulping breaths of the chilly sea air and let it wash down into the depths of his lungs, purging him of the stew of twisted longings and guilt. It worked, for a space at least.

Yet still he stayed there, looking in silence over the boats in the harbour and the stark, undecorated houses on the slopes surrounding it. Too many showed signs of recent flooding, from the ever-worsening storm surges that battered the shoreline. It was easy enough to see the cause from up here. Houses built in the wrong place, too much clearance of the natural plant cover on the outer islands that sheltered the bay, all made worse by the excess draining of the underlying marshy soils in a misguided attempt to increase the area available for houses and combat the natural dankness of the local climate.

The local field staff were building an alternative village farther back from the coast, at the same time restoring the natural state of the shoreline in an area set aside for a public garden. Laughed at initially by the locals, they had persisted and finally the locals started to buy into their housing complex. Freedom from flooding worries and healthier children more than made up for a slightly longer transit to work, they were discovering.

But recently the Survey had changed tactics. Head office ordered a price increase and began an ad campaign. Now, the new, Survey-built suburbs had become fashionable, available only to the wealthier locals and dividing the town. The better off moved away from the old plots down by the harbour, leaving them to the poor and vulnerable.

Even head office should have sensed the slow-burning anger in the local field staff—if they'd ever bothered to visit.

He kicked at a grass clump. Enough brooding. It was only putting off what he'd come up here for. He stepped over the brow, found a sheltered hollow and put a call through to Bob

He'd kept a separate, secure link to his comms man, one Fee didn't know about, and that's what he now used. No answer. He left the call in and sat down to wait. Bob would know from the link that he was on his own.

A buzz.

"Bob, that you?'

"Hey boss. Been expecting you."

Not surprising. He'd gone to school with Bob. "Tell me exactly what happened. The truth without the decoration."

Fee watched Caleb march out and wished she could follow him, but that was no longer possible. Not given the look on his face.

Ben. How could such a vital young man be dead? Aigerach, what did you do? She couldn't even blame her brother. Barely arrived in the plains camp, he'd been hustled off with strangers right after his whole world had tumbled around him.

It changed nothing. Her brother had caused the death of one of Caleb's team; a team he felt responsible for and hated leaving to face risks he dare not.

At least her own group were safe. Seamach had taken them into hiding as soon as this whole thing broke, their reputation blackened even as the Survey set about destroying all they had worked so hard to build.

Frustration did not kill you.

She had to do…something. She thrust back from the table and set off for the comms room. Then changed direction, realising she had a more urgent task. She walked slowly to the room she shared with Caleb, closed the door carefully behind her, and collected every last article of her possessions.

The woman in the boarding house showed no surprise at Fee's request for another room, handing her the new securicard with a pursed lipped grunt. The woman was Survey and Survey Field staff were one; they did not forget those who harmed one of their own. Fee had caused the death of a Survey op, no matter how indirectly.

Her new room was neither large nor comfortable. She set her few things out, hopelessly trying to fill the bare walls and empty shelf.

But she still had a job to do. She sat down and pulled up her screens.

CHAPTER THIRTY-THREE

A slammed door, a curt snaffle of words downstairs, and Caleb had returned. Next, a warning prickle on the back of her neck.

"You moved rooms," he said from the door.

She slowly turned, her clenched fists and the nails scoring into her palms hidden behind her. "It seemed best."

She started to stand and he moved back a step, as if a wild animal threatened with a touch. It was laughable, but she'd never felt less amused. He could bat her away so easily with one of his large hands—or with one, drily pronounced word. But that he wouldn't do, not this man of the plains, not even to the woman he'd been forced to marry. "Found anything?" he said, nodding at her screen.

She shook her head.

He had more to say, it seemed, as he made no move to leave despite his tautly held body poised in half flight. She raised an eyebrow.

"I've been on the com to Bob. He told me what happened."

"Oh." She wasn't ready for this, didn't know if she would ever be ready to talk about it, yet she had to know the truth. She sat down again, his eyes watching her all the time and signalled for him to start.

His voice was as contained as that fist clenching the doorway. "Aigherach left early one morning. His message said he was heading home."

"Could he survive the trip on his own?"

"In that country—no. Ben and Adam volunteered to bring him back." Caleb stopped, his mouth grim. "Your brother only had a few hours' head start, yet it was enough." She lifted a querying eyebrow. "A rock fall. Happens in those hills."

"Is he all right?"

Caleb nodded but she had a distinct feeling he wished it otherwise. "Sprained ankle and lost his water bottle. He set off his com alarm."

"Survey security got there first," she guessed.

"Just. Ben and Adam were minutes behind them. Adam rode shotgun; Ben went in to grab your brother before they could load him into their flyer."

Another of those fraught pauses. This was hard enough for her; Caleb had seen Ben grow up.

"They had a spotter. He shot Ben as he came up behind the flyer."

Her nails bit harder into her palm. "You sure he's …?"

"Dead? Yeah. They left the body in the dust. The team retrieved it later, when they knew it was safe."

"And Aigherach?" she had to ask.

"…was in one piece when they shoved him into the flyer."

"Silas?"

"Safe."

She sat back down and stared at the floor. "Thank you." There was more she should say, though a lump blocked her throat. "You probably don't want it from me, but my deepest sympathies on your loss."

A crash as his fist collided with the door. "Accepted." He shoved his hand in his pocket before she could see if he'd hurt it. She could only guess what the words had cost him. He tilted his head at her screen.

"Anything?"

That was it? Ben's death was a closed topic and they were back to work mode? She took a deep breath. Caleb was the injured party here. If he could manage it, so could she.

"Nothing yet," she said.

A beep announced an incoming message. He waved at her to take it and turned to leave. But then she saw the call sign and the header. Her contact in logistics.

"Wait!"

He stopped at her cry.

The message was pre-recorded and double coded. Her logistics friend was running scared. Behind her, she heard Caleb take a step closer to better see her screen. The message came through, short and brief, but with an even more heavily coded attachment.

'Found this', the introduction said. The logistics man really was scared. She brought up the attached records, and gasped. Caleb leaned forward, his breath heavy on her shoulder. She had to fight hard to give no sign of how his closeness affected her, concentrating intently on the screen instead. "It's the Alliance meeting. A full vid-cast of what our government and the Alliance discussed.

They both watched it, then read the official transcript.

Caleb got to the end first. "Five years and forced assistance if there is no change in our environmental management. Evacuation is a last resort only."

So not two years to change or face the arbitrary evacuation of Arcadia. Not what their Survey briefings had told them. "We'll still have to leave if nothing changes. They'd have no choice."

"Place will be too dangerous to stay if we don't fix it," he agreed.

The level of natural disasters was accelerating too fast. Maybe this generation would be spared, but not the children born today.

"Did you record our briefings with Fox?" she asked.

"Not at the time—it was blocked—but I added it to my journal straight after, and we have the orders from Survey Central on file."

She had a copy of those too, plus her own journal entry. Basic Survey training—if it's not recorded, it didn't happen, and Survey journal records could not be interfered with, even by high up insiders. Not without leaving a forensic trail a cadet could follow. Then there was the first rule drilled into every agent. Always keep a backup copy—and file it safely someplace else. That last bit wasn't in the official training programme, but nor were a lot of the tricks their field trainers had taught them.

"So now to get it out to the public." She stared at her screen. "Any of your media contacts come through?"

"The reporter on Vid05 is interested but refuses to go ahead without any proof to back our story."

Fee rolled her eyes. "Corporate bullies getting their comeuppance didn't excite her?"

A half smile as he took the chair beside her and pulled up his screen, caught in the moment by the problem. Linking her through to his own com unit, he waited till the shimmer of his screen settled into its 3-D pattern then dialled up the major vid channels. "Of the others, these three here are hopefuls, but Anya from *Today* is my best hope."

Anya van Lissen! One of the leading political commentators on the planet; her *Today* a vid-cast no Federal politician could ignore, "Seriously?"

That brief half smile again. "Her eldest son's father was a second cousin of Kal. The boy visits the plains on a regular basis. Anya is a firm believer in her children knowing where they come from."

Kal again. The eco-engineer Caleb had left in charge of the lakes project. A position the man would dearly love to be permanent yet Caleb trusted him.

"You ever meet her?"

A wry twist of his mouth this time. "A few times. She knows my name."

"Oh." She leaned back in her chair. "She wasn't interested in the imprisonment or trumpery charges against your family?"

He frowned. "No evidence, she said. I tried but didn't push it. They didn't seem to be in actual danger—not before this."

"No."

They'd talked about this so many times. All their lives they had fought against their families, fought the corporate powers that demanded exploitation of all available resources to make money for today, with no care for tomorrow's cost. Yet they were still family, still the brothers, sisters, parents who had brought them up in the love, the challenge and wonderful conflict of strong-willed households.

At worst, or so they had believed, their families would be sent off planet till the Survey bosses' control of the Solaris and den Coille assets was firmly in place. Ironically, their best hope of freedom lay in Fee and Caleb wining their battle to save the planet and overthrow head office. Duty matching family needs, and ultimately they had to bring the corporates on side if they hoped to win the environmental battle. Saving their families would help to bridge the current divide blocking all hope of progress.

Ben's death changed everything. Mam and Da, wily Seolta and peaceful Samhchair, Caleb's brothers, father, his terrifying mother, all were now at the mercy of an agency that killed those who got in their way.

It was too much.

Caleb had told her once that her face was like an open reader. She hoped it wasn't true, and the same certainly couldn't be said for him. Not when he set his face closed tight, like now.

"Send that recording through to my personal link. I'll get it played when it's time, I promise."

"Thank you." She looked at the screen, avoiding his eyes. "If word of that vid gets out, head office will hunt us harder than ever. Time we moved on."

He was silent for so long, right up until she looked up and met those eyes of his studying her. Yet all he did was nod agreement, then walk out the door, leaving her.

Moving on. That meant travelling together, just the two of them. It would have to be on foot, the safest method when the Survey turned up the heat, and the next possible refuge was two days' walk.

She took one last look at her screen and sent through the recordings to Caleb's tightly secured, personal log. He'd given her access when they first fled. A privilege she'd rarely used; one she would not contemplate using again except in extreme need.

She shut down her screen and began to pack.

By the end of a second day of Caleb speaking to her only if needed, and that limited to words of work or survival, Fee was near to screaming. He'd halted periodically to log into his search vid, but every time a head shake told of failure. They only once dared link through to Bob and all it did was darken the morass of misery choking her.

"Survey head office arrived here this morning," Bob said. "They've taken direct control."

Caleb linked his com through to share with hers. "Kal?" he said.

"They've done their homework," said Bob. "They know you two aren't mates."

Caleb's face relaxed and for the first time in days, he gave a real smile. It was a good thing their bosses couldn't see it or they wouldn't trust one word Kal said.

"It does mean we're running out of time," she pointed out.

Caleb's smile disappeared. "She's right," he said to Bob. "Tell Kal to keep everyone at emergency status. At the slightest hint of trouble, evacuate immediately."

"And the lake?" said Bob.

"Save it as best you can. That's our future."

"But keep everyone safe," Fee had to add.

Bob signed off and Caleb scowled at her. "We can't do that."

"What?"

"Keep them safe and save the lake," he said. "The plains and mountains both need that lake. It's the key to reversing the damage in the region."

"They need our people more." Fee was absolutely certain on this one. "We can build another lake. We can't train up field staff like ours overnight."

"You think they don't matter to me? I grew up with them and know that every single one would lay down their life for this world." His face closed up again. "We'll have to disagree on this one."

Like too many other things, thought Fee in despair. She shoved her shoulders back and disconnected the link.

"It's time to bring in the politicians," he said as if forced to it. Another matter they had discussed, including the risks. Politicians were too subject to the next vote. Could they trust them?

"Your local Representative?" said Caleb.

"Coinneas den Cleireach? In Da's back pocket—or was. Now, he'll be running scared and firmly in the Survey bosses' back pockets. Whatever works to keep the local money machine turning. But Seilach den Bunachan of the Lower House is a possibility, especially in anything to oppose den Cleireach. They hate each other. She also has a scientific background. What about the Plains?"

"I can talk to Joe Gibbs."

Fee gasped. "He's as hard line conservative as they come."

"Yeah, but he's not in my father's back pocket. He actually believes what he says and will listen to a logical argument. Plus he'll be sore as hell over what happened to my family. *Upsets the natural order,*" Caleb intoned, mimicking the Representative if ever a reporter dared question his stance. He stared into space a moment. "I don't often agree with the man but I do respect him, and he loves this world something mightily."

Which was how she came to be crouching behind a bush in a plush suburb of Dridust, the largest town on the plains. Straddling one of the few aboveground rivers found in this arid region, the town was divided by a swathe of gravel and sand, down the middle of which a brown ribbon of water sketched a slow path. Two bridges crossed the dry bed, joining towering stop banks on either side. Caleb crouched beside her in the shrubby patch of vegetation crowning a high bluff that overlooked the east bank. The Gardens, he called it. It resembled no public gardens of her experience and her look must have shown it.

"It's the only patch of native plants left round here," he said.

They had come in under cover of night, taking the public flyer to the nearest small town then using a local Survey flitter to creep into the outer suburbs before walking the last stretch. Even if the Survey bosses had tracked them to the town, they wouldn't be able to follow them after that. The local groups had given them a sensor to avoid the surveillance cams, letting them slide through the kaleidoscope of brashly lit streets filled with buzzing crowds of people and blend into the hubbub of raised voices, sharp traders and whirling pleasure seekers. For the plains, it was a busy city. Not like Urbis, but enough to let a couple of stray travellers move around at night unremarked.

That changed when they reached the elite suburbs housing business owners and local administrators. The garden plantings here flourished by the standards of this region, a pastiche of the more luxuriant cover of the capital, and they hugged the shadows, moving carefully in the half-light.

From the questionable cover of their shrub, Caleb pointed to a large mansion set on the other side of the brow and commanding the vista below.

The Representative liked to make a splash.

The place was also pocked with multiple surveillance cams and guards patrolled the perimeter, looking far too ready for action against ill-advised intruders. The house looked to be more tightly secured than the Survey Central building.

Caleb stood up and gestured her to follow. Fee looked at the approaching guard and shook her head in a very definite *No*. He pointed at the mansion, waving her on with a curt sweep of his hand, and set off. Every nerve in her body jangling, she got to her feet, swallowed and stepped forward.

"Are you mad?"

"The only way past that level of security is through the front door." He kept walking.

She must follow blindly? Trust her life to this man who had barely talked to her for days? She scampered to catch up.

"You look too guilty," Caleb muttered. "No one's going to hurt you tonight. Not even me."

The rough edge to his voice was more reassuring than any soft words. Caleb Winter made few promises, but those few he kept.

It helped, a bit, and she did her best to match his relaxed stride, yet was heartily grateful for the fitful shadows. Then the full glare of the guard's light hit them.

"Stop there," the man barked, fingering his weapon.

Caleb put up his hands, palm out. "Easy, soldier. Just an old friend wanting to see the Representative."

"Yeah?" The man sounded no less suspicious. "You know the access code?"

"As long as he hasn't changed it in the last few hours."

The guard shoved forward a palm reader, his weapon ready. Caleb laid his hand in the sensor field before entering a sequence. The guard pulled it back, glanced at the pad, stared and his whole face changed.

"Sorry, Ser. Didn't realise."

Caleb waved a nonchalant hand. "I know. Representative Gibbs' friends usually arrive by flyer or unit, but I happened to be in the area and thought I'd call in."

Call in? She seemed to be missing a whole lot here.

Caleb grasped her elbow and propelled her forward. He had to. She was near frozen to the spot in panic.

Before she could make any protest, they'd been shown through the door and into a room. No way out, not now. She still glanced discreetly around, marking exits and searching for anything to use as a weapon if needed. They'd been shown into what was clearly the family study rather than a formal reception room. She'd barely finished her sweep when a man with snowy hair erupting in curled wisps from behind his ears marched into the room, scowling fiercely.

"You've put me in a hell of a spot, young Winter."

Caleb grinned. "Good to see you too, Uncle."

The man's eyebrows jutted forward alarmingly and the scowl barely lessened, but there was a definite quirk to his lips as he turned to acknowledge her. "A courtesy title only," he said, glaring back at Caleb. "Well, you're here now. No doubt you'll be wanting a drink—and who's the pretty lady?"

Caleb pushed her forward. "My wife, Fee den Coille Winter."

At the word *wife*, the man's scowl cracked and he barked in laughter. "I'd heard the rumour, but didn't believe it. You—finally leg-shackled! A pleasure to meet you, Sera."

She forced a smile onto her face. "Thank you, Representative. Fioruisghe ingh Coille beann Caleb den Winter, at your service." She gave a proper bow of honour to his office.

His face sharpened. "Mountain born, hey. So that rumour was true too. You always did choose the prickly path, young Caleb." He waved them to a chair, pulled out a bottle of something that looked to be old and expensive and sloshed an indecently large amount into three equally expensive looking glasses. No more would he say till they had all three taken a sip, at which both Caleb and the Representative closed their eyes briefly and gave a contented sigh of admiration, while she endeavoured not to show the stuff was blowing the top off her head.

He leaned back in his chair, that famous face sharpening again and she remembered too late his nickname. Falk—the large flying predator that once ruled these skies. Razor sharp talons, double-toothed bill and lightning-fast reflexes, changing from swooping hover to downward plunge in microseconds.

"So what can I do for you?"

Caleb leaned back, glass held between his two hands, and studied the man. "You know we're wanted?"

Gibbs nodded, his mouth twisting. "I've got all my ears and eyes out there hunting for news of your families."

Caleb crossed his legs. "The vid-casts report they're being tried in various backwater towns on charges I've never heard of."

Gibbs harrumphed. "Trumped up nonsense, and nothing more than a cover. There's no sign of them in those towns, not now—or of the rest of your folks, young Sera Fioruisghe. You want to tell me what this is really about?"

Fee's hands tightened on her glass as Caleb studiously ignored her, leaning back and settling into his chair. Was he really going to tell this man the whole truth? Her hand shook, a splash of liquid, and she carefully placed her glass on the side table. Both men ignored her, and the knot in her gut wound tighter. How expendable was she here?

Caleb took a sip and put his own glass down. He activated his com unit and set a shimmering screen in front of the Representative. "You need to see this data, Ser."

The man ignored the screen, all his attention on Caleb's face. "That old story you've been peddling me for years?"

"The figures speak for themselves. Read the top report first, then look at the data."

"Report?" The man turned his head back to the screens and set his own glass down with a crack loud enough to have her jump as he read the heading. "This is of a highly confidential Alliance meeting, security rating A1. How did you get this?"

Caleb shrugged. "It's real enough, if that's what you're thinking. Read it, and compare it with our journal entries of what the Survey told us was said at that meeting. "

The man grunted, turning back to the screens.

It took him an hour, interrupted only by the occasional indrawn breath or curse, with a peremptory apology as he remembered her presence.

At the end, he sat back, studying them both, and she suddenly recalled far too clearly some of the vid-caster comments on this man. There was a reason a supposedly rabid right-winger and 'geriatric throwback' held powerful positions on a number of cross-party committees. "He will listen to a logical argument," Caleb had said. Would he consider theirs to be one?

She squirmed in her seat and leaned forward. Caleb put out a hand, stopping her just in time from blurting out a demand for his answer. Taking her hand as a loving husband would. Not that he fooled the Representative, she would guess. The man looked far too knowing. She squirmed restlessly, doing her best to ignore the bite of Caleb's hand as he leaned back in the seat, legs crossed as he waited for the Representative's response.

Caleb knows this man; he must know what he's doing.

At long last, the older man picked up his glass again and took one of those long, masculine swallows. "An interesting collection. I will need to cross-check some of these incidents. And there's the death of this young man. I met his mother once. She came here to petition for a bigger school house." A pause, then a hmmph with a slight quirk of remembrance. "She got it, too."

He was quiet again, staring into his glass, before lifting his eyes to look sternly at Caleb. "Not good that, not good at all. A police matter, possibly. Survey security appears to have exceeded its jurisdiction there, although I will have to examine all the facts, let alone what you claim Survey's senior management have kept from the properly elected representatives of Arcadia. "

"A department is only as good as its Delegate."

"Hmmph. So you've said before, young man," said the representative, "and maybe with merit in this instance." He switched his screen back to the summary of environmental incidents; from flood to drought, landslide to wildfire. "As for this Alliance report; how you got hold of it is one question. Someone either has little regard for state sector confidentiality, or placed the importance of publishing this meeting above his duty to his superiors."

Caleb's fingers pressed warningly on her arm, though his voice remained cool and easy. "Our first duty is to the general wellbeing of the people of this planet, surely? That must override any loyalty to an individual, no matter how highly ranked in government service."

A slight smile touched the older man's face. "Another conversation we've had too many times before, young man, and disagreed on most of them. As for your journal entries…" The smile faltered, a frown appearing on his brow in what she was sure was an uncharacteristic sign of vulnerability. "You believe your bosses lied to you, and for their own gain. A serious charge. Even I will admit that all rules are made to be broken— but never lightly and not when it comes to concealing information from their elected Delegate. That way lies chaos. Yet…?"

He stared again at their records. Caleb's hand eased its grip on her arm, but the Representative was not convinced, not yet.

She glanced at Caleb, who gave a slight nod. *Be careful,* said the set of his mouth.

"Would you care to see the projections?" she said and leaned over to bring up the holo-maps of the plains region. First, the view of the plains as they were today. Next, she set it to scroll forward, stopping just fifteen years from the present. "This is the plains, given no change to the current solar panel designs, and using the lowest estimated increase in area covered by solar arrays."

No change in the man's face, but not surprising. The area of desertification had increased, but not outside commonly held expectations. She dialled it up a notch. "This uses the median increase," the man looked more disturbed, "this is the highest setting," she made one more, minor adjustment, "and this is what happens to the demographics of the region."

The old man gasped. A faint haze of varying shades of red shadings lay over the land. To drive the point further, she added in the actual figures, including the population projection for the city of Dridust.

He stabbed a finger at the figures, eyebrows creased. "These accurate?"

"The projections are Survey standard. We ran them through all its checks and analyses before we had to go into hiding. They are accurate."

He swivelled, fixed his gaze on Caleb. "You showed these to your father?"

"No point. All he would see is the expansion in profit."

"For him, maybe. What about the rest of us?" The Representative peered again at the figures, demanding she cycle back to the median projection. "That's some drop in population. It's right on the edge of minimum Electoral College size. As for the worst case version…"

She scrolled back to the highest setting, and he glared at the new figures. "That's well below. I'd lose my seat. Have to amalgamate with that fool on the northern border."

He stood up and paced around the holo-map, eyebrows bristling. "Where have my voters gone, and why?"

Now it was Caleb who leaned forward. "The increase in solar arrays, coupled with the expansion of festia plantations on the western sides of the mountains, causes a spiralling increase in local aridity. Dryer air, more call on the aquifers for irrigation, and eventually they collapse. Which is no problem for Solaris; solar panels don't need too many workers. For the rest of the locals, though…With no water, no other industries left, there's no choice. They leave, or they starve."

The man paced once more around the holo-vid, glaring at it.

Then came to a halt. "This takes some thinking about. Leave it with me a few days."

"We can't…" began Fee.

"Certainly, Sir," broke in Caleb. "Contact me through my family link with your decision. That is still secure."

The Representative nodded then fixed those sharp eyes on them both. "So, who's your next victim?"

Caleb's lifted his glass. "We're heading over to Councillor Craobh Bunachan."

"Crao…"

Fee butted in. "He means Seilach ingh Craobh beann Stobach den Bunachan."

The nearest to a true smile lit the Representative's face. "I gathered that was who my uncivilised friend meant. Though I would suggest he refrains from using the plains form of honorific to her face; not if you expect help from the lady."

Fee was surprised, and it must have showed on her face. The older man chuckled. "We may be political opponents, young lady, but doesn't mean we can't work together. The lady has a sharp brain and a good heart. A fine choice for your purposes, even if her reasoning can be a mite addled on occasion!"

They left him soon after, staring at the holo-vids and scrolling again through the records. Fee had to admit she liked the man, not what she had expected to feel before they came. But as for surrendering their precious evidence to a man who had voted against too many environmental measures for her liking…

"How can you leave those records with him?"

"He's safe enough," said Caleb. "You can trust the Uncle. He won't betray us, no matter what he thinks of all this."

Fee hoped like hell he was right. Their lives depended on it, and she marched silently beside him back through the security maze of the town to their safe hideout.

CHAPTER THIRTY-FOUR

Another day and a setting far removed from the dry plains. This time, they crouched in the constantly dipping branches of a tree jutting up from the craggy slopes of the western ranges, to the south of their home territories.

"You sure the woman comes this way?"

Fee glanced down at Caleb wedged into a junction below her. He looked far from happy, his chunky boots planted into a hole in the trunk and his hands clinging for dear life round the branch above. She danced back along her branch, setting the leaves above her shimmering in a susurration of sound that set music to her steps. The scent of water on leaves, tangy bark bruised by their scrabble up, the warm must of decomposing loam rising from the base of the tree, all mingled with the brush of moist air against her cheek and the crackle of flaking bark under her feet. It was an old tree, a granddad of the forest, secure, dominant, its broad canopy a camouflage against any ignorant city dweller.

Below them passed a major mountain trail. In appearance, not much more than beaten earth or a carpet of ferns, its importance would be unrecognisable to an outsider.

"You sure about this?" said Caleb. His face was set and he barely looked at her, peering down at the ground and no doubt heartily wishing he was on it still.

"She always does at this time of day. It's the best way home from her office."

He grunted and gripped the trunk harder as he leaned over. She danced back along her branch to get a better view, setting it flexing lightly as if stirred by a breeze.

"Stop that," he growled. "You want to fall? Or let them know we're here."

She did stop, turning in surprise. "Fall? I've been playing in branches since I learned to walk."

He glared up at her, brow creased and mouth straight. "Just—stop."

Her mouth fell open. Could he actually be concerned for her? Whatever he felt, it stopped the saucy words in her mouth.

Zit. Zit.

A puff of bark, a burning in her side. She automatically ducked for cover.

"Fee!"

A scrabble of heavy boots, and a curse. Then his big strong hands shot out and one managed to grab hold of a branch as he toppled forward. She scrambled down, locking tight onto the other arm. He teetered over the edge, one leg slipped down and his weight skewed sideways. She pulled hard, harder than she'd ever thought possible.

The forest floor was so far down.

"You are not going to fall!"

Slowly he rocked back, muscles bulging as he dragged himself up by that one hand gripping the tree.

"I can take your weight," she urged.

"No."

She tugged on his free hand, but he ignored her help, holding all his weight with that other, straining arm. His foot dug into a crack in the bark, he heaved harder, hand tightening on the branch. Slowly, slowly he came back to centre and regained his seat on the branch. To sit back, white and gasping.

So did she.

She had nearly lost him.

She scrabbled down, ran her hands over the scraped palm holding him up and cast her eyes up and down, checking each part of him.

He pushed her away, running a hand over her. "You're bleeding," he said.

She glanced down. "A flesh wound. It'll heal readily enough." Then saw his side.

Red blood oozed from his waist, a lot of blood, drenching his shirt in a spreading crimson tide.

"Sit back. That's more than a flesh wound."

He barely looked down, before pulling them both tight against the junction of tree and branch. "Someone's shooting at us. Any ideas?"

She did, and both were equally dangerous, though not nearly as much as the holes in his side. She snuggled into him, needing to feel the steady, *strong* beat of his heart, then leaned out, ignoring his rattled order to stop.

"Ceardeas," she called out.

Caleb wanted nothing more than to haul her back to safety. Just because he couldn't face talking to her, did the woman think it did nothing to him to see her in danger? She was as at home in these trees as he in the desert, but that was real blood on her arm. Not as much as from the burning agony in his side, but real. She could have been killed.

No answer. Now the damn woman leaned farther out, calling again in a liquid flow of words he couldn't understand, and this time he did grab her back.

Another of those lethal *zits*, and a puff of bark.

"Release her, Plainsman."

The voice came from a patch of bush to his right. Which meant that Fee was fully exposed to the shooter. He reached over to pull her in behind him but suddenly remembered where he was. Ten metres up a damn tree. All he could do was reach in front of her, to cut down the shooter's line of sight, but Fee leaned out to block him.

"Get down, you idiot," he snapped.

"It's you they're trying to hit, not me."

Yeah, like he wasn't counting on just that, and didn't she know she could be hit in the crossfire. The terror of that red tag on her sleeve still raged within him.

He reached to cover her again.

"Sit still. You're hurt," she hissed at him. Then leaned out again regardless of his move to stop her.

"This is my husband, you idiot," she called out in Standard, following up with a string of the unknown language. Though from the look on her face, it wasn't diplomatic small talk she was blasting at their attacker.

Did she have no survival instincts?

A man walked out from the bush below, and a handful more appeared silently from all around them, each carrying the latest in personal weaponry. He and Fee hadn't a chance of fighting clear.

The first shooter spoke again in what he assumed to be the language of these mountains, and while it was directed at Fee, the man kept Caleb in constant view.

"In Standard, Douall, if you please. Did you leave your manners behind in your wife's back pocket as well as your brains?"

Caleb's wife was going to get them both killed, never mind what this man's wife might do.

Fee plonked herself back on the branch, legs swinging from the tree and looking insanely like an errant child.

"Caleb," she said in a suspiciously sweet voice, "let me introduce you to my second cousin Douall mar Ceart duine Caerthida den Coibhneas. You've already met his intelligent half, my team's geologist Caerthida. Douall, my husband Caleb mar Sol duine Fioruisghe den Winter.

Caleb began to feel some sympathy for the man. Not that Fee gave either of them any quarter. "If you've finished playing bandits, we need to talk to the Councillor."

"No."

"What do you mean, no? We have urgent business with her."

"You maybe; not the Plainsman. He's Survey."

Fee began to scrabble down, and every weapon suddenly leapt to attention. Caleb grabbed for her but she was too quick for him.

"Fee, stop." No use. She kept going. Caleb leaned out and yelled at the leader. "Don't shoot. She's unarmed and hurt."

"They're not going to shoot me," she said, throwing a vexed glance up at him.

"Don't tempt me," said the man below. It was the glare on his face that reassured Caleb. That of a man who had played too many childhood games with his disturbing wife. "You better come down too," the man Douall said, looking at him.

With all those weapons trained on him? He shook his head after a pointed survey of the troop surrounding them. Too long a pause, followed by a sharp "Douall," from his charming wife, and slowly but slowly, they half lowered their weapons. Guessing that was the best he could hope for, he went to rise. Then he grunted, swayed and the tree blurred in front of him.

"Catch him," yelled Fee, watching in horror. He was too big to hold. But a rope spiralled up, and she flung it round him. A swarm of Douall's men were up and around them, securing him and lowering him slowly to the ground. Great red globules of blood dripped from his side.

As soon as her feet hit ground, she marched over and punched Douall with every gram of fear inside her. "You shot my husband."

"Your *Survey* husband, from the same organisation that has imprisoned your family and is currently threatening to impeach the Councillor."

"What?"

"You heard me." He glanced briefly at Caleb, laid on the ground beside them. The team medic huddled over him, working to stem the bleeding. Little truly scared Fee, but the sight of Caleb so badly hurt pounded into her heart, fear catching it and strangling it tight in a vice-like grip. Douall grabbed her as a wave of nausea rolled over her.

"Not now," he threatened. "He'll be fine. It's only a flesh wound."

"You don't know that."

"I do. He's tough enough to take you on—he'll make it."

Fee had to laugh, a wild, thready parody, but it broke through the panic. She breathed in, eyes fixed on Caleb. "Thanks," she mumbled, forcing herself to concentrate on the rest of what Douall had said. "What's this about the Councillor?"

"The Survey has filed a complaint against her with the Supreme court. For collusion with your father in subverting environmental rulings. She denounced the Survey's takeover of den Coille holdings in her area."

"So? She can't have been the only one."

Douall gave her that look that had always infuriated her; the one that branded her a naive idiot. He and her brother Seolta had always been close. "Hate to disappoint you, but she was. The Councillor may not agree with everything your father's company does, but outsiders muscling in and taking over our territory is another matter again."

She frowned. "Then it's more urgent than ever that I talk to her. I have important information for her."

For too long, Douall refused. She argued, always watching Caleb out of the corner of her eye as he lay stubbornly unconscious.

"He needs hospital treatment," she finally shouted, worn out and losing all patience. "Get us that at least."

Finally, finally, Douall nodded to his troop to move off. "Only if she agrees to see you," he said, but they loaded Caleb into a medivac flitter and got the bleeding stopped. It was better than nothing.

Her plan for this meeting with the Councillor had been quite different. She'd met Seilach den Bunachan many times before, surrounded by family and in full mountain mode, but today Fee barely glanced at her, too busy checking that Caleb was still breathing.

"You will help us?" she blurted out, her attention on Caleb as she rattled off what they needed and why.

The Councillor had lost weight. Usually elegant in appearance and a fiery advocate, today her hair was pulled back into a serviceable knot at her neck, odd tendrils escaping to be roughly shoved back as she scrolled through the records Fee scanned through to her. Her fists clenched at the report on Ben, but she said nothing, not till the end.

"Your journal entry—you made that on which day?"

"The evening of my arrival on the plains; the same day our local boss gave us the details of our project and the reasons for it—including their claimed deadline."

Just then Caleb opened his eyes. She hurried to his side. "They're part right," she threw over her shoulder at the Councillor. "All the dangers we've been warning about for years; they're real. It's the response to them that's screwed up."

He was trying to sit up, tight pain lines scoring his face. She put a hand on his shoulder, but he ignored it, eyes fixed on the Councillor. "Is she going to help?"

The Councillor heard him. She walked over, crouched down beside Caleb and surveyed his plains uniform, the Survey emblem marked proudly on his right front. Seilach glared at it.

"Marching in with that thing on display, you're lucky my people didn't kill you."

"I wear it too," said Fee.

"Yes, but on a woman clearly dressed and moving as a mountain born. We identified you as soon as you entered the forest. As for you, Ser den Winter…"

She tapped the side of her com unit, considering the display. "Yes, it seems I am going to help you. As soon as my staff have patched you up, and this woman here can string an intelligible sentence together. We'll talk tomorrow."

Caleb struggled to sit up properly. "There's no time."

There would have to be, it seemed. The Councillor had finished listening. She disappeared through a screen of leaves on one side, as Caleb's medivac lifted and moved off in the opposite direction. Fee hurried after the medivac, one hand firmly holding her husband down.

He might want nothing more to do with her, might only be with her out of duty to their cause, but the screwed-up knot of her heart very much needed to keep him safe.

To her relief, he gave in to the medic's orders and lay back down. "You're going to get that cut dealt to as well," he growled.

Once in the medical centre, they peeled off his outer clothes, to reveal the burnt and bloody gouged out furrow on his side. "Put him under," she demanded.

He thrust out a hand to the advancing medic. "Don't you dare."

The doctor merely nodded at the men standing either side of his stretcher. They grabbed Caleb, and held him down. "I am bound by oath to do no unnecessary harm to a patient, Ser den Winter. Not so these men. It is quicker to operate on you anesthetised."

"I can't let you do it. Who knows what's happening out there?"

"Whatever is, "said the doctor, "you need to be treated to deal with it. Knocking you out is the fastest way to do that."

She watched as Caleb studied the doctor, face closed and giving no sign of the pain that scored lines either side of his mouth.

Finally: "Only if there is an antagonist, and Fee stays."

She let out the breath she'd been holding. She hadn't expected the words that said he trusted her still, and had no idea what it meant. But she would not betray him. "I'll be right beside you throughout, and I promise they'll bring you out if you're needed."

He lay back, eyes fastened on her face, and she only wished she knew what he saw. He had become so very precious to her. She had once told him she thought she was in love with him. It was too late for mere thinking, many months too late. She loved this man, body, heart and soul. This man who blamed her and her family for the death of one of his own.

The doctor nodded agreement and Caleb let his hand fall back. The sterile field came down over his face, cutting her off from him, and moments later his eyes closed. She reached through the screen, finding and holding onto that one hand, and her sudden spurt of panic washed away. She was sitting far enough from the doctors' work area to be out of their way, but her hand would be the first thing Caleb felt when he came out, her face the first he saw.

At last the gruesome business was finished. "It's only grade two," said the doctor to her at the end. "The skin and muscle regeneration will be complete within the day, and once dressed he can move about freely. As long as he's sensible."

The woman studied her patient as she spoke. She sounded as wishful as Fee, with as little hope her patient would listen to orders.

Finally, late that night, Fee fell into bed. A field cot set up beside Caleb's med unit, but she was too tired to care, falling deeply asleep with his hand still caught fast in hers.

Too soon after, far too soon, a rough shake of her shoulder woke her.

"Caleb?"

"He's fine, Fioruisghe, but you both need to wake, now."

She shoved a hand at her face, blearily rubbing it and pushing tiredly up.

The Councillor stood beside her cot as a doctor hurried into the room.

"Wake the plainsman," Seilach den Bunachan ordered, her mouth pressed tight.

Fee swung her legs to the floor, as the doctor shot something into Caleb. He grunted crossly, and she leaned over him.

"There you are," he muttered, closing his eyes again.

"More," said the Councillor.

Another shot, and Caleb jolted wide awake, shooting abruptly upright to sit, arms clenched around his knees for support. "What's up?" he said groggily.

Fee set her shoulder against his and looked at the Councillor, a cold beat of fear tapping against her chest.

"Representative Gibbs has found your families—both families. They're scheduled for execution in one week."

She didn't know who yelled, whose the spine tingling screams, till Caleb's arm gripped her tight and she realised they were hers. Then she saw his face, the dark anger and the fear. "What reason?"

"Sedition. Treason, if you want it plainly. The trial kept secret for reasons of 'federal security'. Convicted on evidence presented by Federal troops, but supplied by Survey senior management. In other words, by unimpeachably respectable government officials."

She passed over a transcript. Fee grabbed it and shared it with Caleb.

"They used my field data. They used it against my own family." Her knees wobbled. Shock. This is shock.

"And my team's." Caleb looked ready to destroy— someone, anyone.

He looked up, face set rigid. "Do you have com unit facilities here? We need a full conference call, now."

"Bring ahead the protests, bring in the Representative, release the reports. All at once, immediately? You think that's possible."

"It better be," he said. "There's no other way to beat them. Not in time."

CHAPTER THIRTY-FIVE

Caleb had to give Fee's Councillor full marks for organisation. Within an hour, they were sitting in a secured room facing a full holo-panel of all the field groups who had agreed to help them, plus a glowering Representative Gibbs.

Fee sat beside him, her white face the only sign of her distress.

"It's too soon. We're not ready." The field eco-engineer from the coastal sub-polar region. "And why should we risk everything to save a couple of corporate families who've done as much to cause these problems as anyone?"

"You've lost half your marine species already, Jed, and the rest is threatened by the heavy fishing of karillon in your seas. When is the right time—when you've lost everything?" The very young, very hot-headed leader from a mid-ocean archipelago.

"He's got a point." A river specialist from the other major continent, a woman who had spent her life fighting to save the unique braided rivers of her region from predacious irrigation schemes. "We know Caleb and Fee, know the work they've done, but should we rush blindly into this, solely to help save their families? Sorry," she added belatedly, turning to Fee, "but we're here to stop the Survey bosses' madness, not indulge in feckless games of heroism."

It hurt to listen, hurt to hear the words when images of her brother, her parents kept flitting through her head. Nor could she deny the truth of their arguments. How to combat it? Did they even have the right to ask it of them? Maybe not, but the images of her family would not be banished.

"Our families' actions have been as black as you say. Den Coille's festia plantations are the main cause of the problems of my home ranges."

"As is Winter Solaris on the Plains," added Caleb. "But what happens if we let the Survey kill them? You think the politicians will still back you."

"Or will they start panicking about a department powerful enough to get away with murder?"

"They already have." An angry voice raised, a chorus of murmurs, and a sudden stillness from Fee. Ben's death had been the catalyst Caleb had foreseen, but it felt no better now than when he'd first expected it.

"You forget the other corporate families," he said before the murmurs swelled out of control. "Let our folks die, and you'll have all-out war between the corporates and the Survey, with field staff and the planet stuck squarely in the middle."

"Maybe, but them corporates would finally have to listen to us!"

"But they won't," cried Fee. "We know them; we grew up with them. My family, Caleb's family, they don't come much more stubborn, and the rest are the same."

"Like you two, you mean," called out a wit from the back, and a welcome chortle of laughter rippled around the room.

It broke the building tension, but that was all. Too many set faces still glared back at them.

A chair crashed, and Joe Gibbs rose to his full, impressive height. "Enough," he bellowed in a voice used to beating out challenges in the Federal House. "The den Coille and Winter families are your best weapons. Their arrest was an illegal use of the justice system by senior Survey management. Without them, all you've got is hot-headed opinion."

He glared back at each and every field agent there, and slowly, slowly, the nods began in return.

"There is a full session of the House the day after tomorrow. I will be tabling a motion calling for an investigation into the actions of the senior Survey managers. That motion will fail unless the House is given a reason to pass it. To that end, I need a full scale demonstration in the streets of the Capital that afternoon and a report on all the major news channels during the dinner hour." He turned to Seilach den Bunachan. "Councillor?"

The woman nodded. "As soon as you call the motion, I'll lodge a court enquiry in the Regional House into the illegal seizures of the den Coille and Winter corporation assets. It must hit the House just after the news reports hit the vidscreens."

"Anya is on side," said Caleb, which brought a twist to Joe Gibb's mouth that could have been a smile or a grimace.

He pointed to each of them.

"You clear?" Gibbs scowled at each of the faces in the other screens, finishing with Fee and Caleb. "Organise your demonstrations," he said, "I have work to do," and signed off.

A babble of voices broke out. Fee began to stand, and Caleb shot up to stand beside her, ignoring the stab of abused muscles in his side and the sudden pounding in his head. He banged his cup on the table, and kept banging till silence strangled the uproar.

"I can get my team plus another hundred from neighbouring teams on the streets by midday tomorrow." Or he hoped so. "Fee, you?"

She set her hands on the table edge, back straight and that look in her eye that said she would succeed, come hell or whatever. The look that sent a direct line straight to his gut and lower. "My team, plus the rest of the western mountain ones. Around two hundred"

He nodded, and turned to the hot-head from the archipelago. "Gareth?"

The man gulped, but his face set in lines of dogged grit. "My people will be there."

One by one, around the room, the pledges came through. Edged with caution at first, then cascading to a clamour of support. The streets of the Capital would bulge with people. Fee coughed in a vain grab for attention, so she grabbed hold of his mug and banged it down hard. "If we're to succeed, this demonstration must be a surprise. We have to get everyone there without the media or Survey finding out. Not before it starts."

She was so good, so adept at setting out every point needed. If Ben and her brother didn't lie between them… No, they had a job to do. What lay between them would have to wait—however he felt about it.

He looked at her slim figure standing defiantly beside him. She would do this, would sacrifice everything, even herself. And suddenly he knew he could not allow that. He put out a hand, covering hers. She was still his wife and she would not stand alone.

"Bob and Seamach can work the liaison role, along with Finola Aknutk from central. She knows everyone and can be trusted." He rolled his gaze around the room, collecting in all the disparate representatives of widely varying regions, and called them to join with him, letting his mouth relax into a grin filled with all the cocky assurance he could muster. "Head office top floor are in for one hell of a surprise."

He thrust a fist into the air. "Survey rules!"

A full throated roar of approval rocked the room, the accumulated anger of too many years of frustration. For too long, the senior managers had treated field staff as little more than tokens on their selfish gaming board. But the Survey was more than its managers. The heart of the Survey lay still in those principles that had filled him with pride the first time he'd walked through the doors of the training academy, its purpose unchanged. To protect this world that was home to them all.

Venal managers playing petty games of greedy acquisitions had no part in it. And they were about to be told that very loudly.

It was a very late night, but finally, finally they thrashed it all out. The airwaves were so fraught with messages, Fee wondered that head office didn't pick up on them. Her head drooped and she jerked up, hoping no one had noticed.

On the second, she knew she had to leave. Tomorrow was going to be busy, filled with overseeing the work needed to bring a large body of people from every corner of the planet, all without any hint of it being discovered. She needed sleep. At the other end of the table, a group marched plates and sauce bottles about a pattern of laid cards. Gareth from the islands and Jed from the cold coastal plains up north had laid aside their differences and compared fishing methods, having out-talked everyone else for hours and beaten out any wrinkles possible in the plans. She leaned back in her chair, and the next she knew her legs were swung from under her and a warm pair of arms lifted her high.

"Time for bed, sleepy," said the amused voice of her husband. He was smiling at her.

That was wrong. Her brother had killed Ben. "You can't smile."

His eyes tracked down her body, then up again, and this time there was a decided glint in his eyes. "Yes, I can, Fioruisghe den Coille Winter."

She shook her head. "You don't like me. Not anymore." She wasn't making sense, but nor was the world around her. His arms felt just too good, his hard body a promise of so much more. Arms that tightened on her now, a shimmer of tension running down the length of him.

"Don't think, not tonight, sweetheart. Tonight, let it be only us."

He lifted her higher, closer to his heart. The strong thump of it against her cheek reassured her in a way nothing else could. She let her head fall back, giving in to it. He was right. Tomorrow was too much to consider. Tonight was theirs, for who knew what tomorrow would bring. She shut her eyes and let him take her, opening them only when the sound of a door said they had come to his room. "Tonight," she whispered, and gave herself to the endless light shining from his eyes. He laid her on the bed and began to slowly remove her tunic.

She looked up, and shoved back his collar, yanking at the fasteners on his top. "No, not slow. I need you too badly."

As if her words had released something in him, he burst out laughing as he peeled off her clothes in record time, before throwing off his own. It was frenetic, a battle of warring needs and fraught challenge as they strove for release. Yet always together, each checking and bringing the other to a peak. Then the waves crashed into and through them both. As one, together.

And after, sleep and contentment.

Later in the night, she felt him toss beside her. She put out a hand, eased tighter into the shelter of his body as he held her close, and felt the strain in his locked muscles.

She searched for his face in the shadows. "We will succeed."

At first, he said nothing. Just rolled onto his back, bringing her with him and tucking her into the curve of his arm. "How do you know?"

She didn't, of course. Tomorrow could bring the end of so much more than this sudden togetherness. So be it, but she would not go into it with things unsaid.

"About Ben. Aigherach, he wouldn't have known…but I should have. For Ben's death, I apologise. I can't make up for it, but…"

She hadn't known Ben long, but the young zoologist had been the first in Caleb's team to truly welcome her and to show her what it was about their land they loved so much. That there could be beauty in other than mist and green places. "He was a fine young man, a credit to the Survey."

Caleb's arms tightened on her. "Thank you," he said softly. "One day…" His hand closed on her breast, fingers spread wide. "One day I will be able to forgive your brother. He was a frightened boy, I know that, but Ben…" and there was a catch in his voice even as his arms clamped down as if afraid of losing her. She wrapped her own around his big body, claiming him and the pain she felt as his deep voice rumbled in his chest.

"I saw Ben born," he said. "His mother was my teacher at school, his father one of the most decent men I've met. He was their only son—his sisters will be devastated—and I sent him into danger."

Was that what had driven this stake between them? His guilt, the burden of it as heavy as her own?

She lifted her hands to cradle his face. "There can be only one fitting memorial for Ben. We will succeed."

His gave her back look for look, and his kiss this time was both promise and pledge. "To success." His clever hands brought her to life again, and much later again his breathing told of peace fought for and found. Hard breathing that quickly settled into the quiet huff of sleep.

If only she could join him. Talk of Aigerach, and Ben's death, had brought an uncomfortable niggle of worry keeping sleep obdurately at bay.

She tried hard to lie still.

A hitch in his breathing, a hand reaching around to stroke soothingly down her back. "What's worrying you, sweetheart?"

A choking breath, then the comfort of her head slotted into his shoulder. "Our families. When we make our move, what will happen to them?"

His hand stilled and he lay back. "I don't know. That's the hell of it, but Gibbs is tracking them. He'll keep them safe."

"If he can."

His silence said he was as worried as her, which did nothing to help.

"What do we even know about those at the top of the Survey? We barely know their names."

They had tried hard to find out the truth behind the puffery of the executive biographies, but the senior level were all career departmental managers. Only the top of the Survey knew their real story. The rare head office staff they had risked talking to clammed up tight when asked about their bosses, the stench of fear seeping across the most convoluted of links. The Survey was a big organisation, its numbers always hidden by the low public profile of the department, and the bosses faceless, hiding behind the Delegate and local staff.

Yet these were the people who had brought in their own security service, had killed Ben when he got in their way, and had imprisoned then convicted both their families. What would they do if cornered?

"Gibbs is right. We have to free both families before we go public."

She felt the movement of his head. "We also have to be at that demonstration. I promised Anya van Lissen an interview from the middle of the demonstration. We need it to back up Joe Gibbs' and your Councillor's motions, and you need to be on that podium with me."

A half choke. "Seolta will be laughing all the way to the pillory."

Caleb pulled her up his body. "Shush, sweetheart. We'll think of something."

"Before the march begins?"

His arms tightened again. "Yes." He reached for the light, pulled on shirt and trousers, and hit his com unit. "Patch me through to Gibbs."

Fee shamelessly plugged into the conversation. It was her family, and she needed to know what was being said.

The Representative had been asleep, she guessed, but sat now as formally and unconcerned as if chairing a House committee despite his night clothes and the demands thrown at him by Caleb. "I'll get onto my staff, make sure your families haven't been moved again." Then he cut them off.

Short of calling all kinds of hell down on the man, there wasn't a thing they could do. Fee gave up all pretence of sleeping and banged around the kitchen, making them both drinks and food. Anything to keep at bay the gnawing fear in her gut.

Finally, a ping on the com and Gibbs was back, looking as in control as ever.

"They had been moved, but we've found them. However, getting them out won't be easy. Your parents and Samhchair are in the fort next to the Hondo Canyon."

"Oh." She knew that prison. Not heavily guarded, but there was a reason for that. Surrounded by endless tracts of barren, frost-covered land even in full summer, they would need heavy-duty flyers to make it in and out, the kind of flyer whose passage could not be concealed. "Don't suppose we can knock on the door and just ask to have our families back?"

Dead silence.

"I was joking," she said in a small voice, but the two men completely ignored her. Ominously so.

"Would it work?" said Caleb.

Gibbs' brow furrowed. "If I bring the speaker with me. He owes me a favour, and never did trust these new professional managers peppering the civil service. No proper manners."

They couldn't be serious.

"You don't have time. Not to get up there, release them and get back to speak on your motion the next afternoon."

"It'll be tight," agreed Caleb. At last, some sense.

The representative nodded. "The latest federal shuttles are fast. If I call up a platoon and bring them with me, I can get one released for my use."

She dragged the blanket tight around her shoulders, hugging onto it. "You'll be signalling to every civil department head that something's up."

"Maybe not. The Justice Department never did like your Survey."

"And Uncle here is too far to the right to be suspected," added Caleb. "It's very unlikely the Survey will be watching him."

It was going to happen, no matter what she said. It was insane, but he was going to do it. She glared at the older man, already laying out his plans. "Don't you dare get yourself hurt."

He stopped, looking at her in surprise. "Why, thank you my dear. I don't know when anyone last said such a thing to me."

She forced on a smile. "And our brothers?"

"Ah, now that's a problem. All of them are locked up in a fortified building not far from Capital Central."

Caleb looked across at her. It was clear he knew which building. So did she, and Gibbs was right. The Central Security building had multiple layers of protection and no private entrances. It would be surrounded during the demonstration and heavily guarded. "We have to get them out that morning, before anyone realises something is up."

The hard planning began again, and Gibbs began furiously working his links. At the end, she felt the beginning of hope. Not much, but a beginning.

Two days later, the cold chill of the day matched the bitter chill of fear invading Fee's heart. Huddling in a side street and waiting for the first of the demonstrators, she shivered compulsively. A night of little sleep hadn't helped, a night spent going over and over in her head the plans for today.

Together, in the early hours of that first morning, she, Caleb and Gibbs had mapped out a rescue plan for both families. Gibbs had privately filed with the speaker for the release of their parents and Samchair, the Representative using words so filled with legal authority that she fully believed he'd do as he claimed. As to their brothers, that was a bit trickier. Even now, Federal shock troops were channelling their way into the fortress holding their brothers. Troops who outgunned and could out fight anything the newer Survey troops could put against them. Marco an Fallon still held a grudge over what he'd been forced to do at the time of Caleb and Fee's marriage. The plan was that the height of the riot would cover their brothers' release.

But no, today was a demonstration, not a riot. Please, by all that mattered, nobody begin a riot.

From a hidden nook, Fee watched the business of the capital carry on as usual. A man crossed the street, dropped something and hurried to pick it up before the streetcar bowled him over. On a far corner, a young couple argued. Over what, she wondered. Who was to choose dinner that night or where they would live, the future of their whole lives together. The vital trivia of every day or the big things that overwhelmed you.

A child ran past, her pet rakki chattering behind her.

"Go home, she whispered hopelessly. "Get off the streets." Behind her, the mass of Survey staff swelled to fill the alley. She looked at her com unit. Waited for the signal. Wondered where Caleb was, and if he was safe.

Three blocks away, Caleb glanced at his timer and cursed yet again this insane plan to separate him from Fee.

"We have to make sure at least one of you makes it to the podium."

Fine. Marvellous. Did none of them see how small she was? He'd met up with Adam from his Plains team and ordered him not to let Fee out of his sight. He reached for his com unit.

"Com silence rules, Ser." A hand shoved at his wrist. "Not till the signal comes. "

He glared at the woman beside him, one of Bob's platoon of organisers. He was beginning to suspect the woman had been a failed dictator in a previous life.

"My wife— "

"Is perfectly safe, and will remain so with all the troops she has around her."

He clamped his hand into a fist. The woman might be right, but it didn't help.

Where had this crazy protectiveness of his come from? Fee was a fully trained, highly competent eco-engineer. He'd hacked into her file—she had aced her martial training classes. The woman was as capable of defending herself as he was.

It made no difference. They should have marched together, and once this stupid day was over he was going to personally see to it that every single field op who'd decided otherwise would pay for that decision.

Did they seriously think some future common good mattered more to him than her safety?

Listen to yourself. Fee would laugh her head off.

Just when and how his wife had become so precious to him, he couldn't say. In this one thing, the Survey had got it right.

Fox knew what he was doing when he paired him up with Fee den Coille.

He leaned against the wall, glared at his com unit, waited and dreaded the signal.

Fioruisghe ingh Coille beann Caleb den Winter, don't you dare do anything heroic. Keep safe for me.

CHAPTER THIRTY-SIX

A brrrr of sound and a buzzing on her wrist.

The signal to start. Fee saw the solid determination on her colleagues' faces, men and women who had trained to protect and serve their lands. Staff better suited to laboratories and analysis programmes, not marching down a street in defiance of their leaders.

She raised her hand, took her first step forward. All around her, she felt the calm footsteps of her colleagues moving smoothly into the middle of the street, with the designated warders halting traffic and ushering pedestrians to clear a passageway.

Not one single person stayed behind. Not one. Silence fell on the streets. The silence of shock at seeing a crowd surge onwards and take over the road. All in unison, all proudly wearing their Survey insignia and the field gear of each region. A diverse multitude, today united in a single purpose.

The wave of silence followed them, matching the silence that had fallen on every single field station on the planet. For once, the arrogance of head office was their ally and today, only automated responses fed back along the links. The bosses had no idea what was coming.

She watched her com display, watched the trace lines of other groups moving smoothly towards their objective. Even the red one marching through the busiest thoroughfare in town, Caleb's group, even that flowed steadily.

Please keep it so.

Caleb marched deliberately forward, eyes on the next intersection. Police were manning each corner. Standing at alert, keeping watch, giving no sign they planned to take action, not yet. On one corner, though, a man in a different uniform stood alongside the familiar Urbis police blue.

They marched closer. That policeman looked too nervous.

"Keep ranks. No one gives the police a reason to act."

He walked beside Jed from the Polar Regions. A square, thickset man, as broad as Caleb was tall, the pair of them fronted their squad and he knew they looked formidable. Jed closed on him, followed by a subtle shuffling of the ranks behind. Survey field staff were trained to deal with trouble, their work not always popular.

The biggest and strongest now marched on the outside, those excelling in martial training, while on the wings their sharpest-eyed scanned for trouble.

It was done so swiftly, so subtly that not a hitch appeared in the forward drive of the group.

One of their spotters slipped up beside him. Small, scrawny, easily overlooked, the man looked more boy than trained scientist. "There's a whole heap of Survey security hiding in the left hand alley. They're armed and ready for action."

Head office had sent down their response.

Did it mean they still held their families, or were they already gone? Gibbs' word was good, but that didn't guarantee he could pull off their rescues.

Ahead lay the last intersection before the Central Plaza. There was no way round it.

"We go through?" said Jed, eyes set firmly on the Survey trooper.

Caleb set his jaw. "We go through." Past that Survey guard and the ineffectual policeman standing beside him. "Tell everyone to set body armour to combat strength."

All of them were unarmed, taking weapons to a peaceful demonstration deemed too provocative, but any good scanner would pick up the tell-tale signals of their body armour. It was a risk but the alternative was worse. That someone, one more field op under his control should be hurt in this insane fight.

The Feds were still the key. An Fallon had promised to help free Ethan and the den Coille brothers, but would he deliver? Or had someone nobbled him?

Which side did they back?

He looked at his com unit, at the snaking trails of field staff all converging on the central plaza. Two groups neared the same intersection, one of them leading right past the building holding his brother.

Ethan was rock steady, and gutsy as all blazes. Good or bad? In this situation, he just didn't know.

He should be there, with the federal troops springing their brothers out. No, he should be with Fee. Yet reason and honour said he must be right here, leading his troop safely past the ambush ahead.

He hated the constant wrangle of warring demands. Make a decision and stick to it—that had always been his way. But now, so many needed him at once, so many calling to him and tearing his guts out.

Keep safe, Fee.

The Survey guard up front stepped forward, blocking the policeman and standing square in the middle of the street, hands on hip belt and hovering above his weapons.

"Bring it on," muttered Jed.

Caleb gave him a quick glare. "Just keep walking." Another step forward, the tensions rising. "No one makes trouble," he raised his voice to add. The guard's smirk said he'd heard him.

"No eye contact," he said into his comtab, linked to every single field staffer walking behind him. "We are peaceful demonstrators, walking legitimately through that intersection. The application for permission was lodged and approved by the Urbis Events Department as we set out. They have no reason to stop us."

Or so he hoped. It had been a risk. Councillor den Bunachan had a contact in the chamber, who promised that formal permission would be marked 'Approved' as soon as it was lodged.

"Keep walking." An order to himself as much as to those behind.

They reached the intersection. The incoming traffic ground to a halt, all the route controls set to *Stop*.

A clear pathway for the marchers.

The Survey guard's hands dropped to his weapons. A flicked signal, and the hidden platoon of troops poured out of the side street, forming up behind him.

"Halt," said the man.

Caleb kept walking.

"Stop now or face the consequences."

The man looked too damn happy.

"You have no jurisdiction here. This is a legally sanctioned demonstration of citizens," said Caleb, loud enough for the police manning the street corners to hear.

The four city law enforcers who showed no sign of doing anything about the armed thugs lining up against the marchers.

This was it.

"You better stop right there, if ya know what's good for ya,"

Caleb ignored him. "Keep walking," he shouted again to his group, and raised his hand to urge them on.

The security squad leader spread his legs, braced for action. "This is a direct order from the top. Get back to your stations and return to work."

Caleb slowed fractionally, bracing himself. "Remember signing up for military discipline, Jed?"

"Nope, nothing like that in my contract."

Behind him, the rest of their group angled out in a solid attacking wedge as they picked up the pace.

"Reckon we'll just keep on with our business then," called Caleb, and used his leading shoulder to shove hard against the chest of the idiot with the big mouth before swivelling to let his other elbow collide directly with that mouth.

A hiss of warning. Weapons drawn, fists flying, the Survey guards set to, using stun weapons where they could, but Caleb's squad were on top of them and cut out that option. They retaliated in kind: close up, brutal and very old-fashioned.

What would the police do? Had they moved? Caleb had no time to check. A fist rushed towards his face and he ducked in time, both elbows flying now as he shoved on with head down.

The Survey guards surrounded them, big heavy men intent on dishing out as much damage as possible. Caleb had no time to look back, could only plough on using every trick and sneaky undercut learned in a life time of playing rough on the Plains and honed to an edge by his Survey training. Someone seemed to have failed to tell their opponents that all Survey field staff were taught to defend themselves by trainers who were all ex-field ops, not the hired bully boys leading these troops.

That field staff were sharp witted, tough, committed and skilled in using whatever came to hand to win the day.

A nasty chop to his head, barely deflected but he would have a thumping headache tonight. He shook it off. Swivelled, and kicked out at the guard trying to pummel the woman behind him. Between his fist ploughing into the man's gut and her kick connecting squarely with a far more sensitive part of the fool's anatomy, they sent him crashing to the ground. Caleb stepped over him, pulled the woman up and on to follow him.

"We have a job to do. Revenge can wait," he told her.

His column shoved forward, but still the Survey security held against them.

"Armour, full power," he yelled.

"Are you mad," said Jed. "We'll burn out."

"Do it."

He thumbed the control panel on his side, switched it to full and felt the suffocating pressure of the shield protecting him. A minute at most. That's all they had before the energy drain blew the shield and they were open to every blow.

One minute of invincible power. No seasoned troopers would waste firepower against a full strength shield though some of the Survey guards still tried vainly to aim and fire.

"Full power," he roared out, then shoved his head down and barrelled forward. "Fan out."

Damn, his people were magnificent. Like an unsheathed blade, they swung out, the outliers running full tilt against their opponents. A tidal wave of angry, powerful warriors that crashed against the crumbling wall of Survey troopers. A seismic shock that disrupted their defence once and for all, leaving the troopers sprawled on the ground, battered, unconscious and beaten.

"Grab their weapons, power them off," he ordered, swooping down to snatch the handgun from the man under him, smashing it against the earth and twitching another from the body next to it. Not one field op disobeyed him; every single one smashed the filthy things against the hard ground. Disabled, destroyed, their power vanquished. Grins and shouts, the heady euphoria of victory filled his group.

They roared on, a pack of exultant, triumphant faces. He had to bring them down again.

"Line up. Reform. We've still got work to do,"

A young man on the wing turned, jeered at the sprawl of troopers behind them, turned back on them with arm swinging.

"Arbroath, back in line." Caleb put every ounce of command he possessed into his voice.

And still on the street corners, the police stood watch, still they gave no sign of action—against either side.

Caleb marched down the line, bodily grabbing his people and shoving them back into formation. "Your shields are gone," he reminded them. "We have to move, now."

Jed began to help. Between them, they wrestled their people back into order. Just in time, the streets around them now filling with other groups arriving by their own trails, adding to the crowd of Survey field staffers already massing on the central plaza. Onwards, over the limp bodies of the troopers, past the intersection, with traffic stopped and faces in skimmers gaping in shock at the mass of uniformed people filling the square. Uniforms that before had only represented the living, breathing mass of the ecosystems they promised to protect.

Caleb marched at the head of his group again, the gravity of the demonstration heightened by the ominous silence of the marchers. No slogans, no demands. Not yet. That was for the podium. When he and Fee would tell the world why they were here.

Where was she?

Fee glanced nervously around the entrance to the street ahead. So far, their march had been peaceful. Bemused onlookers stood on street corners and watched them pass, but no one made any move to stop them. It seemed too good to last.

In silence, they neared the central plaza. No more the quiet chatter, the nervous giggles that had marked their march as they headed into the streets. When everything had seemed unreal and like a fragmented afterthought from a waking dream.

Now, reality was the fear crawling in her gut, the held breath of the city as they passed, the unpredictability of what would happen when they reached their goal.

"Keep in the middle of the group, Fioruisghe. No heroics today."

Seamach had joined Adam in riding point on her. No chance to do as she so badly wanted; to march at the head of the team. Not that it stopped her trying.

Seamach pushed her back, shoving her into the middle of the group. "Stay there."

"Or we'll hog-tie you and carry you there." The look on Adam's face said he would do it too, if she forced them.

"Nice to see our teams getting on so well," she muttered gracelessly and stomped into the agreed place.

It was the only conflict so far.

Too easy. All too easy.

A hum began to shiver through the air. A muffled thumping and a base line tremor, felt as much as heard. She glanced at her com unit, bringing up all the other trails marching through the city. The head of each glowing line was millimetres apart on her display, a few streets apart in reality.

The hum became the sharp cut of anger. Cries and the crackle of fighting. To the left somewhere. On the com unit, one line faltered, the red line, slowed and shimmered in indecision. Fear slammed into her.

"What's happening?"

Seamach had pulled up his com unit, swearing as he saw that the flickering trail. "We have to keep com silence. At least till the plaza." The look on his face said how badly he wanted to deny the order. "Keep walking," he said.

She obeyed, but her eyes were fixed on that red line, her ears intent on the sounds coming from that other street. Heart beats of time slowing to an infinitesimal burden.

Finally, finally, that other flickering trail moved off again.

She marched on, through streets lined with onlookers, but an ominous silence greeted them instead of the genial bemusement of earlier. Closed faces watched as they passed, faces that felt like they were waiting in judgement. Word had spread in the city, but just what word, she dared not think.

"Tell our people to keep ranks," she murmured to Seamach. "No giving some idiot an excuse to start something."

A dark line of shadow fell on them, the shade cast by a building. She glanced sideways, then almost stopped in shocked recognition.

The central security building. The prison holding her brothers and Ethan Winter.

Had an Fallon's Feds got them out as promised? If not, this crowd filling the streets spelt their end. Who did the ordinary Federal troops and the Urbis police back?

Adam slowed with her. "Fee?"

She waved him on. "Just a stumble."

She must not look at the building, must not give any sign she knew whom it held. Even now, her brothers and Caleb's Ethan might be lined up inside, waiting that final order.

Trust your colleagues. Trust your fellows. The oldest rule of field staff, now extended to a right-wing, hard-core politician she had met briefly and a Councillor who had been hell bent on securing her own position as long as Fee had known her.

"Fioruisghe?" Seamach turned, grabbing at her elbow as brusquely as he snapped at her. "This is it. Sharpen up."

She looked up, and saw ahead the central Plaza of Urbis. They had arrived. Ahead of her, all those tracing lines of field staff jostled and merged into a silent, purposeful mass. Adam and Seamach both took an arm and drove a pathway through the crowd for her by sheer force of will.

Then an even stronger set of arms gathered her in and she felt the tremor of reaction run through both of them. Caleb. His warm smell surrounded her with a promise of refuge.

"You made it," he said gruffly. He set her back, those light eyes scanning every inch of her.

As did she. Blood streaked his cheek, his shirt was torn on one shoulder and a dark mottling scarred his face. "What happened to you?"

"A few idiots thought they could stop us."

She tugged up his shirt, uncaring of the watching crowds, and winced at the rough grazes and bruises that would turn every colour of the rainbow by evening.

He grabbed at her hand and shoved the shirt back down. "It's nothing. The other man is far worse."

She didn't care a gram about the other man, only the one in front of her. "You sure?"

"It was just a bit of a warm up for the main event." He swooped down, kissed her briefly and quietly asked, "Any word?"

She shook her head. They were still under com silence, but it was good to be asked. Bob slapped him on the back.

"Come on, the crowd's waiting."

"Anya from *Today*?"

"Logged in and ready to go. Showtime, boss."

On the podium, Jed stepped forward, holding up a hand for silence. Not that he needed to. The plaza was packed, every square of it filled with Survey field staff. Thousands strong from every corner of Arcadia, and over them all still that queer expectant hush, broken only by a low humming murmur of nervous rasps.

"You all know why we're here," said Jed. "For years, we've worked without thanks, without expectation of thanks, worked because we believed in what we were doing. Were we wrong?"

"No," they shouted back.

Caleb stepped forward, sliding smoothly into Jed's place and drawing her up beside him.

"Is our world in trouble?"

"Yes," came the full-throated roar.

"But do our bosses know it?" he said.

And dead silence fell.

Jed took the stand again. "For those few who don't know them, let me introduce Caleb Winter, head eco-engineer on the Plains project, and his wife, Fioruisghe den Coille, the western mountains eco-engineer. Two people devoted to the wellbeing of this planet."

He gestured to them, stepping back and leaving them the podium. Fee had never felt so exposed. Caleb squeezed her hand, then leaned forward.

"Betrayed," he said to the crowd. "Each and every one of you has been betrayed, and by whom? By the managers whose duty it was to support you, by senior officials hell bent on their own power and the cost be damned. But you and me, we made a promise—to our world, and to the people of this world."

He paused, turned his head in a slow scan of the crowd, and lifted his voice another notch, the deep timbre of it echoing through the plaza. "Do we work for managers? No. Do we work for the self-serving goal of greedy individuals? No. We are Survey, we work for Arcadia. Today, we're here to deliver on that."

He raised a fist in the air. "For Arcadia!"

She thrust up her own. A sea of pumping fists joined her. "For Arcadia."

Caleb nodded at her and she had to step up to speak, standing on the block someone had adroitly shoved forward. "How many of you have seen your work set aside? Seen it ignored, or twisted from its purpose? That's what happened to us, to me, to so many others here. Do you want to hear our stories?"

"Yes!"

She kept it short, detailing only the destruction of her replanting programme, stepping aside for Caleb to tell of the takeover of the lakes project and the twisting of their cropping regime. The new plants ordered by the bosses that would give short term profit but cause long term ecological failure. Then a succession of others stepped forward, each speaker winding the crowd up a notch.

The last one finished and still the crowd waited to hear more. Caleb stepped forward again.

"Is this the Survey we signed up for? Is this *our* Survey?'

A roar this time that echoed right through her bones. "No," they cried as one.

"What do we want?" he said.

"*Our* Survey back."

"Who do we want to talk to?"

"The managers. The no names," came the shouts.

The no names. That worked for Fee. The senior staffers hiding behind their badges of office while they ignored the field staff and sent out directives that stole the wealth of a planet.

A steady chant began in the crowd, swelling, rising up in a wave to the front.

"Bring them out. Bring them out. Bring out the no names."

Behind the podium were the Capitol steps, the entry to the premier seat of government on Arcadia. Not the headquarters of the Survey, that was in a secretive building a block farther on. A building that held the managers, but also the mid-level support staff all of them had relied on again and again. Staff as much a victim of their seniors' machinations as any of them here today, but who could not be told of this action for fear of a leak of information up the chain of command.

That building the march had left alone. But the Capitol building, the building holding the politicians whose job it was to call the civil service to account; that building was fair game.

"Bring them out."

The chant rose to a near scream of frustrated anger. Fee kept her face strong, but eyed the Feds lining all corners of the square. One wrong word, and this crowd would erupt.

"Someone in there better do something."

Caleb heard her, and gestured at Bob. She didn't recognise the hand signs. Local Plains' variations, she guessed, but Bob moved discreetly away from the stand, down the steps and out of sight.

"Under control," Caleb said softly, but she caught the 'I hope' in his voice.

The chanting continued, ever more frenetic, and the police began to move in, hands settling on their weapons belts.

Suddenly, a change. The noise stopped, and all the faces turned to look in one direction.

Someone had done it, taken their courage in their hands and stepped out onto the Capital steps. She turned slowly.

Isolated at the top and ignoring the offered police escort, Joe Gibbs stepped forward, mouth set firmly and looking as if he was facing just another election rally. He called for a speaker tab.

His voice echoed around the square.

"I am about to present a motion to the House. A motion calling for an investigation into the senior management of the Ecological Survey Department, for the purpose of prosecuting them on the grounds that they have abused their position. That they have illegally alienated private assets, concealed legitimate information from the elected members of this house, and by their actions, endangered the continued existence of humans on this planet. Your managers have abused your trust, your good will and your integrity and I will bring them to account. On this, you have my word."

Another man appeared behind him. Marco an Fallon, the trusted voice of justice throughout Arcadia, but missing today was that grim mask of a man forced down a rotten path she remembered from their last meeting. "Federal troops have taken over the offices of the Survey, under a warrant issued by the Upper Court of Justice. All Survey data banks are secured under full Federal seal and the level one and two managers taken into custody pending the outcome of the Representative's motion in the House. They are also under investigation as to their role in the possible murder of Survey operative Ben Crane of the Plains field staff."

He stepped back, giving the centre back to Joe Gibbs, who lifted his voice in a roar. "Your bosses failed you, they failed their government, and they failed the people of this world—as our witnesses can testify."

He lifted an arm, and from the shadows of the capitol foyer behind him, a number of figures moved forward. Figures she instantly recognised.

"Mam, Da, Samhchair."

"My father and mother," said Caleb beside her, and she heard in his voice an echo of the overwhelming relief filling her. Another walked out, a young man wearing the bruises and dirt of imprisonment. "Ethan." Fee held her breath, then four others followed. Four even more battered figures, one hobbling and leaning on the solid figure beside him, his young face defiantly upright. "Aigherach, what did they do to you? Cumchdach, Seolta, Ceart." She reached out a shaky hand and grabbed her husband's, tears streaming down her face.

The figures came to a halt behind the Representative, to join with him as he brought up his arm in formal salute to the crowd. "Thank you, the field staff of the Survey. Arcadia is indebted to you and the people of this world will not forget it."

A solemn promise, the oath of a man known and respected, and never before publicly aligned with the environmental movement.

As one, the crowd lifted their hands, a unanimous thud of feet hitting the ground as they came to attention. "Arcadia. Ours forever!"

It took far too many hours for Fee and Caleb to escape. With the crowd roaring its approval, they had to stay there on that podium, first to give the promised interview to Anya van Lissen, and after to stay smiling with the crowd as they all waited for the Representative's motion to be passed while Anya's vid-cast played the interview with Caleb over and over on screens hastily set up around the plaza. Stay to rally the other marchers, cursing, laughing with them, whatever it took to stop the tension spilling over. Later, listening in with Bob as their families gave evidence to the House while medics hovered in the wings.

Waiting, waiting, till finally the news came through that the case would go forward. That all the managers were now under arrest, their actions of the last year frozen and under review.

The party would last for hours yet but Fee and Caleb finally managed to slip away from their befuddled entourage. Fee's back was pummelled into agony, the lines on her face stretched beyond comfort and exhaustion battled for supremacy.

A Federal officer materialised in front of them and indicated a nearby alley. "We have an escort waiting, Ser and Sera. Your families have been taken to a secure medical facility."

Fee could not forget that image of Aigherach leaning on Ceart for support. "They're all right?"

"As well as can be expected," was the curt reply.

Caleb gripped her arm, and they hurried after him.

The Federal cab disgorged them into a closed tunnel, which led to a building unmistakable in function; a hospital. Her heart beat faster.

Then a door opened, and there they all were. Winters and den Coilles, huddled together and waiting, even Silas, hurrying in a far door as they arrived, fit, whole and brown as a berry, to be grabbed and pummelled by his family.

Fee flew at her mother and burst into tears at the feel of the thin arms enfolding her. "What did they do to you all?"

"Nothing we can't recover from," said her mother's firm voice, "now you have rescued us."

Caleb stopped awkwardly in front of his father. "I didn't know they would do this," he said, "or not for sure."

"But you did try to warn us." It was Ethan, stepping stiffly forward. "Next time, make it clear. No more of this confidential claptrap."

"Agreed."

"So maybe it's time you came home," said his father.

He had to shake his head, had to deny this first overture in too many years.

"Sorry. I have work to do. Today doesn't change that."

He waited nervously.

His father shrugged and stuck out a hand. "It was worth a try. You're wasted on that outfit, you know. Hell, what you could do in a boardroom!"

His mother said nothing, just held her arms out, and he was home again.

It was Fee's brother Aigherach who brought a halt to the murmur of talk from both families. He stepped out from the treatment room, leg in a long support basket and face white. Of the four brothers, he looked the most battered, and Caleb hated the edge of distress in Fee's voice when she saw him.

But lingering behind the boy was the spirit of young Ben, who had loved the animals of the plains more than his life. A spirit forever stilled because of this boy.

Aigherach saw him, and halted. His mouth stiffened and he lifted his head.

Fee's mother hurried to him. "What did they say?"

"A mess. The bones were shattered and not set right after."

"Did any of those survey thugs even try?" His mother, the depth of anger on her face clear. Aigherach shook his head.

"They will operate tomorrow," said the boy gently then clenched his fist. "What about the men who were with me when I was taken?"

He didn't know. Somehow, Caleb had never imagined that. It must have showed on his face, because the boy's turned grey and pasty.

"They all made it, except one," he said. "Ben Crane, our zoologist."

"No."

"Not now, Winter," said Fee's father.

"No," said the boy. "He tried to save me. Ben stood in front of me. It's why I only have this leg injury. He took the shot meant for me. The man was a hero."

It meant something. "His family will appreciate you saying that," he said.

He wasn't sure yet if he could truly forgive the boy, but knowing he was possibly worthy of Ben's sacrifice did help.

There was only one thing remaining. He reached out his hand for Fee, called her name softly. She met his look, giving it back with all that lay inside her. He stepped away from his family, into the clear space between both den Coilles and Winters. She stretched out her hand, walked across from her family and took his, closing her small fingers tight as he locked his hand over hers.

"We'll leave you now. You must be tired," she said to both families. "The next few days are going to be hectic and we'll be tied up sorting out the aftermath. We'll call you once we get home."

"And where might that be?" said her father, eyeing her with that too-canny look of his. She turned that smile of hers on Caleb, the one that said she was laughing at something only she could see.

"You heard the man, husband."

"Where we build it, that's where it will be," said Caleb. And the sun shone in her face as Fee smiled back at him.

EPILOGUE

Fee let her head fall back, soaking up the spring sun on her face. Under her feet a mix of grass and warm sand beckoned her toes. She closed her eyes and let the warmth waft her away.

"Grandma. Watch me, Grandma."

A small girl with a laughing face jumped up and down in the shallow wavelets of the lake edge. A lake shining clear in the sparkling sunshine, frosted with a sprinkle of diamond bright caps as a light breeze teased the surface.

A crunch of sand behind her. She looked up, to see Caleb walking down the bank towards her. But this was a Caleb with grey in his hair and a face grizzled with age, looking more like his father than ever. Only his father had never looked so handsome, and Sol Winter had never worn a smile like the one on Caleb's face.

The one that told her every morning how special she was to him.

A younger man walked beside him, hair tawny in the sun, and with that spare walk of the plains, yet touched with the lilting flexibility of the mountains. A man with dark eyes who laughed at her like her brothers had when they were children together.

"Watch me, Daddy, GranDa. Watch me," shrieked the child, jumping up and splashing down again in a froth of bubbling waters. The young man marched down to the water, lifting the child high and throwing her up in the air, set her on his shoulders and waded deeper before tossing her into the waters, arms holding her safe till she was ready to swim. She giggled, paddling energetically till she reached the shallows, then back into the waves and her father's arms.

Caleb, this older Caleb, sat down beside Fee and she settled back into arms that held long memories of happiness.

"Think we should join them?"

She shook her head and lifted her mouth for his kiss, emerging long moments later as content as ever. He wrapped his arms around her, and together, they watched the dark-haired girl romping at the water's edge with her father.

"She dances everywhere, just like you," said Caleb.

Fee glanced down, and saw that age had touched her too, her body no long as slim or supple.

"She's the second most beautiful female in the world," said Caleb softly. "She has your spirit."

She couldn't resist. "And who…?"

"The most beautiful?" He looked down at her, those light filled eyes of his twinkling and warm with love. "Her grandmother, of course."

A splash of water, and Fee opened her eyes. The lake water was muddy brown, Caleb a man in his full prime with no touch of grey yet touching that strong head, but the smile was the one of her dreams. "Come on in," he said.

She grinned back, rushing down the sand to jump into the lapping waters. Cool, refreshing, and who cared if it was still brown? One day, one day, that would change.

"Lake Ben, that's what we'll call it," she said to him, then flicked a hand, sending a surge of water over her husband's face. "He would have loved this."

"Yes, he would," Then that grin she had learned to thoroughly distrust. She turned to run, just as he grabbed her up, swung her round, and dumped her full tilt into the water.

"Lake Ben it is."

Thank you for reading TORN. I hope you enjoyed this start to the story of the struggle to restore the planet Arcadia as much as I enjoyed creating it. Please consider posting a review or letting your friends know about this book. I appreciate all honest reviews

Look out for the next story in the Arcadia series. Ethan Winter wants nothing more from life than to run the business he loves so much. But that business has been shattered, he has been imprisoned and brutalized, and to restore Solaris Winter he must make a deal with a woman who challenges everything he thought unchangeable.

For all my news of new releases, including Ethan's story, and special subscriber extras, sign up for my newsletter at:

www.marybrockjones.com

ACKNOWLEDGEMENTS

With thanks to all those who have helped me bring "Torn" to reality. Firstly, to my amazing and hugely knowledgeable editor, Grace Bridges. To Amygdala Designs for my cover. To Victoria who set me on the right path to formatting. And to my fellow writers at SpecFicNZ, RWNZ and RWA, particularly the Auckland specficers and RWNZers: thank you for your generosity, your never-ending support, the laughter and the mutual moans, but most of all for helping me to believe I can do this!

Biggest thanks of all go to my family. To my parents, for raising me in a house full of books, taking us to libraries and taking it for granted that we would all get an education and be able to think for ourselves; to my sons who are always proud of what I do even when it seems weird to them; and most of all to my husband who is always there for me, even though I'm far away in my own world more often than not. Thank you all for your acceptance, for everything you've taught me over the years, and for the smiles on your faces when I really need them.